Thundering Ridge

THUNDERING MOUNTAIN RANCH
BOOK FOUR

NICOLE NEISWANGER

Calico
publications

For questions or and comments about the quality of this book, please contact us at calicopublicationsllc@gmail.com.

Cover Design: Covers and Cupcakes, LLC

Publisher: Calico Publications, LLC

Digital ISBN: 978-1-960600-04-2

Print Edition ISBN: 978-1-960600-05-9

To my mother-in-law, Cheryl D'Angelo
Fly with the angels and know you'll be always loved and forever
missed.

To Eva Torres
While your mother won't let you read this novel today, perhaps one
day in the distant future you'll find as much joy in living your
dreams as I have in mine.

To Caroline Bryant
Thank you for being there for me when I needed it the most. True
friends are rare and to count you as one of those is an absolute honor.

One

June 29, 1900

Luke stuffed the latest piece of news securely in his shirt pocket, and he salivated at what it meant. Hot sweat trickled from his forehead and cheeks, and he wiped it with a worn rag as he finished the morning newspaper run in the basement of the three-story building.

As the typesetter and occasional journalist, Luke straightened his back and stretched his long arms above his head, lifting the sweaty hair from the back of his neck. He had returned late from his brother's ranch the night before and his muscles ached from the quick trip, but he'd still headed into work early to get the day's run complete. Glancing at the clock, he grimaced. He hadn't had the opportunity to talk with Walter, the editor and owner of the *Helena Gazette* and time was passing quickly.

Luke's muscles bulged as he pulled the last of the newsprint into a thick pile and tied it with twine. "Frank, that's it. We're done for the morning. I need to find Walter. As soon as I'm finished, I'll come back and help you in cleaning."

Frank nodded and picked up the broom to sweep the floor.

Walter insisted on a clean press room, and it was a daily part of their work to make sure things were in tip-top shape before they left for the day.

Picking up one stack of newspapers, Luke said, "I'll let the newsboys know they can come and get the rest of these on my way up to see the boss."

"Thank ya kindly, Luke," Frank said. "The missus wants to know if you'd like to come for dinner one day next week. She thinks you ain't gettin' enough to eat." Frank laughed, his grey eyes twinkling.

Frank's wife had been determined to find Luke a wife, and she tried to feed Luke every chance she got. No matter his protestations that he wasn't searching for one, she continued to parade eligible young women in front of him with the hopes he'd set his sights on one and settle down. Until he had avenged his pa's death, he couldn't in good conscience put the woman he married into harm's way. He hated to burden Frank and his wife with his problems, so he smiled and indulged her interference knowing full well he wouldn't court any woman until the time was right.

"I'd like that. Tell her to pick a night and I'll be there." Frank's wife was a kind woman with a good heart, not to mention a great cook, and that alone was reason enough to go. His own cooking was abysmal. He would always appreciate a well-cooked meal, no matter the circumstances.

Frank nodded and continued to sweep up the scraps of paper that were scattered across the floor.

Luke jogged up the stairs, through the spotless front office, to the outside porch where the newsboys sat waiting for the go-ahead to gather the newspapers and sell them. Walter had bought the building just after it was built two years before and it contained the latest modern conveniences of gas-lighting and indoor plumbing. Sometimes, he was afraid he'd track dirt inside the office and Walter would have his head.

Handing the newsboys the stack in his arms, he told them the rest were ready for delivery and then walked up the second set of stairs to Walter's office. A second office was further down the hall, unused at the moment. Luke had been hoping for a permanent promotion to journalist. With any luck, that office would become his when he finally proved himself worthy. He rapped on Walter's door with his knuckles and waited for permission to enter.

"Come in."

Luke opened the door. The sunlight poured in through the dirt-streaked windows, nearly blinding him. Stacks of newsprint lined the far edges of the room. Past issues of various newspapers were stuffed into the tall filing cabinet behind Walter and lay scattered across his desk. It was a wonder Walter could get any work done with the number of papers blanketing the surface.

"Got a moment, Walter?"

Walter raised his eyes from the ledger in front of him and gestured for Luke to come in. Picking up his cigar, Walter sat back in his chair, the leather creaking with movement.

Luke settled in one of the plush armchairs Walter had on the ready for paying customers. Luke likely shouldn't be sitting there, but he didn't think he had much ink on him. Walter didn't seem to mind, as he hadn't told him to get up.

"I kind of have an odd question to ask, Walter."

Walter chuckled. "I can't imagine you asking me anything I haven't heard before. Go ahead." His blue eyes twinkled as he took a puff from the thick cigar that sat between his pudgy fingers. Walter wasn't a small man or a big one, either. He was average size, but he had a large presence. Not afraid to state his opinion on most anything, Walter was a relatively decent man who had given Luke a chance.

"Before I ask the question, I best explain some things about my family and what happened in the summer of 1893." Luke had never told Walter anything about the woman who had caused so much pain and havoc, but considering what he'd just discovered, it was about time if he wanted Walter's help.

Walter nodded thoughtfully. "Go on, then. I don't have all day."

"Yes, well... my older brother, Stanley, married a woman by the name of Connie, or leastways that's what we knew her as. Stanley met Connie in the spring of 1892, and after a few months, they were married. At first, she tried to fit right in with the family, but then things seemed to change. She became demanding and tried to make all these plans to change the ranch."

Luke's gut clenched as he remembered her determination to change the way his pa did things, her snide remarks when she didn't get her way, and the way she chastised his ma over the smallest of things. It still made him sick to his stomach to think about what she had done.

"Pa didn't take to her ideas and things became tense between 'em. Then, Ma and Pa got sick – real sick. Ma went first and then Pa. Pa had been recovering and then he was gone sudden-like. I thought it was strange and part of me suspected Connie, but I had no proof." He rubbed his hands together, a chill running up his spine. "Come to find out, she had everything to do with it. She convinced a ranch hand to smother him to death while he rested on his sickbed." He swallowed back the thick lump in his throat, the heartache very much as real today as it was seven years ago. His voice gruff, he continued, "Then, she manipulated Pa's will to make it seem like Stanley had inherited everything, kicked me and my brothers off the ranch, and then tried to have Stanley killed. Thank the heavens above, she didn't succeed. Stanley survived the attempt."

Walter's eyes were wide with shock. "That's quite the tale. I knew your pa died, but I never knew it was murder."

"Yeah, it's not something I tend to share."

"What happened to her?"

"She managed to escape and disappeared for years."

"So why are you sharing this story with me?" Walter's blue eyes were piercing, contemplative. "I'm sympathetic, but I'm not sure what you need from me."

While they had a good relationship, Luke and Walter weren't the best of friends and rarely saw one another outside of work. Luke shifted uncomfortably in his chair. "My oldest brother, Ben, sent out inquiries, and he received a letter from a friend of his in Texas. We think she might be involved or had been involved in a fancy parlor house." Luke reached into his coat pocket and pulled out the worn and creased letter Ben had given him the night before.

Ben,

I made some inquiries. Connie's real name is Bethany Constance Ashland. She grew up in a Houston brothel. In 1890, when she was nigh on 20 years of age, she left the brothel. It's believed she moved to San Antonio.

She married an older, infirm gentleman in late 1891. He passed six months after they tied the knot and his death was quite suspicious. The law had been questioning her about her husband and a couple other men she was suspected of killing when she disappeared. They followed her trail for a while but then lost track of her.

If she's anywhere in Helena, I'd suggest you look in high-end parlor houses. She ain't one to live simply, and seems to crave attention and money.

Hope you find this information helpful. I wish you and your family the best.

Norman Petterfield

Walter finished reading and handed the letter back to Luke, his face unreadable. "Does this have anything to do with the black eye you were sporting a few months ago?"

Luke folded the paper carefully and placed it back in his

pocket. "Yes. I thought I'd seen her a few times but wasn't quite sure. We never expected her to return to Helena. Toward the end of April, I saw her again and followed her. I was careless and paid the price with a shiner. Since then, I swear I've seen her but haven't been able to track her. Ben gave me this letter last night."

"So, what can I help you with?"

Luke shifted forward in his chair and braced his hands on his knees before raising his eyes to Walter's. "From the letter, it sounds like I need to get myself into a few of the parlor houses in town. It never crossed our minds she might be a lady of the night, so I'd like to start looking there. I can't see her belonging to anything other than an exclusive one, but I doubt I'm part of the clientele that gets a coveted invitation."

"And you think I am?" Walter chuckled ruefully.

Luke's collar suddenly felt tight. He raised a finger to loosen it. "Not exactly, but you know plenty of people, and I hoped you might be able to wrangle me some invitations or point me to someone who could."

Sitting back fully in his chair, the cigar held in one hand, Walter gazed at Luke for a long moment. "I'll see what I can do. Not making *any* promises, but I'll put out some feelers and see what snaps back. Might cost you, though."

"I understand." Luke let out the breath he hadn't realized he'd been holding. "Thanks, Walter. I appreciate it."

"You're welcome. Now get back to work. I don't pay you to sit here idle."

"Yes, sir," Luke said, scrambling to stand.

With any luck, Walter would come back with good news. He was determined to find information on Connie or Bethany, or whatever her name was. With any luck, they would find her and make sure she paid for what she'd done. That way, she couldn't harm anyone ever again.

Two

July 13, 1900

Luke had just finished sweeping the newsroom floor when one of the office boys told Luke Walter wanted to see him in his office. It had been two weeks since he had spoken to Walter about Connie. Maybe today would be the day Walter had some information for him.

Slowly walking up the stairs, Luke tried to calm his beating heart. He had been biting at the bit to ask him, but it wouldn't do to nag the man. If Walter could help, he'd let Luke know.

Walter's office door was wide open, and as Luke approached, Walter waved him inside. Luke stopped in shock. The mess he'd seen weeks before was gone––replaced with order and spotlessness. He could see the top of Walter's mahogany desk and out the now-shiny windows. Even the filthy drapes, once black, had been washed to reveal a navy blue hue. Every surface gleamed.

"Take a seat, Luke." Walter's eyes had narrowed, the wrinkles at the corners of his eyes more prominent than normal. His lips were pulled into a thin line, and his nose flared like a bull ready to blow through a crowd of rowdy wranglers.

Luke's face fell. He'd prayed Walter would be able to assist him, but he had probably hoped for too much. If Walter couldn't help, he'd have to make other plans. Nothing would stop him from finding Connie and making her pay for what she had done to his family.

Dropping into the armchair, he clasped his knees tight to keep them from bouncing.

"Did the run finish on time?"

Luke tried to contain his disappointment at Walter calling on him to discuss business. He'd wanted Walter to have news of a more personal nature, but it wasn't going to happen today. He had to focus on what Walter needed and bemoan his bad luck at home, where he could drown himself in a bottle of whiskey. "Yes, the newsboys picked up the last of the papers ten minutes ago."

"Any issues?" Walter looked back at the ledger on his desk, wrote something, and shuffled the papers around distractedly.

"No, the run went fine."

"Good, good." He pulled a piece of paper from under the ledger and held it out. "Here, take this."

"What is it?" Luke asked.

"It's a lead."

Luke's spine straightened with anticipation. He grabbed the heavy cream paper. His thumb grazed against the gold embossing. Occasionally, Walter would let him work on potential stories. He was good at ferreting out information when given half the chance. It came from him being disappointed and angry at what he hadn't been able to do for his pa. Of course, he hadn't been as lucky with information on Connie as he would've liked. He looked down at the paper and read it aloud.

TUESDAY, JULY 24, 1900

6 PM

MON PETIT AMOUR

"What is *mon petit amour*?" Luke asked.

"A whorehouse."

"Oh!" Luke said, his head raising so fast it was a wonder he didn't break his neck. "You got me into one of 'em?"

"What does it look like?"

"Sorry, Walter. I just... I guess I didn't expect—" His voice trailed off. What an impression he made, looking like a first-class imbecile.

"I asked around, and there are five parlor houses here in Helena. The one I just gave you is having an auction."

"An auction?" Luke asked. "What for?"

Walter grinned with an almost mocking expression. "Have you ever been in a parlor house?"

"Of course I have. What man hasn't?"

"The auction is for virgins."

The words dropped on Luke like a ton of bricks. It was a good thing he wasn't drinking because he'd likely have choked. He was horrified. "Did I just hear you right?"

Walter lost the mocking grin, and his lips turned downward into a frown. "I'm afraid you did. It's a common practice among the more exclusive establishments. They go for high dollars, and men seem to find it exciting *if* they can purchase one."

"Oh," Luke said. Acid rose in the back of his throat at the thought of young women being auctioned like cattle for sex.

"Time for you to grow a thick skin if you really want to investigate these parlor houses and become a journalist," Walter muttered, handing Luke a second piece of paper with four other names scribbled on it. "These are a few other places you might want to look at if Mon Petit Amour doesn't pan out."

"How can I gain access to 'em?"

"Well, that's where some friends of mine have been willing to help, for a price."

Luke grimaced. He didn't have much money after buying a home last summer, and he really didn't want to ask Ben for money.

"Don't worry, it ain't money they're looking for," Walter said.

Walter had an uncanny ability to read him, which was what made Walter a phenomenal journalist and editor.

"What do they want?" He didn't want to put Walter in an uncomfortable position if they didn't want money.

"Kind of varies with each one, but some of 'em want an advertisement in the newspaper free of charge for the next month while others want me to pursue some stories I've avoided."

"Ah, Walter, I didn't expect that. I certainly don't want you compromisin' your integrity."

"Eh, no real skin off my back. They haven't advertised in my paper before, and once the month is up, they'll realize it's to their benefit to pay for an extension. In the end, I'll come out ahead. And you'll pay it back with a good story when this is over."

"What?"

"You heard me. This has the makings of a good front-page headline, especially if she goes to jail. *Madam caught for the murders in a prominent local family.* I can see it now."

"I don't know how to thank you or repay you for this." If this invitation and list of potential parlor houses helped him find Connie, he and his family would be forever grateful.

"Don't thank me yet, Luke. I still expect you to do your type-setting *and* report on the outcome. I'm expecting a good story from you when this is done."

"You'll never know how much this means to our family."

"I've an idea. You come from a good stock. Your parents were fine folk and helped many people over the years. People ain't going to be too happy when they find out what really happened to them, but putting the woman behind bars who orchestrated these crimes will appease many. Speaking strictly for myself, your pa helped me out years ago when I needed it the most. He offered me a loan and a leg up, and I'll never forget it. So, for me, there's no question of whether or not I can help. I'm happy to."

Luke's forehead crinkled. He had no idea that Walter had known his pa. "You've never mentioned this before."

"I never felt the need to. I ain't too proud of my actions back then, but your pa looked past them and saw something in me, saw my potential. If he hadn't given me a chance, I wouldn't be here today. So, in a roundabout way, I owe him. This is the least I can do."

Three

July 24, 1900

As the auction approached, Luke's nerves were strung thinner than barbed wire between a couple of fenceposts. The days crept by uneventfully, but worry gnawed at the back of his mind. Chances were slim that he'd find Connie at this parlor house. If he did, he'd finally be able to put this nightmare to rest once and for all.

When the evening rolled around, Luke dressed in his best suit and favorite black hat. He rode to Mon Petit Amour and showed his invitation at the door. He'd let his mustache and beard grow and run coal soot through his ash-brown hair. There was no way to hide the black mole at the corner of his right eye, but the beard and mustache were a definite change. It had been seven years since he'd last seen Connie. He'd filled out since then, having grown from a scrawny kid to a broad-chested man, but he didn't want to take the chance she'd recognize him.

Luke stepped inside and looked around the house in awe. A glass chandelier hung from the ceiling, its crystals shimmering in the gas lighting. A large, curving staircase swept through the middle of the foyer. It wrapped up and along both sides of the room, connecting to the second floor. Beautiful, scantily clad women were sprawled along the elaborate railing, draped on armchairs and sofas, and in the laps of men. The foyer and the rooms on either side of him were crowded with couples. Essences of rose and lavender competed with the aroma of strawberries and peaches left out in bowls for guests. Plush rugs in a variety of rich, dark colors covered planks of darkened wood that had been scrubbed to a glossy shine. Sofas, armchairs, wingbacks, and wooden-back chairs were scattered throughout, giving the multitude of men a place to relax. Laughter, music, cards, and liquor flowed in abundance. Judging from what he'd seen in one downstairs room, all proclivities appeared to be satisfied.

Luke had been in brothels before––he was a man after all–– but he'd never seen a house so lavish or women so clean and attractive. Their hair was elaborately done up, with blonde, brunette, and red curls cascading across bare shoulders. A few even had hair so black it was like looking at the dark sky with no stars, clouds, or moon in sight. A variety of thoughts ran through his mind, and he chastised himself. His ma would roll around in her grave if she knew what he'd been thinking. He had to remember he was there for one reason only, and it wasn't to bed a woman.

Luke sauntered to the grand staircase and up the shiny wooden steps. Women glided down the stairs, beguiling smiles lifting their plump rouged lips. If he hadn't known what type of establishment he was in, he'd almost believe he was at a summer ball. Most of the women wore fashionable, elaborate gowns, although very revealing ones. Others were not so adorned and wore much less. They touched his arms and shoulders, brushed their chests against him, and stroked the front of him as he walked by. Someone even pinched his butt. He was first shocked at their brazenness, but then thought he shouldn't be surprised.

Once he reached the second floor, he looked around for the auction room. An older lady approached him wearing a dress remi-

niscent of what a housekeeper would wear. It was dark blue and
made of the finest silk with a delicate collar of white lace. She was
tall with grey hair that was pulled back so tight it stretched her
skin, making her cheeks look quite gaunt. She had her lips pursed
thin, and her close-set eyes scanned him.

"You here for the event, I presume?" she asked.

He pulled out his invitation and handed it to her, feeling
nervous. "Yes, ma'am. Thank you."

She glanced at it and then handed it back. He stuffed it into his
suit pocket, his fingers shaking. He needed to pull himself
together. It wouldn't do if he looked out of sorts. He'd have to
blend in if he wanted to look like a member of their clientele.

She huffed. "No need for manners in here, young man.
Follow me."

He was startled by her words but did as she asked and followed
her toward a pair of massive oak doors. The building was bigger
than it had looked outside, but he supposed parlor houses needed
plenty of room for the kind of entertainment the wealthy men
around him desired. The woman rapped her knuckles on the door
twice before it opened from within. She motioned Luke inside.

He stepped forward into a large ballroom with a crude stage on
one end and rows of chairs available for viewing pleasure. The
carpets were thick under his feet, and the music faded behind him
as the door closed. Food and drinks covered the lengthy tables
along the walls, and women sauntered around with trays of cham-
pagne. The hems of their skirts fell way above their knees, barely
covering their derrières. Black silk stockings garnished their legs up
to mid-thigh, held in place by lacy red ribbons. Black and red
corsets adorned their fronts, pushing their chests up full and
center. If one of them coughed, he imagined they'd pop out for all
to see.

He had to swallow back the surge of desire raging through
him. If he hadn't been there for one reason only, he might've spent
the night with one of them. It had been far too long since he had

enjoyed the pleasures of a woman. For the right price, any woman in this place could be his for the night.

He grabbed a glass of whiskey and a pastry from the bounty on display, and picked a seat in the back row. As much as he wanted to be in the front row, he should fade into the background. He'd be less noticeable to Connie if she sauntered into the room.

Settling into his chair, he undid the buttons of his suit jacket and sank into the soft upholstery. He had to admit, they knew how to throw a party. It was decadent––far fancier than any ball, dance, or get-together he had ever gone to. His ma and pa used to throw shindigs at the ranch, but never to this degree of splendor. Luke took a bite of the delicious chocolate pastry he selected and moaned with delight. He'd have to pick up another one on his way out.

Soon, the room had filled with well-dressed men of wealth, and he recognized a few from the society pages he'd printed for Walter. These were not ordinary men; they were some of the richest men from Helena and the surrounding ranches. Lawyers, property owners, bankers, and even the mayor were among those he recognized. Many of them stood alone, kept their faces averted, and didn't engage with anyone. Luke assumed they didn't want to be recognized, but it was hard to miss the most famous faces in town.

He pulled the brim of his hat lower across his forehead. The thought of auctioning off young women made him sick, but he'd have to hide his disgust and paste an ambivalent expression on his face. He was ashamed to take part in it, even if he was trying to find Connie.

Suddenly, the lights dimmed, and the men lingering along the walls elbowed their way to seats. Anticipation lit their faces as they settled in for the show. After a few moments, the red velvet curtains shifted and an astonishingly attractive red-haired beauty stepped into the lights on the wooden platform. Luke's heart dropped. It wasn't Connie. He wondered if this woman was the Madam, but he didn't want to ask. Anyone with a legitimate invitation was bound to know who she was. If he were to blend in, he couldn't ask questions he should know the answers to.

If Connie didn't show up here, he'd have to look around more after the auction. He could find one of the chattier women and sweet talk her into divulging more than she should about the house's management. He had to look around anyway, for he was there for two reasons: to find the woman who had killed his pa and to write an explosive story for Walter's newspaper. Walter had been clear he hadn't been doing this entirely out of the goodness of his heart.

The red-haired woman smiled indulgently at the crowd, waiting patiently for them to quiet.

"Welcome, gentlemen. My name is Pauline. We're so glad you could make it to this invitation-only event. Most of you should know the rules, but for those of you who don't, I'll repeat them." She scanned the room fiercely, as if to convey she had the power to give or withhold their heart's desire at her whim. "One: your bids will be taken at the end of the show for the lady you find most intriguing. The higher you bid, the likelier you'll win, because *only* the highest bidder gets the girl." Pauline sauntered across the stage, her petite hips swaying under the fancy silks she wore. "You will receive your prize once paid in full. Cash or gold dust is acceptable." She halted at the front of the stage and placed her hands on her hips. "We will not hold a woman indefinitely. You have thirty minutes after the auction to provide the funds, or the next-highest bidder will receive what could have been your reward. Two: there will be no obscene remarks. These ladies are innocents, and many of them are nervous. You don't want to scare them to the point of no pleasure, now do you? Three: no touching. You want your prize as innocent as possible, I'm sure. Four: no fighting amongst yourselves. If anyone is displeased with losing, there are plenty of women available downstairs. Five: if you need to see what's under their clothes, ask them or if need be, I'll help so you are satisfied with what you might be purchasing."

Laughter filled the room as if they were in on a joke. Women were going to be auctioned off like cattle. He knew some of these women had no choice, and he wondered if others had known what they had gotten into. How could they? No one deserved to be treated this way. Luke wished he were in a position to help, but he couldn't reveal his real reason for being there.

"Now that we've reviewed the rules, please make yourselves comfortable. The maids will be happy to refill your drinks before the show begins. We will start in approximately ten minutes." She slipped back through the red velvet curtains.

Men stood and mingled, gesturing for the maids, their hands lingering on the women's hips and backsides. They laughed and ribbed one another in anticipation of what was to come. That anyone could to this to an innocent young woman was inconceivable.

Luke needed another drink if he were to survive. He stood and headed to the whiskey decanters, and poured himself a healthy amount. Downing the drink, he wiped his hand across his mouth before filling his glass again. Then, he went back to his seat and waited for the show to begin.

Once it started, Luke's outrage grew, yet his body betrayed him as young women were paraded onstage. There were rules, but nothing was truly off limits. Women with confidence removed their clothing and danced proudly, not minding that they weren't wearing a stitch. Others trembled in fear, shaking as Pauline forced them to unimaginable things. He couldn't wait to wash the stink off him from the perfume, smoke, and degradation he witnessed.

They were nearing the end when Pauline introduced her--a woman named Louisa. Luke's jaw dropped and his senses sharpened. For a moment, it was as though they were the only two in the room. She looked at him, and he held her gaze--green eyes wide with fright yet steeled with a determination he hadn't expected. Auburn hair hung down her back in a mass of thick curls that begged for a man's touch. Louisa stumbled but then caught herself, her eyes flitting back to Pauline before she came to a halt in the middle of the stage.

Louisa was gorgeous, likely the prettiest woman he had ever seen. She was thin with full pink lips, high cheek bones, and curves in all the right places. Black stockings with rose-colored ribbons covered her long, shapely legs. A light pink corset accentuated her small waist and draped over her hips where it met a short, ruffled skirt. She was every man's dream.

He wanted her with a fierceness that shocked and unnerved him at the same time. She was a harlot. Yet, according to the rules laid forth earlier, she was still an innocent and as such hadn't fallen. Perhaps he could save her.

Luke scoffed at himself. The thought was ridiculous. He wasn't there to save anyone; he was there to find Connie, and he would do well to remember that.

It became plain, however, that he wasn't the only man infatuated with her. A scruffy, older man stumbled to the stage. He was short and round with ears that stuck out and a grey beard that hadn't been shaved in some time. Pauline directed Louisa over to where the man could see her closely. When he demanded Louisa remove her clothing, she shook her head. The man hollered for Pauline to show him her wares. Pauline sauntered to Louisa and whispered in her ear. The look she gave Louisa was purely venomous, as though daring Louisa to defy her.

Louisa bowed her head in acquiescence and undid the ties to her corset with shaking fingers, letting it drop to her feet. She moved to lift the chemise over her head but stalled. Disgusted, Pauline stepped behind Louisa and before Louisa could object, she yanked it up and over her head, leaving her standing in nothing but stockings. Louisa tried to hide her body behind her hands, but it was useless. She was mesmerizing, but he was horrified. He couldn't believe what had unfolded right in front of his eyes.

Luke balled his hands into fists. It was all he could do to not jump up and stop everyone from looking at her, humiliating her any further. The man walked around her, smacking his lips. Her arms hung limp at her sides. Her face was red and defiant, but she didn't fight. She had no other choice but to stand there, for Pauline wasn't going to let her escape.

Anger swelled inside him. She shouldn't be treated this way. He had to protect her. Bidding seemed to be his only choice without blowing his cover. He had a sinking feeling it wouldn't be enough, but he had to try.

He wouldn't hurt her; he was determined to give her a choice. She could leave this place, and he'd help provide her with a future if she so desired. If she wanted to stay, then he would let her make that decision. Either way, the choice would be hers. Men could only bid on the virgins for the night. The price of a second night would be negotiated in the morning, so she would have to choose quickly.

Eventually, Pauline ushered Louisa off the stage, and the final two girls paraded in front of the men. They were nowhere near as alluring as Louisa, but the audience sat entranced. There would be no shortage of money flowing here tonight. The thought of bedding a virgin made men pull wads of cash from their billfolds and bags of gold dust from their pockets.

The curtain closed, and Pauline sauntered to the front of the stage. "I hope you've enjoyed the show... for we surely have."

The men clapped, whistled, and stomped their feet, showing their eager enthusiasm.

Pauline smiled. "Please place your bids within the next thirty minutes. Once your initial offers are listed, they will be read, and you can up your bid if you so choose. Once we determine the winners and payments are final, your prize will escort you to her room." She paused while the men applauded. "For those who aren't lucky enough to secure one of our treasures, we have plenty of more experienced young ladies who can grant your every desire. We don't want any of you leaving empty-handed, even if you don't win tonight. If you have questions, please consult with Bruno."

The man who'd shown interest in Louisa immediately staggered in Bruno's direction. Fearful the man would win, Luke headed their way and stood to the side, listening as he gave his bid to Bruno. Horror spread through Luke at the amount this man offered to pay. It was more than Luke made in a year. He could not come up with that kind of money.

Frustration filled every part of him, but then reality hit. He had come to find Connie, not to save a woman who'd let herself be auctioned off as a virgin. He tried to ease his mind by putting in a bid, but he wouldn't win. It would be better if he forgot about her and concentrated on his mission.

Men returned to their seats as the time arrived to discover who had won and to finalize the bids. As the winners were announced, there were cries of joy, and shouts of anger and frustration as men won or lost their prizes. Some upped their bids, but most accepted the outcome. When Louisa's name was called, the man who had insisted she undress won. Louisa didn't conceal her disgust. A deep frown pulled at her lips, and she shuddered when the old man touched her. As she was led off the stage, Luke saw fear in her eyes. Her eyes met his and begged for him to save her, but he couldn't do that. Despair swept through him at his inability to be her savior.

The final ladies were taken offstage, then Pauline quieted the men once again. "Thank you, gentlemen. It's been an exciting evening. For those of you who didn't win the prize you were looking for, remember there are plenty of women who are ready and willing." Women began pouring into the room, their smiles wide. "Please make your choice and enjoy the rest of your evening. But before you leave, our very own Madam Lafoe would like to speak a few words."

She pulled back the curtain, and a woman with light yellow hair emerged. *Holy cow!* It was Connie. His forehead beaded in sweat, his heart raced, and he gripped his knees hard. He had hoped to find her but hadn't expected to. Sinking back in his chair, he tried to relax, and prayed she hadn't seen him. He had to let Ben know he had found her, and he had to notify the sheriff as soon as possible. His nightmare might finally end.

Connie cleared her throat. "I'm pleased to see that all of my girls have been so generously offered for. I'm sure you'll enjoy your evening with your nubile prize. And for those of you who were not so lucky, please remember there are plenty of young ladies to pick from. If none suit your fancy, please let me know and I'll be happy to find someone who fulfills your needs. We have plenty here to satisfy all your desires, so don't be shy."

The men clapped and cheered, and a few sloshed whiskey into their laps and onto the floor. They loved the show and had enjoyed every minute. Connie had a presence of grand elegance and an aura of aloofness that men were drawn to. She would purr like a kitten all night long yet divulge none of her deep, dark secrets. He remembered how she had swept into his brother's life, her allure intoxicating. If she hadn't been married to Stanley the first time he met her, he might have chased after her himself.

She laughed, waved at the crowd, and then disappeared behind the curtain; leaving many wanting her, which was exactly what she'd planned. Connie was devious and manipulative, and his suspicions had been confirmed. She had returned to Helena.

Luke trembled with both relief and exaltation. She hadn't noticed him. He would leave the stink of this place behind when he contacted the sheriff. She would finally pay for her crimes.

Standing, he shuffled through the crowd when he saw the man who had purchased Louisa out of the corner of his eye. He stumbled out of the room, his eyes wide with lust and anticipation, his hand holding Louisa's as she led him away from the ballroom. Fighting his instincts to leave them well enough alone, Luke followed the pair at an unassuming distance and saw them enter a room at the end of the hall. He couldn't stop himself. He had to know what would happen to Louisa and whether he could still save her.

With all the parlor house staff milling around, he needed a

reason to be in the vicinity, so he grabbed a cute blonde and pulled her to his side. From this vantage, he could watch for trouble and hear what happened inside that room.

Keeping one ear open, he half-heartedly paid attention to the woman in front of him. She murmured words he ignored, placed kisses on his neck, and tried her best to entice him, but his mind was entrenched firmly on what was happening behind the door Louisa had disappeared behind. The woman didn't notice, or if she did, she didn't care. Payment was her only concern. He couldn't blame her. He used her as much as she used him.

The hallway soon quieted as couples disappeared behind doors. The woman in his arms tried to lead him away, but he kept her by his side until she got fed up with him. He gave her a few dollars and ushered her on her way. The house was quiet except for the occasional moan behind doors.

As Luke contemplated his next steps, the door to Louisa's room flew open. She stumbled out into the hall and straight into his arms.

Four

Tears streamed down Louisa's face, dripping onto her chest. Black streaks of mascara marked her cheeks. She wore nothing more than a shortened shift that barely covered her body, and she trembled in fear. When he took a deep breath, the fresh scent of roses tickled his nose, her floral perfume heady. He tried to steady her, but she fought him harder than expected for someone barely as tall as his shoulder. Her eyes were wild and her movements erratic.

"Let me go! Oh, please let me go."

"Ma'am, it's all right. Can I help?" He let go of her, his body missing her touch as soon as she stepped away. He gave her the space she needed to feel in control.

She retreated a few more steps and backed into the door frame. Her fist was clenched at her mouth as she gazed at him, searching his face for something. After a long moment, she must've decided she could trust him because she yanked him into the room she had just escaped from. In one glance, his eyes took in the frilly bed covered in white and yellow blankets, a wooden wardrobe, and white lace curtains.

"Please help me, mister. I didn't mean to hurt him, but he... he..." She gulped back a sob, her green eyes filled with desperation.

The man who had purchased her was sprawled on the bed, not moving a muscle. This would not go over well with the madam and her goons, who guarded the place like a prison. He broke a sweat. If he didn't get her out of there quick, all hell would rain down on them.

Luke strode to the bed, flipped the man onto his back, and bent to see if he breathed. The old man's chest moved and hot onion breath infused with strong moonshine blew from his open mouth and nose. Shards of glass from a lamp and an empty bottle of moonshine lay on the floor. The man was out cold, whether from the booze or from being hit with the bottle, it was hard to say.

Louisa stood shaking against the far wall. Grabbing a threadbare quilt from the foot of the bed, Luke placed it around her quivering shoulders, being careful not to startle her. She raised her head, her gaze unfocused, but she gripped the fabric between clammy fingers.

Not wanting to scare her, Luke maintained his distance. She didn't know him and had no reason to trust him, but she must've found something in his eyes if she trusted him enough to show him that she'd fought off the drunk old man.

She shuddered and took a deep breath. Her pink tongue darted out to wet her lips, dried from her rapid breathing. "Is he, is he—"

She couldn't say the words, so he finished them for her. "Dead?" He shook his head. "No. Drunker than a skunk and passed out, but he's still alive."

Her shoulders sagged with relief. "Oh, thank the lord above," she said. "I didn't mean to hurt him, but he started to, well, he started to—"

"It's all right, ma'am. You don't need to explain nothin' to me. I understand."

"Do you?" she said, her green eyes piercing, probing as if to glean his intentions. "You're in this place. I saw you in the crowd earlier. You were there to buy one of us?"

"No. I mean, yes. I mean..." He took a slow breath. "Yes, I was there, but no, I wasn't there to buy one of you."

Her brows snapped together. "Why else would you be at a virgin auction?" Her head tilted to the side, her eyes wide with unasked questions and disbelief. "The invitations were exclusive, and if you had one, then you had to know what was happening."

"Well, I—"

"Yes?" she said, waiting patiently.

He wanted to chuckle at the sudden interrogation but didn't think she'd appreciate him laughing at her, so he held his chortles at bay. "My boss got me an invitation, but I wasn't here to buy anyone. I'm looking for someone."

Her eyes darted back and forth between Luke and the man on the bed. "Who?"

"It's a long story, and I'm not sure we have the time."

"What do you mean?"

"I mean, eventually, he's going to wake, and it'd cause a ruckus if I'm found here, not to mention what they might do to you."

"I didn't mean to drag you into this." She glanced down at her scant clothing and pulled the quilt tight around her slim frame, nervously shifting her feet. They were in a parlor house, so a lack of proper clothing wasn't unusual, but his blood boiled as a streak of jealousy burned through him. He didn't want any man to see her this way.

"You didn't drag me into this, but..." He shouldn't get involved, but he couldn't help himself. He didn't enjoy seeing a damsel in distress. "I'd like to take you, if you'd let me."

Her eyes widened with horror.

"No, I don't mean it like *that*," he said, shoving his hand through his hair. "I mean, I'd like to help you escape this place if... if you'd accept the help, that is."

She snorted and emitted a painful laugh. "I can't leave. I have nowhere else to go."

"You don't have any family?"

She looked at him as if deciding what to tell him and what to hide. After a long moment, she murmured, "No, I'm alone. Besides, if you want to have me, then I might as well stay here and let you pay Madam Lafoe. Then, at least I'll get some of the money."

He stumbled back a few steps. "No, no." He held up his hands, shaking his head vigorously back and forth. It was a wonder it didn't swivel off his neck. "I'm not looking to have you. That's the last thing I'd ask." Although, if he were honest, he'd hoped she might've showered him with thanks.

She scoffed. "Why would I believe you?"

"I don't know." He shifted uncomfortably, realizing he had to give her a reason to do as he asked. "If I were you, I wouldn't believe me either, but I'm not here to hurt you or take anything from you. I just want to help."

"I don't know." She paced back and forth, the quilt dragging across the wooden floor.

"My family owns a ranch outside of Helena, and I'm sure my sisters and sister-in-law wouldn't mind having you stay with them until you can get back on your feet. That is, if you want to leave."

She had a shocked yet hopeful expression, but then it disappeared so fast he wondered if he had seen the hope after all. "I don't want to stay here, mister, but I don't have a choice. Madam will never let me leave, especially after what she's spent to get me ready"--she paused--"for all of this."

"I wasn't thinking of asking."

"It's not that easy." She sighed and lifted a hand to adjust an auburn curl that had fallen across her cheek, the quilt dropping from her creamy white shoulders.

Lust swirled through him in a blinding haze, and he had to force his gaze back up to her face.

"She has guards at all the doors. They'll never let me leave with you, unless you pay them. Even then, I'm not sure they'd let me go."

"You let me worry about that. I'll get you out of here."

"I appreciate that, but I don't think you realize how difficult it is to leave this place."

"Let me try, all right?" He let his fingers graze her cheek as she looked up at him with those big, dazzling green eyes framed by long, dark lashes. Her cheeks were pink, her lips plump. He could drown himself in her if he weren't careful. This wasn't the time or the place, and if he offered to help her, that was all it could be. Otherwise, he would be no better than the man sprawled unconscious on her bed.

She finally nodded in agreement. He wanted to help her, and he'd be darned if he'd let anyone harm her.

A door banged closed down the hall and startled them. He stepped away, and she pulled the quilt back around her bare shoulders.

"Pack your things and be ready to leave when I return. We may only have a few minutes, and I'll need you to be ready. Can you do that?"

She looked at him with innocent hope that tugged at his heart, then nodded. He had to succeed for anything else was not acceptable.

"I'll be back soon. Oh, and Luke Seymour's the name, but *you* can call me Luke," he said, winking at her. He opened the door, looked both ways, and slipped out without a sound.

Louisa had just agreed to leave Mon Petit Amour with a stranger. She didn't know Luke or what he wanted. He could be the same, or worse, than the man she had just fought off. *Am I out of my ever-lovin' mind?* She had nowhere to go and was worried she wouldn't be able to put a roof over her head. Luke said she could stay with his family. He seemed sincere in his offer to help her escape this place, but he could be lying.

She had chosen this path and knew what was expected. But when that old man had stumbled into her room, he'd looked at her like she was a piece of chocolate cake he couldn't wait to devour, and her stomach had tightened with revulsion. In that moment, she knew she had made the wrong choice, and she'd hoped plying the man with whiskey would help. She had kept him talking, all the while giving him drink after drink.

Finally, fed up with her maneuvering, he'd tried to take her into his arms. He had kissed her––slurpy, smacking motions that filled her with disgust. He moved violently, struggling to undo the ivory buttons of his shirt and trousers. Ardor oozed off him in spates, and that frightened her more than anything else she had ever experienced. He would not be gentle or kind, of that she'd been absolutely certain.

He'd demanded she remove her tiny shift. Instead, she'd scooted back on the bed, shaking her head as fear drove through her like a thundering storm. Enraged, he'd slapped her face and yanked at her clothing, ripping her stockings in his attempt to get what he wanted––to get what he'd *paid* for. It amazed her that the man was still conscious and fighting, considering the amount of liquor he'd consumed. She didn't know what it would take to keep him from hurting her. She'd reached for something to stop him, and her hand brushed against the heavy lamp on the bedside table. She'd grasped it and swung with all her might, hitting him on the back of his head and knocking him out cold.

Louisa hadn't known if it was luck or coincidence when she'd run straight into Luke's arms. She had looked into his bright green eyes, almost the same color as hers and something spoke to her––a kindness, a compassion she hadn't expected, and she'd instinctively known she could trust him. Now she wondered if she'd seen real kindness or if she'd seen what she wanted to see.

As much as she appreciated the thought of being free, going to his family's ranch was not reasonable. Her troubles would follow her no matter where she went. Pursuing a life in a parlor house had been wrong, but she'd had no other choices. Leaving might not solve her problems, but she couldn't carry through with being a woman of the night. She had to find a different way.

The old man stirred and she jumped back. If he woke and found her there, he was bound to hurt her more for daring to stop him. She pulled on a low-cut dress featuring a slit up to her thigh, obviously sewn with a man's pleasure in mind. Then, she grabbed a satchel from under the bed, throwing her belongings haphazardly into it. Time was of the essence. She just hoped she wasn't jumping from a blistering hot pan into the fire.

Once she finished packing, Louisa paced back and forth, the minutes ticking by as slow as a snail crossing the road. She glanced at the clock. Only ten minutes had passed but it felt like forever. She held her black cloak tight around her shoulders, her fingers twisting the fabric this way and that.

The old man snorted and moaned. She hoped Luke would return before he awakened. Perhaps he'd left her to handle the aftermath of trying to stop the old man. She wouldn't blame him if he had, for there was no reason a perfect gentleman would help someone like her.

Finally, the door creaked open. Louisa held her breath, hoping it wasn't a guard, Madam Lafoe, or the floor mother. She'd seen firsthand what happened to girls who disobeyed, and she had decided from the beginning she wouldn't be one of them.

Luke peered around the corner and whispered, "You ready?"

She nodded, picked her bag off the floor, and scampered to his side. He looked her over and grimaced. "Do you have a better pair of shoes?"

She lifted her skirt and looked at them. She owned nothing outside of the fancy slippers on her feet. They weren't practical and would likely cause her to slip and fall. She furrowed her brows. "I know they aren't the best, but I'll make them work."

He shrugged. "Can you trust me with what happens next?"

Do I have a choice? She was trapped between a desire to do better and the inability to live how she wanted. It was either him or suffer the consequences. "Yes," she whispered.

"Stay close behind me. I've got a plan, but it's tenuous at best and requires you to cooperate, no matter what."

Not sure what she had just agreed to, she followed him. She didn't know why she trusted this man, but she knew she could.

Louisa followed Luke closely as they crept down the hall. Luke paused every time he heard a moan, a rustle, or a creak in the floorboards. They reached a set of hidden stairs behind a door that blended into the wall. Unless you knew of its location, it was difficult to notice, but somehow he had found it. He pushed the door open and looked down the dark stairs before pulling her behind him. When they reached the bottom, he let go of her hand and whispered in her ear, his breath tickling her, sending shockwaves along her spine. "Stay here. I'll be right back."

He disappeared and she stood silent, holding her breath. Before she could guess what they were doing and how likely they were to make it out of the parlor house alive, he returned and pulled her into the bright, open hallway behind the kitchen. She shivered. This was a dangerous place to be. If anyone saw them, an alarm would be raised. She shouldn't be anywhere near the kitchen unless it was time for the morning meal, the only time working girls were allowed there.

Luke suddenly halted, pushed her up against the wall, and threw her bag a short distance away to a nearby nook in the wall. He braced one hand against the wall while the other pulled her hips against his. It all happened so fast she hadn't had time to take a breath before his mouth brushed against hers. He scattered kisses along her cheek to her ear before whispering, "I'm sorry. I heard someone's footsteps, and this just makes sense."

Men laughed somewhere nearby, but her attention was focused solely on Luke. Like a bow against violin strings, her body hummed in tune with his. Her spine tingled as his lips rested against her ear. His hand rubbed gentle circles on her lower back, her skin warming under his touch. Before she could form another thought, his supple lips touched hers again softly. Then, he deepened the kiss, sending a surge of fire to her toes. She leaned into him.

When she didn't think she could take it any longer, he released a small groan, lifted his lips, and rested his forehead against hers. Their breath mingled, hot and heavy, before he pulled away slowly. She raised a hand to the round, black mole at the corner of his eye and caressed it gently. He grinned at the tender touch.

No, she wanted to scream, *you can't stop*, but he had. Her heart begged for him to return, but common sense prevailed. She couldn't rut with him like a common whore. Her escape from this parlor house was her chance at a new future, and she had to make the best of it.

He peered over his shoulder before he grabbed her bag, snatched her hand up in his, and tugged her with him down the short hall, through the empty kitchen, and to the back door. Her mind whirled. Everything happened so fast that her breath caught with wonderment. He pushed open the door and gazed outside. With a satisfied smile, he pulled her to a waiting horse and lifted her atop it. Then he quickly mounted behind her and urged the horse forward.

His arms held her close, shielding her, protecting her. Just as they were almost free, someone yelled, "Hey, you, stop!" A gun exploded, the sound reverberating off nearby buildings. A bullet slammed into Luke's shoulder, and he slumped against her. The heaviness of his weight made her worry that the man who had helped her escape, who had evoked something brilliant, might have just been killed for trying to save her.

She yelped in fear and tried to turn to see how bad it was, but his powerful arms kept her in place. He muttered curse words under his breath but stayed upright and forced the horse into a gallop. Clumps of dirt flew behind them as the wind whistled through her hair, blowing it behind her. He urged the horse forward, keeping her safe.

Five

"Ow," Luke muttered.

He thought they had escaped unnoticed, but he had miscalculated and a bullet had ripped into his upper arm. It burned something fierce but had presumably gone through, leaving a jagged mess behind. Blood trickled from the wound, staining his good shirt and suit. He had to get somewhere safe to stop the bleeding.

He hadn't expected to take it as far as he had with Louisa while standing in the hallway of the parlor house, but her sweet essence had been his undoing. As soon as his lips had touched hers, he had been lost. The only thing keeping them from rutting like wild horses right there in the hallway had been the realization that she could've gotten killed if he hadn't gotten her out of there. Men cackling as they had gone down the hall had pulled him from the intoxicating yearning he had for her.

He shifted in the saddle and lifted his arms to urge the horse forward when a sharp pain erupted down his arm. He didn't think he'd die, but it sure would hamper his movements for some time. There were too many things he wanted to do, one of which was to bring that witch, Connie, to justice. He had to remember that.

Blowing out a deep breath, he said, "I've been hit."

"Yes, I know," she said, her voice soothing, calming in the face of danger. "We should stop so I can look at it."

"Can't stop now. I'll be fine." He grimaced as she bounced back against him and hit his arm. It certainly wasn't her fault, but darn if that didn't hurt. They had to disappear fast.

He dug his heels into the horse's flanks and bent over Louisa. His energy started to wane. As the pain in his arm continued to build, the severity of this situation hit him hard. He didn't know where to go because he wouldn't make it back to his place and his younger brother, Michael, lived on the other side of town. Judging by the loss of blood, he was afraid he'd pass out soon, but he had to stay conscious long enough to get Louisa to safety. Luckily, they were near Walter's place. He hoped his boss was around to help.

Reaching Walter's two-story home, he nudged the horse around to the back and tried to dismount without falling. It wasn't graceful, but he got his feet on the ground, the world swirling around him. Taking a moment, he leaned his head against the horse's flank, his pulse racing, his breath labored, his limbs shaking with fatigue. He raised his head to meet Louisa's eyes and she winced.

Her body swam before him as she swung her leg over and slid down the horse's side. She grabbed a handkerchief she had stuffed in the top of her dress and placed it against the wound, trying to stop the flow of blood. He took it from her and swayed on his feet but somehow stayed upright.

The horse smelled his blood and pulled at the reins, anxious and uncomfortable. Louisa grabbed the reins and calmed the horse with a few whispered words. She stroked his muzzle with her palm, soft and comforting.

Louisa was a fascinating woman, and her scant clothing hid nothing from his perusing eye. Even though his arm hurt something fierce, he couldn't help but remember her against him in that hallway. He hadn't intended on kissing her, but he'd been lost in her heady floral scent and her wide, trusting eyes. He had gotten more than a taste, and he desperately wanted more; but he was losing blood, and she had just survived an attack by a dangerous man.

Louisa tied the horse to the fence, grabbed her bag, and put her arm around his waist. She nestled against him, her head next to his good shoulder. "Lean against me." She looked around the back of Walter's home, her head swiveling this way and that. "Is this your home?"

His vision blurred, and he shook his head to clear it. He didn't know if he would make it to the door, but she stood warm and strong next to him.

"Luke?" She turned her head to gaze up at him.

"No, it's my employer, Walter's place." He muttered obscenities under his breath, sharp pinpricks shooting down his arm. His energy was draining fast. "I was afraid I wouldn't make it to my house before I passed out."

"Will he help?"

"I surely hope so." Luke stumbled along the rocky stone path to the back porch. The only thing keeping him upright was Louisa by his side, holding him up as they climbed the porch steps.

She dropped her bag on the porch and held him tight as she pounded on the door. After a few moments, a light appeared in the window and the door cracked open.

"Do you know what time it is?" Walter glared at him, bright light silhouetting him from behind.

"Sorry, Walter." Luke's tongue grew thick in his mouth, and he struggled to talk. "I didn't know where else to go."

Walter's lips moved and the gas lights shone on Luke's face, but nothing penetrated the fog as he slipped into the black abyss.

∾

Louisa gasped as Luke slumped against her and slid to the ground. She took the full brunt of his heavy, muscular frame and tried to keep him from falling, but it was too much. She stumbled and fell to her knees, her dress ripping under their combined weight. With sheer determination, she kept his head and shoulders from hitting the wooden boards of Walter's porch. Sharp pains shot up her knees and thighs, but she ignored the ache. The man in her arms needed her.

She looked up at Walter. "Please help."

He grabbed Luke under the arms, pulled him off her, and hollered, "Marie, come quick!"

When Luke's weight lifted, Louisa scrambled to her feet and gathered his limp legs under her arms. Grunting, she helped Walter drag Luke inside. Together, they lifted him onto the tall kitchen table. Tinware plates and cups scattered and cutlery clattered to the ground, but Walter barely glanced at the mess.

Throwing her cloak on the nearest chair, she raised her eyes and caught Walter looking at her. His gaze roamed her frame, and his eyes lit up with obvious pleasure. Disgusted that all men reacted the same, she ignored him. Luke needed to be tended to, and she'd deal with Walter later.

"Can you help me remove his suit jacket?" she asked.

Walter grunted as he lifted Luke to a sitting position with his head lolling forward while she undid the buttons on his jacket and shirt. She pulled the clothing from his upper body, his good arm first and then his injured one, careful not to disturb the wound any more than necessary.

When freed of both garments, she got an eyeful of his broad, sculptured chest and had to remind herself he was hurt. She shook herself free from the heat that rested inside her. Walter's presence further reminded her of where she was and what she needed to do. He guided Luke's limp form to the table and stepped away to give her room to work.

She found a small paring knife resting on the counter against the far wall and picked it up between her fingers, the movement familiar and comfortable. She had assisted her father while he worked on patients in his home surgery, so she knew what to do. The bleeding had slowed to a small trickle, but he had likely lost more than he should've.

Lifting his arm, she examined his flesh. The bullet had exited through the front of his upper arm. How it had missed her, she would never know, but relief filled her. If she had been injured, she wouldn't have been able to help him and things could have turned out much differently.

A young woman with hair the color of the midnight sky came rushing into the kitchen. She stumbled to a stop and stared at Louisa and Luke, her mouth wide open before shaking herself out of her stupor.

"What happened, Walter?" She reached inside a large cabinet against the far wall, retrieved clean rags, and dropped them on the table next to Luke's head before she placed her hands on her hips, her eyes flitting back and forth between the three of them.

"I can't say for certain, but it appears Luke here has been shot," Walter said.

"And who is this?" Marie said, tilting her head to Louisa.

"That I can't answer, sister dear, but I think we need to worry about Luke and his injury before we ask too many questions."

Marie let out a little *humph* of dismay. She grabbed an apron and handed it to Louisa, but then chuckled when she saw Louisa's blood-covered hands.

Louisa tried to hide her grin. This wasn't a laughing matter, but the expression on Marie's face made her want to giggle. "Not sure I'll be able to put it on and not make an even bigger mess, but I appreciate the thought."

Marie smiled wide, a dimple piercing her cheek. "Let me help." Marie held out the straps and helped Louisa slip it on before tying the apron strings securely around her waist. The apron would protect her clothing from blood, but Louisa didn't care if her dress was salvageable. With any luck, she'd discard it soon in favor of clothing that hid more than it revealed.

Marie scurried to the cast iron stove, opened the grate, and started a small fire. She filled a large, black pot with water from the kitchen pump and then placed it on the stove without being asked. Meanwhile, Louisa continued to inspect Luke's wound, using the knife to peel back the blackened skin.

Marie raised her eyes to Louisa's, her gaze full of questions. "What can I do?"

An understanding of their shared determination passed between them, giving Louisa a measure of comfort. This woman wouldn't judge her and could become a friend if they were given the opportunity. She took a deep breath and returned to the task at hand.

Looking back at Luke's arm, Louisa said, "Do you have needles and thread? He's going to need stitches." Her fingers continued to probe the area around the wound, making sure there weren't any remaining pieces of bullet under the skin.

"Shouldn't we call a doctor?" Marie asked, peering over Louisa's shoulder.

Before Louisa could respond, Walter said, "No, this situation requires us to be discreet. Am I wrong in that, young lady?" He stared hard at Louisa, his gaze unwavering, the ardor that had been there when they arrived replaced by something akin to respect. She didn't want to read anything into it as he hadn't seen her in action yet, but she hoped she'd prove she was more than what she was wearing.

"No. I believe Luke would agree we need to keep this quiet." Straightening her posture, she turned back to Luke's wound. Luke had saved her from a fate worse than death, and she would do everything in her power to make sure he was well taken care of.

"Do as she says, Marie."

Marie left through the swinging door and returned moments later, with needles and thread in one hand and more rags in the other. She dropped the items on the table, then went to the stove and poured boiling water into a ceramic bowl. Gripping the bowl carefully, she brought it to Louisa.

"Can you put two of those rags in the hot water, Marie? May I call you Marie?" Louisa asked.

"Yes," Marie said. "And you are?"

"Louisa."

Marie nodded and did as she asked, her movements swift and efficient.

"Do you have any whiskey?" Louisa asked.

"Don't you think you two have had plenty to drink tonight?" Walter said, a mocking tone to his voice. Louisa had forgotten he remained in the room.

Louisa glared at him. "It isn't to drink. It's to clean his wound."

"Why would you waste good whiskey?" he asked, raising an eyebrow.

"Are you a doctor?" she snapped back. When he didn't reply, she asked again, "Do you have *any* whiskey?"

Glaring at her, he snatched a bottle from the cabinet and dropped it onto the table. Louisa looked for something to grab the hot, wet rags. Marie handed her a pair of tongs before she could ask. Walter's sister was a gift sent from heaven. She didn't ask questions, and she understood exactly what Louisa needed.

Using the tongs, she lifted a rag from the water and let it drain for a moment before wringing it out. Her fingers protested the heat, but she ignored it. She cleaned the blood and dirt from the wound before picking up the whiskey bottle. Saying a quick prayer, she poured the liquor straight into the wound.

Luke's eyes flew open. "What are you trying to do to me, woman?" He shoved the whiskey bottle away, the liquid sloshing onto the table and floor.

Stumbling back, Louisa struggled to hold on to the bottle, made slippery by her bloody fingers. Using his good arm, Luke pushed to sit and swung his legs over the edge of the table. His face was bright red and sweat lined his brow. He looked at his arm, moved it, and grimaced. "You trying to kill me?"

The wound bled freely again with his erratic movements. Ignoring his question, Louisa dropped the whiskey bottle back on the table and picked up another rag, shoving it against his upper arm.

Glaring at her, Luke said, "Can you be a little more abrasive?"

He reached to push her away, but she slapped his hand. "Don't touch. I'm trying to stop the bleeding. You need to lie down so I can stitch it closed."

"No, I'll stay where I'm at, thank you very much." His eyes flashed with irritation and pain, but at least he was more alert than he had been moments before.

She bit her bottom lip. "Have you always been this stubborn?"

"Stubborn." He laughed but winced with the movement. "I'm not stubborn, just determined to watch what you're doing to my arm."

Shrugging, she stepped away, wiped her hands as clean as she could on another rag, and dug through the needles and thread. She found a long needle, threaded it, and soaked it in whiskey. Holding the needle up, she dabbed at the wound to wipe away more blood. "Are you ready?"

"Give me the bottle first," Luke said.

Eyes flashing, she bristled at his tone but wouldn't argue with him. She put the rag down and snatched the bottle with her free hand, then handed it to him. He lifted it to his full lips and took a long swallow. Her eyes focused on the movements of his slim neck as the liquor made its way down his throat.

Wiping his mouth with the back of his good arm, he placed the whiskey bottle on the table, his hand still wrapped around the neck. "Let's get this over with, shall we?"

Louisa bowed her head to hide her smile and quickly sewed the wound closed, first on the front and then on the back. He sat still, his arm twitching only once or twice when she pulled the needle through his thick skin. Once done, she poured more whiskey on the wound, apologizing for the sting before wrapping his arm in clean bandages.

"There. That should work," she said, coming around to face him. Sweat dripped off his face, but he hadn't uttered a word during her ministrations. "You'll need to clean that at least twice a day to keep it from oozing any pus."

"Thank you," he said, holding his arm to his side. "I appreciate you taking care of it." His lips lifted into a dazzling grin, and her heart pounded. He had to know how a woman would swoon at that gaze, his green eyes twinkling as though he had all kinds of secrets to share.

To distract herself, she said, "You'll need a sling." She grabbed another rag and looked it over carefully. "This should work." She draped it around his neck, her fingers grazing his soft skin. He shivered, the only sign he gave that he was affected by her touch. She gently placed his arm in the fabric before scooting around him and tying it behind his neck. Her fingers brushed against the silky ash-brown hair that curled at the nape of his neck.

When she finished, Luke said, "I didn't realize I had stumbled across a doc in..." he hesitated and looked at Walter and Marie, who stood watching them both. "Well, where I found you."

"I ain't a doc." She tried to contain the blush that had snuck out of nowhere.

His gaze went deep into her soul, and her skin tingled as she remembered their brief interlude. She knew he had done it only to keep Madam from discovering what they had been up to, but she couldn't help the furious blush that rose up her neck and into her cheeks.

Walter cleared his throat and Louisa chastised herself. They were not alone, nor was this the time to let wayward thoughts overtake her. Marie and Walter's gazes were full of questions she wasn't prepared to answer. She put distance between herself and Luke, and rubbed her hands on the apron around her waist.

"You wouldn't have been hurt if you hadn't... well, if you hadn't helped me leave. I should be the one thanking you."

Luke's lips lifted into a wide, handsome smile. "I aim to please." Then he started to sway. His lips fell. What little energy he had disappeared at an alarming rate. Louisa grabbed his good arm. "You should lie down. You've lost a lot of blood, not to mention all that whiskey you just drank."

Luke's eyelids drooped. "I'll be all right," he said, his words slurring. He fought to keep his eyes open.

"I don't think you will," Louisa said.

Walter used his elbow to gently nudge her out of the way and helped Luke stand. "Let's get you to bed before you fall asleep on my kitchen table."

With Walter supporting most of Luke's weight, they headed down the hall and up a set of stairs to the second floor. Walter pushed a door open to the first room on the right. The moon shined through the tall windows and onto a large four-poster bed. Louisa scurried to the bed and pulled back the coverlet.

"Are you sure you want to put him in here?" she asked as her hands ran across the decadent, silky sheets and soft blankets. She gazed in awe at the mahogany furniture and plush rugs under her feet. This room was far nicer than any place she had ever stayed.

Walter muttered something under his breath and half dragged, half encouraged Luke to the bed where he unceremoniously dumped him onto the plump mattress. Luke's head flopped like that of a newborn baby, with no strength and no support. She gasped and pushed Walter out of the way to tend to Luke, but his eyes were closed. Gentle snores emerged from his wide lips.

She reached for his legs and yanked off his boots. Reaching for his waist, she went to undo the buttons of his trousers when Walter cleared his throat loudly behind her.

Whipping her head around, she tried to see where he stood, but the darkened room made it difficult.

"What do you think you are doing?" Walter drawled.

"I..." she stopped. *What am I doing?* She shouldn't be undressing a man. She had no right. "I'm sorry. I shouldn't be doing this."

A match was struck, and a flicker of light shone from his two fingers. It barely illuminated Walter's face, but what she saw made her wish he had never lit the match. The desire was back, and it'd serve her to leave the two men alone.

She backed away from the bed. "I'll... I'll let you get him undress..." she swallowed hard. "Undressed, that is. Better that way. I'll... I'll head downstairs to... to clean up the mess we made."

She turned and ran out of the stuffy room.

Six

Louisa rushed into the empty kitchen and breathed a sigh of relief. Walter's gaze hadn't been unfriendly, but it wasn't exactly welcoming either. With Luke out cold, it appeared she was on her own once again. She should be grateful Luke had gotten her out of the parlor house, but she had no money and nowhere to go. She couldn't go back to the parlor house. They'd either kill her, force her to be with that man, or beat her until she agreed to whatever they demanded. Now that she had escaped, she had to stay far away.

She braced herself against the kitchen table, her fingers digging into the soft wood, her heart beating erratically in her chest. *Where can I go?* She couldn't stay here. Walter gazed at her the same way as every man in that horrible parlor house. She didn't know if he would expect something more or if he would be as kind as Luke was. She prayed she hadn't stepped from one viper's nest into another.

She had mistakenly believed she could survive a life as a harlot when her other options had been ripped from her. When she agreed to give up her innocence for the funds she needed, she thought she could take her mind elsewhere, let a few men do what they needed to do, and then disappear with the money she had earned. She couldn't help but descend into the memories of the chilly May morning when her life changed, and not for the better.

May 28, 1900

Louisa stood in the ballroom of the finest parlor house in Helena, shivering with fear over what her life had been reduced to. She clutched the small bag containing her worldly possessions. Her clothes were worn but clean, and her shoes barely hung onto her feet. She owned nothing but what was on her person. Everything else had been taken, sold, or given away. Her pride was all she had left, and that was being tested as she swallowed the revulsion that threatened to overwhelm her.

She knew what Mon Petit Amour was and what would be expected of her. Her pa had treated enough women of the night in his home surgery office. She knew what could happen, but she was still unprepared.

Her mother and father had never hidden the finer details of what went on between a woman and a man. Her father had given medical details regarding the human form, what went where, what its purpose was, and how it functioned. Her mother had described the act as loving, giving. She had wanted Louisa to find the love she so deserved.

Now, instead of having the loving relationship they both had wanted her to have, she would give her body to men for money. Her parents would've been appalled and disappointed if they were still alive. Her life had taken unexpected turns, and immense responsibilities left her with few choices and even fewer opportunities. She had tried to gain employment as a governess, a laundress, and even a seamstress. That had been a disaster. She wasn't even remotely talented when it came to piecing together fabric.

The door to the ballroom opened and a confident, elegant blonde swept into the room. A stern and burly man followed at her side. When she glided to a stop, he folded his arms across his chest. His eyes were cold and menacing as he stared at the young women standing, waiting for their fate.

Most of the young women knew why they were there, but there was a small group who didn't speak English. Louisa feared they had no idea what they had gotten themselves into. Her compassionate side wanted to warn them, but she knew it was too late for them all. The men guarding the doors were not friendly or cuddly, and were not there for their entertainment. They were there to make sure the girls never left again. She had been told when she walked through the front doors that once she entered, she would forever be a whore.

Clapping her hands to get their attention, the blonde looked at them, firm and determined. The titters in the room quieted until they all but disappeared.

"Ladies, welcome," she said. "My name is Connie Lafoe. I'm to be your madam. This"––she pointed to the burly man next to her––"is Nathan. Please don't let his stern expression scare you. You should be more afraid of me."

Connie explained their next steps. They were going to be invited into her office––as though any of them had a choice in the matter. Then, they would be interviewed, and Connie would decide where and how they would work in the house. Nathan opened the wide ballroom doors and invited more rough-looking men inside. Nodding to Nathan, Connie sauntered to a door discreetly built into the wall, opened it, and disappeared into another room.

Over the next few hours, each girl was led to the door and disappeared behind it. Some returned with wide smiles, others with tears in their eyes, and some were never seen again.

When it was her turn, Louisa's fingers cramped as she clasped her bag, her knuckles burning. She had made this choice, and she would have to live with it. There was no other way to pay off the debts she had accumulated since her father's death, not to mention the ones he had left for her to handle. With any luck, she could close her eyes, endure whatever men wanted from her, and earn enough money to escape in the future. They said she couldn't leave, but she would find a way. They couldn't keep her here forever.

Nathan pushed the door open and when she hesitated, he shoved her into the room hard enough that she stumbled and barely kept to her feet. She shuffled to the wide, intricately carved desk and stood trembling in front of it. Bright sunlight nearly blinded her from the sparkling windows. Heavy purple drapes were tied back with gold tassels, and a thick purple rug lay under her feet. Connie studied the papers on her desk and waved her to sit. Another man with a scar along his right cheek stood behind her, looking just as evil as the man she called Nathan.

Louisa dropped into the wooden seat, her bag held in her lap like it would stop the train wreck that was happening in front of her eyes. After what seemed like hours but was only a few seconds, Connie pushed the papers aside. She leaned back in her chair, raising her fingers to her lips as she looked Louisa over.

"How old are you?"

"I... um... what?" *Why would she ask that?*

"Don't make me repeat myself, young lady. Time is of the essence, and I don't have the patience or the desire to deal with someone who can't answer simple questions. How old are you?"

Swallowing hard, Louisa said, "Twenty-five."

"That old?" She scrunched her nose in disgust. "What's your name?"

"Louisa."

"Hmph. An old name for an old maid."

"I'm not an old maid." Louisa regretted her words when Connie's eyebrows snapped together. This was not a woman she wanted to anger.

"So, you do have a backbone, I see?"

"A backbone?"

Connie sighed and pinched the skin between her eyebrows. "Have you ever been with a man?"

"No, never."

Connie laughed, but her eyes were hard and displeased. "Then why are you here?"

"Why am I here?"

"Yes, why are you here?"

"To make money." It wasn't to find a husband; she wouldn't be looking in a whorehouse if she wanted to get married.

"I guess that's as good a reason as any."

Connie stood and headed to a wardrobe alongside the distant wall, opened it, and withdrew some items. She threw a silk robe, shift, stockings, and a corset at Louisa. "Remove your clothing and put these on."

Louisa held the items in shock. "There's no dress." She raised her eyes to Connie's crystal blue ones.

Connie laughed again. "This isn't a high-society event you're at, young lady."

"But—"

"But nothing!" She slammed her fist on her desk. "You're lucky, girl. I'm not altogether sure you're an innocent."

What difference did that make? "I've never—"

"That's what they all say, but if you're lying to me, I'll find out soon enough, and if you're smart, you'll come clean. If you're an innocent, then you're worth something to me. If you aren't, you won't like what happens next."

Not knowing what to say, Louisa sat stunned. Her eyes were likely wide with alarm.

"Bruno will take you to your room. Change clothes, and take what you're wearing and whatever's in that bag, and give it to him."

"But this is all I have," Louisa protested, shaking like a leaf.

"And you won't need it here."

Louisa opened her mouth to argue again, but as Connie glared at her, Louisa knew it would be useless. She had stepped into this mess and now she'd have to live with it for the rest of her life.

The kitchen door swung open, pulling Louisa back to the present. She'd become lost in memories that were best left in the past. Pushing a strand of hair from her cheek, she took a deep breath and plastered a smile on her face.

"There you are," Marie said. "You must be plumb tuckered. Let's get you upstairs and into one of the guest rooms."

"I shouldn't." Louisa gazed around the room, looking for her bag, and found it against the wall. "I should leave."

"And go where?" Marie asked, her fingers gently touching Louisa's arm.

"I—"

"Luke wouldn't want you to leave. If he went to the effort of taking you from... Well, from wherever he rescued you, then you should stay here until he decides what he wants next."

"You're right, but I..." Louisa's words trailed away as Walter ambled into the room. She backed away from Marie.

"You're still here," he said, staring pointedly at her.

"I was just leaving." She picked up her bag. "Please make sure Luke watches that wound carefully. It could get infected if those bandages aren't replaced at least daily."

"You can't go," Marie said, her voice pleading. "It's late."

"I'm sorry, I shouldn't be here."

"Don't let us stop you," Walter said.

"Walter," Marie snapped. "Quit being rude to her. She saved Luke's life."

"And he wouldn't be in this mess if it weren't for her."

Marie gasped, stalked to her brother, and pulled him to the

other side of the room. She whispered harshly in his ear, her face
growing redder with each word. He scowled, and eventually threw
up his arms and moved away from his sister.

Staring hard at Louisa, he said, "Put her in the room next to
Luke's. That way, she can watch over him if he has"––his eyebrow
lifted––"needs in the middle of the night. If he brought her here,
then she can surely watch over him." With that, he pushed past his
sister and stalked out of the room.

Marie sighed and rested her hands on her waist. "I apologize,
Louisa. He usually isn't such a bear, but the few nights when he
isn't working, he likes to sleep and if he's disturbed, he can be a bit
cantankerous. He works a lot, you understand, and—"

"It's all right. I'll just leave. It's clear he doesn't want me here,
and—"

"Nonsense," Marie said. "It's late and there's nowhere for you
to go. Besides, Luke would never forgive me if I were to let you
leave."

"Oh, is he your—"

"Luke?" She laughed. "No, we aren't like that. He works for
Walter. I don't have time for men. Too many things I need to do.
Now, come with me and let's get you settled." She walked to the
kitchen door but then stopped. "Oh, heavens. Are you hungry? I
didn't think to offer you anything to eat or drink." She marched to
the icebox under the counter and pulled it open, peering inside.
She drew out a platter of ham and a bowl of chilled potatoes.

Louisa's mouth watered at the thought of eating, and her
stomach grumbled when she caught a whiff of the fresh bread
Marie grabbed from above the stove. Louisa hadn't had a decent
meal in days. The house mother believed Louisa was too voluptuous and had her on a diet of water and stale crackers. She hadn't
eaten well in months and hadn't had meat in some time.

Feeling as though she should be useful if she were to eat their
food, she grabbed a clean rag and went to work wiping the table.
Blood and filthy rags were scattered everywhere. Within a few

minutes, Marie and Louisa had cleaned the table, and picked up the plates and cutlery that had been thrown to the floor. They worked well together.

Sitting, Louisa took a piece of ham and a scoop of potatoes.

Marie looked at her plate and shook her head. "Louisa?"

Louisa had just picked up her fork. Lifting her eyes, she caught Marie's gaze. "Yes?"

"Is that all you're going to eat?"

Louisa looked at her plate and blushed.

"There's plenty. Please take as much as you'd like," Marie said as she filled her plate with far more food than Louisa had.

Louisa nodded and put a few more pieces of juicy ham on her plate, another generous helping of potatoes, and a thick piece of bread slathered in warm butter.

Marie laughed. "Now that's more like it." She took a bite of bread. "I'm starving, and I ate a few hours earlier. Nothing like a little excitement to whet the appetite."

Before long, the two of them were laughing and talking as though they had known one another for years. When Louisa didn't think she could eat anymore, she swallowed the last piece of ham, leaned back in her chair and groaned with pleasure. "Thank you. That was purely delicious. I haven't had anything this nice in months."

Something flashed in Marie's eyes, but it was gone before Louisa could examine it. "We have plenty. Have as much as you please."

"I have. You might have to roll me out of the kitchen." She yawned, her face near splitting in two from the depth of her exhaustion. Blushing, she said, "I'm sorry. That was awfully rude of me. It's been a long day, and it's caught up with me."

"Let's get you to your room."

"Let me clear the dishes first," Louisa said, stacking the plates in her arms and placing them next to the water pump.

"Nonsense," Marie said. "I can get them in the morning."

"But—"

"There was plenty in here from our dinner that I didn't clean up, so a few more dishes won't make a difference. It's late. You're tired, I'm tired, and they'll keep." Marie's tone suggested Louisa not argue. Not wanting to offend her host, she did as Marie said.

She would get up early in the morning and clean up the kitchen so she wouldn't burden Walter and Marie with her presence. It was the very least she could do.

Seven

July 25, 1900

It didn't take much more than an hour to get the kitchen back to rights after Louisa had woken in the nicest bed she ever had the pleasure of sleeping in. She hadn't been raised wanting for a thing, but there hadn't been a need for the nicer things in life, either. Her father had made a good living working as a physician, but he'd spent more time helping those less fortunate, and so the money, while scarce, had been plenty to keep them from starving. There had been a lot of love and a dry roof over their heads, but not much else.

Taking one last swipe at the now clean kitchen table, she brushed away the sweat that had gathered on her chest. It trickled down her neck and she scratched at her corset, trying to stop the incessant itching. Her dress wasn't made for cleaning. It wasn't made for much more than tantalizing, but she didn't exactly own anything proper. At least it was clean, albeit scandalous.

They had taken her modest clothing in the parlor house, but now she wished they had let her keep something. Shaking her head, she admonished herself. The past was in the past, and now that she had left, she had to decide on her future. Making the choice to enter the parlor house had been a mistake, but at least she could recover from that choice. She just needed money to put a roof over her head and to pay off her and her father's debts.

The door to the hallway swung open behind her, startling her from her musings. She dropped the wet rag and knelt to pick it up. Black boots shifted and caught her eye. The legs were stiff, unyielding, and closer than she'd liked. Raising her head, she followed the legs up to a waist, and further up to Walter's broad chest. He had an unobstructed view of her chest, and his eyes were bright with hunger. She squirmed under his perusal. In a different time and place, she wouldn't have hesitated to give anyone who looked at her like that a scathing rebuke, but considering where she had just come from and what she wore, she held her tongue.

He crouched and touched her elbow, helping her stand. His fingers were firm, but gentle as his thumb rubbed against her skin.

Marie walked into the kitchen from the hallway, allowing Louisa to pull away, and Walter's hand fell. She didn't want to give Walter the wrong impression of her but feared her clothing was saying more than she'd like.

"Louisa," Marie said. "You didn't have to clean in here, but I'll be honest, I'm most appreciative. I hate doing housework, but Walter here doesn't believe in hiring for help. He thinks since I'm still living here, I should clean up after him." Her retort was made in a laughing tone, but the words were far from light. There was clearly a dynamic here that Louisa didn't want to get in the middle of.

"It was the least I could do," Louisa murmured. "Although, I really need to get something more appropriate to wear." She laughed, trying to make light of her revealing dress.

The room grew silent, and Louisa knew she had made a mistake. She placed the wet rag near the water pump and dried her hands on her soiled skirt before grabbing the clean bandages she had prepared. "I'm going to head upstairs and change Luke's bandages. See if he needs anything." Meeting Marie's eyes, she said, "Thank you again for last night. I appreciate your thoughtfulness. Excuse me."

Sharp pains in his arm woke Luke from his slumber. He shifted, his hands brushing against the silky sheets. *Where am I?* He struggled to remember what had happened the night before. His eyes snapped open, and his gaze roamed the room. Bright light poured in through the tall, squeaky-clean windows. Yellow silk drapes framed them, but they'd been pulled to the side. He wasn't in his bed, that was for sure; it wasn't nearly as tall, wide, or comfortable as the one he found himself in.

The night before was a blur. Blood, bullets, sweaty men, Louisa. *Oh, Louisa! Where is she?* He hoped she was all right and that Walter hadn't thrown her out. His heart warmed at the thought of her being in his arms as the events of the night rushed back to him. He remembered getting her away from the parlor house, a bullet ripping his upper arm, and seeing the scowl on Walter's face.

He sat up in the bed and noticed he was only wearing his drawers. He grimaced, the pain in his arm sharp. He must be at Walter's, which was decidedly not a welcome thought. Walter would tear into him for coming to his home and bringing Louisa there. A stickler for propriety, Walter protected his younger sister, Marie, with a vicious fierceness. Bringing someone like Louisa into Walter's home would not go over well, no matter the circumstances.

A soft knock sounded on the door.

"Come in," Luke said. He pulled the blankets to his waist. He wasn't sure who waited behind the door. Someone had undressed him, and he prayed it had been Walter. He could only take so much embarrassment in a twenty-four-hour period.

Louisa walked in, and his jaw dropped. She was just as desirable in the light of day as she had been the night before. He had to swallow the surge of passion that roared through him like a freight train. Memories of her from the night before came to the forefront of his mind. He couldn't bear the thought of her seeing how much he desired her, for he had rescued her from a man who had been determined to take her innocence. He couldn't be the same. He wasn't the same.

"Good morning, Luke." Her voice low and tentative, a definite difference from the way she ordered him around the night before. "May I come in?"

"Yes," he said, adjusting his back against the hard wooden headboard.

"Did you sleep?"

"I think so. Don't remember much," he said.

"I'd like to check your arm, if that's all right with you." She moved toward him, her steps hesitant.

"I ain't going to bite, you know." He lifted his lips into a smile.

She giggled, her eyes sparkling with delight. "I didn't think you would."

She leaned across him and gently touched his arm. His skin grew warm. Trying to tamp down his urges, he sucked his chest in to pull away, but it was no use. Her chest draped across him like a hot blanket as she tried to examine his wound.

Taboo thoughts roared through his mind. He might have found her in the parlor house, but she'd never had a man, or at least that was what Pauline had said during the auction. He imagined they wouldn't have been able to sell her to the highest bidder if she hadn't been an innocent. Between his inappropriate thoughts and the memory of their embrace the night before, he grew more uncomfortable with each passing second.

He had never had such a reaction to a woman before. Ben and Elizabeth, his brother and sister-in-law, had paraded plenty of women in front of him, but he'd never been interested. Sure, there had been a few crushes long before his pa was killed but since then, he hadn't had so much as a passing interest in any woman until Louisa. He wasn't quite sure what to make of it.

She untied the knot of his sling, but from the muttering under her breath, she couldn't see or reach the wound as well as she would've liked. She mumbled something unladylike, hitched up her skirt, climbed onto the bed, and straddled his lap. He hadn't had time to stop her before she settled against him. He had to force his mind to what she was doing, not what he wanted to do. Her movements were methodical, nurse-like, and she likely had no idea the havoc she created.

She lifted the bandage and examined it carefully. She then probed the wound, and he barely contained the harsh grunt coming from his lips.

"Heaven help me, Louisa." Any desire he might've had was now squashed by the pain shooting down his arm, into his fingers, and up his neck.

Pulling clean rags from the front of her bodice, she lifted onto her knees and placed them on the wound, then quickly re-wrapped it. She tied the top of the bandage, sat back on her heels, and took a good look at him. "Did you want to ask me something?" A quirky smile played on her lips.

Luke couldn't tell if she was laughing at him. "You are... well, on my lap."

"You just now noticed." Her eyes twinkled as she looked down and then back into his eyes. She crossed her arms. "Is that a problem?"

"Um, well, no." She was quite forward, but it amused him and made him smile.

"How else was I supposed to tend to your wound?" She cocked her head to the side, an impish grin lifting her lips.

Well, she had him there. "You pulled the bandages from the top of your... um, dress," he said.

She laughed. "Yes, this dress has no pockets. It was that or at the top of my stockings. Got to make do with what you've got. Besides, you've got nothing any other hot-blooded man doesn't have, so nothing surprises me."

His eyes widened in shock. *Did she just... Oh, yes, she did.* The grin on her face told him she knew exactly what she had implied. He shouldn't have said a word. His face was likely red as a fiery flame from a smithy. His gaze dropped but then immediately returned to her face. She didn't seem to notice.

"I've embarrassed you," she said. "I shouldn't have been so blunt. I've not exactly been living the life of a proper young lady of late, so I forget how I should act in the presence of a gentleman."

"That's all right. It's been an interesting twenty-four hours."

"It has been." She stared at him for a moment, looking as though she wanted to ask him something.

"Is there anything wrong?"

"No," she said, "but can I ask you a question?"

"Absolutely. I'm an open book."

"Why were you at Mon Petit Amour if you weren't there to get... well, you know."

He chuckled but stopped when he saw the look of consternation on her beautiful face. "I'm sorry, I shouldn't laugh." He shifted his arm and cursed under his breath. His arm hurt like the dickens. "It's a long story, but suffice to say, Madam Lafoe hurt my family. I'd gone there hoping to find her, to bring her to justice."

Her eyes were wide, almost shocked at his words. "She's a criminal?"

He grimaced. "She's that and more." Swallowing back his pain, he continued, "She killed my pa and tried to take my family's ranch. I've been looking for her for years."

"Oh my." She held her fingers against her lips. "I'm so sorry, Luke. How did you know to look for her there?"

"I didn't exactly. We had gotten a letter from a friend of ours who mentioned she had grown up in brothels and that she had a propensity for high-end ones. I asked Walter if he could help me and he got me an invitation to the place." He raised his good hand to his face and wiped his eyes. "I went inside Mon Petit Amour hoping to find her, but found something else entirely." He cleared his throat. He'd said too much, but he couldn't seem to help himself. He had found something that he had never expected and wasn't willing to lose it if he had a choice.

She blushed. Her tongue licked her pink lips, and his mind flashed back to the kiss they had shared in the parlor house's hallway. Chemistry crackled between them now as it had then. Luke leaned forward, his lips inches from hers when the door slammed open, and she startled on his lap. Her eyes wide, she scrambled off of him and leapt off the bed.

Walter stood in the doorway, his arms crossed and glaring at both of them. Her being in his lap might have started as innocent, but it was extremely inappropriate. He had gone too far.

Eight

Louisa's breath came fast and furious. The interest in Luke's eyes had been unmistakable. She had wanted to kiss him, to feel his lips against her once again, but straddling Luke's lap had been wrong. Walter's look of disgust had said it all. Sure, she'd done it to tend to his arm, but she had acted boldly, completely unlike herself. Her shameful behavior was a sure sign she had fallen further than she had realized. It was inexcusable, and she was ashamed of herself. Standing near the window, her back to the men, she tried to hold back tears. She didn't want either of them to see her cry.

Louisa shifted her feet on the hardwood floor, her toes curling in her stockings as her unease grew. She tried to adjust her skirt so it covered her leg, although it was pointless; Luke had seen more than he should have. He might have found her in a parlor house, but she wanted to go back to being a proper lady. She had to change her behavior if she ever wanted to be accepted into polite society again. If she continued to kiss Luke, she would fall hard and fast. She had to remember her priorities, and they didn't include an unwedded romp with this man.

Behind her, harsh words were being spoken between Luke and

Walter—a disagreement she had caused. The time she'd spent thinking about her actions had removed her from the conversation, and she'd missed what they had said.

The room grew silent. Seconds passed and no one spoke. When it became too much to bear, she turned and brushed her fingers against the top of the armchair as though removing nonexistent dirt. "You'll need to keep changing the bandages every couple of days. If you see any green or yellow pus, seek a doctor at once. I tried to remove the dirt and grime, but you can never be too careful." The words came out in a rush, her face as hot as the bright sun. "I... Thank you for getting me out of there last night, but I need to gather my things and leave."

"Louisa, I don't know if that's a good idea," Luke said, his voice soft and hesitant. His gaze met hers.

"If she wants to leave, Luke, you can't make her stay," Walter said.

"Walter." Luke's voice held a threatening tone, and the men glared at one another. "Can you leave us? I'll explain everything later."

Tension crackled like a thunderstorm ready to explode. She hadn't wanted to cause friction between Luke and his boss. Her existence in this house was proving to be a mistake. Walter muttered something under his breath, but he did as Luke asked. His receding footsteps allowed her to breathe a bit easier.

When he was gone, she said, "I need to leave."

"Do you have somewhere to go?" Luke asked.

She hadn't the slightest clue where to go, but he had to know that already. He wasn't stupid. Women didn't find themselves in brothels because they had options. She had no one to turn to and no one she could trust. She'd survived this long, so she would live through today and worry about tomorrow later. "Promise me you'll find a doctor if you need one."

"You didn't answer my question."

Louisa stepped to the door frame and gripped it for steadiness, her body weary as the weight of the world crushed her spirit. She didn't want to cry in front of the man who had saved her from a life of misery. It wouldn't be right to ask more of him.

"Don't go."

She stilled but didn't turn to face him.

"Please don't go." His voice was so warm and sincere, it made her want to trust him.

Trying to keep her voice from betraying the tears that were threatening to fall, she said, "I can't stay here. I don't belong."

The bedcovers rustled and he muttered a few curses, which made her smile. It shouldn't make her smile, though. This man couldn't mean anything to her until she fixed the problems she had created.

Before she realized it, he had climbed out of bed. "Where are my trousers?"

"At the foot of the bed." She had seen them folded there when she had entered the room.

From the sounds he was making, he was likely pulling them on. He then moved across the room and stood behind her, his hot breath running across her neck. He placed his hand on top of hers and pulled her fingers, one by one, away from the door before he closed it. He shifted to stand in front of her, and his good hand lifted her chin. "Please, don't go."

He bent his head as if to kiss her, but she pulled away. This wasn't the right time. She had to find a way to live, to put a roof over her head, to put food in her mouth before she could explore a relationship.

His hand dropped away. "I shouldn't have done that. You don't have anywhere to go, do you?"

"That really isn't any of your concern." She scooted around him and went to the window again. She peered outside, her hands grasping the yellow drapes, the silky fabric something real to hold onto.

The window faced the street. People bustled to and fro,

heading to work, to run errands, and to enjoy the beautiful weather. A large black dog ran along the dirt road, a young boy in ragged clothing laughing as he chased it. What she wouldn't give to be that carefree again. Dropping the fabric, she turned to face him, his trousers hanging low on his hips. She had to quit looking at him like he was a piece of moist cake. "What do you want from me?"

He rubbed his forehead. "I want nothing from you."

"We both know that isn't true, but if you want *that*, it's not on the table. I'm done with that life. I made a mistake thinking I could do that, but I can't."

"I would never presume."

She scoffed at his words and crinkled her nose. "Wouldn't you? You know exactly where I've been and what I was to do, so why wouldn't you presume?"

He took a few steps forward. "Louisa, I—"

She held her hand out to stop him. "Don't. I'm not blaming you. Whatever this is"--she waved her hands in front of her face--"isn't good for either of us. Thank you for everything, but I have to find someplace to live and some way to earn a few dollars."

"What if..." He ran his good hand through his hair before resting it behind his neck. "What if you came to work for me?"

She shook her head. "I said I wouldn't do that."

"I didn't say *that* was what I wanted you to do," he bit out, his voice harsh. "I'm not like that."

"I..." she hesitated. He'd explained why he was in the parlor house, and it hadn't been to buy a young woman like all the others in the room. She didn't know if she should trust him, but he had seemed sincere. "You're right. You told me why you were there, but—"

"Please, consider my offer."

"To do what?" The thought was ridiculous no matter what he offered, but she stayed to listen against her better judgment. Living on the street was too horrifying to contemplate.

"I..." He chuckled. "I have no idea, but I'm sure we can come up with something." He smiled wide. "Can you cook?"

Louisa chuckled to herself as she headed down the stairs, the bloody bandages from Luke's wound held tight in her hand. She couldn't believe she had just agreed to his cockamamy plan. She could cook, although it wasn't her strong suit or something she enjoyed for that matter.

Her ma had tried to get her into the kitchen to learn the basics, which she had fought at every turn. She had always wanted to be with her pa and to learn at his hand, but her ma had wrangled her into learning a few things. When she had pointed that out, Luke told her he needed nothing fancy. Meat and potatoes were good enough for him.

Cooking didn't seem enough for room and board. He asked her if she had other suggestions. That's when she'd had the idea of being his housekeeper, both cleaning and cooking. He had agreed, almost too readily, but she had made it clear she would do nothing more. She didn't want to take advantage of this good fortune, nor did she want to fall any further into the depths of debauchery than she already had.

She stepped out onto Walter's back porch, dropped the dirty rags in the trash bin, and stared at the world in front of her. Trees stood still, the blistering sun burning bright, and the stifling heat nearly suffocating her. Midsummer was upon them, and the days were scorching hot. It was a wonder fires didn't burst forth from the dry hay and grass. A few hairs had fallen from her makeshift bun and stuck to her neck. Sweat dripped and settled on her shoulder blades after just a few minutes of standing outside.

When she had woken yesterday morning, lying in the bed she had been assigned in the parlor house, hearing the moans and groans of the customers in the rooms next to hers, she hadn't expected the strange turn of events her life had taken since. Her head screamed she was making a big mistake, that she wouldn't be able to deny Luke's soulful eyes, but she didn't know if she had any other choice. It had to be better than returning to the parlor house or living on the streets. As much as she hated to admit it, she was stuck in a quagmire of her own making. This was far better than letting men have their way with her. She shuddered at what she had narrowly avoided.

She had no father or older brother to protect her. She had nothing except the clothes on her back and memories of her parents, who meant the world to her. Their lives had ended too soon. Even the people she'd thought were friends had disappeared when she couldn't keep a roof over her head. It also hadn't helped that most thought she was wrong for trying to be a physician like her father. They didn't find it appropriate behavior for a young lady.

Sighing, she brushed back a lock of hair. She couldn't stay outside all day, even if it was easier than facing the uncertainty of her future. She should head back inside and find Marie to ask about borrowing a modest shirtwaist and skirt. The two of them appeared to be the same size. It would be a relief to wear something not only more comfortable but which didn't show every inch of her skin. Louisa didn't want to spend the next few days wearing the clothes she'd taken from the parlor house. She wasn't even sure why she had grabbed the dresses when she left, other than a need to have something with her. They had taken everything from her when she entered, and she had felt it was only right to take something when she left.

Walking back inside, she wandered through the hall, peering into different rooms. When she reached the library, she couldn't help but stop and look at the books lining the walls. What a veritable treasure trove of information. She'd love to sit and read, but now wasn't the time, as she had to find Marie. She turned to leave when Walter's voice stopped her in her tracks.

"Going so soon?" he drawled. "You don't need to leave on my account."

She whirled around and saw Walter sitting behind an elaborate wooden desk that took up much of the other side of the room, far from the books she had been admiring. A large decanter of liquor rested in front of him, and a glass tumbler rested in his hands. Focused on the books, she hadn't taken a moment to see if she was alone.

"I didn't mean to intrude. I'm looking for Marie."

"She's in her office, most likely."

"Her office?"

"Down the hall, last room on the right." He waved his hand, the liquor sloshing over the side of the glass, but he didn't appear to notice.

"Thank you," she said and started to leave.

"Would you care for a drink before you go?" He held up a second tumbler. "Join me. She's probably buried in one of her multitude of causes and doesn't like to be bothered."

Not sure what she should do, she hesitated.

"I apologize if we've gotten off on the wrong foot. I've had a few late days recently, and being woken up in the middle of night isn't one of my favorite pastimes." He laughed. "I'm a bear at the best of times, but last night I was particularly rude."

Louisa was shocked at his words. While he hadn't been overtly unpleasant, she had thought he hadn't wanted her around. "You don't need to apologize. I'd be unhappy, too, if a stranger came knocking at my door with a wounded man in their arms."

"Perhaps, but as Marie informed me, I should learn to be more polite."

Louisa smiled. "It must be nice having such a sister as Marie."

"It is," Walter said, his eyes softening. "She is a force to be reckoned with, what with her pet projects and her enthusiasm for women's rights."

"You must be very proud of her."

"At times, yes. Other times, I wish she'd be more mindful. Not many men are as accommodating and accepting of women having more rights."

"Do you have the same thoughts as your sister?"

Walter stared at her for a long moment and took a sip of his drink.

She wondered if she had overstepped. "I apologize, I shouldn't have asked that question. It certainly isn't any of my business."

He waved his hand and leaned back in his chair. "No, it's a perfectly reasonable question. I agree with some of her causes. In others, I don't. I do think she should chase her dreams and do what she is passionate about."

Nine

"Damnit!" Connie snarled as she threw a vase against the wall behind Bruno. It shattered, and water and flowers fell to the ground, but Bruno barely flinched, the scar on his cheek red and prominent in the afternoon light. "What happened last night? Where did she go?"

"Not sure, ma'am. The fire chief came roaring out of her room, screaming she'd hit him and raising all kinds of hell. He demanded to know where she'd disappeared to. We think she was shuffled out with the help of a man. Nathan shot at 'em and believes he wounded him, but they gots away."

"I cannot believe this. The fire chief is one of my best customers." She swung around and stalked to her ornate wooden desk, ignoring the mess on the floor. This was her sanctuary, her place of business, and the missing Louisa had sullied it. One small woman was going to ruin everything if they didn't find her fast.

"I've had my men out looking all morning, but we haven't found any sign of 'em."

She sank into her squeaky leather chair. One more thing to add to her list. She couldn't stand a noisy chair. "Do we have any idea who helped her?"

"No. We think he was here for the auction, but no one knows his name."

"How did he get inside? I only invited certain men."

"He had an invitation, and after speaking with the girls, it seems he messed with Cora Lee for a time. But she says he didn't want to come into her room. Instead, he paid her and sent her on her way."

"Did she get his name?"

"No, but she gave a description."

"Give it to me, then. I don't have all day."

"He's got green eyes, is about this tall"--Bruno held his hand out--"and he has a black mole at the corner of his right eye."

"What color was his hair?"

"Looked black but he might've put something in it. Cora Lee said it didn't look right," Bruno said.

A sick feeling grew deep in the pit of Connie's gut. Luke Seymour had a black mole at the corner of his *green* eye. The similarities were uncanny. He had spotted her in April and had been a pain in her backside. Having some of her more trustworthy men rough him up hadn't worked, and he'd been hunting for her ever since. She didn't want her business to suffer because of men from her past, but clearly, she had underestimated him.

She had evaded capture for seven years, and now it could come tumbling down around her ears, all because she had returned to Helena. Even though the ranch was just an hour outside of Helena, she had mistakenly believed it was far enough away that she wouldn't run into any of the Seymours. If only Luke hadn't seen her that night, she wouldn't have to make these decisions. She slammed her fist onto her desk.

If it had been Luke who had spirited Louisa away, she'd have to be extra vigilant. She didn't want to disappear again but she might have to. She could run the parlor house from a distance, but that wasn't what she wanted. Her baby sister, Pauline, had wanted to take a more active role in the parlor house and had taken the lead in playing hostess. In fact, Connie had let her lead the auction the night before. Perhaps it was time for her to take a more prominent role. If she left Mon Petit Amour in the care of Pauline, she could establish a new house in San Francisco. Once that was producing a fair amount of cash, Pauline could close this one and follow Connie.

She'd think on it a bit. If and when she found it necessary to leave, she could pick up some Shoshone and Bannock girls in Pocatello on her way to California. They'd be perfect for exotic appeal to some of her more discerning customers. A friend of hers had been begging her to visit and if things didn't resolve here in Helena, then she'd just take a little trip. But she would return. She had unresolved business in Helena.

She would end the Seymour family––all of them––but it may take longer than she'd like. It had taken years to rid herself of Luke's pa, Cole. She could be patient a bit longer.

Thundering Mountain Ranch and all of that gold should've been hers. If Cole Seymour hadn't interfered in her ma and pa's relationship, then she would've been the one raised proper like. Instead, Cole Seymour had convinced her pa, Howard Seymour, to marry Pauline's mother. She had missed out on everything the Seymour family had to offer, all because Cole had wanted his brother to marry someone else. Her pa had then left her and her ma to rot in that Texas saloon.

The Seymours were the reason for all of her pain and heartache. They were a noose around her neck, but one day she'd eliminate them, just like she had their pa. She'd be the last relative standing. Then she'd get everything she deserved and more.

Ten

Late that evening, Louisa and Luke left Walter's. After her discussion with Walter, she felt far more comfortable in his presence than the night before. He wasn't quite the bear she originally thought him to be, but Luke wanted to be in his own bed, so they had said their goodbyes.

There had been little to be grateful for over the past few months and few who had been kind to her. Marie would be a friend, of that Louisa was sure. She had been a godsend, lending Louisa a modest skirt and shirtwaist, allowing her to shed the parlor house clothing once and for all. She had felt more like herself when she had dressed in the worn but clean clothing.

When Louisa told her she would return them soon, Marie insisted she keep them. "I've plenty and I'd rather they go to a good home, to someone who'll appreciate them. I'm sure you would do the same if our roles were reversed." Her smile was warm and generous. Why hadn't Louisa encountered women like her before she'd made the choice that landed her in a parlor house?

Louisa gave her a quick hug, then mounted the borrowed horse. Trotting through the dirt roads, she saw new homes in all shapes and sizes surrounded by wild grass and wilting flowers from the hot July sun. Luke led the way to a large three-story home in a respectable Helena neighborhood far from the parlor house. His house was some distance from other homes but nestled in the foothills of Mt. Helena, six blocks North and three blocks West of Walter's place.

Louisa now understood why Luke had not continued to his home the night before. It would have been dangerous for them to have tried to go such a distance and if they had gone too far, they might have stumbled down the ridge along the left side of the house. If he'd have fallen unconscious, she wouldn't have known about the sudden drop. There were no railings or signs to indicate that the road abruptly ended in a rocky ravine. The house itself, though, was surrounded by a white picket fence and a small red barn. A corral sat to the right and behind the barn. There was even a small sign above the trellis that said Thundering Ridge.

When she asked Luke about the sign, he had chuckled and stared at it for a long moment before responding, "My pa named his ranch Thundering Mountain. As each of us boys got older, we each decided that wherever we settled, we'd name our homes, ranches, or businesses to each begin with Thundering. Ma always loved thunder, so it seemed fitting. I don't know if I'll stay here forever, but it honors my ma. I named it Thundering Ridge due to the mountain ridge right there." He pointed to the ridge she had seen just a moment before.

"That's beautiful," she said. "Your pa must've been so proud."

His eyes darkened for a brief moment, and he said nothing. She groaned inside. She hadn't meant to make him sad, but he brushed it off and a moment later, he was back to his devilish and carefree self.

She hadn't expected Luke to have such a nice place, but if she were honest with herself, she didn't know what she should have expected. She hadn't been thinking too far into the future, only of getting out of harm's way. Fears regarding Madam Lafoe and her men were foremost in her mind.

She yawned wide, her jaw cracking. It had been a long day, and while she wanted to go to bed, she didn't even know where that bed was. Plus, she still needed to care for Luke and his injured shoulder. She had to determine what he expected of her as his housekeeper and cook, as they hadn't really spoken of the details yet. She couldn't mess up this opportunity. It was her chance to fix what had been broken.

Holding the reins, she looked over at Luke and grimaced. He was hunched over, fatigue in his shoulders and pain in his eyes. Leaving Walter's so soon was not good for Luke's health, but they'd both agreed it was time. He hadn't wanted to stay at his boss's house, and she hadn't disagreed. In hindsight, she should've insisted they stay and considered Luke's pain, but it was too late now. The only thing she could do was care for Luke the best way she knew how. He wasn't the first man she'd helped nurture back to health.

Throwing her leg over the pommel, she slid down the horse's side and tied him to the hitching post. She would care for the horses after Luke was inside and in his bed. She touched his leg. He jumped and then winced.

"Do you need my help, Luke?" She was going to give it to him regardless of whether he agreed or not.

He shook his head no, but as he dismounted, his legs collapsed. She wrapped her arms around his waist and held him up. His injured arm bumped into his side, and he uttered a curse. It was a repeat of the night before, but at least he seemed to have more energy than he'd had last night.

She smiled into his chest, knowing he would be all right. He might be weak and in agony, but he hadn't passed out and still had grit remaining. It was a good thing, too, as she didn't have Walter standing by to help her get him inside.

Luke tried to push her away, but she held tight. "I can walk on my own, you know," he muttered, leaning into her.

She shook her head and didn't let go. "You almost fell. Let's get you inside, where you'll be more comfortable."

He tried to pull away but was unsuccessful. His lack of fight told her he was weaker than he wanted to admit. Slowly but steadily, they made their way up the dirt path until they reached the wooden front door. He reached into his pocket with his good hand and pulled out a large black key. He fumbled and couldn't place it in the lock.

Louisa removed the key from his limp fingers, inserted it, and pushed the door open. The drapes were drawn, so she could barely see her own fingers.

"There should be a gas lamp on the table to the right," he said.

She let her eyes adjust for a moment before finding the lamp and pulling the chain. It took a moment for the mantle to become hot before it illuminated the front entrance. He leaned against the wall, his eyes closed, his chest rising and falling with the effort of walking inside.

"Where is your bedroom?"

He opened his green eyes, taking a moment to focus on her. "Up the stairs, second door on the left." His words slurred from exhaustion.

As the light continued to brighten, Louisa noticed the staircase mere steps in front of them, what looked like a parlor to the left, and perhaps a formal dining room to the right. The other rooms were dark, so she could just make out faint outlines of the furniture. "Do you think you can get up the stairs, or should I gather a few blankets and make a pallet for you down here?"

He pushed away from the door. "I can make it upstairs. I'm not that weak." He swayed and slumped back against it.

Louisa held back a chuckle. She didn't think he'd appreciate her laughing. "I'll come with you, just in case." She wrapped her arm around his waist once again while he draped his good arm over her shoulder, this time not giving her any lip.

Once they reached the top of the stairs, Luke stopped, sweat pouring down his face, but he was stubborn enough to continue. After another moment, they stopped in front of the second bedroom on the left. She presumed it was his.

She pushed open the door and fumbled for the lamp next to the wall, then pulled on the chain. As it lit, a soft glow shone across the masculine room. Not a frill in sight. Dark wood furniture with thick brown bedding – a fine room made for a man. She helped him to a chair before pulling back the patchwork quilt and plumping the pillows. The room was warm, plenty warm for summer. Pulling back the brown drapes, she opened the window. No breeze filled the air, but with a little luck, it would cool once the sun set. If nothing else, it would help relieve the stuffiness.

His eyes were closed, and his forehead wrinkled with pain. She didn't want to move him again, but he would be more comfortable in his bed.

"Luke," she said, nudging his uninjured side.

He stirred and looked up at her with hooded eyes. "Yeah."

"You need to climb into bed."

He stood but wobbled on his feet. She held out her hand, and he clutched it to keep from falling. "I'm likely to fall flat on my face if I'm not careful." He forced a chuckle.

"Let me help." She led him to the bed. Kneeling, she began to pull off his boots.

He pulled his feet away. "I can do that. I'm not an invalid. Besides, I don't want you to do anything that could be deemed improper."

She studied him for a moment and placed her palms against his lower legs. "We have gone far past propriety. You rescued me from a parlor house." She gently pulled one leg back. "I think that for tonight, we can forget what is proper and just get you into bed. Tomorrow, we can be appropriate and forget everything that's happened. I'll become your housekeeper and cook, and I'll never venture into your room again unless it is to clean it or care for you."

He eyed her intently for a moment, but she couldn't identify the thoughts running through his mind. After a long moment, he nodded.

She pulled off his boots and placed them to the side. Then she stood and gently removed the sling until she could get him undressed. She undid the buttons on the shirt Walter had let him borrow, as his had been soaked through with blood. The borrowed shirt was big across his chest, but that had been helpful with his bandages. He tried to shrug it off but couldn't move the sleeve across his hurt arm. Pushing his hands away, she pulled it off and dropped it to the floor. She'd wash the shirt in the morning so he could return it to Walter.

His eyes were unfocused and hazy, but he stood, undid his trousers, and let them drop to the floor. Heat flared up her chest and into her face, likely causing her to blush fiercely. She had seen plenty of men in their drawers, but not a man as handsome and fit as the one standing in front of her. She itched to run her fingers across his sculpted muscles.

Glad the light from the lamp was dim, she glanced at him, but he wasn't gazing at her. He dropped to the bed and laid back, his wounded arm resting on a pillow. She pulled the blankets over him as if she were tucking in a small child. She had the urge to kiss his forehead but resisted the impulse.

"If you need anything, Luke, just call out. I'll be close." She brushed the ash brown hair from his forehead, her fingers lingering longer than they should've.

His eyelids looked heavy and closed within seconds. She didn't know if he understood what she'd said, but he was sleeping for now. Rest was what he needed.

Giving him one last glance, she grabbed his soiled clothing. She had wanted to change his bandages again, but there didn't appear to be any sign of blood. She would check on him later, once he had gotten time to rest.

Louisa closed the door behind her and leaned against it, her shoulders relaxing for the first time in weeks. She knew Luke hadn't anticipated having a housekeeper; he had only offered the job to help her, so she was determined to be the best housekeeper and cook he ever had. She would do everything in her power to ensure he didn't regret giving her this opportunity. Having this chance would give her the ability to earn the money necessary to pay what she and her father owed to many debt collectors.

Stifling another wide yawn, she decided to find a room and sleep for a few hours. Morning would be here soon enough, and she wanted to show her worth so Luke wouldn't have any regrets about offering to help her.

Eleven

July 26, 1900

Louisa forced herself out of bed. She hadn't slept more than a few hours, tossing and turning with thoughts about what would happen if Madam Lafoe and her thugs ever found her. Her eyes gritty and her body sluggish, she would have preferred to stay in bed, but she needed to check on Luke's arm and get something to eat. It was early, and while she hated to wake him, it needed to be done.

Running a comb through her hair, she pulled it into a loose bun at the back of her neck. Before she had fallen asleep last night, she had cleaned his messy kitchen and soiled her borrowed clothing. She hadn't wanted to wash clothes so late at night, so she had found a man's trousers and shirt. They'd lay folded in a washroom next to the kitchen at the back of the house. It wasn't exactly proper clothing, but it was better than one of her dresses from the parlor house.

She ran down the servants' stairs she had found at the end of the second-story hall to the kitchen to find fixings for Luke's morning meal. Rifling through the larder, she found the makings for ham and biscuits, but it wouldn't be complete without some eggs. Remembering she had seen a chicken coop behind the barn the night before, she grabbed a basket and went outside to see if the hens had laid any eggs. She also imagined the chickens and horses would need feed and water. She'd care for them, too, while Luke was laid up in bed. It was the least she could do.

An hour later, eggs, bacon, coffee, and fresh-baked biscuits were ready. She put generous helpings of food on a plate and poured the strong brew into a large mug, placing it all on a tray she'd found stuffed in a wide cabinet. It proved to be full of several cooking implements, all covered in dust. Someone had at least stocked the kitchen well. She carried the fully laden tray up the servants' stairs, stopping in front of Luke's room. Holding it with one hand, she knocked firmly on his door. After a long moment, he muttered, "Come in."

She pushed the door open. Luke lounged against his headboard, his injured arm held tightly against his side.

"Good morning, Luke. I hope I didn't wake you."

"No. I was awake, just hadn't made it out of bed yet." He smiled. His brown hair was in disarray, his wide chest catching her eyes, sending a tingle through her.

"Well, no reason to get up." She walked to the bed holding the tray of food. "I hope you're hungry. I made bacon and eggs. When you're done eating, call me and I'll change those bandages."

"You didn't have to do that. I'm perfectly capable of coming downstairs."

"Perhaps you are, but no reason if I could bring this to you." She lifted the tray and placed it on his lap.

"You'll spoil me to death at this rate." His eyes twinkled.

Trying to ignore her attraction to him, she took a few steps back. "I wasn't sure what you'd prefer, but you had plenty of bacon and eggs, so I assumed you wouldn't mind them both."

"It smells downright delicious and looks better than any plate of food I could rustle up." He picked up a fork and took a big bite of the fluffy yellow eggs. He groaned as a look of pure satisfaction covered his face. "These are scrumptious. Did you eat?"

She wanted to giggle. His cooking must've been pretty awful if he thought her cooking was that good. "Not yet. I have a plate waiting for me in the kitchen. I wanted to get you fed first. Can I fetch you anything else?"

"No, this is plenty."

"I'll leave you be. Holler if you need anything. I'll leave the door open so I can hear you."

"Thank you."

Smiling, she turned to leave the room when he cleared his throat. Turning, she looked back at him. "Yes, Luke?"

"I hate to mention this, but um, what are you wearing?"

Looking down at her attire, she chuckled. "I hope you don't mind, but I found a shirt and trousers of yours. I soiled the clothing Marie let me borrow, and I have little else."

"I don't mind, but we might want to get you something a little more..." he paused, "becoming."

Clasping her hands in front of her, she raised her eyes. "It'll have to wait until I—"

He dropped his fork and looked at her with an expression she couldn't identify.

Before he could say a word, she said, "It's all right, Luke. I don't mind wearing the trousers. They are kind of freeing." She tried to smile to let him know it didn't bother her, and she hoped he believed her. It was a lie of course; it embarrassed her to know she had been reduced to this, but what choice did she have?

"Louisa, I'm sure we can outfit you with some fabric for dresses, or perhaps some ready-made clothing."

Heat crept into her cheeks. "I can't pay for them."

"I'm not worried about that. I've got enough to pay for a dress or two." He lifted an eyebrow, and it made him even more handsome.

"I don't want to take advantage of your generosity." Louisa

shuffled uncomfortably. She hadn't been prepared for this conversation.

"You aren't. I offered."

"But—"

"I've made up my mind. I'll ask Marie to go with you. She's involved in plenty of local causes for women. I'll send her a note in a few days and see if she has a moment to go shopping with you. The dry goods store might have some ready-made clothing. If not, you can always order something. If you're worried about the money, we can come up with a suitable arrangement for you to pay me back, but I wouldn't lose sleep over it."

"I am worried, Luke, and I will pay you back."

He raised an eyebrow. "If you insist, but I'm happy to do it."

"I appreciate that, but I'll feel better if I do." With that, she left him, her embarrassment complete. She appreciated his kindness, and she had planned on asking him for help, but when he offered, it was like he could see deep inside her soul. He knew she had nothing and depended on him and him alone.

Twelve

July 29, 1900

Luke walked into the parlor at the front of his house and found Louisa dusting the shelves along the back wall. Her hair was up in a loose bun, and she was singing a tune softly.

"We need to talk, Louisa."

"Ahh!" The dust rag in her hand flew into the air as she whirled around to face him. "You almost scared me to death." Her hand rested against her heart.

"Didn't mean to do that. Thought for sure you'd heard me clomping down the stairs." It had been a few days since they had returned from Walter's, and his energy had returned.

"I was in my own little world, I suppose."

He gestured to the armchairs. "Can we sit?"

"I'm quite filthy. I don't think you want me sitting on your nice chairs." She swiped at stray auburn hairs that had fallen from her bun, pushing them behind her ear. Her cheeks were rosy and a streak of dirt ran across her chin. It made her all the more adorable to him.

"I'm not worried," he said, smiling.

"Clearly, considering the state of this house," she muttered.

He cocked his head. "Are you saying my house ain't clean?"

"Oh, I'm sayin' it all right. I ain't seen nothing this filthy in years." She smirked.

Surprised at her forthrightness, he grinned. She was refreshing and different from any other woman in his life. "I haven't been the best housekeeper."

"You're right about that."

He laughed. "I don't see any clutter."

"It ain't clutter that's a problem. You've got dirt, dust, and grime on every surface of this place. When's the last time anyone dusted? Have you looked out the windows lately?" She pointed to the ones in front of them and he grimaced. They were quite filthy.

"Now that we've established I'm not the best housekeeper, I think hiring you might've been the right decision, if you can get me back to rights."

"We need to negotiate my pay considering the mess I've found," she muttered under her breath.

She was quite fetching with her bright green eyes and red cheeks.

"Let's sit, and you can tell me what you think you deserve for taking care of my home. You can tell me about yourself, too."

She reluctantly sat in an armchair, her feet crossed at the ankles and tucked under the chair. If she hadn't been wearing his trousers, she would've made quite the picture of propriety. Although truth be told, he enjoyed seeing her in his trousers, not that he'd ever tell her that.

"What do you want to know?"

"A lot, actually." He really wanted to get to know her.

"There isn't much to tell, and there's plenty to do around here. I shouldn't be wasting the day away." Her hands rested on the armchair as though she were going to stand. She wouldn't make this easy.

"Tell me what led you to..." The collar around his neck seemed to tighten. He didn't want to have this conversation, but better to get it on the table and over with. "Well, to the parlor house."

She looked at him for a moment, as if trying to decide what to tell him. She sighed, her hands releasing the arms of the chair. "I'm not that interesting."

He could see the wheels turning in her head, but he stayed silent. It was her story to tell.

"I needed to find work. There isn't much for a twenty-five-year-old female outside of marriage, and there weren't eligible men knocking down my door with proposals."

"What about your ma and pa?"

"What about them?" Her eyes shuttered closed for a moment before she opened them again, this time containing a clear pain she was unsuccessful at hiding. She tapped her fingers on the table between them, clearly a nervous gesture.

"How do they feel about your decision?"

"They..." her voice broke. "They don't know about it because they passed away a year ago."

He reached across the table, sitting between the two chairs, and placed his hand over hers. Her long, soft fingers jumped at the touch. Her eyes downcast, she didn't look at him. After a long moment, she removed her hand from under his, placing it on her lap.

Luke could empathize with her pain and decided if he were to question her, he could be honest and forthright with her. "I mentioned the other day that my pa had been killed, well, my ma had died right before then, too. It's been seven years, but it still feels like yesterday." He had to take a breath. It was harder to talk about them than he recognized, even now. "There are moments when I'm at my family's ranch, and I turn to say something to my pa or my ma, and then realize they're no longer with us. I made things difficult for my pa when I was young, constantly arguing with him, trying to be a man when I was just a boy."

She said nothing, and he knew he'd have to give her a moment to compose herself. "I remember this one time I wanted to go to a neighboring ranch to see a friend. We'd made plans the Sunday before to meet up at the local watering hole to go fishing. My pa, though, had a different idea. I hadn't been doing my chores, thinking I was above it." He tapped the side of his mouth. "Pa told me I couldn't go, but instead of listening, I slipped away when he wasn't looking. When I returned that night, boy oh boy, did we have quite the argument. I think ma thought pa was going to beat me within an inch of my life."

"Did he?" she asked, her eyes wide.

He chuckled. "No. He wanted to, even pulled off his belt to give me a good one, but ma stopped him. She was afraid he'd do me real harm in his anger. After he calmed down a few hours later, I did get a whipping' but nothing I couldn't recover from."

She shook her head, smiling at him. "You loved your pa, didn't you?"

"Yes, I did, and it's real hard sometimes knowing they're gone."

"I know the feeling. At times, I can't believe they're gone. I go to say something to my ma and realize I'll never be able to again." Her voice broke for just a moment.

"Did they not leave you with any means to care for yourself?" he asked.

She hesitated, her fingers running circles across her trouser-clad thighs. "Yes, but it didn't last long. We moved to Helena three years ago, so my father could help those less fortunate, and he hadn't anticipated the high costs. We lived in smaller towns before, but once we moved to Helena, he got in over his head. When I couldn't make the rent, I was thrown out."

"No other family could've taken you in?" He couldn't imagine what she had gone through.

"No, there was no one else." Her eyes were wide with unshed tears.

"Didn't you try other avenues, perhaps becoming a governess or a seamstress?"

She grimaced and lowered her eyes. "I tried, but no one was hiring. No matter how hard I tried, no one would take me on."

"But why a... A lady of the night?"

She smiled ruefully. "They offered a bunch of money, food to eat, and a roof over my head. I figured I had few choices."

"Everyone has a choice, Louisa."

"That's easy for you to say." She raised her eyes. They were flashing with irritation, her voice stern with anger. "Men can find employment so much easier than women. Short of marriage, there wasn't too much I could do."

"Well, why didn't you marry, then?"

She scoffed at his words. "Like I said, not too many men were asking for my hand."

He was making her uncomfortable, but he couldn't seem to stop questioning. "Did your parents introduce any men to you?"

"Yes, but they were looking for something I wasn't willing to give."

"And what was that?"

She shifted in her seat and avoided his gaze. "They wanted a traditional wife, one who cooks, cleans, and stays at home. I didn't want to do that."

Surprised, Luke scratched the back of his head. "What *did* you want to do?"

She gripped the edges of the armchair, her fingers growing red. "Why are you asking so many questions, Luke?"

"I want to know who I've hired to work in my home." His eyes were pointed. He was being too aggressive but couldn't stop.

Sighing, she said, "I wanted to be a doctor... like my father."

"Really?" he said, shocked. He had never met a woman who wanted to be a doctor. Of course, he had heard women were interested in the medical field, but they were typically nurses or midwives, not doctors.

"Yes, really." She stared right back at him as though daring him to say something. "My father took me on many of his visits, and I loved it. He taught me many things, but not too many medical schools allow women. He tried to get me into one before he died, but once he passed away, I had no one to advocate for me."

"I'm sorry to hear that. I never thought of a woman being a doctor. A midwife, yes, but not a doctor."

"What is wrong with a woman being a doctor?" She sat straight in her chair, her feet moving from underneath the chair to right below her knees as though she were going to jump up and throttle him if he weren't careful.

"I didn't say there was anything wrong with a woman being a doctor. It just ain't common."

"Perhaps not, but I learned a lot and read every medical journal my father had. I would've been a great doctor, but I no longer have that option."

"Are you content enough to be a housekeeper?" He was afraid she was settling for something that wouldn't make her happy.

"It's employment, Luke, and since I'm not willing to become a whore any longer, I guess this is as good as anything else."

"I get the feeling you don't want to be a housekeeper."

"Would you want to if you were passionate about something else?" She held up her hand to stop him from answering. "It's honest employment, and I'm grateful you're giving me this opportunity. I didn't know what I was getting into with the parlor house, but the money sounded good, and I was desperate. If you don't want me here, I can find something else."

"You don't have anywhere to go." She offered him an excuse, a reason to let her go on her way, but he couldn't do it. No matter how it appeared, he wanted her in his home. That was reason enough to scare him, but he consoled himself with the fact that he was helping someone in need. Besides, he had plenty to keep him occupied with his chase for Connie, so he wouldn't get distracted with the beautiful woman in his home, sleeping just down the hall from him.

"If you don't want me here, I understand. I just ask that you give me a couple of days to look for a job and someplace to live. Perhaps I'll try the employment office I tried before the parlor house. Maybe something new will have come their way. I can always try the laundry, or maybe a hotel will let me wash dishes."

He had to stop this now. "I'm not asking you to leave, Louisa. I just want to make sure you are happy with your choice."

"Happy?" She laughed, the sound hollow. "I don't have the luxury of considering happiness. Honest employment is enough."

He paused. Her words spoke of pain, and while he wanted to know more, it wasn't his business. He had pushed her too far in his desire to justify why he really wanted her there. She was there to work for him, nothing more, nothing less, and now seemed the perfect time to discuss their roles and her place in his home. He took a deep breath. "I'm happy to have you, but we need to establish some guidelines."

"Such as what?" She tilted her head to the side, her back still straight as though she expected the world to drop out from behind her.

"I think it'd be best if we don't mention to anyone that you lived in a parlor house. It would portray an image I don't want, and I'd hope you'd feel the same."

"I'm not ashamed of the choice I made. Could I have made a better one? Possibly, but when you're hungry and have no place to live, you do what you have to do."

He was shocked, but he couldn't judge her. He was the last person to do that. "I don't disagree with you, but I'd rather we keep that part of your life between us."

"If that's what you want, I won't tell anyone I lived in a parlor house." She shifted in the chair, her eyes downcast now. "It's not something I want to shout from the barn tops."

He hadn't meant to embarrass her, but it was best they air

everything now, so there would be no miscommunication. He also had to remember that his sole purpose these days was to find Connie and bring her to justice. He didn't have the luxury of being distracted, not when he was this close to ending his family's pain.

"Thank you. I think it would be easier for you as well. People won't approve, and I don't want you to be embarrassed or shunned." But if he were honest with himself, he didn't want to explain to anyone, including his family, why he wanted a former harlot in his home. He'd had a taste of her, and he wasn't willing to let her go, at least not today.

Thirteen

***

July 31, 1900

A few days after his uncomfortable conversation with Louisa, Luke left for the courthouse. He should have gone sooner, but between being shot in the arm and having a new woman in his life, albeit a housekeeper, he had lost sight of why he'd gone to the parlor house in the first place. Connie had been skirting the law for quite some time, and now it was time for her to pay.

After reaching the courthouse, he headed inside, a jaunt to his step, his arm still in a sling. It was healing but still pained him when jostled. Quite jovial, he was biting at the bit to tell Sheriff Fleming he had found the woman who had ruined his family. The sheriff had known his pa and had been just as angry when they'd discovered Connie's involvement. Luke would never forgive the woman for killing his pa and attempting to kill his older brother, Stanley. Because of Connie's machinations, they hadn't seen Stanley in months. He came home occasionally but only for a few days at a time, and Stanley wasn't the same man he was before he'd married Connie. Luke prayed that if they ever got Connie behind bars, Stanley would finally come home and start to heal.

Pushing open the door, he said, "Fleming, you won't believe what I..." his words trailed away because the man sitting behind the desk was not Sheriff Fleming.

The strange man looked up and leaned back in his chair, his large body oozing over the sides. He had round, ruddy cheeks and a balding head. This was obviously a man who had enjoyed life too much and certainly didn't fit the mold of a man who upheld the law. His stained white shirt strained across his belly, the buttons gaping. One had even popped off. Who would have thought he was the man for the job?

"You aren't Sheriff Fleming," Luke said.

"No, I'm not," the man said, his voice contemptuous as a scowl spread across his thick lips.

Luke looked around the room. "Will Sheriff Fleming be back soon?"

"No," the man said, offering nothing more.

Luke stood, discomfort in his bones. "Can you tell me when he'll return?"

"No."

"Will he be back?"

"No."

Luke ran his hand through his hair, frustrated. "What happened to him?"

"Not sure it's any of your business, son. Did you have any business here?"

"Who are you?"

The man shifted in his seat, the chair groaning under his weight, and leaned forward. He rested his bulky forearms heavily on the desk in front of him, raised his eyebrows, and stared at Luke for a long moment. "I'm the new sheriff. Who are you?"

"What? What happened to Fleming?"

"Don't matter none. He ain't here anymore. I am. Now what did you need? I've got more important things to do than have idle chitchat with a stranger."

Luke looked around the room. No one else was there besides them. No papers, pencils, or knickknacks covered the desk. He wasn't sure what the new sheriff was doing, but the thick tension in the air told him he'd be wise not to argue.

"I apologize. Didn't mean to sound abrupt. I just wasn't expecting Sheriff Fleming to be gone. He's been the sheriff for some time and—"

"And what? He ain't here now."

"Yes, I realize that, but—"

"I don't have time for this. What is it that you need?"

Irritation climbed up Luke's back and into his shoulders. This new sheriff was not someone he should trifle with, so Luke swallowed back his ire and smiled instead. It wouldn't serve him to get on this man's evil side.

"I don't want to take up much of your time, so I'll get right to the point."

The sheriff waved his hand for Luke to continue.

"In early 1893, my pa was killed by my older brother's former wife, Connie. She also conspired with a ranch hand to have him try to kill my brother. She got away years ago. Now that she's back, it's time she paid for her crimes."

"So, where is she?"

"She's the madam at Mon Petit Amour."

The sheriff's eyes widened. "Nah, I don't reckon that's right. I'm a close personal friend of Miss Lafoe. You've gots to be mistaken."

"I'm not," Luke said. "That woman tore apart my family and—"

"I don't think so, Mister?"

"Seymour. Luke Seymour."

"Miss Lafoe is a fine, upstanding woman. She'd never do as you suggested. She's a sweet little thing, always pleasant, and doesn't have a mean bone in her body."

"You're wrong—"

The sheriff slammed his fist onto his desk. "I'm done here. You'll not besmirch her name. If you continue to do so, I'll throw you in the clink."

Luke's mouth fell open in shock. He didn't understand what had just happened. Who was this man, and what had happened to Sheriff Fleming?

"Now..." The sheriff stood, pulling his pants farther up his wide belly. "I've got things to do, so if there's nothing more—"

"I apologize, Sheriff. I've taken up too much of your time. Have a good day." Luke swallowed back his anger. Clearly, the sheriff wouldn't be of any help. He needed to find Sheriff Fleming, for this man was either in Connie's pocket or so enamored with the woman he couldn't see straight.

Luke doffed his hat and retreated. He should head to his family ranch and let his brother, Ben, know that Sheriff Fleming had disappeared. They needed to find him, and fast. Otherwise, Connie might escape once again. They were coming too close to let her slip through their fingers.

Louisa had laundered the skirt and shirtwaist Marie had let her borrow the day before. Luke had told her he was going to the courthouse and left her to her duties. She had been wearing the button-down shirt and trousers of Luke's. They could stand a good wash as well, so she'd clean them today. Luke didn't want her wearing those trousers, and she didn't want to give him a reason to ask her to leave. She'd be happy to get back into the skirt of Marie's.

Louisa grabbed her apron off the chair next to her vanity, slipped from her bedchamber, and dashed down the steps to the kitchen. She stepped inside the warm room, pulled out some pots, and looked through the pantry when a knock sounded at the back door. Wiping her hands on her apron, she wondered who it could be.

It was Walter.

"Louisa, may I come in?" He held a bouquet of flowers in his hand and lifted the brim of his black hat from his face, highlighting his ruddy cheeks.

"Oh, um, yes." She stepped away from the door to let him inside.

He handed her the flowers. "These are for you."

"Thank you, Walter. You shouldn't have."

"It's the least I can do after my behavior the other day." He smiled wide and strutted to the other side of the room. He reminded her of a peacock, showcasing his colorful feathers, or in this case, a pretty bouquet of flowers.

"I don't know if Luke is home or not, Walter," she said.

"I'm not here for Luke." He straightened his suit coat.

"Oh, then why—"

"I came to see you."

"I... I don't understand." She turned her back to him, placed the flowers in a vase from under the sink, and filled it with water before looking back at him.

He pulled out a chair and sat, his hat resting on the table. "I'd like to see if you'd do me the honor of attending the opera with me next week."

"The opera?"

"You're beautiful," he said.

Louisa blushed. She wasn't plain, but she wasn't the belle of any ball.

"I... that is very kind of you to say, Walter, but I think I'd need to make sure Luke doesn't need me here first."

"Why would he need you here? You aren't his wife." He stood and came near her. "Honestly, Louisa, it probably isn't appropriate for a young lady such as yourself to be staying in a bachelor's home. Perhaps you should come live with Marie and me instead?"

"Oh, what? No, I mean..." she swallowed and moved toward the pantry door to put some distance between them. She did not want to live with Walter. She saw the appreciation in his eyes, and while he had apologized for his behavior, she feared he'd gotten the wrong impression. "Luke has offered me a position as his house-keeper and cook."

"You shouldn't have to work, Louisa. Where are your parents?"

"There's nothing wrong with working, and I'm very apprecia-tive of Luke's willingness to offer me a job."

"But you wouldn't have to work if you came to live with us. There would be no cause for people to gossip, not with my sister there to chaperone."

"While I appreciate your concern and very well-meaning offer, Walter, I'm going to have to decline."

He sighed. "Well, if you change your mind, you are always welcome."

She smiled, relieved he didn't seem upset with her declining his offer. "Thank you. I'll keep that in mind."

"Now, about going to the opera. What do you say?" He placed his hands on her arms and squeezed them lightly

"Can I think about it?" she said.

His grin dropped a bit, but then he brightened. "Of course, just let me know by the end of the week. I'll need to get tickets before they sell out."

"I will," she said.

Before she could stop him, Walter leaned in and kissed her on the lips. She felt nothing for the man, but before she could pull away, the kitchen door opened and Luke walked inside. His wide smile dropped when he saw her close to Walter.

"Walter, I didn't expect to see you here. Is everything all right?"

Walter brushed his fingers across her cheek before turning to look at Luke, acting as though nothing had just happened. She was horrified she hadn't stopped Walter sooner.

"I came by to talk to you and ask Louisa to go with me to the opera next week. You'll let her take a night off, won't you?"

Luke's gaze widened, but he nodded after a long moment. "She's welcome to go anywhere she pleases."

Walter nodded and then walked out of the kitchen toward the hallway, whistling as he left. Luke had a stormy look on his face, but she wasn't sure if it was from Walter appearing unannounced or the fact that Walter had just kissed her. Either way, unease crept up her back. She prayed she hadn't just jeopardized her position as his housekeeper. Kissing his friends was not going to be looked upon favorably.

Luke glanced at her, a hurt expression on his face, before turning and following Walter out of the room.

Louisa's heart sank. She shouldn't have invited Walter inside, but she had never expected him to ask her to the opera let alone kiss her. The only man she wanted to kiss was Luke, but she was sure that would never happen again.

Luke and Walter seated themselves in the parlor's armchairs.

"What are you doing here?" Luke asked. He was being curt and shouldn't be. His arm ached, and finding Sheriff Fleming replaced by someone completely enamored with Connie had put him in a foul mood. The last thing Luke had expected was to find Walter kissing Louisa. Considering Walter's powerful feelings about propriety between men and women, he was shocked to find Walter alone with his housekeeper.

Guilt suddenly burned hot in Luke's gut. *This is ridiculous,* he thought. He shouldn't feel angry or jealous. Louisa was his employee, nothing more. In fact, he couldn't afford to have a relationship with anyone. He had too many things to do without being distracted by an independent, bull-headed young woman who would give him a run for his money.

"It seems your presence at the parlor house caused quite the uproar," Walter replied. "My contact is furious. Madam Lafoe is questioning everyone at Mon Petit Amour, trying to figure out how you got in. So far, my contact is keeping mum about their part in the arrangement because of dirt I have on them, but if I don't assuage their fears, they won't have any problems letting her know who you are." He didn't make apologies for being alone with Louisa and acted as though kissing her was perfectly acceptable behavior.

Luke walked to the decanter and poured himself and Walter a drink. Maybe Luke had misinterpreted what had happened, but his gut told him he hadn't. He took a healthy swallow of the whiskey and placed his glass on the table before handing one to Walter.

"That ridiculous sheriff will no doubt let her know it was me if she doesn't figure it out before then. So let 'em tell her who I am. I know who she is, and I'd be happy to tangle with her. That madam is Connie. She's responsible for my pa's death."

"You saw her? Are you positive?"

"As positive as I can be. She walked out onto the stage. I would've gone after her if things hadn't spiraled out of control. She disappeared, and then before I knew it, I... well, let's just say I got sidetracked."

"Does this involve Louisa?" Walter asked with barely concealed fury.

Luke swallowed. He could lie to Walter and tell him it wasn't, but Walter would expect the truth. Taking another sip of his whiskey to give him courage, he gave Walter a step-by-step explanation of what had occurred that night and how he'd ended up with Louisa.

When Luke finished, Walter said, "So I was right. She *is* the woman Madam Lafoe is looking for." Walter shook his head in disbelief. "They are determined to find her. Lafoe has put a large reward out for Louisa's return. It's enough money to make anyone want to return her if they knew where to find her."

Luke looked at Walter deliberately. Although Luke had been

working for Walter for some time, he didn't really know him. He hadn't even known that Walter knew his pa.

"You aren't thinking..." Luke let the question hang there in the air, staring intently at Walter.

"No, that's ridiculous. I'd never do that. I do have some honor, Luke. You can trust me. Louisa is a beautiful young woman who got caught up in something she shouldn't have."

"Can I trust you?" As soon as he'd said the words, he cringed inside. Walter had given him the ability to find Connie, and he had as much stake in this game as Luke did. "I shouldn't have said that, Walter. Forgive me?"

"Nothing to forgive." Walter appeared to brush off his words, but his eyes were defiant. It was as though he knew he had more to offer Louisa than Luke had and was going to do his best to get her. "How much evidence do you have that she's responsible for your pa's death?"

"Enough."

"Is it enough? She's been in Helena for some time. That parlor house has existed over a year, and the most influential men in the state frequent it."

"Yeah, I learned that this afternoon."

"What do you mean?" Walter asked.

"I just came from the courthouse. What happened to Sheriff Fleming? Some other sheriff is in his place. The man has no desire whatsoever to believe that Connie, or should I say Madam Lafoe, was responsible for his death."

"I don't know what happened to Sheriff Fleming but the mayor, the fire chief, and the current sheriff are frequent visitors to Mon Petit Amor."

Luke shook his head. This had gotten more complicated than he could have ever imagined. "That doesn't mean Connie isn't responsible and shouldn't head to prison."

"I understand that, but you're going to have a tough time

proving she had anything to do with it unless you have hard evidence."

"She confessed everything to my brother Stanley."

"Her husband?" Walter asked.

"Yes."

"So, it'd be her word against his."

"Are you calling my brother a liar?" Luke asked, rage building.

"Of course not, Luke, calm yourself. I swear you're like a cannon ready to explode. Always reacting without thinking."

"I don't need to calm down. That woman killed my pa, and she *will* pay for it if it's the last thing I ever do."

"If she is responsible, I'm sure she will, but right now, we have a bigger problem. My sources are telling me she's extremely influential and has many powerful men in her back pocket. Not only will it be hard to prove she had anything to do with your pa's death, you'll be hard-pressed for the law in this town to put her behind bars."

"Then I'll contact the US Marshals and have them do something about it."

Walter chuckled sardonically before responding, "And what makes you think the US Marshals will be any more impartial than the law here in town?"

"I'll find Sheriff Fleming, then. He'll be able to substantiate everything I've said."

"I'm not sure that'll be enough."

Frustrated, Luke poured himself another drink. "So, what do you suggest?"

"I'm not sure, but going off half-cocked ain't the answer."

"I won't do something stupid," Luke said.

"I'm not too sure about that."

"I can't let her get away with it. My brother, Stanley, said it hadn't been the first time she had killed. Not to mention the letter I shared with you showed she likely killed her husband back in Texas. And I wouldn't put it past her to do it again."

"If that's the case, you need to investigate. Get proof of her actions, other witnesses to prove she's committed similar crimes. Then you might have enough evidence to convince the US Marshals and the governor if it comes down to it."

"I worry she'll take off again if she thinks I have her in my crosshairs."

"You said it's been seven years since she killed your parents, and yet she came back to the scene of the crime, so to speak. Besides, if she's the madam of Mon Petit Amour, she isn't going to give up that cash easily."

"I don't know—"

"Think about it, Luke. You said you wanted to become a journalist. This just might be your avenue to that."

"What are you saying?"

"Write a good story that gets picked up nationally, and it might persuade me to make you a full-time journalist. You've wanted it, and I haven't given you the opportunity. This is your one chance to prove yourself." Walter held up one finger as though Luke didn't know this was his only chance.

"I—" Luke stopped. He was torn between what he wanted for his future and putting Connie behind bars. His anger at the thought of Connie getting away again was a hurt so deep and personal that it tore at him. He so wanted it to go away. He wanted to remember his parents with fondness. His ma passing right before Connie killed his pa was a hard thing to forget. He wanted his parents to still be here, and they deserved to be here. That's what hurt so much. He hadn't had enough time with his parents. His siblings needed them. He needed them.

Luke also wanted to be a journalist—a dream he hadn't forgotten. If Walter gave him the chance to fulfill that dream, he didn't want to squander it. Raised on a ranch, he didn't mind hard work, but he enjoyed ferreting out stories, tracking down information, and letting the truth of corruption be known. Walter's expectations were high for those he hired. He required them to be the best, and he was giving Luke a chance to prove his worth.

Taking a deep breath, he said, "I'll do as you suggest. I'll find more evidence to prove her crimes and give you the best newspaper story you've ever had."

Grinning, Walter said, "You better, 'cause I'm counting on you to do this right."

Fourteen

August 16, 1900

"Have you found any evidence of where she went?" Connie asked, her fury simmering just below the surface, ready to explode. She prided herself on not losing control, but she would lose her temper if something didn't go right for her today.

Bruno and Nathan stood glowering in front of her ornate cherry desk. She ordered it special and loved running her long fingers across the shiny, smooth surface, but considering the state of her affairs, she might have to leave it behind.

It had been weeks since Louisa had disappeared, and her life had been a nightmare. She hadn't been able to appease the fire chief with her offer to give him another virgin. He wanted Louisa and demanded that Connie find her, or he'd pull his patronage and shut her place down with fire hazards. That man was a very unhappy, disgruntled pain. He was influential, albeit not the most desirable of men. She had too much to lose if she couldn't calm him fast.

Bruno finally spoke, "No ma'am, not yet, but we're still lookin'. We'll find her."

"You better. I invested money in that one, and I stand to lose quite a bit if I can't produce her soon."

"Yes, ma'am." He shuffled his feet.

Bruno was all muscle, but he had little between the ears. He was good for keeping the girls in line and enforcing the rules of the house, but not much else. She expected more of Nathan and was surprised he'd said little.

She directed her gaze at him. "Nathan, you have nothing to say?"

Nathan looked at her sheepishly. He'd bungled his duties by letting Luke in her house without the proper vetting, and likely knew it was best to keep his mouth shut unless he could tell her where Louisa was.

"Find her," she said, her words pointed and harsh. "It has to be Luke Seymour who took her. He comes from a well-known family, and it shouldn't be too hard to find him. You understand me?" Her eyes narrowed as she looked at each man.

They nodded and lumbered out of the room. They grated on her nerves, and nothing infuriated her more when they made a mistake. She picked up the vase of flowers that sat on the corner of her desk and threw it against the wall. The glass shattered and water splattered everywhere, trickling to the floor. At this rate, she was going to break every vase in the house, but it was better to break something in the confines of her office than lose her composure in front of the bumbling idiots she employed.

The door to her right flew open, and Pauline rushed into the room.

"Connie, is everything all right?" She looked horrified at the mess on the floor.

"No, nothing is," Connie spat, the venom in her voice startling her sister.

Pauline paused for a moment, looking between the mess on the floor and Connie. "What happened?" Her voice shook.

"Nothing! They still haven't found her. How hard can it be?"

"They'll find her, I'm sure." Pauline wrung her hands in her lap. "I still can't believe she left without help."

"Oh, she had help, and I know exactly from whom."

"Who?" Pauline asked, a quizzical look on her face.

"Someone I never thought I'd have to deal with again. It was a bad idea to return to Helena, but I couldn't resist the opportunities. It may have been a big mistake, unless I can rectify it as soon as possible."

"What are you going to do?"

"What I should have done years ago. Rid myself of the Seymours, starting with Luke."

Fifteen

August 25, 1900

T he night had been long and by the time the last guest had left for the evening, Louisa's feet and back throbbed. Her head was splitting with sharp aches that radiated across her forehead and down her neck, and she couldn't contain the nonstop yawns.

It had been a few weeks since moving into Luke's home, and she had gotten comfortable with her duties when he invited a few men over for the evening. He had sent out the invitations a week before heading to his brother's ranch for a few days and had left the planning to her.

After the men had finished dinner, they moved to the parlor, where they smoked thick cigars and drank bottles of whiskey, bourbon, and rum. She had been on her feet for hours, scurrying back and forth between the kitchen, dining room, and parlor, and she was exhausted.

As she closed the door behind the last of the stragglers, she leaned against it and sighed. She ran her hand across her eyes and rubbed at the fatigue. She so wanted to climb into bed and sleep, but it'd have to wait. The kitchen wouldn't clean itself.

Luke's friends were quite rowdy but friendly. They must have had a great time, judging by the conversation and laughter emanating from the parlor. However, Luke had seemed quiet, almost sad, when he had returned from his brother's ranch. He'd had little time to do more than run up to his room and do a quick wash before his first guest arrived, so she hadn't had a chance to ask him how his trip went. She had spent the week getting ready for the get-together, and although she had prepared large amounts of food, she hadn't expected how much work it'd be in serving them.

A part of her wished to join in on the fun, but she knew it wasn't her place. She missed the parties and events her parents had held, as well as those she had been invited to before her life had taken such a hard turn. Once her parents had died, the joy and contentment she experienced were buried under endless responsibilities she hadn't been prepared to handle.

She couldn't dwell on that now. It would just reduce her to tears, and she didn't have the time or inclination for them, especially tonight. She had cried for months before entering the parlor house, and she didn't want to start again, not when she could fix her mistakes.

Pushing away from the door, she retreated to the kitchen, where she grabbed a basket to gather the dirty plates, glasses, and cutlery scattered throughout the house. Heading to the parlor, she pushed open the door and cringed. They'd definitely had a good time. She had spent days cleaning the rooms that week, and it hadn't taken them but a few hours to turn them into a disaster.

She picked up the discarded dishes scattered on the tables, the floor, the fireplace mantel, under the chairs, between the seat cushions of the sofa, and even in the bucket of ashes next to the fireplace. She shook her head. His guests hadn't thought twice about where they'd dropped the items when they were done with them. She wondered if she'd been that thoughtless when she attended parties or even when her parents had events at their home. Having one's circumstances shift changed one's perspective.

She was on her way to the kitchen when banging on the door almost made her drop the basket. It was late, after midnight. Placing the basket on the low table in the foyer, her fingers just touched the doorknob when it was pushed open with tremendous force, and it threw her back.

Her head slammed against the wall, and she slid to the floor, her ears ringing from the impact of the blow. The gas lights were blackened within seconds, and black boots were all she saw. She couldn't tell how many men had invaded Luke's home, but something was terribly wrong.

Her heart pounded fiercely in her chest. A couple of pairs of boots pounded up the stairs. Apparently, they hadn't seen her. She had to warn Luke, but she'd be in danger if she were discovered. These men weren't here to party, they were there to do some damage.

She scooted quietly across the floor until she felt the door to the hall closet. Pushing it open, she scrambled inside and closed it softly behind her. She moved behind blankets and coats in a heap on the floor. Pulling them over her head, she prayed harder than she ever had before. She knew deep in her bones that those men were here for her. Somehow, Connie's men had found her.

She strained to hear what was going on in the rest of the house. Smashed glass, furniture breaking, drawers removed and thrown to the floor, doors opened and slammed closed. If they looked in the closet, they'd see her. She pulled her knees to her chest and shuffled the blankets more closely around her, trying to pull herself into a tight ball when the closet door was yanked open. She held her breath, peeking through a rip in one of the blankets. A large hand reached toward her. One by one, the blankets were being removed from the pile. Then, he abruptly stopped.

"Hey," a man's voice yelled. The blankets were dropped on top of her, forgotten, and the door slammed shut. If he had continued to look through the blankets, there was no doubt he would've found her.

"Look what I found," a different man's voice said. It sounded like Nathan from the parlor house. Madam Lafoe's men had indeed found her.

The two men walked away from the closet door, and she breathed a sigh of relief.

She didn't know where Luke had disappeared to, but she prayed he was safe. The men continued to storm through the house, wreaking havoc wherever they went. Just when she believed they'd never stop, the mayhem came to an abrupt end. The men hammered down the stairs, their footfalls heavy before they stopped outside the closet door, where she huddled in fear.

"She ain't here," Nathan said.

"She's got to be. This is Seymour's place, and he hired her as his housekeeper."

"Wherever she is, it ain't here."

"She was here early this morning. Bruno saw her then."

"Maybe he took her to his family's ranch," Nathan said.

"That's a possibility, I suppose, but Madam is gonna be furious. There's no way we can look for her there. That ranch is tighter than Fort William Henry Harrison. Heard just today they hired a bunch of gunslingers and ain't lettin' anyone near the main house."

"I'm sure we can find a way. We just have to find the right time. I'll send Bruno out there tomorrow to have a look around. We'll find her. There are only a few places she could be hiding," Nathan said.

A few moments later, boots stomped down the hall before they rushed out the front door. Louisa sat frozen, her ears ringing in the silence from the real possibility that if they'd found her, they would have dragged her back to the parlor house. She struggled to find the courage to crawl out of the closet until she knew for sure they were gone. After hearing nothing for well over ten minutes, she pulled the blankets off her head one by one, dropping them on the ground, and when no sounds met her ears, she stood, taking care to not make a sound. She grasped the door handle, turned it slowly, and pushed it open a crack.

She peered through the room, hoping against everything the brutes were gone. All was quiet. Nothing moved, and she saw no one. She crept out, taking cautious steps on her tiptoes, cringing when she stepped on a creaking floorboard.

The front door was wide open, the wind whipping through the entrance, but save for a streak of light from the moon, all was dark. It appeared the intruders had knocked out the gas lights on the street near the front of the house to hide their intrusion. She pushed the door closed, threw the lock, and took a deep breath—not that the locked door would stop them if they came back, but it gave her a small measure of comfort. On guard, she walked down the hall, holding her skirts in her hand so they wouldn't swish on the floor.

Just as Louisa reached the kitchen, a loud noise made her jump. Startled, she stifled a scream and ran the rest of the way to the kitchen, not caring if they heard her now. She had to get out of the house. Yanking open the back door, she scurried down the steps to a well-worn path between Luke's place and his neighbors'. She shivered, not from cold but from fear. Holding it together became too much, and it bubbled to the surface. She forced it back again. She couldn't let the panic take hold, for there was too much to lose if she did.

Louisa ran to the back door of the neighbors' and banged on it for eternity. It was really only a few minutes later when Mr. Rodgers yanked the door open. His hair stood on end, and he clutched a blue, worn robe around his wide belly. She had met him just a few days before, and he was a nice old man.

"What in the world are you doing here, young lady?" he barked. "Do you know what time it is? What's a man to do when he can't get a good night's sleep?"

"I'm so sorry, Mr. Rodgers, but I need your help." Her words came out in a rush. It was a wonder Mr. Rodgers understood any of it. "Some men broke into the house, and I don't know where Mr. Seymour is, if he's hurt, or if they—" She swallowed back the lump that had grown wide and thick in her throat. She couldn't finish that sentence. The thought of Luke being hurt or dead was too much to bear.

"Oh." Mr. Rodgers expression changed instantly from disgust to concern. "Come in, come in." His eyes scanned the black path behind her as though looking for any danger that might've followed. "I'll send one of my boys to get the doctor and the authorities."

"I'm fine. They didn't touch me." The kitchen she stepped into was large and inviting. A small table sat in the middle of the room, surrounded by four wooden chairs.

"It ain't for you, young lady. If something happened to Seymour..." He trailed off when he saw the horrified look on her face, and his face burned bright red when he discerned what he had said.

She restrained her sigh. "Thank you, Mr. Rodgers. I'm grateful for your help, but I should really go back."

"No, no, young lady. Not while I have breath in my old bones."

"I have to go back, I can't leave... I can't let Luke—"

His eyes widened at what she was saying. "Let me send my oldest, Charlie, with you. He can stand guard 'til Henry alerts the authorities."

"I don't know, what if..." her words trailed off. She didn't want to think about what she might find.

Mr. Rodgers nodded. "I understand, young lady, but it'd make me feel a whole lot better if'n you let me send Charlie with you. Will you give an old man that much?"

Mr. Rodgers was only trying to protect her, so she sank onto a kitchen chair. He went down the hall and disappeared. A few minutes later, Charlie came stumbling into the brightly lit kitchen, his eyes heavy with sleep, a sliver of dried drool on his pink cheek as he shoved his light brown shirt into his trousers and pulled up his blue suspenders. He stumbled to a halt when he got a good look at her, his mouth wide open with shock.

"Well, don't be standing there, son. We ain't got all night. Times a wastin'." He pushed his son to keep him moving. Behind his son, Mr. Rodgers hid back a grin that Louisa might've missed if she hadn't been watching.

Her heartbeat had slowed somewhat, but still thumped in her chest. He was taking too long. "I should go back, see if I can find Luke, I mean Mr. Seymour, inside somewhere. What if he's hurt and I—"

"Now, young lady, you ain't goin' back there without Charlie goin' with you." He stared pointedly at his son. Charlie shoved his feet into his boots, hopping on one foot as he tried to be quick. His father watched his every move. Once ready, Charlie righted himself and stood tall. "Don't forget the rifle, Charlie," Mr. Rodgers said. "Best not take this young miss back without it. Who knows what you'll find."

He patted her arm before she turned and ran down the steps with Charlie by her side.

Once they reached Luke's back door, Charlie held out his arm and stopped her. He held a finger to his lips, put a bullet in the chamber of his rifle, and motioned for her to stay behind him. She shuttered her feelings of irritation at the assumption that a woman had to be protected, but considering what had happened this evening, she was relieved Charlie was there in front of her.

He pushed open the door, slipped inside, and listened carefully. The wind blowing behind them was the only sound in the murky, creepy night. He whispered, "Stay here. If you hear a sound, run."

She grabbed him by the arm. "Be careful, please." Desperation filled her voice. She wanted nothing bad to happen to him, and prayed he'd find Luke alive and well.

His smile grim, he patted her hand and then, with a firm determination to his gait, he left her alone in the kitchen. She tried sitting but was too anxious. Instead, she paced back and forth across the room. The minutes ticked by slowly. There were no sounds, no movements, nothing except the harsh breathing from her dry lips.

Then she heard doors being opened and closed. Footsteps pounded up the stairs and above her on the second floor. What was taking so long? When she couldn't take it any longer, she decided she had to find Charlie. She couldn't be responsible if he had been hurt as well. Before she could open the door to the hallway, it swung open and Charlie stepped inside.

"Did you—"

He shook his head. "All's quiet, although whoever came here did a number on the place. It's a frightful mess."

She shook her head. "Where is he?" she muttered, more to herself than to Charlie.

"Who?" Charlie said, appearing confused at her question.

"Luke."

"There's no sign of him or anyone else."

She sighed with relief. He had to have left before the men stormed the house. Hopefully, he would return soon. That both frightened and comforted her at the same time. She wanted Luke to be safe, but she feared he would regret his decision to have her under his employ after what the men had done to his home.

"You don't think they'll come back, do you?" Fear crawled up her spine. *What if they came back?*

"Nah, I think whoever it was won't chance it, at least not tonight. Don't you worry none. I won't let anybody hurt you."

"Thank you, Charlie."

He patted her arm, giving her reassurance. "I'm going to go wait out front for the authorities. I'm sure they'll be here soon. My brother, Henry, has a fast horse, and I'm sure he rode him as hard as he could."

Pulling out a coffee pot, she filled it with water and put it on the hot stove to boil. It was the least she could do for the lawmen when they arrived. Grabbing the remaining pastries from the party that she had been saving for the morning, she placed them on a tray when her energy faded and her limbs shook uncontrollably. Chills ran up and down her spine. She stumbled into a seat before her legs collapsed underneath her.

Resting her elbows on the table, she put her hands on her face, trying to stop the erratic beating of her heart. They had warned her what the madam would do if she tried to escape, and she hadn't heeded their words. They had invested a lot of time and money in her, and they were determined to have her back. As soon as Luke returned, she'd explain why it wasn't safe for him if she stayed. She couldn't put him in danger. Madam Lafoe and his men were determined to catch her, and perhaps it would be best if she left. She didn't know where she would go, but she would find a solution.

Calming her frayed nerves, she went to the sink and threw water on her face. Her shaking hands settled. She picked up the tray and went to the parlor. She saw Charlie standing near the window, keeping watch. When she stepped inside, he turned and crossed the room, took the tray from her, and placed it on the nearest table.

"Are you doin' all right?" he asked, his eyes crinkled with concern.

"Yes," she said, although she clearly wasn't. "No sign of the law yet?"

"No, but I'm sure they'll be here soon. Do you think those intruders took Luke?"

"I don't know. When the last guest left this evening, he headed upstairs. I started cleaning, and I just assumed he had gone to bed. He must've slipped away without saying a word."

A loud knock reverberated through the room, and Louisa

jumped. Charlie put his finger to his lips and crept to the front door. Opening it with his rifle ready, he spoke a few words and then opened it wide, letting in the law.

What happened next was a flurry of questions asked by men in black and brown suits with bright, yellowish silver badges on their chests. They roamed around the house, looking for what she didn't know. They questioned her about what she saw and heard. She didn't want to confess that the men had been after her but knew she'd have to tell them if they didn't figure it out first.

The front door slammed open and Luke burst inside. The law men grabbed his arms to keep him from coming further into the house. When he told them he was Luke Seymour, the owner of the house, they let him continue inside. Shaking them off, he strode into the parlor and looked around in disbelief.

"What's going on? What happened? Why are they here?" Luke said.

The sheriff stepped forward. "It appears we meet again, Mr. Seymour. Your housekeeper claims there was a break-in tonight. As far as we can gather, there were at least two burglars but likely more. They broke in and ransacked your house, looking for something. Your housekeeper hid and stayed out of sight until they were gone."

"What were they looking for?" Luke said.

"That's what we're trying to decide," the sheriff growled, growing impatient with Luke. "Do you have any idea who would do this?"

"I have an idea, Sheriff, which was the reason I came by your office a few weeks past."

The sheriff scowled. "I need to know who your enemies are, Mr. Seymour."

"I told you before, Sheriff. It's Madam Lafoe's doin' here tonight."

The sheriff shook his head and growled, but before he could

give Luke a piece of his mind, one of his men interrupted, and he stomped off, muttering expletives under his breath.

Sixteen

August 26, 1900

L ouisa came downstairs the next morning and grimaced at the mess from the intruders. Luke hadn't wanted her to touch anything the night before and told her they'd tackle it in the morning. The rush of energy she'd had before the sheriff and his deputies arrived had dissipated quickly. She had been glad when Luke sent her to bed, relieved knowing Luke would protect her from harm. Despite her exhaustion, she had tossed and turned all night.

Stepping into the parlor, she grimaced. Broken furniture and glass littered the floor. Books from the bookshelves lay ripped and scattered as well. It pained her to know that Madam Lafoe's men had done this all in an attempt to take her back. Footsteps sounded behind her, and she turned to find Luke standing at the opening to the parlor.

His eyebrows scrunched in concern. "How are you feeling?"

"All right, I suppose." She was alive, and that was all that mattered. "Not looking forward to cleaning up this mess, but better to be alive than dead."

His grin was so wide it twinkled in the sunlight. "Glad to hear you have a bit of humor after everything that's happened."

"It's my fault they ransacked your house. I'm so sorry. If I hadn't left the parlor house, none of this would've happened." Her voice cracked under the strain.

He would likely send her away now. She had caused him much turmoil. The amount of money it would take to replace the items destroyed made her sick.

"No, Louisa." He walked inside the parlor and picked up a few chairs, righting them. Some furniture was ruined but not all of it. "It isn't your fault. Whoever did it must've planned everything. A courier arrived just after the party ended and gave me a message. It sent me on a fool's mission but kept me gone long enough for those men to get inside. They almost found you." He picked up a few books that weren't too damaged and placed them on a still-standing table. "I didn't even tell you I was leaving. If you hadn't hidden, who knows what might've happened."

Shame pierced through her. Her poor decisions were piling up and engulfing those around her. She should have left Luke's the moment he'd been able to care for himself. If she hadn't been there, none of this would have happened. "This is all my fault."

"Why would you think that?" he asked. He moved to stand in front of her and pushed away strands of hair that had fallen across her forehead. His hand brushed against her cheek before he realized what he had done, and he pulled away. She almost wished he hadn't.

"Because I heard them." There was a tremor to her voice.

"You did?" He tilted his head to the side.

"Yes..." her voice broke, and it took her a moment to continue, "when they pushed inside. I hid in the front closet. I heard their voices and recognized one of them. His name is Nathan, and he's one of Madam Lafoe's personal bodyguards. As they were leaving, they said they were looking for your housekeeper."

His shoulders tensed. "Still, it isn't your fault."

"Yes it is, and I'm so sorry." She gulped, and then more of the men's words came back to her. "Luke, you need to send a message to your brother. Let him know they're going to look for me at his ranch. He needs to be ready for that. I should've told you last night, but I forgot."

"I'll send a message, but he's hired guards for reasons unrelated to this. No one'll get close. Not now."

"I don't understand."

He turned and looked out the window, pushing back the drapes. "Someone set fire to the ranch last week. They took my sister, Anne, and my brother-in-law's children."

"Oh, no. That's horrible. Your family must be worried sick. How can I help?" Then a thought occurred to her. "Madam Lafoe's men must've already gone to your family's ranch looking for me. What if they were the men who took your sister?"

"I appreciate your concern but I don't think so, not if you overheard them talking about going to the ranch last night," he said. "There's no reason to believe that mess has anything to do with you. My brother thinks it's because of legal troubles my brother-in-law's wife is facing."

"But—"

"Shh," he said. "Please don't worry. Besides, my brother's ex-wife, Connie—"

"Connie?" This couldn't the same woman she knew as Madam Lafoe. It would be too much of a coincidence

"Oh, yeah, you know her as Madam Lafoe." He ran a hand across the back of his neck. "She went by Connie while she was married to my brother."

"Married to your brother?" Louisa's eyes widened in shock. She grabbed the back of a chair to steady herself. He had told her that Connie had killed his pa and tried to take the family's ranch, but she had never thought to ask more. "I'm so sorry, please excuse my shock but... but is your brother all right?"

He smiled, although it didn't reach his eyes. "Stanley hasn't had it easy, especially when he realized the extent of her duplicity. It almost tore our family apart, and Stanley still hasn't forgiven himself."

"Is there anything I can do?"

"No, but I appreciate the thought. All of that to say, Connie doesn't have a problem causing havoc for me or my brothers, especially if she's looking for revenge. Her plans were thwarted. To add insult to injury, I was responsible for helping you escape, so she's likely after us both."

Louisa was horrified. While she appreciated Luke's help, she hoped she hadn't made the situation worse by staying with him.

"Let's just get this mess cleaned up. I'll start cleaning up my study if you'd like to stay in here?" Luke said.

She nodded.

He hesitated as though he wanted to say more. Instead, he walked past her, leaving her alone in the ruined wreckage of his front parlor.

An hour later, she had piled what couldn't be salvaged in the hallway for Luke to dispose of. Her mind hadn't stopped churning as she thought over everything she had learned about Madam Lafoe--Connie--but her stomach was screaming at her. It would be best if she found something to eat. Before she could leave for the kitchen, a knock sounded at the door. She paused, her body tensing, but she reminded herself it was the middle of the day. The men who had attacked the house probably wouldn't do it again now.

Louisa walked to the window beside the door, peered out, and breathed a sigh of relief. It was Marie. Opening the door, she welcomed her friend inside.

"What are you doing here?" Louisa asked.

"Well, ain't that a howdy-doody welcome for you," Marie said, smiling.

Louisa blanched, but Marie's laughing grin made her relax. "That was awfully rude of me. Please, come inside."

Louisa ushered her into the foyer, and Marie's eyes widened in shock when she saw the pile of debris. "Are you all right, Louisa?"

"Yes, I'm fine. Had a bit of a scare, but nothing I can't recover from." She led Marie down the hall to the kitchen, where she grabbed a loaf of bread from the breadbox and a crock of butter.

"I can see that," Marie said.

"Please sit. Would you like a piece of bread or perhaps a cup of coffee?"

Marie pulled out a chair and sat at the table. "A cup of coffee would be nice."

Louisa filled a pot full of water and placed it on the cookstove to warm. "To what do I owe the pleasure of your visit?" Louisa grabbed a knife and cut a large slice of bread for herself, her stomach growling with anticipation.

"Luke sent Walter word this morning and asked me to come by to check on you. Perhaps to make sure you really are unharmed after what happened."

"He did?" Louisa asked in disbelief. She didn't need someone to watch out for her.

"Now, don't let all those bees in your bonnet. He wasn't trying to do any harm. He was concerned, and rightly so, considering what those men could have done to you. You'd think we're living in Deadwood, South Dakota with how much damage those men did."

Louisa swallowed back her ire. "At this point, I'd think he'd want me to disappear after all the commotion I've caused him."

"I think you *disappearing* is the last thing he wants." Marie's eyes twinkled, and Louisa couldn't help but blush at the obvious implication. Marie must have misinterpreted their relationship. She was nothing more than a woman in his employ.

Marie held up a finger. "Before you say a word, I can tell what you're thinking. Luke cares for you, whether you believe it or not."

"I'm his housekeeper, Marie. Nothing can ever happen between us. It ain't proper."

"Says who?" Marie asked.

"Society. It's just not proper for a house—"

Marie slammed her fist onto the table. "To hell with what society says. It's men who think to dictate what's proper and what's not. They have no right to tell us women what to do or how to act. You should have every right to decide your future, whatever that might be."

Louisa's eyes widened with shock. Marie's eyes were blazing with fury, her hands in fists, and her face red and splotchy. This was clearly a passion of Marie's.

"I'm sorry, Marie, I didn't mean..."

Marie took a visible deep breath after she raised her eyes to Louisa's. She forced her hands away from the table and gripped her skirt between her fingers, seeming to realize she had lost her composure.

Smiling, Marie said, "No, no, you have nothing to apologize for. I'm a firm supporter of women's rights, and I'm going to help bring the vote to women here in Montana. Sometimes I forget that not everyone believes the same way I do. Walter tells me I need to be considerate of how others feel and not push my beliefs on them."

Louisa was intrigued. She had heard of women getting the vote in some places. It seemed so far out of reach, but if women got the vote, then maybe––just maybe––she could realize her dream of becoming a doctor. "Can you tell me more, Marie?"

The pot of coffee was ready. She poured them both a cup, as she realized that the two of them might be there for a while.

Marie's eyes widened, and a bright smile lit up her face. "You've been through so much. Don't you think you should be resting after all that commotion?"

"I am resting"––her finger pointed to the table––"right here."

Seventeen

∽

August 30, 1900

Over the next few days, she and Luke removed all the broken furniture and cleared the mess that had been left behind. They even visited a furniture store to pick out a few new pieces to replace the ones that had been ruined beyond repair. It had been a delight to help him and for a few moments, she had pretended she was decorating her own home, giving suggestions and steering him in different directions when he picked out outlandish items.

He had been careful, though, wearing his gun belt and insisting she wear a bonnet that covered most of her face. He even had her pull her hair up into a tight bun so no one could see the color. While it wasn't a great disguise, he insisted she do it if she were to go with him.

He'd also bought her a hat she'd admired in a window on Main Street and took her to a new soda and ice cream shop. They had laughed and talked about his dreams of becoming a journalist, as well as her thoughts of becoming a doctor one day.

However, as the days wore on, Louisa grew more anxious. Luke hadn't said anything more about Connie and her goons ruining his home. Still, she felt guilty for the amount of money he had to pay for all the damage they'd done.

Stepping inside the kitchen, she found Luke at the table eating biscuits from the night before. Marie had brought them, although she'd admitted she wasn't the greatest cook. Louisa smiled at the memory of seeing the consternation on Marie's face when she had said that. Louisa wasn't much better, but she could cook a few passable things, and Luke didn't complain. In fact, he seemed to relish whatever meal she put on the table.

Marie had also been wonderful over the past few days, coming by to entertain her and to tell her about suffragist work. Louisa hoped that once she had shown Luke he hadn't made a mistake in hiring her, she could volunteer with Marie. It would give her something to concentrate on, and she could give something back to the community in Helena. Although, she feared if she were seen out and about, Connie or her goons would try and take her again.

Luke stood and wiped his mouth with his napkin. "Louisa, you're up. I hope I didn't wake you."

"Nonsense. I should have been up sooner, but I must've been more tired than I thought. It's my duty to cook."

"Louisa—"

She held up her hand to stop him. "No. You're paying me to do a job."

He looked at her for a moment, then shrugged. She wouldn't budge and wouldn't argue with him. While he had been kind and generous, she couldn't take advantage of that. She had this one chance to make a better life for herself, and she wasn't about to ruin it.

"Sit and eat. From the sounds emanating from your stomach, I'm thinking you're hungry," he said.

Louisa laughed. "I am, but if you don't mind, I'd prefer something more than cold biscuits. Would it be all right with you if I whip us up eggs and ham?"

"Would I mind?" Luke's smile widened. "I'd be thrilled to eat anything warm and not *my* cooking."

She giggled. "To be honest with you, I would too."

He snorted. "While you warm up the ham, I'll scoot out to the chicken coop and see if I can find us a few fresh eggs."

A few minutes later, he ambled inside with a handful of brown eggs tucked between his large hands. Placing them carefully on a clean rag on the table, he waved to her in the larder. "Can I help you?"

"No, no." She grabbed an apron and tied it around her waist. "You sit. Enjoy that cup of coffee, unless you need me to start a new pot?"

"Nope," he said. "The only thing I can do well in the kitchen is coffee."

Within a few minutes, she had thick slices of ham sizzling on the cooktop and fluffy eggs ready to serve. Serving up the food, she sat across from Luke, placed a cloth napkin in her lap, and raised her eyes. He was gazing at her intently, his green eyes growing dark with what appeared to be an intense longing. She recognized the look and before long, a hot blush climbed up her chest and into her cheeks. She worked for him and couldn't encourage this kind of behavior, not if she wanted to make up for her mistakes.

"Eat," she said in a futile attempt to distract him.

He grinned but picked up his fork and dug into the warm food.

When they finished, Louisa took a deep breath. "Luke, can I talk to you about something important?"

"Of course." He reclined back in his chair, his arms folded across his chest.

"I... um, well."

"Are you nervous?" His eyes sparkled with mirth.

She chuckled. "Nervous, yes. I need to ask you something, but you've done so much for me, I'm afraid it'll be enough for you to throw me out on my ear."

"If you want to go to the opera with Walter, you don't have to seek my permission."

"What?" she said and then remembered Walter had come by, asking her to go to with him. Walter had sent a note just the other day about whether they could attend the opera the following week. She had never replied.

"No, I'm not asking about that, although I do need to let Walter know one way or the other." She crinkled her nose.

"Are you going to go with him?" He avoided looking at her, a frown marring his handsome looks.

"As much as I'd like to see the opera, I don't want to give Walter any ideas. If I write him a note declining his kind offer, would you mind giving it to him when you head into work this morning?"

Luke nodded, a smile brightening his face. It seemed as though her decision not to go with Walter had changed his countenance. "So, if it wasn't going to the opera, what did you want to ask me?"

"I... I just don't want your opinion of me to change."

"I'm not that cruel and heartless." His expression shifted again, a frown pulling at his otherwise congenial countenance. "Don't be afraid to ask me for anything. I'll help if I'm able."

She didn't know if she could ask. Maybe she should wait.

When she said nothing, he filled the silence. "Louisa, whatever it is, it can't be as bad as you think. You don't need to be afraid."

"I'm not afraid," she said, although she really was. He didn't need to know that, though. Taking a deep breath, she placed the napkin on the table and her hands in her lap. "I owe people." She paused. This was going to be harder than she had expected.

He waited patiently for her to continue.

Just spit it out, she told herself. "When my parents passed, I struggled to keep a roof over my head. When it got to where I couldn't pay anything, the landlord kicked me out, but they are expecting to be paid what I owe."

His forehead crinkled in concern, but he said nothing and waited for her to continue.

She cringed in embarrassment and blinked back hot tears. "I didn't want you to think ill of me, truth be told. I already made horrendous choices and wasn't sure if you'd decide I wasn't worth it." She took a breath before continuing. "And considering everything that's happened, I wouldn't blame you if you did. We've never really discussed what my wages are and then, after Connie's goons ruined your home, I was afraid to ask for anything."

"All right." His thumb and forefinger rubbed at the bottom of his rugged chin, grazing against the dark shadow of hairs that graced his face. "How much do you owe?"

She mumbled the amount and Luke's eyes widened in shock.

"That's quite the sum, Louisa."

"I shouldn't have said anything." She pushed away from the table and turned toward the dishes in the sink to hide her tears. Asking Luke to pay off her debts was too much. She stared at the dirty dishes and wished her life would be as easy to clean as the mess in front of her.

Luke's chair scratched against the floor. He didn't say anything. She feared he was disgusted with what she owed. The amount was staggering. She didn't want bill collectors showing up at his doorstep along with everything else.

She jumped when Luke's hand rested on her shoulder.

"We'll find a way to pay off your debts," he said.

"I know it's a lot and with..." Her voice broke.

He turned her slowly and pulled her into his arms, providing a comfort she hadn't known she needed. She held onto his shirt front, silent tears streaking her cheeks. He held her close, murmuring words of solace for the loss of her parents, her home, and the life she had always wanted.

When the tears finally dried, she said, "I've made such a huge mess of my life."

He pulled back and rested his hands on her shoulders before

wiping stray hairs from her still-wet cheeks. "I don't want you worrying about anything. While I can't pay off your debts, I'm sure we can come up with something reasonable."

"I can't ask you to do that."

"You didn't ask. I offered." His eyes filled with tenderness. "I also need to pay you for the work you've done so far. My house hasn't been this clean in... well, ever." He chuckled. "How about every Friday? We can even set up an account for you at the bank, if you'd like that?"

She didn't know what to say. He was being more than generous. Swallowing hard, she said, "Thank you."

He leaned forward and kissed her on the forehead, but lingered for a long moment before he stepped away. She had an overwhelming urge to throw her arms around his neck but held back. He was paying her to be his housekeeper and cook, but if this had been another time and another life, she wondered if she might have pursued him in a different way.

Eighteen

August 31, 1900

The next morning, Luke said his goodbyes to Louisa before leaving for work. She smiled and waved him away. She told him today was laundry day, and she didn't need to be distracted. He chuckled at the look of irritation on her face. Laundry didn't appear to be her favorite pastime, and he couldn't blame her. He had seen his ma do it on numerous occasions. It was hard work bending over a large cauldron of hot water, lifting the heavy blankets and sheets in and out. Between the heat of the day and the heat from the fire, she wanted to get an early start, and so he let her be.

He felt a great responsibility for Louisa, even though he had nothing to do with her decisions. From the moment he saw her on the parlor house's stage, the gas lighting illuminating her pale skin, he'd wanted to protect her, to shield her from harm. Although if he were perfectly honest with himself, he wanted her to stay in his home so he could see if the chemistry he felt was mutual.

Staying up late the night before, he thought through everything that had happened. He had pulled her out of the parlor house, promising her a life as his housekeeper, but he hadn't even discussed how much she would earn. He had selfishly thought that being in his home was enough. He had no idea she owed that amount of money and could see why she felt desperate enough to choose a parlor house.

What he hadn't expected was for Connie to send men after Louisa. He shouldn't be surprised, considering how diabolical Connie was. She likely believed that Louisa belonged to her and would do everything in her power to get her back. He had believed that once Louisa was under his care, she'd be safe from harm, but he'd miscalculated.

He closed the front door and walked to the dirt road toward Walter's office. He could have ridden his horse, but it was cool enough that morning that he decided to walk. Besides, it would give him time to think. He shouldn't leave Louisa alone, but he had to speak with Walter and get back to work. It had been some time since he had been at the newspaper office, and while Walter had been fine with him leaving unexpectedly for his family's ranch, his goodwill would only extend so far. He also needed to earn money if he were to pay for an unexpected housekeeper and cook that he was now responsible for.

Walking briskly along the dirt road, his thoughts elsewhere, he almost found himself dead on the ground. His friend, Harry, appeared and pulled him back from a large, brown freight wagon that had careened around the corner at a high speed. The horses were agitated, and the owner tried to gain control but failed miserably. They disappeared around the corner, leaving Luke grateful for Harry's intervention.

"Luke, what the hell?" Harry sputtered. His curly black hair flopped over his short forehead, and his ears stuck out more than normal. "You could've been killed."

Luke braced his hands against his knees, huffing and puffing before looking at the dust the wagon had left behind. "Thanks for that. I wasn't watchin' my step."

"I've been yelling your name, and you didn't turn even once to look."

"I didn't hear you."

"That was clear, especially when you tried to get buried underneath those horse's hooves. It's a good thing I was close enough to pull you out of the way. Otherwise, you might be a pile of dead meat lying on the street."

Chuckling at Harry's exaggeration, Luke said, "I don't know about that, but I'm grateful you were near enough to pull me aside. I was preoccupied. I didn't even see or hear that wagon."

"Everything all right?" Harry asked, his thumbs resting in the belt loops of his trousers.

"Yes, yes." Luke rested his hand on his friend's shoulder.

It had been a few months since he had seen his friend, and while Harry was aware of what Connie had done to his family, he didn't know that Luke had found her.

"I've got much to tell you, Harry. Why don't you come by the house tonight for dinner?"

"And eat *your* food? Not sure I'm right excited about that." He grinned.

Luke laughed. "It's not that bad."

Harry's wide eyes and exaggerated expression told him otherwise. "Did you hit your head when you fell?"

"Maybe, but you don't need to worry about my rank cookin' any longer. I've got myself a housekeeper who cooks better than me."

"In that case, you've changed my mind. A housekeeper? Is she pretty?"

"Always looking for the pretty girls, aren't you, Harry?" Luke would need to keep an eye on Harry around Louisa. He didn't always act as he should.

"Can't seem to help myself."

Luke shook his head. "I don't need a housekeeper, but she needed help. Although my house is cleaner now that she's there."

"Sounds as though there's a story here?"

"Yes, there is, but as much as I'd love to stay and chat, I need to get to the newspaper office. I'm late, and Walter's gonna have himself a fit."

"Walter's surely a stickler for timeliness. Don't wanna get on his evil side. Go, I'll see you tonight."

Luke shook Harry's hand and waved him away. This time, he noted his surroundings and made sure no wagons were running unchecked down the street before he crossed it. Everything in his life was colliding at once, and he needed to have a plan of attack.

Luke got home later than he would've liked. He'd been running late and, with any luck, Harry hadn't arrived yet. Not seeing him inside, he placed his hat on a chair in the front parlor and poured himself a healthy splash of whiskey. It'd been a long day, and he needed it. Walter had been in a foul mood, and Luke had withstood his anger and frustration.

He didn't know what bee had gotten in Walter's trousers, but Luke couldn't fix it. Walter had stomped around the office, yelling at both him and Frank over not finishing the press run as fast as he would like. Then he about lost it when he saw some old, ripped newsprint on the floor that Luke hadn't cleaned up fast enough. Luke stopped trying so hard when he realized it didn't matter what he said or did; everything still irritated Walter. Luke enjoyed working for him, but when he became obstinate and hard to work with, Luke found it easier to avoid him.

On his way home, he realized Harry might be the perfect person to help him. Harry had connections that were far more reaching than Walter's and delved into areas that were occasionally questionable. He should've thought of it sooner, but he had been so wrapped up in trying to find Connie on his own, he didn't consider Harry. Perhaps it was fortuitous to have run into him this morning.

He took a swallow of his whiskey, grimacing as it burned his throat. He wandered to the window and pulled away the damaged drapes to gaze outside. The intruders had taken knives to the drapes, piercing them in several places and leaving them a mangled mess. He and Louisa had removed most of the ruined furniture and broken glass from the room, but they hadn't replaced the drapes. Why, he didn't know, but he'd have to add it to the list of things that needed to be purchased. If he wasn't careful, he'd eat through his life savings quicker than he could skin a snake.

It was a nice evening. No clouds were in the sky, and a gentle breeze caused the thick green leaves to ripple on the tree in his front yard. The days were long and had grown hotter. He enjoyed summer, although it didn't last long. Working in the newspaper office didn't allow for much time outside, so when fall came around, he often got melancholy. Pondering the things in his past led him to consider what he should do about his future. He knew one thing for sure: he couldn't move forward until Connie was where she belonged, rotting in prison or hanging from the end of a rope.

He finished the rest of the whiskey and placed the glass on the table. A knock sounded at the front door. Opening it wide, Luke grinned and welcomed Harry inside.

"I'm so glad you could make it," Luke said.

"Thanks for havin' me. It's been some time."

"Yes, it has. Come in, come in." Luke led Harry to his study. The intruders had ransacked it but hadn't done near the damage as they had in other rooms of his house. It was his favorite room, featuring mahogany wood, books that lined the walls, and a wide leather chair that enveloped him like a glove. This was one room he hadn't felt the need to change. It fit his personality and reminded him of his pa.

"Would you care for a drink?" Luke asked.

"Yes, a brandy if you've got it."

"I do." Luke walked for the decanters of liquor. He reached for the bottle of his expensive brandy, pulled out a glass, and poured a healthy amount. Luke handed Harry the drink and gestured toward a seat.

"Make yourself at home."

"Nice place you have." Harry looked around the room in astonishment. "You've definitely come a long way since living in the boarding house."

"I stumbled across the place about six months ago, and it was such a great deal, I couldn't pass it up. I figured it was time I settled down. Need to think about a family, Ben tells me. Not that I'm ready for that, but I figured maybe buying my own place would stop his yammering for at least a few months."

Harry chuckled. "It might, for a week or two, but you know Ben. He'll bring it up again if he doesn't feel you're moving fast enough."

"You know my brother well. For now, though, he has stopped introducing me to every girl he and Elizabeth find suitable."

"And how are the rest of the family?"

Luke grimaced. "Some better than others."

Harry's hand stopped halfway to his mouth. "What's going on, Luke? If'n you need my help, you only have to ask."

He didn't know how much he wanted to tell Harry. He'd been a good friend for years, knew his family well, and would help if he could. Sighing, he told him what had happened to Anne and his brother-in-law's children, and the fire that had taken portions of the ranch house and barns.

"What can I do to help?" Harry asked.

"Nothing for now, but I appreciate you offering."

Nodding, Harry changed the subject. "I saw Michael the other day, and he seems to be livin' high on the hog."

Luke chortled at the description of his younger brother. "Yes.

He's expanded into a full-service livery, although with those new wheeled machines, I worry he'll regret doing so."

"They are the new fandangled thing, but they won't become popular. Nothing can replace the reliability of our four-legged friends."

They both laughed.

"Tell me about this new housekeeper of yours," Harry said. "You've certainly come up in the world if you have one now."

"I didn't need one, but the opportunity arose. She needed help, and it just seemed the right thing to do."

"Well, I can't wait to meet the old woman."

Luke smiled. Louisa wouldn't appreciate being called an old woman. "She ain't old."

"Oh, really?" Harry said, sitting up straight in his chair. "You need to tell me what's going on there."

"Nothing to tell. She needed a job."

"And you thought you'd be kind and offer her one, I'm assuming."

"Something like that." Seeing the interest in Harry's eyes prompted Luke to move on to why he had asked Harry over that evening. Louisa and her past weren't topics he wanted to share with Harry, at least not yet. "I need your help."

"What do you need?" Harry asked, the laughter draining from his eyes. Taking a drink of his brandy, Harry settled more comfortably into his chair. "Go on."

"You know I've been looking for my pa's killer for some time."

He nodded. "Have you come across any new leads on her whereabouts?"

"As a matter of fact, I have." Luke shifted and placed his glass on the table next to him and braced his elbows against his knees.

"That's good to hear."

"Well, yes and no."

Luke told Harry about the last few months and seeing Connie at Mon Petit Amour. Luke didn't mention finding Louisa in the same parlor house. Harry wasn't a gentleman with women of ill-repute, and if he knew the truth, he might try to take advantage of her. Harry didn't have respect for women who had fallen in the eyes of society. Luke, on the other hand, always treated women well regardless. Harry, on the other hand, wasn't as generous or kind, so it was best to keep that information to himself.

"Why didn't you grab her when you had the chance?" Harry asked.

"I got distracted."

Harry raised his eyebrow. "I'm sure you did." He took a sip of his brandy, a slight smile on his lips. "Did she see you?"

He knew what Harry was thinking, but he wasn't about to indulge that line of inquiry. Brothels and parlor houses were full of scantily clad women, and it would be easy to get distracted. "I don't think so, but I'm not sure she didn't either."

"Do you think she'll take off again?"

"I hope not. I believe she owns the parlor house, so I can't imagine her leaving behind a lucrative business. But that's where I need your help."

"Doing what? Why haven't you gone to Sheriff Fleming?"

"I tried, but they've replaced Fleming with another sheriff who isn't inclined to help."

"Not surprising. There's been a few changes in the local government with that new mayor that was elected."

Luke would keep that information handy when and if he could get the evidence to throw that witch behind bars.

"What do you have planned?" Harry asked.

"I thought you could frequent the place and see if you can't find out more about what she's up to, her activities, where she lives. Those kinds of details."

"I'm always up to frequenting brothels. They're delightful on so many levels."

Luke chuckled. "I'd hoped you'd say that."

"Which one is it?"

"It's the one on High Street, Mon Petit Amour."

Harry winced. "That might be a problem."

"Why's that?"

"I'm not sure how you got in, but I don't have the cash that place requires. I've tried, and you need a recommendation and plenty of money."

"Don't worry about the money. I'll cover it."

Harry scratched a spot on his neck but didn't ask more. "That takes care of the money, but I still need a recommendation from someone who already has an invitation."

"I'll arrange that as well. Give me a couple of days."

A knock sounded on his study door, and it opened a moment later.

"Sorry to interrupt, but dinner's ready," Louisa said.

Harry choked on his brandy. His face turned bright red.

Luke looked at him, alarmed. "Are you all right?"

Harry took a few deep breaths, shuddered, and said, "Yeah, sorry about that. I swallowed wrong."

"I guess so. Well, if you're sure, let's head to the dining room."

"Who's this?" Harry asked, gesturing toward Louisa.

"Harry, this is my housekeeper, Louisa."

"Nice to meet you," Harry said.

Louisa nodded.

Luke looked at Harry again. "Ready to eat?"

"Yes, am I ever." Harry's eyes ere wide as he followed Louisa out the door.

Louisa's unease grew within moments of meeting Harry. He initially gave her no overt reason to be uncomfortable, but his piercing gaze followed her every movement, and the hair on the back of her neck stood on end. Something about the man warned her to be mindful.

It had been a rough afternoon, but she salvaged it when she found a salted ham hanging in the larder. She warmed it up to replace the beef she had burned to a blackened crisp while preparing dinner. She almost wished she hadn't saved the meal with the way Harry's eyes undressed her with every step she took.

Harry grinned and laughed, raising his glass in toasts, but when Luke's attention was elsewhere, Harry's eyes bored into her. She placed a dish in front of him, and Harry's hand caressed her leg through her skirt. She shot him a dirty look, but he just licked his lips like he was getting ready to feast on her instead of his hot plate of food.

Louisa shuddered and scooted out of his reach. Her father had warned her about men like him. They seemed jovial and kind, but when no one was watching, their eyes would shift and their body language would transform into something far from harmless. While she wanted to believe Luke wouldn't be friends with someone evil, she knew she had to be wary of Harry. She'd make an effort to never be alone with him. It wasn't worth the risk.

Her eyes swept the table. It looked as though they had everything they needed, so she turned to leave when Luke's husky voice stopped her. "Louisa, stay. Eat here with us."

"I've eaten, but you enjoy your meal."

"But—"

"I'll be in the kitchen. Call me if you need anything." Not giving him a chance to say anything more, she scooted through the swinging door and into the kitchen, away from Harry and his wandering hands.

Twenty minutes later, when the kitchen sparkled, the door opened. She turned with a welcoming smile, but it immediately dropped into a frown. It was Harry.

"Oh, it's you." *What was he doing in here?*

"My, my. Not so enthusiastic, I see." He strutted around the room like a rooster, one hand resting against his chest, his other running across the warm, smooth top of the wooden table.

"I apologize. What can I do for you?" She scooted around the small wooden table, wiping at an unseen crumb in an attempt to put any object between them. His gaze was disturbing.

"We finished with dinner. I told Luke I'd come in here and help you with dessert."

"No need for that. I'll bring it out in a minute."

"Oh, but I'm sure you'll need help."

"I can carry an apple pie."

"I'd like to spend time with you, Louisa."

The sound of her name across his lips made her skin crawl. Tingles of fear and repulsion raced along her skin. She couldn't let him know how much he frightened her. Men like him could smell a scared mouse from ten miles away. If he sensed any fear, he would pounce.

He moved close and blocked her from escaping. His hand moved a curl from her chest and pushed it behind her shoulder.

"You certainly are one ripe cherry, aren't you?" he whispered.

She swallowed her disgust. "I don't know what you're talking about, but if you'll excuse me, I need to cut the apple pie."

He stepped away. She maneuvered around him, her breath escaping in a relieved whoosh when she was free from his touch.

He chuckled. "It sure has been a pleasure, young lady. We'll have to continue this conversation later." He winked before leaving her alone.

Now she knew more than ever that she would have to stay away from that man. If he got her alone, there was no telling what he would do.

Nineteen

September 14, 1900

"Louisa, where are you?"

She was upstairs on her hands and knees, scrubbing the wooden floors. Her black skirt and white shirtwaist were covered in dust and grime. The rooms were filthy, and she'd been tackling them one at a time for the last two weeks. She gripped the side of the nearest chair and stood, her knees popping from being bent so long. She placed her hands against the small of her back and stretched before meeting Luke on the second-floor landing. The elaborate wood railing gleamed under the sun from the tall window that had been scrubbed clean just hours before. There were five bedrooms on this floor. Outside of the two she and Luke were using, the others were still a mess, both from lack of cleaning and the damage Connie's henchmen had done to the place a few weeks past. She hadn't even looked at the third floor yet.

"Oh, good. There you are." His face was red with exertion.

"Is everything all right?" she asked, tucking a stray hair behind her ear. He was bouncing on the balls of his feet and looked plumb thrilled with his news. It made her want to smile at the sweet picture he made. He was like a small child who had just gotten the best present from St. Nicholas.

"Yes, yes, it is. I just wanted to let you know I've got news about Connie." He rubbed his hands together in glee.

Her heart burst with excitement for him. It had been a week since Harry had come for dinner. Luke hadn't expected him to find information this soon, so he had to be thrilled.

"Come with me, and I'll tell you what I know." He reached for her hand and led her down the stairs, into the front parlor. Goose pimples raised on her skin at his touch, and her cheeks flared hot, but he seemed single-minded in his focus and didn't appear to notice.

Pulling her onto the plush cream-colored sofa, he sat next to her, his thigh nestled against her. Turning to face her, he took both her hands, his thumbs running across the tops of her knuckles. She looked at him, his green eyes gazing devilishly into hers. His rugged good looks and sweet nature could cause her to fall head over heels for him. She itched to run her fingers through the light brown hair that curled just below his collar. It begged to be touched, and she'd love to be the one who did it.

Stop! *What am I doing?* She had to quit looking at him like he was a piece of cherry pie she wanted to lick off her fork.

"Louisa?"

She had missed what he said with her inappropriate musings and shook her head to clear it. "I'm sorry. I was thinking about something else. What did you say?"

He smiled at her, and she practically swooned at his feet. Heat curled deep within her belly, like a rose opening up to the sun for the very first time.

"Nothing important," he said.

"Did Harry find Connie at Mon Petit Amour?" Luke had been watching Mon Petit Amour whenever he got a free moment, but she never showed her face there. He had gotten quite despondent, thinking he had lost his chance to catch her.

"No, but she might be at another one on the seedier side of town. I'm this close to taking her down, Louisa."

"Oh, Luke." She let go of his hands and threw her arms around his neck. His woodsy scent enveloped her like a day in a wet, warm forest. Suddenly, she realized what she had done. She pulled back, the heat running up her chest and into her face. "I'm sorry, I shouldn't have done that."

"It's all right. No harm done." He patted her knee, sending more tingles down her spine. She had to gather herself or she might melt into a liquid pool at the bottom of his feet.

Sitting back, she scooted ever so slightly away from him. If she stayed near him, she might do something more than just hug him in exuberance, and she really wanted to. She had believed for so long that she wasn't good enough for him, considering everything she had done. When he looked at her with those green eyes and dark lashes, her belly clenched with desire. She wanted more and if he gave her half a chance, she would jump at it. At the same time, she wondered if her past would be something he wouldn't be able to ignore.

He gazed at her. "Louisa? What are you thinking?"

He had caught her mooning after him like a lovesick calf. She chuckled to hide her embarrassment. "I'm sorry, I must be tired from all that cleaning I've been doing. When are you going to go after her?"

"Not so fast," he said. "Harry thinks she might be there but isn't positive."

She moved her head to the side, her gaze intent. "Why isn't he positive?"

"It's only a rumor, but he thinks she owns a few brothels, and she was seen at this one just the other day."

"Then let's go there and see if it's her."

"We can't all just waltz in and demand she come with us, Louisa."

"Why not?"

"Because she has too much to lose. If I can catch a glimpse of her, then I'll reach out to the US Marshals and have them arrest her."

"You don't trust the sheriff?"

"Absolutely not." He scowled. "He's under her thumb. I'm not sure how, but he has no desire to put her behind bars. It's likely she's giving him something, and he won't want to lose that. I also don't want her to know I'm this close. I'm afraid she'll retaliate against me by trying to take you back."

"You shouldn't worry about me. They weren't able to take me the last time they tried, and I won't let them do it if they try again." Her words were full of bravado she didn't really believe, but she didn't want him to worry about her. He had too many other things weighing on him.

"We have to be careful and do this methodically."

As much as she hated to admit it, he might be right.

"We?"

"Me and Harry."

"Oh," she said, disgust filling her voice. She didn't know why she was surprised Luke would rely on him to help.

"Is something wrong?" he asked.

"No, I... You haven't told Harry that you found me in a parlor house, have you?"

He looked surprised at the sudden change in topic, and she hoped she hadn't displeased him. "No," he said. "I thought it best not to tell anyone. It would cause too many questions and could hurt your reputation."

He meant it would hurt his reputation, but she understood and couldn't blame him. "I'm sorry. I didn't mean to offend by asking."

"You didn't, but I'm surprised you'd think I might've told your secret." He looked hurt at the suggestion.

"I... you're right. I shouldn't have doubted you. But Harry, well, he appeared to know."

Luke winced. "I should've warned you. He's had a hard life and sometimes forgets himself when he's around ladies."

"You don't need to explain. I shouldn't have asked." She regretted letting her derision toward Harry show. Luke had too much going on to worry about how she felt about one of his friends.

He patted her hand, his touch soothing. "It's all right. You have every reason to worry about something like that, but I'll never betray your trust."

She smiled. "I appreciate that. What's your plan?"

"We need to get inside and see what we can discover without asking too many questions."

"Do you think that'll work?"

"Honestly, no, but we've got to do something." He ran a hand over the back of his neck and leaned up against the sofa.

"How about I go instead?" she said.

"Definitely not," he said, almost angrily.

"And why not? I could ask questions."

"You don't need to be exposed to the atrocities inside of a brothel."

She laughed. "Exposed? Luke, I was going to become a whore. I'm not an innocent who doesn't know what goes on in them."

"This is so much different." He scowled.

"I don't see how. They're all the same, I'm sure."

"That's where you're wrong." His mouth pursed into a straight line, and he took his time in continuing. "They're different, very different. You were lucky. The one you were in is exclusive, and only customers with significant amounts of money are allowed in."

"Men are men. Doesn't matter if they have money or not," she said.

"It makes a huge difference. You have no idea how bad these places can be."

"It can't be as bad as you believe."

"Yes, it can, and you won't go back inside one. Not while I have breath in my body." His back straightened, his hands drew into fists, and a stern expression rested on his face.

"That's ridiculous, Luke. If I can help, you should let me. She won't be expecting to see me in there."

"Perhaps, but I don't want to see you hurt."

"I won't be."

"You don't know that and besides, this is my fight, not yours."

Frustrated, she stood and stalked to the window, pulling back the drapes. She shouldn't interfere, but she really wanted to help. Sighing, she looked back at him. "All right, I'll not argue."

"I'm sure Harry and I will find her."

"I'm counting on it," she said.

Twenty

September 15, 1900

The next evening, Luke and Harry left for another brothel. They didn't have a plan other than to inquire discreetly, and with any luck, they'd find valuable information. When Harry had inquired at Mon Petit Amour, Pauline claimed to be the madam, and many girls in the house said they had no knowledge of Connie. It was all a lie, of course. Pauline had introduced Connie as the madam in July when Luke had gone to the auction, but they were claiming otherwise now. Not wanting to appear overeager or to explain why he was in such a hurry to find her, Harry had left it alone and extended his search to other brothels and parlor houses in the area.

It was dark when Luke's carriage pulled up alongside the brothel, and he groaned internally. This place was decrepit, with sagging window sashes, cracked glass, and a patched roof. The entire building listed to the side. One forceful wind gust might erase it from this earth.

Luke studied Harry. "Are we in the right place? I expected something different."

Harry slapped Luke on the back. "You've been in plenty of brothels with me, Luke. This ain't no different."

Luke shrugged. "Maybe, but—"

"Not all places are as nice as Mon Petit Amour." Harry laughed, and the smile lit up his drab face.

Luke chuckled. "You're right. I guess I got spoiled going in there."

"I'm sure you did, but now that you're back in the land of us common folk, this is more like it." Harry's grin dropped into a slight frown. "But before we go in, I should warn you... they cater to all sorts, if you know what I mean."

Luke looked at Harry for a moment and wondered how much worse this place could be than what he had seen and experienced at Mon Petit Amour.

"You need to be aware of what you'll see."

"But you—"

"I don't partake in that kind of degenerate debauchery, but there are plenty who do, so beware."

A chill ran up Luke's spine. Harry was rarely inaccurate with the information he gave Luke. He'd been a reliable source for several newspaper stories, and had seen and heard things in the underbelly of Helena that those in polite society never knew existed. A lot of it had to do with Harry's upbringing, but it was more to do with those he consorted with. While Luke appreciated his friendship and the information he shared, Harry was involved in things that Luke stayed far away from.

"Why do you think she'll be here?"

"I don't know if she will be or not, but someone with her description was seen leaving here yesterday afternoon. So, maybe we'll get lucky."

The two of them ambled up the walk when two drunk men stumbled out of the house, followed by a voluptuous woman in a blue dress that had seen better days. Her scowl disappeared into a beaming smile when she caught Harry's eye.

"Gentlemen, welcome, welcome. Please come inside and make yourselves at home."

"What about us?" one of the drunks said. He laughed hysterically at something his companion had muttered.

The woman turned her gaze on them, her eyes narrowing. "Not until you settle your bill. This ain't a charity house. Go on, now git!" She then gestured for Harry and Luke to follow her, her eyes skimming them from the tops of their heads to the tips of their boots as though measuring their wealth as potential customers.

The warm scents of honey and lavender competed with cigar smoke and unwashed bodies. The cloying scent did little to mask the unpleasantness permeating the large, open room and the shoddiness of the furnishings. They were far from the opulence of Mon Petit Amour.

The room was dimly lit, likely to hide what it lacked. Low, sensual laughter filled the air. Women in all stages of dress lounged on the chairs, in men's laps, across their shoulders, against the walls, and even across the upright piano that had seen better days; giggling, whispering. A long bar lined one edge of the wall, spittoons on the floor at either end of it, with dark brown liquid dripping down their sides. The burly bartender slapped large mugs of beer and whiskey on the wooden bar top for the unkempt men who leaned against it.

Once inside, an older, handsome woman approached. Her smile was wide with pleasure as she pulled Harry into her arms. She kissed each cheek, the smacking noises loud enough to be heard over the low roar of the crowd.

"Mister Harry, so glad to see you. It's been some time since you've graced us with your presence." She took Harry's hands and winked at him. "Millie is available, if you so desire. She was quite heartbroken the last time you left and has been anxiously waiting for your return."

She waved to a woman on the other side of the room who

quickly approached them. She had long blonde hair, large breasts that were barely contained under her dress, and a narrow waist. She embraced him enthusiastically.

"Oh, Mister Harry," she squealed. "It's been way too long since you've been here. Come with me. Abby will be done shortly, and we can begin where we left off." She pulled Harry close and whispered something in his ear. Harry's cheeks reddened like a schoolboy with his first crush.

Speechless, Luke had never seen Harry blush. With barely concealed pleasure, Millie led away Harry, not a single word of protest leaving his lips. They left Luke to fare on his own. He almost called out to stop him but halted. It had to look realistic, so letting Harry head off with two women was unfortunately necessary.

The older lady watched Harry and Millie leave and then turned her attention to Luke.

"Mister?"

"Seymour," he said. "Luke Seymour."

"Welcome, Mister Seymour. You can call me Miss Josie." She grabbed Luke by the arm and took him to an empty table. "Now, Mister Seymour, what can we help you with tonight?" She sat, her blue dress revealing a leg covered in a sheer black stocking. She didn't even appear to notice she was flashing it.

"Um." He pulled at the buckle around his waist. He didn't know how to approach the real reason he was there. He wasn't sure they'd take too kindly to his reasons.

"Don't be shy, lovey. We cater to everyone's desires." She winked at him. "No matter how..." she licked her lips and left the words hanging, letting Luke make his own interpretations.

"Can I just have a drink and... observe, then decide?"

"Of course," she said. "Whiskey?"

He nodded.

She waved to the bartender and before he could blink, a young woman brought him a glass and handed it to him, bending low giving him a view he'd never forget. He swallowed. It was going to be difficult to keep his mind on his task.

"Once you've decided, you just let me know, and we can work out the particulars."

"The girls themselves don't... let me know that?"

"If you become a frequent customer and we establish a quality relationship, then yes. But until that point, I like to make sure my girls are protected, if you know what I mean." She said it pointedly, her gaze direct, her voice inviting no argument.

"Yes, ma'am. I understand."

He swallowed a sip of whiskey, and the liquid burned his throat. He could hardly contain the cough that swelled from his gut.

"Well"--her hand dropped to his knee--"I'll let you... observe." Her eyes twinkled at the absurdity of that statement. "Tell me when you're ready to partake of your every wanton wish." She squeezed his knee before running her fingers up his thigh, then smiled at him and stood. "Please let me know if you have questions and... when you've made your choice."

Luke sat rooted in his chair, unsure of what to do next. It wasn't as though he didn't know where he was and what was expected. He had come with clear intentions, but it was hard not to get distracted. He had walked into the den of iniquity, and it wasn't church on Sunday.

His eyes wandered across the room. Coarse laughter and booze poured freely, and cash and gold changed hands quickly. Even though this was not Mon Petit Amour, there was no shortage of money being made.

Once done with his drink, he stood and strolled up the rickety staircase along the wall opposite the bar, trying to act as though he was looking for the woman to fulfill his dreams. Once he reached the second floor, the doors that were open showed things he would've rather not seen. He wasn't innocent, but he preferred to keep his business behind closed doors.

A few women looked him up and down like he was a ripe melon, and he felt like one as they licked their lips and undressed him with their eyes. Trying to focus on why he was there, he scanned the hallway. He wondered if Harry hadn't gotten the wrong information, and this had been a wasted effort.

Twenty-One

September 16, 1900

The next morning, Louisa ran down the stairs to the kitchen to see if Luke was awake. He had come in late the night before, long after she had gone to bed, and she was curious to know if they had discovered anything. Ever since the attack on Luke's home, she'd been afraid that if Connie still believed she was there, she would come after her. Once she was behind bars, both she and Luke would be able to breathe easier.

Of course, the threats hadn't stopped her from leaving the house and visiting Marie whenever she had the chance. Luke would prefer to have her locked up tight, but she was not going to let anyone ruin her new life. She always wore a bonnet that covered her hair and didn't stop to talk to anyone unnecessarily.

She burst into the kitchen and found Luke looking inside the pantry.

"Luke," she said.

"Ahhh," he yelped, banging his head on the door.

"Oh, no, Luke. Are you all right?"

He rubbed the top of his head and grimaced but gave her a

small grin. "Yes, I'm fine. My head might have a knot the size of Mt. Helena on it but I'll survive."

Horrified that she had caused him to get hurt, she ran to the icebox, ripped it open, grabbed the icepick and hit the ice block a few times, breaking off a couple pieces that she gathered in her skirt. Dumping the ice on the table, she grabbed a clean linen rag and wrapped up the pieces.

"Louisa, you don't need to do that. I'm fine."

She grabbed his arm and led him to the table, forcing him to sit. Then, she picked up the ice pack and handed it to him. "Put this against your head."

When he didn't move, she placed her hands on her hips. "I said, put it on your head."

He grinned but picked it up and did as she said. "Now you want to tell me why you came careening into the kitchen in an all-fire hurry?"

"What?" She watched him place the ice against his head and when satisfied he was doing as she said, she sat across from him. "I wanted to know how last night went, but it can wait. I feel so bad for causing you to hit your head."

"I'll be fine. It's not the first time I've hit my head, and certainly won't be the last, I'm sure." He winked at her.

A hot blush ran up her neck and into her cheeks.

"So, want to tell me what's on your mind?"

She began to fidget and shoved her hands under her thighs. She didn't want to look nervous, but she couldn't seem to help herself. "I... um, I was hoping you could tell me what happened last night. If you had discovered anything more on Connie's whereabouts."

He dropped the rag-covered ice onto the table and crossed his arms, leaning back into his chair. "We didn't find any evidence she was there, and no one we talked to admitted to ever seeing her before."

"Did you believe them?" She was afraid she sounded needy and didn't want to be that way, but she couldn't seem to help herself.

"I don't know. Harry thinks she was possibly there at some point, but either they're afraid to say she was or love her enough to protect her. Either way, no one is talking."

"Are you going to go back?"

"Yes, tonight."

"How about you take me tonight? I can blend in and ask questions you haven't been able to." She could do this. They wouldn't suspect another woman in a brothel.

"Absolutely not," he said.

"Why not?" Her back stiffened at his brusque tone.

"You can't do that."

"I can do plenty, and this is one thing I can do."

"No!"

Louisa shoved away from the table and glared at him. "You can't tell me what to do."

"Yes, I can. You work for me." He cocked an eyebrow as though his word was as good as gold.

"During the day. The nights are my own, and if I choose to do this, then there's nothing you can do to stop me."

"If you want to have a job during the day, then, yes, there is."

She glared at him, shocked and angry. Her throat tightened, and she struggled to take a deep breath.

"Are you really going to fire me because I want to help you? Because I want to help myself!"

"I didn't mean—"

"Yes, you did. You're like all the other men who think that a woman has to stay at home and have a protector. I had a protector, and look what happened to him. My father was killed and left me with nothing!" She slammed her fist onto the table, bending over it and shooting daggers at him with her eyes.

He held his hands up in surrender. "I certainly didn't mean to get you all riled up."

"I'm not riled up," she yelled.

His eyes widened, and he scooted back away from the table. "Clearly, I misunderstood and said the wrong thing."

Her chest heaved with anger. She curled her fingers against the wooden table and hung her head, trying to gain control of her emotions. She hadn't lost her temper like that before.

"I know you want to find her as much as I do, but there are better ways to do this without you having to compromise yourself again." He tried to soften his tone, but her blood boiled at his domineering stance on whether or not she should go to the brothel.

She slowly raised her head. "She hurt me too, Luke, and while I may not have experienced as much pain as you and your family, I still want her behind bars. If I can help, I should have that right."

"I know you do. Please, let me try again tonight. The madam knows her girls. How would you hide from her? Not to mention, the men are ruthless. They take what they want and you're—"

"I'm what?" she asked.

He stared at her for a long moment, his eyes boring into her soul as if he were trying to peel away her layers to see what lay beneath.

"Please don't take this the wrong way. You work for me, and I don't want to make things uncomfortable between us."

"You won't."

He sighed, rubbed his eyes, and stared at her for a long moment. "You are... you are the most beautiful woman I have ever met. I'm afraid the men in that house will take advantage of your innocence and your beauty. I don't want that to happen."

She was shocked at his words. He thought she was beautiful. Her anger dissipated as quickly as it had arrived, leaving her limp with fatigue. She hadn't expected those words to come out of his mouth and pressed a hand to her throat. "I—"

"Please, just do as I ask and stay here."

She nodded, letting him believe she'd agreed. As flattered as she was, she wouldn't let him stop her. She'd follow him to that brothel. She was tired of waiting for others to do what she was capable of doing herself.

Late that evening, Louisa sat in the dark, looking out her bedroom window, waiting for Luke and Harry to leave. She had wrapped herself in a black cloak, the hood pulled over her head, and serviceable brown boots on her feet. The dark blue dress she wore was long enough to cover the boots, and the men in the brothel wouldn't notice. Their eyes would focus on her low-cut neckline. The dress she wore was one she had taken with her when she'd left Mon Petit Amour. She never thought she would put a scandalous garment on again, but she needed to blend in and it worked well for her mission tonight.

She had saddled one of Luke's horses when Harry arrived and had it waiting for her in the barn. The two of them had been distracted with their conversation in Luke's study, and it had given her time to slip outside unnoticed and ready the horse for when she needed to leave.

As soon as Harry and Luke ambled toward Harry's buckboard, she ran down the stairs, through the kitchen, and out the back door, taking care not to let it slam shut behind her. She led the horse from the barn and saw the edge of the buckboard as it turned the corner at the far end of the street.

She used the mounting block Luke kept outside the barn and quickly climbed into the saddle. Shoving the cloak around her legs, she nudged him forward, not wanting to lose sight of Luke and Harry. Once she turned the corner, she saw them up ahead but made sure to keep a fair distance between them. She followed, her eyes and movements furtive, but it was late and there was little activity on the dark streets. She didn't encounter anyone on her way to the brothel. This was a good thing because she certainly didn't want to be caught wearing this dress by anyone Luke might know.

Harry and Luke seemed engrossed in their conversation and never looked behind them. When they reached the brothel, she dismounted behind an empty building, and watched around the corner until Luke and Harry entered. Once they disappeared from sight, she weighed her options. She couldn't go through the front door, but there should be a door around back where she could slip in unnoticed.

She led the horse to the back of the brothel and tied it to a hitching post far from the lights pouring out through the wide windows. She watched as women sauntered in and out, smoking cigars, laughing and groaning before being called back inside to meet with their customers.

Finding the right opportunity, she slipped inside and stared in shock at how rundown the place was. There were holes in the walls, dirt covered the floor, and a tall stack of filthy dishes rested in and around the sink. A rat scurried across the floor, and she had to hold back a squeak. She shuddered and remembered why she was there. She couldn't lose sight of that now.

Louisa saw a wall full of cloaks near the door into the main part of the house. Pulling the tie open, she removed hers and hung it there for her to grab when she left. She tried to tug the neckline of the dress up, but it was no use. Clearly, she had put on some weight while living with Luke. It had been a tight squeeze getting into the dress and as she tightened the corset, it had only accentuated her curves. She took a shallow breath to calm her beating heart and slipped through the swinging door into the hallway after putting her ear to the crack to ensure no one was nearby.

The hallway and back stairs were quiet and empty. Most of the activity would be out front and in the bedrooms upstairs. The powerful madams wouldn't allow any woman to dilly-dally when there was money to be made. They'd demand each woman earn her keep.

Going up the rough stairs at the end of the hallway, she peered around the corner. An older gentleman with a younger woman, clad in nothing more than a short shift and stockings held up by white ribbons, drifted into a room. They were so entwined around one another, they wouldn't have noticed if lightning struck the place.

She started down the hall. Not sure where to begin, she figured she had nothing to lose by opening each of the doors. The last thing she wanted to do was interrupt anyone and see more than she had seen in Mon Petit Amour, but she wouldn't find what she needed if she didn't at least look. If she intruded, she could pretend it was an accident. She wanted to find some sign of Connie so her clandestine trip to the brothel wasn't a complete waste of time. Luke was going to be upset with her when he found out she had followed him, but with any luck, she'd find something useful. Then perhaps he wouldn't be as angry.

After searching all the rooms on the second floor, discouragement settled in. She had found nothing more than what you'd expect in a brothel, although this brothel wasn't nearly as glamorous as Mon Petit Amour. The men inside were singularly focused and hadn't noticed her, but it had been difficult to hide her cries of distress. While she wanted to stop the atrocities, she couldn't expose herself, not without putting herself in more danger than she was already in.

This wasn't a place where women were in safe hands, not that she'd been protected in Mon Petit Amour. At least they stopped angry men from beating the girls. Here, beatings were considerably more commonplace, and no one was around to stop them. Determination straightened her spine. She wouldn't leave until she was convinced Connie wasn't here.

A group of scruffy men appeared at the top of the stairs. They laughed and stumbled down the hall toward her. She lifted her lips into a smile. She had nowhere to go and had to play the part. A tall, skinny man approached and put his hands on her waist. Before she could stop him, he had pulled her close. His mangy, black beard brushed against her chin.

She recoiled from his touch. Placing her hands on his chest, she began to push him away but then stopped. Playing this role required her to be accommodating and sweet, but she didn't want to encourage his behavior. She was here on a mission, and she'd do anything to complete it.

"Hmm," he said, leering at her with half-hooded eyes and the stench of liquor on his breath. "Who are *you*, and why haven't I met you before?"

She tried to slow her rapidly beating heart. "I'm new."

"Miss Josie didn't tell me about you when I inquired earlier."

"I'm not supposed to be out here yet," she said, her voice high-pitched. "I'm to be displayed in a week. She'll be awfully upset you caught me."

"Now, don't ya concern yourself with that." He forced her back until she was against the wall. "Miss Josie and I have an understandin'. Why don't you and I find ourselves a nice, quiet corner?"

Louisa was in a quandary. Not knowing the rules of the house could be her downfall. She wondered what kind of diseases she might pick up from this man. She'd have to take a scalding hot bath when she returned home tonight. "How about you find that corner and wait for me? I'll find Miss Josie and ask for her permission." She tried not to gag on the words. His hands moved from her waist, one cupping her backside, the other moving to her neck, running a dirt-crusted finger across her chest. She shivered from revulsion and had to swallow hard to keep the acid in her throat from releasing all over his greasy face.

He grinned, leaned in close, and kissed her roughly on the lips. "Darlin', that sounds perfect. I can't wait to see what you have to offer."

Stepping away from him, she grabbed his hands and pulled them to her lips, kissing the knuckles. She tried to remember what she had been taught at Mon Petit Amour, but it was difficult when she was swallowing back the bread she'd eaten earlier. "Wait for me. I'll be back in a moment."

He grinned, his hand slapping her butt, causing her to jump before laughingly joining his friends. "Don't be long," he sang.

All the men chortled, expecting a romp with her of which she would *not* satisfy.

"I won't." She gave him a small wave when what she wanted to do was run as far from him as she could get. Louisa resisted the urge to spit and wipe her mouth to remove the foul taste from her lips.

She was running out of time. Walking briskly down the hall, she turned the corner to the stairwell, falling out of sight of the men. She glanced down and then up, weighing the risks. If she didn't leave now, she'd take the chance of being discovered and violated by that man, but if she left, the trip would have been all for naught. She decided the search was worth getting caught.

She rushed up the stairs. Once she reached the third floor, she discovered one door at the end of the hallway was closed, and the others were open and empty. Perhaps she had finally found a room with some useful information. She reached for the door handle, twisted it, and stepped inside, closing it behind her. A single candle flickered in the dark room, but it was completely empty--just like all the others on this floor. She muttered a curse and stomped her foot on the floor, dust flying around her. She had found absolutely nothing, and she had a man below waiting, not-so-patiently for her.

Suddenly, the door opened. She whirled around and covered her lips with her hand. A tall man stepped inside, closing it behind him. The lone candle didn't shine enough of a light for her to tell who it was, but it was likely the man from earlier. He hadn't waited and had come to find her.

Pasting a smile on her face, she had to be quick on her feet and maneuver around him to the door. If she could slip past him, she might have a fighting chance. She started forward, then saw it was Luke who stepped into the dim light of the candle. It took him a moment to realize who she was, and when he did, his eyes flashed with rage.

"What are you doing here?" he said, his voice low but full of anger. He glared at her, stopped, held a finger to his lips, and stepped to the door. He leaned his ear up against the wood. His hand hovered above the door handle. Then, he relaxed and turned back to her.

"What does it look like?" she hissed, now free to speak.

"Do you realize how dangerous this is?" he muttered. His eyes flashed dangerously.

"No one knows I'm here."

"You ignored my wishes, but now that I've found you, it explains what's going on out there." He glanced over his shoulder again. He was twitchy.

Her spine tingled with dread. "I don't understand."

"The madam is trying to convince a man there's no one new in the house, but he's belligerent and quite convinced he saw a new girl, one with auburn hair and green eyes. Know anyone that fits that description?"

"Um." She swallowed. "I might've run—"

"You can explain later. We don't have time." He scowled. "They're about to search the house, looking for you." He paused and raked his fingers through his hair. "We need to leave now."

Louisa followed Luke out the door. His anger simmered just below the surface, but his need to protect her seemed to take precedence. The hallway was quiet, not a soul in sight, but Louisa feared they'd be unable to leave without running into someone.

Their luck disappeared after they ran down the two sets of stairs and the hallway toward the kitchen. The door to the kitchen flew open. Two men stood in front of them, their guns drawn.

Holding his hands out, Luke dropped the knife he'd held, and it clattered to the ground. It appeared to be the only weapon he'd had on him. She hadn't seen a gun belt on his hip and had failed to ask him before they left the room upstairs if he had anything else.

The two men herded them into the kitchen. The taller of the men moved in front of them and crossed his arms over his massive chest. A long scar ran down his cheek. "You've caused a great deal of turmoil, Louisa." The other man stood behind them, a loaded gun at their backs.

Trepidation filled her. *How did he know my name?* Looking at him more closely, she groaned. It was Bruno, one of Connie's men.

"You owe Connie a great deal, and you're going to pay––one way or another." His voice was ominous like muffled thunder.

He grabbed her arm and pulled her near him. She struggled to pull away, but he held fast, restraining her arms behind her back, his head near her ear. His breath smelled like a dead, rotting skunk.

"Let her go or you'll live to regret this," Luke snarled.

Fear slithered up Louisa's spine, but she wouldn't let them know how scared she was.

The man holding her chuckled. "Seems to me"––the laugh fading into a low growl––"you're going to be the one to regret this."

A rag was stuffed in her mouth, a black hood dropped over her face, and her hands were tied behind her back. Her throat closed and dread pulsated through her limbs. She tried to take a breath, but the thick fabric in her mouth, over her face, and around her neck was tight. She was lifted like a bag of flour over someone's shoulder.

"Stop," Luke yelled. "What are you doing with her?"

Bruno didn't say anything, just laughed viciously. Her head bounced against his back, her legs held tight so she couldn't kick. She was trussed up like a baby calf who was on its way to get branded. There was no way to move and no way to fight.

A few moments later, she was tossed into the bed of a wagon. It shifted as Bruno climbed in beside her. He grasped her neck and whispered in her ear, "Don't ya go anywhere, little one. We're going to have us a fine time. If you try and leave, that there man of yours won't live to see another day." He fondled her backside before the wagon rolled and shifted as he left her.

Louisa struggled to undo her hands, but failed. She couldn't scream. She could barely breathe.

Tears fell down her cheeks. She desperately tried to shove the rag out of her mouth with her tongue but only gagged instead. She'd made another blunder in the long list of mistakes since her parents had passed. *What is wrong with me? Why do I insist on making stupid decisions?*

If she'd listened to Luke, none of this would've happened. She didn't know where she'd be taken but one thing was clear: she had bungled this. If anything happened to Luke, it would be all her fault.

Twenty-Two

Luke watched in horror as Louisa was taken by Bruno, one of Connie's men. He had recognized him from the moment they had been shoved into the kitchen. There wasn't a thing he could do to stop it. The man behind him had grabbed him by the neck and shoved the gun into the back of his spine. If he fought, he was sure the man would've pulled the trigger.

He hadn't expected to find Louisa when he went upstairs until he heard the skinny man getting frustrated with Miss Josie. When the man had described Louisa, Luke knew she had followed them. When he left his home earlier, he'd believed she'd listened and stayed behind. He should have known better. His own sisters, Anne and Katy––and even his sister-in-law, Elizabeth––did what they wanted, especially when the stakes were high. Louisa was the same, and while he admired her strength, she'd taken unnecessary risks.

Luke suddenly thought of Harry. He hadn't seen his friend in some time and had no idea where he'd disappeared to. With any luck, he was safely in a room with a girl.

After Louisa had been taken by Bruno, the other man pushed him out of the kitchen and down the hall. Luke wasn't sure what this guy would do to him, but he had no doubt it'd be unpleasant. The man pushed Luke into what appeared to be a study. The lights were low, the furniture dark and heavy. While the other rooms were shabby, this room was not. It was clean, not a speck of dust anywhere. The rugs under his feet looked new, and the sofa and armchairs were covered in a soft velvet fabric.

Someone tied Luke's hands behind his back and forced him into an armchair, the velvet fabric soft against his fingertips. His knife was gone and his hands were secured. He'd left his gun in the buckboard, believing he wouldn't need it, and chastised himself for not bringing it anyway. He could hold his own in a fight, but with his hands useless, he didn't stand a chance. His captor stood firmly behind him, his thick fingers digging into Luke's shoulder, the gun jammed into his neck. If he made the wrong move, he'd be killed in an instant.

A moment later, a woman walked forward. It wasn't Miss Josie; it was someone else, but Luke couldn't tell who until she stepped within inches of him.

It was Connie. Harry had been right. She had been there, only now he was unable to get to her. She had the upper hand, and he'd let her take it.

"Luke," Connie drawled. "You haven't been a simple man to deal with." She walked back and forth, her body in a dark green gown that seemed out of place in a brothel. Her blonde hair was like a beacon in a dark sky. She pursed her lips into a thin slit. "What are we to do with you?"

Luke squinted and held her gaze. He had no desire to say a word.

"Have nothing to say?" Connie asked. She tapped a finger against her eyebrow as she sauntered around the room. "I'll admit, I didn't see you during the auction. My mistake, of course, but now it'll be rectified. If only you hadn't seen me, we wouldn't be in this position, but you're forcing my hand. Little did I realize what havoc you'd play in my plans." She slowly raised her crystal blue eyes to his. "I'll *never* make that mistake again."

He smirked, glad he was disrupting her plans.

"You've caused me nothing but grief, and I'll be glad to be rid of you."

Luke stared at her in stony silence. "You deserve everything you'll get."

She laughed, the sound musical, a stark contrast to the evil radiating from her eyes. "You're right, I will. But not the way you think. Oh, and don't let me forget." Her grin was sinister. "Thank you for bringing that little brat back to me."

Luke winced. He had played right into her hands. While he hadn't brought Louisa with him tonight, he had led Louisa straight into Connie's arms by not ensuring she wouldn't follow him. He knew she wanted to help, and he had believed she'd listen to him. Now Louisa would pay the price.

"This little game of yours is ending tonight." She looked at the man behind him and said, "Take him away. Beat him until he knows that this is no longer a game. Next time, he will die."

Luke grimaced and tried to stand, but the man's grip was strong. His options were disappearing fast. He didn't want to give up, but if something didn't change soon, he'd be dead and rotting in the ground.

She disappeared quickly into the dark corners of the room. The sound of a door opening and closing was the only noise indicating she had left.

Luke was jerked out of his seat and pushed toward the door. "Enjoy your last moments, as they might be your last. No telling how far I might go."

Louisa lay quiet in the wagon long after Bruno left, his ominous words keeping her from trying to leave. She didn't know if he would carry through on his threat to kill Luke, but she didn't want to take the chance. If her cooperation saved him, then she would do as Bruno demanded. She had caused this mess and now Luke could be killed, all because she didn't do as he asked.

All of sudden, shouts and gunfire exploded around Louisa. She startled and tried to sit, but the wagon shifted and lurched forward. The wagon careered down the road, hitting divots and ruts, throwing her from one end to the other, her body slamming into the hard wooden sides of the wagon.

Then everything stopped. She flew forward and hit something hard, groaning at the impact. All grew quiet. She shivered with fear. Was she going to die now or something far worse?

The hood was pulled off her head and the rag yanked from her mouth. She licked her lips, trying to moisten them as her eyes fluttered open. As her eyes adjusted to the dark, she saw the side of the wagon, tall trees, and twinkling stars above her, but didn't see who had removed the hood.

"Who... what... where am I?" The words jumbled out of her mouth. She couldn't get a coherent thought. Her body hurt from being thrown around the wagon.

"Shh," someone whispered.

Other noises circled around her––distressed horses neighing and stomping their hooves, wind whistling through the trees, and the creaking of the wood under her body as she tested her limbs.

A hand touched her shoulder, and she scooted away. Fear pierced through her.

"It's me, Louisa." Gentle fingers reached for her hands. With the quick swipe of a knife, her arms were free. She flipped around, her curls a tangled mess around her shoulders and in her eyes. She shoved it away to get a good look at who had untied her. Louisa's savior struck a match.

Her eyes widened. It was Luke. A bloody cut ran down his cheek and his clothes were covered in blood, but he was a most welcome sight. She hurtled her battered body into his arms. His grunt was a sign he was hurt, but he pulled her close, murmuring against her ear. All she heard was the pounding of her heart.

Luke feared the worst when Connie's man had dragged him outside, but luck was on side. Harry had been skulking in the shadows and subdued the man holding Luke by hitting him over the head with a frying pain. It knocked him out cold. Harry grabbed the man's gun and cut Luke loose from his bonds. Together, they dragged the man into a closet. With any luck, he'd be out long enough for them to rescue Louisa.

Once free, Harry handed him a sharp knife and another gun. He shoved the knife in his boot and pulled back the hammer on the gun. They crept to the door leading outside.

"She's in the wagon outside," Harry hissed as he pulled the door open slightly to look outside.

"Why didn't you get her?" Luke asked.

Harry turned his head slightly to glare at him. "The man who took her left her in the wagon. I thought she'd be fine 'til I found you. Better for two of us to fight back, than just one of us. Besides, my loyalty is to you, not her."

Luke placed his hand on Harry's shoulder and squeezed. The two of them shared a glance and stepped outside when Harry gave the all clear. Then all hell broke loose. Bruno had just rounded the corner with another man. They saw Luke and Harry, and Bruno opened fire. Luke dived behind another wagon while Harry ran in the other direction. Both of them shot back.

Bruno jumped into the wagon and took off with Louisa's limp body in the back.

Luke yelled, "Stop," but the man didn't listen and looked back at him, an evil grin on his face.

Luke ran to a tethered horse, but before he could jump on, the other man came running toward him and tackled him to the ground. The two of them rolled, trying to get the upper hand. Luke's gun flipped from his fingertips. He grappled for control, shoving an elbow into the man's side. The attacker groaned but seemed determined to end him. The man managed to grab his neck and had Luke in a chokehold. Luke's throat closed and his vision blurred, but he wasn't going to let this man end him. He tried to buck him off but had no luck. Remembering the knife in his boot, he bent his knee and reached with his hand, finally grabbing it after a couple of tries. He shoved it up and into the man's side.

The man grunted, his eyes wide, his hands relaxing from around Luke's neck. He glanced down and grabbed his side, blood leaking from the knife wound. Luke pushed him off and scrambled to stand. He found the gun and shoved it into his pants. Not caring if the man lived or died, Luke jumped on a horse, grabbed the reins, and took off. He didn't know where Harry was, but he couldn't think about that now. He had to find Louisa and prayed it wasn't too late.

A moment later, he caught sight of the wagon bolting down the street. Retrieving the gun from the back of his pants, he pulled back the hammer and leaned over the neck of the horse, urging him forward.

"If you give me all you got, I'll give you a nice carrot and a full bucket of feed," he whispered into the horse's ear. The horse seemed to understand and pushed forward faster.

Luke got closer and closer to the wagon, raised his gun, and took aim, hitting Bruno in the back of the shoulder. He fell forward and to the side, over the edge of the wagon. The horses were agitated and seemed to grow more anxious with every second. They dashed down the road, not wanting to stop. Luke pushed the horse under his hips until he came alongside one of the wagon horses and managed to snatch the reins before he yanked all the horses to a stop. His muscles strained with the pressure, but he had to do everything in his power to save Louisa.

The horses neighed, their chests heaving. They shook their muzzles but stayed in place as Luke jumped off his horse and ran to the back of the wagon. He found Louisa lying prone against the wooden side slats. His heart fairly jumped from his chest, his breath coming in short bursts. Was he too late?

When he ripped the hood and rag from her face and mouth, she looked confused. Her body was shaking, but she was alive. When she got a glimpse of him, she flung herself into his arms. His heart was lodged firmly in his throat, and he had to swallow hard a few times before he could speak. Tears burned his eyes, but he blinked them firmly back. This woman was special, and he had almost lost her. He didn't know what he was going to do next, but now that he had her, he couldn't lose her to Connie's skullduggery. He had to keep her safe until he could determine what was going on in his heart and his head.

Louisa fainted and he hugged her tight, her body limp in his arms.

"Is she all right?" Harry asked, breathing hard as he ambled over to him.

Luke jumped. Somehow Harry had caught up with him, his eyes wide with envy and desire. Before Luke could say something about it, he blinked and the look was gone. He wondered if he'd imagined it.

He'd consider what he thought he saw later. Now, he had to get her home safe. Lifting her from the back of the wagon, he held her close, one arm around her waist, the other under her knees. "She's alive, but I'm not sure of much else. She'll be black and blue from bouncing around the back of that wagon. Who knows what else might be wrong."

He'd never forgive himself if anything more happened to her.

Luke needed to find a safe place for her but wasn't sure where that would be. Perhaps stashing her at Michael's place, or even with Walter and Marie, would be better than his home. She wouldn't be safe with him, especially now that Connie knew for certain he had been the one to take Louisa from Mon Petit Amour.

Twenty-Three

September 17, 1900

The next morning, Louisa groaned when she stretched her bruised body. She couldn't forget how Luke's large, warm hands had lifted her gently onto his horse before he mounted behind her the night before. He had held her close but said nothing as they rode home. Harry had stayed behind to clean up the mess. She had been ashamed at her actions and trembled with worry over whether or not Luke would send her away.

When they'd arrived home, she'd tried to apologize, but he clenched his jaw and just ushered her inside, up to her room. He still treated her with care and concern, but he'd avoided looking her in the eye. Instead, he'd asked his neighbor, Mr. Rodgers, to send for the doctor, not willing to leave her alone in the house.

Once the doctor had looked her over and cleaned up Luke's gash, Luke had left her alone to consider all she had done. His anger was clear. She could sense he was doing all he could to keep it at bay, but she had pushed him too far. Because he had been trying to keep her safe, Connie had slipped through his fingers once again. That was the second time his protectiveness over her had cost him.

Moving slowly so as to not jolt her sore body, she drew on clean clothes and gingerly walked down the stairs. Her arms ached from being tied behind her. Her shoulders, back, and legs were covered in bruises from being thrown around in the wagon.

She had just poured herself a cup of hot coffee when the door from the hallway swung open and Luke walked in. The gash on his cheek only enhanced his rugged good looks but was spoiled by the firm set of his mouth. He'd likely throw her out this morning. She prepared herself for the worst.

"Good morning," he said. "Did you rest?"

She shrugged, avoiding the question. "I'm so sorry my actions caused you problems last night."

"We'll find her." He picked up a mug and filled it with hot coffee.

"Has there been any news?" she asked.

"No. Harry never came by, and it was late by the time the doc left."

Her heart sank. The longer they waited, the greater the chance Connie would disappear. Because of her, he hadn't been able to catch his former sister-in-law.

"I've sent word to Harry. I'm sure he'll be here soon."

"Can I go with you?" she asked, although there was no chance he would willingly let her after what had happened the night before.

"No." His eyes flashed with irritation. "I'm taking you to Walter's. You'll be safer there than here with me."

"I—"

"Don't argue with me, Louisa. Not after what you did last night. I just..." He placed his mug of coffee on the table. "I can't do this. You'll go to Walter's, and you won't argue with me about it."

She wilted under the harsh glare of his eyes.

A knock sounded at the front door. "That's Harry or my

brother, Michael. Can you bring coffee to my study? We'll be there."

"Would you care for something to eat?"

"No, I ate earlier."

She nodded, sadness pinching her throat. She wasn't sure how much longer she'd be able to keep it together. He was angry with her and wasn't afraid to show it. Louisa couldn't blame him, but she had some soul-searching to do. She needed to decide what kind of relationship she wanted with Luke and if that would even be possible.

Twenty-Four

September 19, 1900

Louisa paced back and forth. Marie sat at her desk scribbling notes and ignoring her, for which Louisa was grateful. She didn't know if she could carry on a rational conversation with anyone.

She had been furious with Luke when he deposited her at Walter's two days earlier. That was the last place she wanted to be, but he'd been insistent and wouldn't budge. She reluctantly went along with his plan, but her irritation was high.

After welcoming her with open arms, the three of them had eaten an early supper and then Louisa and Marie had settled into Marie's office. Marie had offered to visit, but Louisa knew she had been dropped on her and Walter unannounced. She told Marie to ignore that she was there and to continue with her normal activities. Marie looked at her carefully for a moment before deciding she was sincere, then nodded and went back to work, raising her eyes occasionally at Louisa's frantic pacing.

Sighing after she had looked out the window for the tenth time in as many minutes, Louisa sat on the sofa and tried to calm her fiercely beating heart. She'd feel awful if anything dreadful happened to Luke. She couldn't bear knowing she had caused him harm. Her parents would be appalled if they had been alive today. Going into a brothel, not once but twice, and then going against the wishes of someone who had offered her a safe haven. No wonder Luke didn't want anything to do with her.

"Are you sure you wouldn't like to talk about whatever it is that's bothering you?" Marie asked. "I can make us a pot of tea and grab some of those cookies my neighbor made the other day. They're surely delicious."

Louisa raised her head and sighed. "No, it's all right. I'll just sit here and consider all the stupid decisions I've made recently."

Slapping her hands on her desk, Marie stared at Louisa defiantly. "Are you through?"

Startled, Louisa grimaced at the glare in Marie's expression. "I'm sorry, Marie. I've been an annoyance and—"

"You don't need to apologize, Louisa. But pacing, sighing, and staring out the window won't fix anything."

"I know that, but I just can't seem to help myself."

"There's nothing you can do about Luke's decision, so I'd suggest you determine your next steps."

"What do you mean?"

Marie shook her head, straightened her shoulders, and pushed back into her chair. "What are you going to do when Luke brings that woman to justice?"

"Do?"

"Yes, do."

"I'm not sure I understand," Louisa said.

"Are you going to stay with Luke? Are you going to find employment elsewhere? How are you going to put a roof over your head?"

"Oh," Louisa said and shriveled under Marie's glare. "I... I guess I hadn't thought much past today."

"You need to come up with a plan, Louisa."

"You're right, I do."

"All right then. Let's make a plan." Marie pulled out a piece of paper and picked up her pencil, licking the tip of it before asking, "Are you going to stay working for Luke?"

"I... I don't know. I'm not sure he wants me to."

"Why would you think that? Has he said he doesn't want you to continue to work for him?"

"He dumped me here and couldn't get rid of me fast enough, Marie, so I'm not sure he wants me."

"He wants you, all right," Marie said, a grin lighting up her face.

"Not like that, Marie," she said, blushing. While Louisa wouldn't mind finding herself in Luke's bed, she didn't want to be his mistress, and he certainly wouldn't make her his wife. "I need to find my own way."

Marie nodded. "Go on. What would you do if you could?"

"I don't know. There isn't much a woman without a father or older brother can do."

"That's a load of horse manure," Marie spat out.

Louisa startled at the harshness of her tone.

"Tell me the truth," Marie said. "What would you do if there was no one or nothing stopping you?"

"I—" Her dreams were too unrealistic. While her father had been trying to get her into a medical school, there were few schools that would take women.

"Quit overthinking, Louisa," Marie said.

"You're right." She grinned. "I'd be a doctor."

Marie smiled. "A doctor. I have to say I didn't expect that, but considering how you patched Luke up the night we met, I guess that isn't surprising. You know it won't be easy, right?"

"I know, and I'm not sure I'll ever be able to achieve that, but if I could, that's what I would do."

"So, until we can get you into medical school, do you want to work for Luke?"

"Yes." She wanted to stay with Luke as long as she could.

"All righty then. Step one, get into medical school. Step two, work for Luke. Looks like we got the start of a nice plan."

Louisa laughed. While it wouldn't be easy to get into medical school and certainly not something she could do tomorrow, she could at least try. That was more than she had done in all the months since her parents had passed. She knew the medical schools her father had reached out to, and there was one or two that had let a few women into their hallowed walls each year. Perhaps with a little luck, a lot of patience, and some pure determination, she might just make that dream come true after all.

Twenty-Five

October 3, 1900

It had been two long weeks, and Louisa felt like she had overstayed her welcome at Marie and Walter's. Marie had been kind, but she had plenty of things she was involved in, and Louisa didn't want to be a burden. She spent most of her time in Marie's office, trying not to die of boredom. She tried darning some socks, and ended up creating a bigger hole than she started with. Then, she tried reading a few books, but those too didn't hold her interest. She'd even tried cleaning, but both Marie and Walter had been less than thrilled when they found her scrubbing the hallway floors. So she sat, staring out the window, twiddling her thumbs. She did write two letters to the two medical schools back east and had Marie post them. She had taken what Marie had said to heart and was reaching out. Once she heard back from them, she would know whether or not they would be feasible options for her.

Marie had much to do, and was often gone long before she woke and didn't come home until after Louisa had gone to sleep. Even Walter wasn't home much, being busy with his newspaper. She had offered to help Marie with her work, but Luke told her she wasn't to leave their house. Marie and Walter agreed, and they sequestered her like a parakeet in a birdcage. She could have left easily. The last thing she wanted to do was disappoint Luke, but she might have to if he didn't release her from the cage soon.

She had heard nothing from Luke since the moment he had sent her to Walter's. He'd been angry, but she thought he would have sent word or at least visited. She missed him and hated feeling so useless. Marie insisted she rest, but she was done resting.

Tonight after dinner, she was going to Luke's. She'd be careful and mindful of her surroundings. It was time to discover where things stood and to see if Luke was done with her. She couldn't live with Walter and Marie forever. She already felt like she had overstayed her welcome. He had to give her answers, even if they were ones she didn't want to hear.

After eating a rich stew that had been simmering all day, Louisa left a note for Marie and walked to Luke's, bundled in a cloak she had borrowed. While it wasn't freezing outside, it was chilly, and she wanted to hide her appearance as much as she could. If anyone were watching, they wouldn't suspect it was her. The leaves were turning, and the days were getting shorter. It wouldn't be too long before snow fell.

Once she reached his home, she took a deep breath, squared her shoulders, and marched up the walk to his front porch. Grabbing the railing to give her courage, she pulled herself up the steps and rapped her fist on the hard wood before she could change her mind.

As soon as her hand dropped away, she second guessed her decision. Luke was going to be furious with her for coming here after the way things had ended between them. He wanted her to be far from danger, and he'd think her wandering the streets of Helena as foolhardy. She didn't want him angry with her, so she backed away from his front door and turned to leave when it opened. He stood there, just as handsome as the day she'd met him. She should not have come here.

His welcoming smile dropped into a frown. "What are you doing here?" Luke swiveled his head back and forth. Then he grabbed her arm under the cloak and unceremoniously dragged her inside before slamming the door shut behind her. "Did anyone follow you?"

"What? No."

"Are you sure?" He hadn't released her, but his fingers loosened and skimmed along her arm to her elbow.

"I..." She gulped at the look in his eyes. The anger at her arrival disappeared in a flash, and a pulsating heat replaced it. His desire was so intense it nearly bowled her over.

His heavy breath hit her skin, and he backed her up against the door. His other hand braced against the door near her head and leaned his forehead against hers. "Why are you here?" he whispered. Luke raised his fingers and brushed them against her cheek before they fell to the hollow in her neck, resting there. He was bound to feel her fast-beating heart.

She gulped again, her hands gripping her skirt. When he looked at her, she saw past the pain in both their lives and to what might be. He was affectionate, caring, kind, and fiercely protective of her when he didn't have to be. She wanted more from him but couldn't find the words to tell him. "I just wanted to..." Her words trailed off.

His fingers untied her cloak, letting it fall unheeded behind her. Then, he ran them down to the edge of her bodice, skimming along the buttons until he reached her waist, where his warm hand circled to her lower back and pulled her body close.

Louisa shivered, but it wasn't from the cold. It was from a fire blazing uncontrolled under her skin. She hadn't come here for this, or at least she hadn't intended to, but now that she was here, she didn't want to step away.

He continued to stare at her, his eyes seeming to see straight through to her soul, as though he could read every thought she possessed. But what did he see? She didn't want him to see her as the woman who chose to enter a parlor house. She wanted him to see her as the woman who could become a doctor--who was strong and independent, but who could love him with a fierceness as strong as his protective instincts toward her. She wanted him to cherish and adore her, but she wasn't sure she had the right to ask.

His red lips lifted into a wide grin. "You wanted to?"

Banging on the door startled them apart. He sighed, dropped his hand away from her waist, and stepped away. She immediately missed the warmth his body had provided.

She rubbed her hands against her skirt, her palms wet with sweat. The knock sounded again, and she jumped. She bent and grabbed her cloak from the floor. She then scooted away from the door and around Luke.

"Go into my study, Louisa," he whispered, "I don't know who is behind that door, and I'd rather be safe than sorry." Any tenderness he might have had in the moments before vanished when the real world interrupted. She nodded and headed away from him, slipping inside his study before he opened the front door.

A moment later, Luke joined her. She jumped to her feet, her hands clasped in front of her.

"Who was at the door?"

"Harry." His previous congenial attitude was replaced with irritation.

"Is he out there?" She pointed to the hallway. She did not want to be around that man and if he was still here, she'd head upstairs, away from his beady eyes and wandering hands.

"No, he's left."

"Is there any news on—"

"No, there's no news on Connie," he snapped. "She's disappeared again, but I've caught her goons watching the house, which is why I didn't want you anywhere near here."

She dropped into a chair, her fingers covering her mouth. "Is that why I haven't heard from you?"

He crossed his arms over his chest and let out a long breath.

"There are many reasons, Louisa. Being near you is far more diffi-cult than I could've ever imagined, and I'm afraid I'll lose control around you."

Her mouth opened in shock. Then hope bloomed inside her. Perhaps he would be willing to explore more, but she had to be sure. "I don't understand." She berated herself for the lie she just uttered. She knew exactly what he meant, but she wanted more from him than a housekeeping job. It was complicated. She needed to know if he could live with the choices she had made.

He raised an eyebrow. "Don't play coy. It doesn't suit you."

She shrank back in her chair. He was right. She was trying to hide her actual reasons because she feared how he would react. Louisa was better than that. She never used to hide behind lies and half-truths, so she didn't understand why she was doing it now. "I'm sorry. You've been nothing but kind to me, and I shouldn't play games."

"Why are you here?"

Straightening her back, she looked him dead in the eyes. "I wanted to know if you had heard anything and..." She was scared. He said he wanted her, but she wanted more than a romp in his bed. She wanted a loving husband, partner, and protector. Did she have the courage to ask him? "And I wanted to know if... if there was something more between us than me being your housekeeper."

He stared at her hard. "This isn't the right time for this conversation."

"But—"

"It isn't safe here. That's why I had you go to Walter's."

"Why won't you answer my question?" she cried, jumping to her feet. "It's because I was in a parlor house, isn't it? You'll never want anything to do with a woman who would sell her body?"

"No, of course not. I would never hold that against you. I know your reasons, and you never actually, well, you never——"

"Then what is stopping you?"

"This really—"

"No"--she pointed a finger at him--"we've been bouncing around this for months. I understand you don't want me to get hurt, but do you want me to be more than just your housekeeper?"

"Damnit, Louisa. Yes, I want you, but until Connie is behind bars, I can't give you what you need." He ran a hand through his hair, his chest heaving up and down.

"Then what do you want me to do?" Sweat beaded across her brow.

He shook his head. "I want you to go back to Walter's, where you'll be safe from harm."

"I don't want to be there, Luke."

"I can't have you here."

She stalked toward him. He took a few steps back, stumbling against a chair. "You're not being honest with me."

He held his hands up as though he could ward her off.

"Why don't you want me here?" She stepped even closer, until only a hair's breadth stood between them. "And don't tell me it's for my safety. There's more to it than that. You know it. I know it. You wanted me to be honest. How about you be honest?"

He retreated once again, but she wouldn't let him put distance between them. He had held her at the front door just minutes before. It was her turn.

Her green eyes darkened with every word she spoke, and it was all he could do to keep his hands to himself. Luke had made a mistake backing her into the front door just minutes before. He had been so close to kissing her, the pounding at the door the only thing stopping him. He could've kissed Harry on the cheeks for inter-rupting them if he hadn't been just as irritated that he had.

It'd been two weeks since he last saw her and not long enough to squash his feelings. He'd told her it was because he couldn't keep her safe while she stayed in his house, but there was more to it. He couldn't stop thinking of her.

Every waking moment of every day, he was consumed with thoughts of her. Her smile, the sway of her hips, the way she lifted a duster, the way she fluffed his pillows. He remembered how he had found her stretched across his bed, trying to fit the bottom sheet. She hadn't seen him and had picked up a pillow, singing a little ditty. The sound of her voice reminded him of his ma. She would have loved Louisa.

Luke enjoyed her laugh, and the way she didn't back down while still being considerate of his feelings. She may have jeopardized her safety by following him to that brothel, but she had done it with good intentions. He couldn't fault her, not if he was honest with himself.

Leaving her with Walter and Marie had been for both her safety and for his sanity. He couldn't be consumed with thoughts of her. He was too close and if he gave into what his head wanted, he'd be distracted from his mission. He couldn't let his family down.

With Louisa standing in front of him once again, all he could think about was her lips under his and her soft body in his arms. He couldn't forget that night in the parlor house, no matter how hard he tried.

"Please forgive me." He placed his hand around the back of her neck, bent his head to hers, and pulled her into a kiss that torched him from the inside out. She tasted of honey, her lips soft and moist beneath his.

Her arms wrapped around his neck, and he pulled her to him until she fit perfectly into his embrace like she had been made for him.

He deepened the kiss, not able to get enough of her. One hand went to the small of her back, the other nestled into her soft auburn hair. Luke didn't want to let her go. He moaned, his excitement at finally having her in his arms making him ache. He lifted her into his arms and strode with two giant steps to the sofa. Luke sat with her in his lap, her arms still wrapped around his neck, her head resting against his chest. His breath was hot and heavy as he tried to gain control of himself.

"I should apologize and tell you I shouldn't have done that," he murmured, his voice low.

Her fingers curled into the hair at the back of his head, sending shivers down his spine.

"Don't apologize," she said, her face buried in his neck.

He grinned and pulled her close, the fire crackling next to them. It was a moment he wanted to savor, to cherish. The real world would come again tomorrow, but for tonight, it was just the two of them.

Twenty-Six

October 11, 1900

It had been a week, but she still couldn't forget that night. It had been a few hours of lighthearted but serious conversation with sweet kisses interspersed before Luke had agreed to let Louisa return. He had done delightful things with his lips that left Louisa tingling with a heady heat, but he was a gentleman and it hadn't gone any further.

She had listened patiently as Luke explained his hesitation at letting her return. Afraid the danger wasn't over, he had told her he feared Connie wouldn't stop until they harmed her. He thought they were gunning for him now as well, and he hadn't wanted Louisa to get caught in the crosshairs.

While she understood and appreciated his concerns, she hadn't wanted to impose on Walter and Marie's hospitality any longer. She had to earn her keep and unless Luke was willing to let her come back, she needed to find alternate employment. She had told him he was paying her to do a job, and she needed to do it.

Louisa was convinced it wouldn't matter where she was. He

could hide her deep in the mountains, in a fortress with guards aplenty, but if Connie wanted to hurt her, she would find her. In her mind, it made sense for her to stay with the one man who could protect her, although she insisted she could take care of herself if it came right down to it. He had grinned at that pronouncement but acquiesced with the promise that she would not follow him if he had any more leads. While she wanted to argue, she had agreed to his demands so she could come back to his home and work for him again.

He'd also told her if she were to stay, their relationship had to be put on hold. She had already gone outside proper social graces with her foray into a parlor house. While she didn't want to agree, she knew he was right. They would keep their feelings at bay until Connie was behind bars.

Smiling once again at the memory of his lips, she headed to the kitchen to prepare their morning meal. She opened the back door onto the porch to breathe in the fresh morning air. The sun was rising over the distant mountains, streaks of orange and yellow across the horizon.

Heading back inside, she saw a basket full of fresh eggs on the kitchen table. Luke once again showed his care and concern for her by doing a simple deed to make her life easier. A few minutes later, she had them sizzling on the stove top when the door to the hallway opened behind her. Not wanting him to think that she was desperate to lay her eyes on him, she took a deep breath to calm her thudding heart. She had to learn to not swoon breathlessly whenever he was in her presence.

Grabbing oven mitts to protect her hands, she opened the oven door, let the heat touch her skin, and gave a quick glance at the biscuits. They were coming along nicely and would be ready soon. She dropped the mitts on the counter, wiped her now-sweaty palms on her apron, and turned to face him.

Luke stood in the doorway, his eyes twinkling and a devilish smile on his face. She could imagine herself jumping into his arms and him swinging her around, but they had an agreement and she'd stick to it.

She wet her lips with her tongue and then opened her mouth to say something. Only a soft squeak emerged. Embarrassed, she tried again. "Good morning. Breakfast will be ready soon."

Instead of responding, he stepped forward, backed her into the counter, and kissed her quickly on the lips, sending a zing straight to her toes. He reached around her, picked up the pot of coffee, and grinned mischievously. "Coffee ready?" He held up the pot, his body still near hers, and she nodded.

She blushed furiously and turned back to the stove, trying to calm her rapidly beating heart. "Are you hungry?"

She could hear the splash of coffee as he poured it into a mug. "Yes, but I'm late. Walter's bound to be irritated I haven't arrived yet. I *would* like some of those eggs, though." He brushed a hair away from the back of her neck, his fingers lingering for a moment. "Can you do me a favor?"

She turned back to him. "Of course, whatever you need."

"Please stay inside, lock the door behind me, and..." He pulled a revolver from the waistband of his trousers and placed it on the table. "Keep this with you at all times."

Her excitement at being back in his home had overshadowed the threat that was still hanging over their heads. She picked up the black revolver, the handle smooth and checked the chamber to make sure it was fully loaded. Her fingers felt sure and solid while her heart raced with dread. Once done, she raised her eyes to his. "I'll be ready. Do you think I'll need it?"

His hand covered hers and squeezed. "I wish you didn't, but there's too much at risk. I don't trust that they aren't watching the house, hoping for a glimpse of you. For all we know, they've already figured out you're here."

"All right, if you believe that's best," she said.

"I do." He furrowed his brow as though surprised at her quick agreement.

Louisa didn't want to disappoint him again and would do anything to keep that from happening. Pulling open the oven door, she removed the hot biscuits. She dished up a plate of warm eggs, a piece of sizzling ham, and a hot biscuit and placed it on the table for him.

"Have you heard anything more about Connie?"

"No, but I think we're getting close. I can taste it." He pulled out a chair, picked up a fork, and then waved for her to sit. "She's going to make a mistake, and I'm going to be there when she does."

"I hope you aren't being reckless." She piled food on her plate and sat in front of him.

He chuckled. "Reckless? I wouldn't say I've been reckless, but perhaps not as careful as I should. It's been years since she killed my pa, and I'm determined that after all this time, we'll get her. She's right in our grasp. I just have to reach out and grab her."

"I would think you'd want to notify the sheriff."

He chewed a bite of egg and swallowed. "I'm considering reaching out to the US Marshals, but I want to run it past Harry, see what his thoughts are."

Louisa shuddered and dropped her eyes. Harry made her extremely uncomfortable. Every time he came by and Luke wasn't looking, he ran his eyes down her body and licked his lips. Her distaste for the man only grew with each encounter.

"What?" Luke leaned forward in his chair and narrowed his eyes.

She looked up and realized he must have seen her disgust. "It's nothing."

"It's something," he said. "As soon as I mentioned Harry, you squirmed."

"I did?" she said, trying to sound as though she didn't know what he was referring to. Her fingers played with an ivory button on her blouse.

"Louisa, I'm not addlebrained. Something's bothering you."

"No, no, you're mistaken. Nothing is bothering me."

"You're lying to me." His voice deepened with displeasure.

She stared at him, trying to decide if it was worth it to say how she truly felt about Harry. After a moment, she decided it wasn't. Harry was Luke's friend, and no matter how she felt about him, it wasn't her place.

"I—" A loud pounding on the front door interrupted Louisa. Her shoulders sagged in relief. She didn't know what she would have said, but now she didn't have to tell him that Harry made her skin crawl, and she'd be happy if he never came near her again. With Harry helping Luke, she'd be best to keep her opinions to herself.

Luke stood, pushed his chair back, and raised an eyebrow before going through the kitchen door to the hallway, leaving her to her food.

Hopefully, he would forget what he had seen and wouldn't question her further about Harry. She didn't want to explain and was determined to avoid doing so at all costs. She would not come between Luke and a friend, even if that friend would never be a friend of hers.

Hours later, Louisa paced back and forth in the parlor, nervously waiting. The day was half over and she still didn't know what was happening. Luke had left without saying much and hadn't told her who'd been waiting at the door. She hadn't recognized the voice and didn't believe it was Harry or Walter.

A loud banging at the front door startled her. She raised a fist to her lips, and her thoughts raced as to who it could be. Every time she turned around, someone was knocking on Luke's front door, and it was never good news. It wouldn't be Luke. He had his own key. Was it Connie's men coming back to take her? She grabbed the revolver Luke had left her, pulled back the hammer, and held it behind her back. She wasn't sure she'd be able to fight them off, but she'd give it her best effort.

She peered out the side window, but all she saw was an empty porch and a bright blue sky. The person was just out of sight. Her gun-toting hand trembled. She didn't know if she could do this again. While she tried to be strong, fear poured through her veins, and she had to take a few deep breaths before she could breathe solidly again.

"Who is it?" she called.

"It's me, Harry," he yelled. "Open the door, Louisa."

Irritation crawled up her spine. She did not want to be alone with the man. Releasing the hammer, she relaxed her grip on the revolver and placed it in the pocket of her skirt. She didn't trust him, and it gave her a measure of comfort to have it on her person. She twisted the lock to release it and pulled the door open a crack.

Harry pushed inside and closed it behind him, throwing the lock. His coat billowed around him. He pulled it off and handed it to her before stalking into the parlor. Irritated at his disregard for her, she hung the coat on the coat tree and reluctantly followed him.

"What are you doing here?" Louisa asked.

"I'm looking for Luke." Harry's blue eyes raked over her.

"I thought he'd gone to work," she said.

"He never showed. Walter's fit to be tied. I thought maybe something happened to him, so I came here to see what you knew."

Louisa gasped. "What do you *mean* he never showed up to work? Where could he be?"

"If I knew that, I wouldn't be here with you." He glared at her.

Louisa cringed at his ominous tone, but she wouldn't let him scare her. The weight of the revolver in her skirt reminded her she could protect herself. "Go look for him, then."

"Don't you worry your pretty little head. You're just his house-keeper, not his wife."

"I'm well aware of what I am." She balled her hands into fists at her sides.

He rubbed his hands together. "Louisa, we both know you're more than you want to admit."

"I don't have any idea what you're talking about," she said, her back straightening. Unfortunately, she knew all too well what he was suggesting. Ever since their first meeting, she'd felt uncomfortable in his presence.

Harry walked to her, stalking her like a lion after his prey, licking his lips as if preparing for a bloody feast. His piercing eyes were ripe with desire. She knew that look. She had seen it way too often at Mon Petit Amour, and she didn't want to let him know how much it made her skin crawl.

He stepped closer.

She slipped around one of the side tables.

He chuckled. She grabbed the duster lying on the table and held it up as if it were a sword.

"You aren't as innocent as Luke would like to believe, Louisa, are you?"

He took another step forward, closing the distance between them.

If she could distract him, maybe she could stop him in his tracks. "Luke isn't here. I think you better leave."

He shook his head, the salacious grin on his face growing wider with each passing second. "I shouldn't leave you alone, considering everything that's happened."

"I'm perfectly fine."

"Are you?" He pushed the table aside, forcing her up against the wall. He glowered at her, his bulky body preventing her from escaping. His hot breath brushed against her cheek, and his hands braced against the wall, keeping her trapped with nowhere to run. He had never tried anything while she had been staying in Luke's house. Why was he after her now?

"I have work to do. Excuse me."

He studied her before whispering breathlessly. "I'm sure you do, but perhaps you should do for me... what you do for him."

She recoiled in fear. Her body seemed to shrink back inside itself. *Grab the gun!* But her hands refused to cooperate, dangling uselessly at her side, the duster falling from her fingertips and dropping to the floor.

"I don't know what you're blathering on about," she said.

His fingers skimmed her cheek and brushed against her ear, pushing a lock of hair away. Then he let one pudgy finger slide down her chin, settling his hand there delicately as if he were holding a teacup.

Trying to hold back her panic, she jerked her chin away, his rough fingers scraping at her skin. "Don't touch me!"

He ignored her, chuckling mirthlessly under his breath. His hands dropped on the wall next to her waist, his body shifting, pushing his hips into hers. She swallowed the lump growing in her throat.

He leaned toward her, his lips brushing her ear.

"You're something to behold." His voice was anything but kind as his teeth darted out and nipped at her earlobe.

She wanted to push him away, to claw at his cheeks, to kick him hard, but she was frozen in place. Her limbs wouldn't move, no matter how hard she wished they would. *What's wrong with me? Why can't I move?*

"I believe we can come to an understanding, don't you?"

Thick body sweat, peppermint, and cigar smoke fought for dominance in her nostrils. Louisa swallowed back a gag that was rising with intensity. She refused to answer him, but he didn't appear to care if she answered or not.

"Hmm," he said. "Don't be shy, now. I think we could have fun. I don't see any reason we can't enjoy ourselves."

The doorknob rattled.

"Louisa! Why's the door locked?" Luke was shouting. He sounded angry, belligerent--a delightful and most welcome sound to her ears.

"I guess we'll have to continue this another time," Harry murmured.

Finding the strength to move her hands, she finally shoved him away.

He chuckled and walked to the chair near the fire, settling into the plush cushions as if he had been patiently waiting all this time.

Taking a deep breath, she tried to calm her racing heart. She patted her hair to make sure it was still in its tight bun and straightened her shirt before stepping away from the wall and letting Luke in.

Luke came inside, opened his mouth, and said, "Why was the door locked?" Then he saw Harry, and his attention was diverted.

"Where have you been?" Harry asked. "Walter said you didn't show up to work this morning."

"I got another useless message about Connie."

"Well, I might have something a little more promising," Harry said. "But it can't wait, we need to leave now." Harry stood and marched toward the door. "Let's go."

Luke followed Harry toward the door, but then stopped when Louisa said his name.

"Yes, Louisa?"

"Where are you going?"

"Luke, are you going to explain yourself to your housekeeper?" Harry muttered.

"He's right. Go to bed, Louisa."

Red, hot anger flared up her chest and into her cheeks. He had some nerve talking to her like that. "Luke, I don't think—"

"No, Louisa. Do as I said." With that, he looked back at Harry. "Give me a minute. I need to run upstairs and grab something. Then we can go." He headed out of the room and up the stairs.

Harry watched him leave before turning back to her. Before she could stop him, he had grabbed her arm and pulled her close, a menacing whisper in her ear. "You aren't special, my dear. You're nothing but a whore. You mean nothing to him. The sooner you realize that, the better."

Twenty-Seven

November 1, 1900

L uke leaned on Harry as they stumbled inside his house, his head and sides throbbing from the blows he had received from Connie's goons. Harry had found him on the street in front of Mon Petit Amour an hour past, blood running down his arm, cuts and scratches on his face and arms, his legs having just collapsed. If Harry hadn't arrived when he had, Luke would be lying on the street, waiting for a wagon or horses to rumble over him.

They tried to be quiet, but Luke feared they'd wake Louisa. Harry propped him up against the wall, closed the front door behind him, and then dragged him into the parlor. Once inside, he helped Luke to the sofa. Harry dropped him onto the cushion's edge and bent over, bracing his hands on his knees, breathing heavy. Luke wasn't a large man, but he was fit and weighed far more than Harry had likely ever carried.

The single gas light on the table cast a dim glow in the dark room. It was late, and the sun had fallen hours ago. Groaning, he slowly checked his ribs. He didn't think they were broken but they were certainly bruised. He had been cocky and unprepared, and he didn't want Louisa to see him like this. There'd been unresolved anger and tension between him and Louisa for weeks, ever since he had found Louisa and Harry in his parlor. He had spoken to her harshly and as a result, she'd barely spoken to him, avoiding him by claiming she had cleaning or cooking to do. They hadn't shared a kiss, a touch, or even a tender glance since.

"Luke!"

Louisa's voice pierced through his skull and increased the severe pounding in his head. She rushed to his side, her revolver held firmly in her small hand.

"What happened?" Her voice quivered and squeaked. "You're hurt!"

"Yeah, he's hurt, Louisa. Go get some hot water and rags to clean him up," Harry ordered.

Louisa seemed to hesitate and looked over her shoulder. Harry had been standing just out of sight. He moved forward to help Luke sit more fully on the sofa after he'd gotten a breath.

Louisa visibly bristled at Harry's tone, but she stuffed the revolver in her skirt pocket and ran out of the parlor.

Lifting a hand to his pounding head, Luke said, "Did you have to be so harsh, Harry?"

"I wasn't. Just letting her know what to bring to help you. She's your housekeeper, so she should be comfortable with being ordered around like the servant she is." Harry put his hands under Luke's armpits and helped him sit back against the sofa.

Luke was angered at Harry's tone but held back a sharp retort. The man had helped him after all. "Thanks. I feel like an old man whose bones don't work no more."

"Well, you went in there, guns blazing, without any help, thinking you could actually take her down by yourself. What were you thinking?"

Luke winced, both from the pain and in shame. "Not my best

moment. Besides, I actually didn't expect to find her. I had every intention of confronting Pauline, and instead I found her."

"If I hadn't shown up when I did, what do you think would've happened?"

"Nothing pleasant, I'm sure." He tried to grin, but it was more like a grimace.

Louisa burst back into the room, rags and a bowl of water in her hands. She put the bowl on the table next to the sofa and dropped the cloth rags beside it. She reached into her pocket and pulled out a pair of scissors, a bar of soap, and a bottle of whiskey.

She elbowed Harry out of the way and knelt in front of Luke. "What hurts?" she whispered.

"Everything," he mumbled.

"Is there anything that doesn't?" She reached for the bottle of whiskey and held it up to his lips. He gratefully took a swig. Maybe if he drank enough, things would start to hurt less.

Louisa then went to work cleaning his cuts and bruises. Her touch was tender as she probed his wounds, washing them with the soap and clean water, and even dabbing them with a rag soaked in whiskey. The wounds stung, but she assured him that it was the only way to get them clean. She used the scissors to cut off his good shirt. When he protested, she pushed his hands away.

"The shirt's covered in blood and has rips in it already. At this point, it's meant for the rag bin." She pursed her lips into a thin line as she concentrated on cutting. She examined his chest and ribs carefully, her fingers skimming across his bare skin. Grabbing a long piece of cloth, she placed one end against his hot skin and began wrapping it slowly around him. Her body was flush against his, her breath warm against his chest and neck, sending tingles of awareness through him. He had missed her touch and craved her with an intensity that fought with the pain from being beaten to a bloody pulp.

When she finished, he breathed hot and heavy. Having her this close to him was near torture and if Harry hadn't been watching their every move, he might've pulled her into his arms and kissed those beautiful pink lips. Harry's growl was enough to keep him from taking advantage of the situation. She was trying to help him, her movements methodical and purely nurse-like, nothing romantic in them.

Once done, she stood, brushed the back of one hand against her forehead, and then placed both on her hips. "Well, you'll hurt for a few days, but I don't think any of your injuries are life-threatening."

"Thank you," he said. "I appreciate your doctoring."

She nodded. "So, mind telling me what happened?" Her words were laced with a ferociousness that surprised him.

"He doesn't need to tell you a thing, Louisa. You're just his housekeeper. Why don't you take your pretty little behind up to bed and let the men talk," Harry said.

"Harry," Luke said, surprised at his ugly tone. "What's come over you? You're not normally so rude."

Harry's face twisted into an evil scowl before quickly being replaced with a congenial smile. Luke had to blink several times. He wondered if he'd hit his head one too many times tonight. It appeared Harry had been angry, but the look had disappeared so quickly, he might've imagined it.

"It's been a rough night. I'll head back to Mon Petit Amour and see if I can figure out where Connie went." He rubbed his chin. "Louisa, please excuse my bad behavior. I'll see you in the morning, Luke." Harry turned, striding out of the parlor and through the front door. He'd opened and closed it so fast if Luke hadn't watched him leave, he might's missed it. It was as though a wolf had chased him.

Louisa dropped into an armchair across from him. "I don't like that man."

Surprised, Luke gazed at her. "He's a little rough around the edges, but he's been a good friend."

"Perhaps, but he... Well, I just don't particularly care for him."

"You'll get used to him over time."

"No, thank you. I'd rather not." She raised her hands to her hair, pulled out the pins holding it up, and scratched at her scalp forcefully. A look of pure pleasure came over her face. She caught his eye and blushed. "Sorry, it's been a long day, and sometimes I just need to let my hair down. It's so heavy at times."

She leaned forward, her gaze pointed. "I think you're avoiding my questions from earlier."

He sighed. "I'm not trying to, but it ain't important. Things just didn't work out the way I thought they would."

"Why don't you tell me what happened, then?"

"Were you going to shoot someone?" He ignored her question and tried to hide his smile but was sure he'd failed.

"What are you talking about?" she asked, her eyes narrowing.

"You were carrying your revolver when you roared in here."

"If you hadn't made so much noise, I wouldn't have grabbed it," she muttered. Her face was set in stone, and she had never been so appealing as she was in that moment.

"You could've hurt yourself." As soon as the words came out of his mouth, he knew they were the wrong ones. Her cheeks bloomed red, not with embarrassment but with anger.

"I can't believe you," she said. "You're the one who gave me this revolver." Louisa yanked it out of her skirt and waved it in front of him before she stood and stalked across the room. She placed the revolver on the side table. Stopping at the fireplace, she picked up the poker and jabbed it into the logs, stoking the flames higher, and then turned back to face him. "I'm not the one who was beaten today." She raised the poker and pointed it at him, huffing, and shoved it back where it had come from.

"Well, I—"

"Well, what?"

He snapped his lips shut. She needed to say her piece, and he could let her considering she had taken care of his wounds.

"You're so infuriating," she said.

"I don't—"

"Don't even say it. They hurt you once *again,* and I'm sure it has something to do with me, doesn't it?"

"I—"

"I don't want to know, Luke. I've become a hindrance to you, not a help."

"Louisa."

"Once again, you got yourself into a pickle, and you could've been killed."

"Uh—"

"You can't even tell me. You're confused and hurt." She paced back and forth in front of him, her hands going from her waist to clenched balls in front of her. Her movements were erratic.

"I—"

"I have to leave. I should've never come back here. I should have left Marie's and found myself a job at the hotel or the laundry, but coming back here was a mistake." Her voice had risen with each word. She stalked away from him toward the window, pulling back the drapes. Her fingers were white with the force of her grip.

"Louisa."

"What?" She spun away from the window. Her auburn hair lay in a mass of curls down her back. He itched to run his fingers through the thick, luxurious length and bury his nose in the rose-scented fragrance.

"Can I say something?"

"Of course. I haven't stopped you."

"Well, I wouldn't say that," he said, a grin lifting his lips and causing the cuts and bruises on his face to stretch painfully.

"And what is that supposed to mean?" she snarled, her anger and frustration growing to a boiling point.

"It means..." He pushed to stand and limped toward her. His right hip was tight, his ribs were aching something fierce, and his head pounded, but he was determined. "It means you're an amazing woman who I'd be honored to have by my side in my fight against Connie."

He reached for her hands, and she looked at him in astonishment. His eyes burned into hers, and energy sizzled between them.

"None of this would've happened if you'd never met me. This is all my fault," she said.

"You realize that's ridiculous, don't you?"

"No, it isn't," she said, trying to pull her hands away.

"Yes, it is." He held onto her hands and pulled her close. Gently, he wrapped his arms around her waist until her head nestled under his chin. He never wanted to let go. "It's all right, I'm fine. A little bruised but still kicking."

Hot tears fell down her cheeks, wetting the front of his chest. He only wore the cloth rag around his ribs. Having her near him, even when things were spiraling, made him feel like he could have everything he had ever wanted. He let her cry, and he murmured reassuring words into her ears, his hands rubbing the small of her back.

Louisa's sobs eventually subsided to hiccups, and then she quieted altogether. He didn't want to let her go, but she was restless. Not wanting to scare her, he gave her the freedom she needed. She bowed her head and wiped her face with the back of her hands. He handed her a handkerchief he had stuffed into his trouser pocket. She took it, the fabric twisting between her fingertips.

"Thank you. I'll wash this and get it back to you," she said.

"I've got plenty, so don't hurry on my account."

"I'm sorry. I didn't mean to lose my composure. That's not like me." She avoided looking at him, her hands trembling.

"It's been a stressful few weeks. You have every right to shed a few tears."

"Oh..." She looked at him and touched his forehead, her fingers gentle. "You should be resting, not standing here trying to comfort me." She cradled his hand and led him back to the sofa.

"I'd really like you to tell me what you got involved in tonight," she said, her voice quiet with concern, still holding his hand between her soft fingers.

"I'm not sure that's a good idea."

She dropped his hand and scooted to the other end of the sofa, his body strangely chilled. "I'm not leaving until you do." She folded her arms across her chest.

He chuckled softly and winced. Laughing didn't help ease the aches. Connie's men had surely done a number on him.

"You certainly are an intriguing woman." She was much more than that. Every single moment he spent in her company only reinforced how strong and delightful she truly was.

Luke feared he was treading dangerous waters. He needed to silence the demons that had been chasing him for seven long years if he wanted a life with Louisa.

She tilted her head to the side as if trying to decide whether what he'd said was a compliment or an insult. The mixture of emotions on her face was lovely to watch, and his heart fluttered. Her lack of guile made her even more endearing.

"Don't change the subject." She bounced her knees and glared at him.

He rubbed his hand across his eyes, tried to get comfortable on the plush sofa, and then rested his palms over his eyelids. "Not much to tell. I went to Mon Petit Amour. I thought maybe I could convince Pauline to tell me where Connie was at."

"Did Pauline tell you anything?"

He laughed, but it wasn't filled with joy. "No, I found Connie instead."

Luke had been stunned silent when he'd slipped into what he thought was Pauline's office on the second floor of Mon Petit Amour and found Connie resting on a sofa. She turned her head and smiled, although it didn't reach her eyes. She didn't even appear surprised that he had invaded her sanctuary. It was almost as though she'd been waiting for him.

He had convinced a black-haired beauty on the main floor that he desperately needed to talk to Pauline once he'd moved past the burly guard at the front door. A group of drunk men had stumbled outside, distracting the guard. It had been easier than he anticipated and made him think he was invincible. Luke had slipped the young woman a gold coin, and she had willingly told him where he could find Pauline.

He had scooted up the gleaming wood staircase, past scantily clothed women, and turned down the hall to the right to a room at the end. The woman had told him to look for double doors, and he saw them at the end of the hall.

When he stepped inside, he saw Connie's stocking-covered feet draped across a small, padded stool, her blonde hair loose around her shoulders, and clad only in a black satin robe. All the rage, anger, confusion, and sadness he'd felt over his parents' passing flooded back to him. His eyes were focused only on her. He hadn't noticed the men who burst from the corners of the room. They quickly grabbed him by the arms and divested him of his weapons.

She sighed, brushed the strands off her shoulder, and faced him. She had stood just as elegant and put-together as she had years ago when she had married his older brother, Stanley. For a moment, he was that young boy who had watched his brother marry a sophisticated woman. Her mere presence had made him tongue-tied and insecure, but he was no longer that boy. He was a man who didn't have to cower in front of her.

Her thugs stood next to him, their hands holding him firmly. He glanced over each shoulder. He didn't recognize them. They looked cutthroat and thoroughly dangerous. He thought for just a moment that he might take one of them down, but not both.

As if reading his mind, she shook her head. "Don't even consider it, Luke. We both know that you can't fight them. Now, why don't you sit, since you were kind enough to visit." A sly smile played on her pouty lips.

He looked at her with disdain. "I'd rather stand than sit in your presence."

"Is that any way to talk with your beloved sister-in-law?"

He curled his lip. "Beloved isn't the word I'd use, and you're no longer my sister."

"Oh, did your weak-minded brother finally do something about our short-lived marriage? I didn't think Stanley had it in him." She quirked an eyebrow, one hand on her satin-clad hip.

He ignored the slight against his brother and kept his mouth shut.

"Hugo, why don't you escort our guest to the chair? Lance, you can watch the door. I'm tired of watching him stand." She didn't wait to see if her men did as she demanded. Instead, she turned and sat gracefully on the sofa.

Furious at finally finding her but not being able to get his hands on her, he didn't fight the men. He didn't want her to know how much she'd unsettled him, but he feared he couldn't hide a thing from her. With as many years as he had spent hunting for Connie, the fact that they sat facing each other as though this were an after-supper party was surreal. He didn't know what to do, but he was a bit curious about what she would stay.

She leaned back against the plush sofa. The edges of her satin robe opened, but he only felt disgust for her. Seeing her act as if she were safe from imprisonment was more than he could bear. It was all he could do to not claw her eyes out.

"I think it's time we resolve this, don't you?" she murmured. "I'd hoped to see you dead by now, but you're like a rat, always rising to the surface."

"Resolve what? That you killed my pa, or that you attempted to kill my brother and steal our family ranch?" He rubbed the back of his neck, his arm brushing against the man she called Hugo, who held him in place. Lance had moved to stand guard on the other side of the room. "You deserve to be hanging from a rope, not running around free as if you've nothing to lose."

"Tsk, tsk. So much anger and resentment. Don't you think you should let it go? It has been over seven years. You should move on with your life. Your brother is alive, your family still has the ranch. You didn't lose a thing."

"I didn't lose a thing?" He started to rise, but Hugo held him in place and Lance reached for one of two revolvers hanging under his waistcoat. Grunting, he dropped back into his seat. "I lost..." he grimaced, the pain as real now as ever. "I lost my brother and my parents because of you. Stanley hasn't been the same since."

She draped one leg over the other, her foot swinging back and forth as she smiled at him. "Technically, it was because of Beau, the ranch hand, not me. I had nothing to do with your mother's death —that was all due to the illness. Your father, on the other hand, well..." She rubbed the edge of her robe. "All of that's in the past. It's time to move forward."

Hot rage burned through Luke. He'd love to wrap his hands around her neck and squeeze every last breath out of her. His hands gripped the arms of the chair instead. When the moment was right, she'd pay dearly for everything she had done to his family. He had made that vow years ago, and he'd not stop until she was behind bars or rotting deep in the ground.

"Nothing to say? Hmm, I would've expected you to jump out of that chair and come for me with your uncontrollable temper."

Holding back the disgust, he said, "I don't think you're worth it."

She chuckled. "Luke, you never could lie. Not sure why you're trying to do it now."

He curled his lip and crossed his arms.

"Nothing to say now?" She shifted on the sofa and settled more into the soft cushions. "You were never one to control your temper very well, so I'm surprised you're quiet now."

"I'm surprised you're still in Helena, Connie. I would've

thought you'd have ran with your tail between your legs like you did after you tried to kill Stanley."

"I would've succeeded in killing your sniveling brother, but he was surprisingly resilient. I must admit, he surprised me. I didn't think he had it in him to take out Beau."

"He should have ended you then."

"But he didn't. Now, it's time for this to be over with, don't you think?"

"The only way things will *ever* be over is when you're hanging dead from a noose."

"My, oh my, so angry." She twirled a blonde curl around her forefinger.

He gritted his teeth. "What a horrible person I must be for not thanking you for your generous nature. I have no reason to despise you, do I?"

She chuckled. "Perhaps you do, but that is neither here nor there. What we need to do is solve this. I can't have you continuing to besmirch my good name."

"Your good name?" He snorted. "Are you serious?"

"I'm a respectable business owner now. I don't need this headache."

He laughed, not with mirth, but with disdain. "I'd hardly call a parlor house madam a respectable business owner."

"Owning a parlor house is only one of my many ventures, and considering my clientele, it's more respectable than you might believe. But enough about that. Your vendetta against me needs to stop." Her eyes narrowed contemptuously.

"It'll never stop—"

"Enough." She swung her legs to the floor. She stepped around the sofa and toward the other side of the room, where she ran her hand along a wooden desk. "I'm done with this. If you don't stop, I might have to get angry, and you certainly don't want that. Think of what it could do to you and your family." She paused and lifted her eyes toward him, the gaze menacing. "Or perhaps Louisa."

Unease crept up his spine. It was bad enough she was threatening his family, but it was something else to bring Louisa into this. "Leave Louisa alone." His tone grew harsh. "You don't scare me. In fact, I relish the opportunity to end you."

"You're still thinking with your heart, not your head. I'd thought a little honest conversation would let us resolve this as sensible adults, but I might be wrong." She continued to wander around what was quite possibly her office, her back to him as though she had all the time in the world.

He laughed sardonically. "What world are you living in?"

She turned back to him, her blue eyes narrowed into thin slits. "I would've thought that with all that I've done, it would've given you an inkling into what I can and *will* do to you if you don't stop."

"Are you threatening me?" His collar grew tight around his neck.

She smirked. "I wouldn't call it a threat, my dear. I'd call it more of an unfulfilled promise." Her hand pushed back a yellow curl that had fallen across her shoulder.

"A promise?" He stared at her incredulously. She had audacity, and it infuriated him more. He'd bring her to justice if it was the last thing he ever did.

"I never threaten, but I keep my promises."

"What are you suggesting?" he said. A part of him was curious to see what she was up to.

"There, now. Was that so hard? We *can* have a reasonable conversation."

He laughed inside. She was delusional if she believed that.

She stepped close to him, bending near his ear. "You have something I want, and I only think it's appropriate that you return it. Once I have it, you give up your vendetta against me and go back to your life as it was."

"It doesn't sound as though I'm getting anything if I agree," he hissed.

"Why, of course you are." Her fingers ran down the front of his shirt, flicking at the button near his throat.

"And what is that?" Her cloying scent made him want to gag.

"You won't have my men coming after you or hurting any member of your family."

"You've already hurt my family in ways that can never be forgiven."

"Are we going to do this again?" Her palm dropped on his chest, the pressure so uncomfortable he wanted to push her away, but he wouldn't give her the satisfaction. "It truly is unfortunate things had to end the way they did. I do hold a special place in my heart for Stanley, but ultimately this was his fault." She moved away, her hand dropping to her hip.

"You're crazed."

She cackled. "I'm far from that. He made promises to me when we married, and he broke every... single... one... of them."

There was a hint of something in her voice, but he couldn't pinpoint what it might be. "And what promises were those?"

She sighed. "The biggest was giving me a home of my own. He knew what I wanted and what I expected. I was clear about that from the beginning. Instead, he forced me to move to your parents' ranch and live with your *mother*."

"I don't see how that was a problem. The ranch is massive. There would've been room enough for both of you."

She shook her head. "That is something you men can never understand." Connie rubbed at a spot on her forehead. "No woman wants to start her new life living with her mother-in-law. That was her home, her domain, and I had no say. That was unacceptable."

Connie's face turned ugly, potentially from memories of something he couldn't possibly understand. His mother had been loving and kind, but the ranch had been his ma's home, her mark on every inch of the place.

"What am I supposed to give back to you?" he asked.

She sauntered to the rose-colored sofa, running her fingers across the top of it as though he should know exactly what she wanted. "Why, your dear Louisa, of course." Her smile was anything but generous and was filled with a calculated evil more dangerous than the men guarding her back.

Hysterical laughter built inside of him. She was living under an illusion if she thought he'd give in to her demands, but he could continue to play her game. "She isn't an object I can return."

"Oh, she is." Her mouth turned into a vile frown. "I invested in her, and she owes me."

"She doesn't want to return."

"I don't care what she wants." Connie's voice went from congenial to disgusted. "I've lost money because of that slip of a girl, and she *will* fulfill her part of the bargain." She braced herself against the back edge of a chair, her fingers digging into the soft upholstery. "We can do this the easy way or the hard way. It's up to you."

Her cheeks had turned bright red, and her arms trembled slightly. If he hadn't been watching her carefully, he might have missed the signs. As his eyes caught hers, she took a few deep breaths, walked back to the sofa, and sat, calming her angry nerves.

"Now, you need to bring that young *lady* back here," Connie said with disdain. "Let her know she owes me and she will pay, one way or another."

A slither of dread crawled up his spine. There was no way he was going to turn Louisa over to them. "I can't say where she's at."

"Now, Luke. Where would she be if not here in Helena with you?"

"She went to the ranch." The lie slipped past his lips. She wouldn't believe him, but perhaps it would give him time to end this without Louisa getting hurt in the melee.

"We both know that isn't true."

"It is."

"Now you're going to make me angry, and I *don't* think you want to do that."

"I don't care what you want, Connie. I have no reason to do anything for you."

She looked at him for a moment and then did an almost imperceptible nod toward Hugo, but Luke was prepared. He had his hands braced against his knees, his legs ready to fight. Hugo moved in front of him, his fist raised, but Luke blocked him with his right arm. Luke shoved his hips back, and the chair crashed behind him. He exploded upward, his other arm ripping an arc across to Hugo's face. His head swiveled, blood spurting from Hugo's lips, but it didn't stop him. Hugo emitted a growl and punched forward but Luke ducked, avoiding the blow.

Luke had nothing to lose and wouldn't let Connie or either of her henchmen stop him. He bent down and rammed his head into Hugo's chest. Hugo stumbled back and crashed into a table. Wood splintered under him, his head bouncing against the floor. Hugo, confused from the fall, shook his head. He appeared disoriented, allowing Luke to concentrate on the other guard.

Lance ran toward Luke, a revolver in his hand. Luke snatched his wrist and pushed his arm up, keeping the gun from being pointed at him. They wrestled for control, Lance not as brawny but just as angry. Luke grunted and elbowed him hard, trying to rip the gun from Lance's hand. A gunshot blasted through the window, but Luke managed to knock the gun from Lance's fingers. It clattered to the ground, forgotten as the two of them wrestled for the upper hand.

Out of the corner of his eye, he saw Connie scurry away from the fight. It became clear Luke was not a match for either brute, but Luke gave as much as he took. Fists flew, blood spurted, and grunts roared from Luke's lips. Lance pushed him into the wall, and his clenched hand popped one, two, three times into Luke's gut. Luke's head swam, the pain growing, but he wouldn't give up.

By the time Luke knocked Lance back, Hugo had risen and burst back into the fight.

When Luke's body grew weary from the strain of the blows and he began to wonder how much more he could take, the door to Connie's office flew open. Pauline ran in, screaming in fright. It distracted Hugo, and Luke pushed him away again. This time, he fell into Pauline.

Luke wouldn't win this fight, not tonight. He stumbled for the door, pushed past the women crowding the hallway, and ran down the stairs. He burst out the door and into the road in front of the parlor house. His eyes were losing focus. A gash down his cheek and various other wounds leaked blood all over him. He floundered, tripping over his feet, and his legs collapsed. He fell to the ground, his head hitting the dirt road with a hard thwack.

Twenty-Eight

November 2, 1900

A loud knock sounded on the door, interrupting them and making Louisa jump in her seat. After everything he had told her, she wouldn't be surprised if it was Connie's men coming to finish what they had started tonight. "Who's that?"

Luke shook his head. "For all I know it's my sisters coming to town wanting me to take them shopping," he said, making a poor attempt at lightening the mood, of which she didn't appreciate.

"None of this is funny," Louisa snapped. "Let me go see who it is."

"No." He reached for her hand and stopped her in her tracks. "I'll go. If it's Connie's men, I don't want them to see you. I told them you weren't here, but they didn't believe me."

She reluctantly nodded. At the entrance to the parlor, he turned and said, "Close and lock the door behind me. If it's them, you'll hear me yell. Go out the back and into the hidden cellar off the kitchen." He had shown her the room after the last attack. It was stocked with food, water, and a rifle with plenty of bullets. "They shouldn't find you there."

Louisa did as he said and didn't argue. However, she wouldn't run without a fight. She still had her revolver and wasn't afraid to use it. She checked the chamber and then patted her pocket. The clinking and warmth of bullets made her feel strong and in control.

She stood at the door, her ear against it. Unfortunately, the door was thick, and it was difficult to hear anything but murmured voices. She heard nothing loud or dangerous. No gunshots, raised voices, or fighting.

"Louisa, it's all right. You can let me in."

She opened the door slowly and was relieved to see it was only Luke and Walter. Shoulders relaxing, she stepped back and let them both inside the room.

Walter turned to Luke and said, "What has been going on, Luke?"

"It's quite the long story, and I'm not in the mood to repeat it."

"I think you better. I was interviewing the sheriff about the recent wave of crime when Madam Lafoe burst into the room. Two men were with her, looking like they'd taken quite a beating. She demanded that he arrest you. What did you do?"

Luke shrugged.

"Luke?" Walter's eyes narrowed. "I had to pay the sheriff so he wouldn't come here and drag you to jail. I don't like wasting my money without knowing why. What did you do?" His face had gone red, his cheeks blowing out like a balloon.

Luke ran his hand across his chin. "I'd like to see them try. Besides, they have no grounds to arrest me." Luke growled.

"You had to have done something tonight. You look as bad, if not worse, than Madam Lafoe's two men."

Luke sighed and waved to the sofa. "You might as well sit. Would you like anything to drink?"

Walter yanked off his coat and dropped it across the back of the sofa before plopping down. "Coffee, black."

"Louisa, would you—"

"Yes, I'll put a pot on now and perhaps a little something to eat?"

Luke nodded and hobbled to the armchair. "Yes, that'd be most welcome. Thank you."

Louisa walked to the door. Hesitating in the opening, she glanced over her shoulder to reassure herself he'd be fine. He met her gaze and smiled. She nodded and headed down the hallway to the kitchen.

Luke had his own reasons for chasing after Connie, but Louisa's escape from the parlor house had only caused problems for all involved. She feared that Luke was being rash in his judgment and in trying to protect her. From all accounts, he had been more cautious in his pursuit at the beginning, but from the moment he rescued her, his need to end Connie had taken on a new meaning.

Swinging open the kitchen door, she filled a pot with ground coffee beans and water, and put it on the stove to warm. She pulled out some cookies she had baked just the day before and arranged them on a platter.

Sitting down at the table, she considered her options. Perhaps she could convince Luke to let go of his vendetta, but she disregarded that notion. He wasn't going to do that, not for anyone. He wouldn't get any peace until he dealt with Connie or until she left Helena. Either one would be dangerous.

The sheriff wouldn't help. It was clear he was on Connie's side. Luke had mentioned reaching out to the US Marshals, but he would've done that already if he'd had enough evidence. She wondered if she could confront Connie, get her to admit her involvement in Luke's pa's death. She scoffed at that idea. Who was she to think that Connie would admit anything to her?

The water boiled in the coffee pot. She pushed to stand and grabbed a cloth to protect her hands. Carefully, she put the pot and three mugs onto a tray with a plate of cookies and went back to the parlor. She didn't know what she could do to help Luke, but she had to help him somehow.

Luke waited until Louisa left the room before turning his attention back to Walter.

"I didn't think things would blow up like this. I went to Mon Petit Amour to look for Pauline. I thought perhaps I could bribe her to tell me where Connie was. The last thing I expected was to find Connie in her office, but she didn't seem surprised to see me."

Walter leaned back on the sofa and draped his arm along the edge of the sofa. "She claimed you burst into her office tonight and harassed her. Since she has a lot of dirt on those with power around here, she's pulling in markers. If you don't back off, they're going to throw you in the slammer, and they'll trump up charges to keep you there."

"I can't deny I went there, but her men disarmed me quickly. They definitely had the upper hand."

"Then how did it get out of hand?"

Luke grinned. "Let's just say I wasn't willing to let them kill me, and I gave as good as I got. Besides the law has got to be on my side."

Walter shook his head and leaned forward, resting his elbows against his knees. "The law isn't. You went there, not the other way around. The sheriff was ready to arrest you on her word alone."

"Then why isn't he here?"

"Because I paid him, remember?"

"Oh, yeah. Thanks for that."

"Also, I convinced him that arresting a member of the Seymour family wasn't in his best interest when the woman who was making the accusations was a whore. I reminded him that your family is well-known and well-liked, and with the mayor up for election next year, the scandal alone wouldn't be in anyone's best interest."

"Sounds like you handled it, then," Luke drawled.

"Yes, I did but the sheriff's goodwill is only going to last for so long. The sheriff made it clear you're to leave her alone or he won't hesitate to find a way to end you."

"He can certainly try."

"Are you always this hardheaded?"

"Walter, you know what she has done to my family. Would you stop if she had done the same to yours?"

"I understand your motives, but you've got to be smarter than this."

"I can't disagree with you, but there's something you need to know. She wants Louisa, and I'm afraid of what lengths she'll go to get her."

"Maybe I should just return to Mon Petit Amour." Louisa walked into the parlor, a tray held firmly in her hands. "It would stop her from coming after you. Maybe I can get her to confess to killing your pa."

"Absolutely not," Luke said. "She isn't going to say anything incriminating to you and even if she did, it would be your word against hers. The sheriff isn't going to arrest her based on that alone."

Louisa placed the tray on the table between him and Walter, and poured them both a mug full of hot coffee before sitting on the sofa next to Walter.

"You don't know that for sure, Luke," Louisa said. "We've got to do something different. You running into different parlor houses and brothels isn't working."

"But—"

Walter interrupted him. "She actually might have a point, Luke."

"I don't think—"

"You haven't been thinking, that's the problem," Walter growled.

Luke bristled at the implication, but he didn't want to look a fool in front of his boss, so he kept his angry retort to himself. "I can't write that headliner for you if I don't continue going after her."

"The only way you're going to get Connie behind bars is if you have irrefutable evidence. The mayor and sheriff won't disrupt her business unless they have something to lose."

"Or something to gain," Louisa said. "I don't want to go in that place. It makes my skin crawl, but you can protect me. Reach out to the US Marshals. Perhaps they can station a man or two inside. If someone can overhear her confessing, then it wouldn't be just my word against hers."

"That's a ridiculous idea," Luke said. "It would never work. She would be expecting something."

"Would she?" Walter asked. "She wants Louisa, and her single-minded focus on that might make her say something out of turn." Walter leaned forward, his forefinger rubbing against his cheek, lost in thought. "Louisa could claim that the two of you had an angry fight, one in which you called her a whore."

"I would never do that," Luke said, angry at the implication.

"Of course you wouldn't. This is just a story Louisa could tell her to make the return to the parlor house credible."

"Why would Louisa return just because we had a fight?"

"The same reasons that Louisa went there in the first place. Do you think Connie cares about why as long as she gets her perceived property back?"

"I just don't know if she would believe that," Luke said.

"Connie wants me for her own reasons." Louisa paused, her face red with embarrassment. "The man who bid on me probably wants Connie to uphold her end of the bargain. If I go back, she can satisfy her customer."

"You know what'll happen if you go inside that place again, Louisa. She isn't going to let you leave so easily, even if I did agree to this harebrained plan," Luke said.

"I don't need for that to happen. I'll go in there long enough to get her to confess while someone listens on the other side of the door. As soon as she does, they can arrest her, and then I'll leave."

"This isn't a silly parlor game," Luke said.

"Of course it isn't." She stood, one hand on her hip and the other braced against her neck. "Do you really think I want to go back? I made the mistake of going to Mon Petit Amour because I thought I had no other options. I have options now. I'd only be doing this to help you."

"I don't need your help, Louisa," Luke said. "I can't sacrifice your safety just because I want to end her. She's my problem, not yours."

"She's my problem, too," Louisa said.

"She wants you back, and she is going to do everything in her power to achieve that," Luke said.

"Then let's play into that," Walter said.

Luke opened his mouth, but Walter held up his hand to stop him.

"We will be there. We can wait outside and have men we trust inside Mon Petit Amour along with the US Marshals. If Louisa plays it right, Connie will make a mistake and say something incriminating, and it'll finally end. She'll be arrested and Louisa will be safe."

"How can we ensure her safety?"

"Luke, I want to do this. I need to do this. All of the choices I've made have put you and myself in danger. I'll carry a knife in the boning of my corset, perhaps one on my hip. I know how to use them. No one will get close."

"You don't know that. There is no way we can guarantee something won't go seriously wrong."

Louisa walked toward him and knelt in front of him. She

grabbed his hands and held them softly in hers. He couldn't let her do this. Putting her in danger wouldn't be right.

"You'll protect me, Luke. Just like you have all along. I have no doubt you'll keep me safe and not let anyone harm me. We have to do something, and this may just be the answer."

Twenty-Nine

November 4, 1900

Connie slapped her black silk gloves onto her desk. For the past two days, she had fumed over what Luke had done and the sheriff's refusal to arrest him. That influential newspaperman had been in the sheriff's office when she had gone there to request he do something about Luke. Instead of listening to her, the sheriff had been convinced it wasn't in his best interest to do so, at least not now.

Her hold on both the sheriff and the mayor was tenuous. Both of them feared the newspaperman would unleash secrets that could jeopardize their bids during the next election. Although she too held secrets on the men, it seemed the mayor was holding his cards close to his chest. She didn't want to play her hand unless she absolutely had to. There were too many benefits from keeping it as a threat instead of exposing him for the deviant he was. She couldn't do anything that would garner unwelcome attention.

She would have to go after Louisa differently, change her approach. She was ensconced safely in Luke's home regardless of Luke's claims to the contrary. Bruno had been watching the place for days and had seen Louisa on numerous occasions. It would just take her time to find the perfect solution.

Nathan had followed her into her study at Mon Petite Amour. He stood behind her, waiting patiently, or at least pretending to do so while she thought of her next move.

"Connie, what do you want us to do next?" Nathan asked after the silence became too much for him.

She raised a hand to her forehead, pinching the skin between her brows, the other on her hip as she stalked back and forth behind her desk. "Let me think on this."

"I can send Bruno to Luke's house and have him grab her when he leaves."

She stopped and held out her hand, her fingers drifting up and down. "No. He'll have safeguards in place, and I don't want to attract any more attention."

"Attack his family's ranch?"

"No, you just told me she's still at Luke's home. That would serve no purpose." She braced her hands against the back of her leather chair.

He shrank from her words and muttered, "You don't trust me any longer, do you?"

She groaned inwardly and turned toward the window, trying to put her mask of coquettish innocence back on her face. It was challenging keeping the men under her control satisfied and compliant. Nathan was just another man in a long string of them who believed they were in love with her. To her, he was an over-grown oaf who needed his ego stroked just as often as her Beau had. Beau had been a nuisance, but man, he'd satisfied her. The memory of him caused her eyes to glaze over, and a dreaminess covered her features. Remembering him was perhaps a good thing because Nathan would believe her gaze was all for him. Unfortunately, Beau had died at the hands of Stanley Seymour.

Pulling on the long metal pin holding her black and white feathered hat in place, she removed it and placed both on her desk.

Then she turned back to Nathan and pasted on a sweet smile. She sauntered to stand in front of him and ran her hands across his chest. She brushed her body up against his.

"Now, Nathan, you know I trust you with my life. I want nothing to happen to you or to foul up our plans." She arched her back, so he could admire her. "Luke has become a nuisance, one which we can control. We just need to find the perfect opportunity to do so."

She wrapped her arms around his neck and placed her lips on his. He groaned with satisfaction and dragged her close. After giving him a taste, she pulled away. His slurpy kisses were enough to make her gag, but she could play the game. She had done it often enough over the years.

"Mmm, don't go away, baby. You taste delicious, like fruity wine, and I—"

"Shhh." She placed a finger against his lips to quiet him. "Now isn't the time, although you know I would love nothing more than to finish what we've started. We need to rid ourselves of this problem before we can enjoy ourselves."

Connie ran her hand from his lips down to his chest. His breath quickened, and his eyes darkened. He placed his hands on her waist and tried to move her close. She laughed quietly and kissed him on the cheek before she stepped away. Nathan breathed hard with frustration. She knew what he wanted, but she wasn't inclined to jump between the sheets with him. She had a business to run and frankly, Nathan didn't excite her. Such was the life of the calico queen.

She went to her desk and sat, patting her hair. It wouldn't do to look disheveled.

Nathan grunted and adjusted himself, trying to control his breathing before sitting in the wooden stiff-backed chair in front of her desk.

"What should we do now?" he asked.

"There's got to be a way. I just need to come to it."

He grunted again. "What do you want me to do in the meantime?"

"Go check on the new batch of girls and send Pauline in here. I'll send for you once I have a plan."

He nodded and started toward the door when he turned back to her. "I—"

"Shh, I know. I feel the same way. Now go." She waved her hands to send him on his way.

Connie watched him leave. She slumped in her chair. "What do I have to do to end this madness?"

This was frustrating. She was finally rolling in money. Helena had been a virtual gold mine, and she didn't want to let it go, but she might not have a choice. If she couldn't get Luke under control and get Louisa back to fulfill her promise to the fire chief, she stood to lose everything. The mayor was up in arms, and the fire chief was threatening to shut her down if she didn't produce Louisa soon. She had to get her back. Once she did, she could rid herself of Luke.

If she could make it look like an accident and make sure nothing led back to her, she might stand a chance. The last thing she wanted was for any of his brothers to think she had anything to do with his disappearance because that would be her downfall.

A knock sounded at her door. Schooling her features so she didn't appear as furious as she felt, she said, "Come in."

The door opened, and Pauline stepped inside her office.

Connie's fake grin disappeared. She didn't have to pretend in front of her sister. She waved Pauline forward. "Close the door. Sit."

Pauline did as she was told. She was a striking woman. Connie still couldn't believe they were related, but they had the same father. They'd only found each other a few years before, and all because Pauline had found letters sent to her pa about his other daughter. Pauline had grown up in a world far different from hers. Connie was jealous of what opportunities Pauline had versus what she'd experienced. Pauline had lived in a world of wealth and privilege – never wanting for anything, going to balls, being courted by the wealthiest of gentlemen – until everything fell apart. The only thing that kept Connie from taking her anger out on her sister was that Pauline depended on her, and Connie got a perverse sense of pleasure from that.

"Did Nathan tell you what happened?"

"Yes," Pauline said.

"Then you know we've got a problem. Has the fire chief been by today?"

"Yes." Pauline scowled. "He's here, complaining and raising all kinds of havoc. I gave him one of the new girls."

"Was he happy with his choice?"

"Temporarily, but he still wants Louisa. He said if you don't produce her soon, he'll shut down the house citing fire hazards. We're at his mercy, and he enjoys the power."

"Infuriating, pompous ass. I'm doing everything in my power to get her back. I just need more time." Connie's voice rose with anger.

Pauline shrunk in her chair. "I know you are." Her voice was quiet and controlled, and it infuriated Connie to no end.

"Oh, for hell's sake, Pauline, I won't bite. You've got to get a backbone if you're going to survive in this business." Connie glared at her sister as Pauline tried to gain her composure.

It was probably time for Connie to consider a move to San Francisco, but Pauline had to be ready to run the parlor house and brothels she owned. Mon Petit Amour was the nicest one, but the real money came from the brothels she owned on the seedier side of town. Men came in droves and paid plenty to get their desires fulfilled. There was no way Connie would lose money on this venture.

Pauline would be the perfect person to run the parlor house if she could just gain a bit of confidence. She had made strides over the last few months, shown a bit of grit. Still, there were moments when she was that scared socialite who'd had her world torn out from under her.

There were times Connie wanted to shove Pauline in a room with her roughest customers to see what she would do. It might do Pauline a bit of good to have her innocence taken so she would know what it was like for the girls. It was what Connie's mother had done to her, after all. But because Pauline presented a semblance of sophistication to the parlor house, Connie had convinced herself it wouldn't do to harden her that way.

Looking hard at Pauline, Connie asked, "Have the new girls settled in yet?"

"Yes, they're all in their rooms. The doctor's coming by tomorrow to inspect them."

They were due to have another virgin auction in a few weeks, and this last batch had been slim pickings. It was getting harder to find tempting young women to fulfill the needs of the powerful men in town. Many of them preferred women who had never lain with a man before, and she could price them at a premium. The problem was, they weren't coming in droves any longer.

Times were changing, and Helena was becoming respectable. The gold rush had ended years ago. More families were settling and making the town their home. Pastors and preachers were bringing their flocks to the area. Less-than-stellar bars and brothels were being closed at an alarming rate. Only the high-end brothels and parlor houses were left alone. The powerful men still had their needs and weren't willing to give them up, at least not yet.

"Good. What is your first impression of them?" Connie watched as Pauline tried to form the words. This was part of her training: the ability to describe the girls on both a physical and performance level. As a madam, she had to match her girls with the correct customers, especially in the higher-end market. Desires needed to be satisfied if they were to expect repeat customers at higher prices.

"I... well, that is to say, they... um... well, they seem fine." Pauline fiddled with the lace on the bottom of her bodice.

Connie shook her head. "Is that the best you can do? We've discussed this. Describe them."

"I know that, but it's just—"

"It's just nothing. Now describe them to me." Connie's voice was harsh and unyielding.

"They're young, pretty. We only have five." The words came out in a rush, as though it was hard for Pauline to utter them.

"Only five?" That wouldn't be enough to satisfy these men who were clamoring for more.

"Yes."

Connie slammed her fist on her desk. "I was told to expect at least double that."

Pauline jumped in her seat. "A preacher *rescued* a few of them before they reached town. Somehow, he convinced them they would have a better future if they stayed with him."

"Damnit," Connie muttered. "I need at least ten for the auction. We've got to find five more, and soon."

"Bruno told me he has some potentials but isn't altogether sure they are still... well, you know."

"No, I don't. Tell me."

Pauline had to learn what was expected of her.

"He isn't sure they are intact." Pauline's face turned a bright shade that matched her dark red hair.

Connie chuckled under her breath. It was still difficult for Pauline to say the words, but she would have to learn. This place was no society matron's parlor. This was a parlor house, and there was no room for embarrassment. If Pauline wanted to stay in Connie's employ, she either had to embrace being a madam or become one of the girls. She was positive Pauline wasn't interested in spreading her legs.

"I'll deal with that later, but tell me about the ones we have," Connie said.

Pauline stumbled over her explanation of the physical features and potential abilities of the new girls when a knock sounded at the door.

"Just a minute, Pauline. Come in."

The door opened, and Bruno stepped just inside.

"What is it? I'm busy."

"Sorry, ma'am, to interrupt, but I thought you might want to see this."

"And what's that?" she asked, barely looking up from her desk.

"This." He dragged a woman into the room. A long black cloak covered her from head to toe.

She sighed. "Bruno, couldn't this have waited? I thought you knew how to handle them."

"Ma'am, you're gonna want to look at this one. She showed up at our door just a few minutes ago."

Frustrated, Connie dropped her pencil and glared at him. "She's covered by a cloak. Am I supposed to guess who it is?"

Bruno grinned wickedly before snatching the hood off the young woman's head and uncovering her slender body wrapped in a purple velvet gown. Long, curly auburn hair hung down her back and in front of her face, covering her features.

"I still can't see who she is."

Bruno looked at the young woman. He forced her chin upward. Bright green eyes flashed in front of her. A wide grin lifted Connie's lips.

"Well, well, well." She pushed back her chair and stood before walking from behind her desk and toward Louisa. "My night has just improved. You're the last person I expected to see." Connie placed a finger on Louisa's chin, forced her face to turn, and examined her like a horse. "You do look a little worn, but nothing a little rouge won't fix."

Connie wasn't stupid and knew there was a reason why Louisa had returned. For now, the fire chief would be satisfied. If this was a little plan between her and Luke, it wouldn't work. Connie grabbed the front of Louisa's dress and ripped it away from her. The fabric was flimsy and tore with little effort.

Louisa shrieked and tried to grab at the remnants of her dress, but Connie slapped at her hands and said, "Don't even try it." Without taking her eyes off the woman who had caused her heaps of irritation, she said, "Hold her."

Bruno grabbed Louisa's arms and held her in place. The rest of her dress fell to the floor. She stood clad only in her silk chemise, elaborate corset, silk stockings, and satin slippers. Her expression was defiant.

"It's a good thing you came here on your own, otherwise this would've been much worse for you."

"I did come here on my own."

"I wonder why?" Connie said. She shouldn't care, but she was curious as to why Louisa had finally capitulated to her demands. "Did Luke convince you to come here as part of his vendetta against me?"

"No." Louisa's eyes flashed with anger. "That stupid man can get himself killed for all I care. He called me a whore and told me to leave his house when he found me with one of his friends. Not a thing happened between us, but Luke chose to believe otherwise."

"I don't believe you."

"I don't care if you believe me or not," Louisa snarled. "I was wrong in leaving here. Men are all the same. He didn't want me for his housekeeper. He just wanted what all the men in this *place* want. If that's the case, why shouldn't I get paid for it?"

Connie chuckled. "My, oh my, this sure is interesting."

"I'm not here for your entertainment," Louisa said. "I aim to get paid the same way I should've if he'd never entered my room and taken me in the first place."

"He didn't take you—"

"Yes, he did. I was getting ready to please that old man when Luke busted in and insisted I come with him. That wasn't my choice."

"You're lying."

"Why would I lie? I have nothing to gain by doing that." She squirmed in Bruno's arms, but he held firm. "Can you ask this big brute to take his hands off me? I'm not going anywhere. If I didn't want to be here, I wouldn't have come."

Connie studied her for a long moment. While she wasn't inclined to believe her, Louisa had come back, so Connie could grant a bit of leniency to the woman. She could be compassionate when she wanted to be.

"Let her go, Bruno."

"But, ma'am—"

"I said, let her go." Connie glared at him.

Bruno reluctantly released her but stood right behind her, placing his hands on his gun belt.

Connie strode back to her desk. She was interested enough to know more. "Why don't you sit, my dear?"

Louisa pulled her shoulders back and walked to the chair near Pauline, acting as though walking around in little was a joy. She didn't seem to be concerned about it. Perhaps she'd be a good little whore after all.

"So tell me, Louisa, what really went wrong between you two?"

Crossing one leg over the other, Louisa leaned back into the chair and appeared to get comfortable. "He called me a whore. I called him a stupid man. He told me I'd either behave or I could leave. So, I left." Louisa lifted a hand and pushed back a curl that had fallen across her cheek. "You can kill the man for all I care."

"Now, why would I kill him?"

"The same reason you killed his pa, I suppose."

Connie's eyes narrowed. What was she up to? "Who says I killed his pa?"

Louisa laughed, her eyes full of mirth and unrestrained anger. "You did, of course. Not that I can blame you. If all the Seymours are as egotistical and as mean-spirited as Luke, then I'd have done the same thing."

Connie tapped her fingers against the top of her wooden desk. Either the girl was really stupid and thought she could bamboozle her or there really was some truth to her words.

"Are you prepared to do as you're told?"

"Within reason," Louisa said. "Before, I didn't realize what my innocence was worth. Now, I have a better idea."

Connie leaned back. Well, this was an interesting turn of events. "And what idea would that be?"

"I heard how much some of those men were willing to pay during the auction. That tells me you're getting far more than I was going to get. So, I wonder what my cooperation should cost you?"

"So this is a negotiation, now?"

"I'd call it"--Louisa paused--"a discussion between two strong women who know what they want and will do anything to get it."

"And if Luke comes back for you?"

"Then you can turn him away. I want nothing to do with him. I had no idea what he was really like. He pulled the wool over my eyes, made it seem as though he could be my savior. He talked about how his pa was always saving this person and that person." Louisa shifted in her seat and lifted a finger to her lips. "Made me wonder if his pa wasn't as big a liar as Luke turned out to be. They do say the apple doesn't fall far from the tree. Stands to reason that's where Luke got his savior attitude when in reality he was only out for himself."

"Cole Seymour was the man who ruined my life," Connie snarled.

"Sounds like you knew the man quite well," Louisa said. "Guess you know exactly how I feel."

"Oh, I knew who that man was and what his soul was like long before I laid eyes on him. After what he did to my mother, he deserved having his life snuffed out by a mere pillow. I enjoyed knowing it was me who finally ended his pathetic existence." Connie spit out the words, her anger palpable, looking beyond Louisa and Pauline into the memories of the past. "Cole Seymour was the cause of all the pain and heartache I endured when I was a child. I waited years to get my revenge, and it was so sweet."

Dropping her eyes to Louisa, Connie's mask slipped.

Louisa smirked. "I wondered how long it would take you to reveal what you had done to Luke's pa. Luke wasn't convinced you'd say a word, but I told him it wouldn't take much. I was right."

Connie stood, her back ramrod straight as she leaned against her desk, her palms on the hard wood. "What did you do?"

Louisa crossed her arms over her chest. "Oh, you'll find out soon enough."

"Bruno, get her out of my sight."

Thirty

Louisa didn't fight Bruno as he dragged her out of Connie's office and down the hall. It had been quite satisfying seeing Connie spill her secrets. With any luck, one of the marshals stationed throughout Mon Petit Amour had caught her slip and this farce would end tonight.

Bruno's hands were all over her, but she knew she had little to worry about. Not only would Luke keep the man from hurting her, she knew Connie needed her to stay innocent. She also had the knife in the boning of her corset. She had decided at the last moment to not put one in her stocking, and that had proven to be the right choice. They would've seen it when Connie ripped the dress off her.

It was only a matter of time before the Marshals and Luke and Walter's men raided the place. She just had to keep her wits about her and not do anything foolish. It would be quite gratifying when Connie got everything she had coming to her as well as knowing Luke would finally have peace. She'd wanted to cackle with glee the moment Connie realized the mistake she had made. All Louisa had to do was make her angry enough to say the words.

Finally, they came to a stop. Bruno opened a door and threw

her inside. She fell against a bed and onto a hard mattress, musty pillows and blankets flying around her.

She scrambled back and pulled her legs underneath her, grabbed a blanket to cover herself, and pushed her hair away from her face. Bruno stood grinning at the foot of the bed. He wouldn't touch her. Connie would be furious if he did. Not wanting to take the chance, however, her gaze raced around the room, trying to find a weapon, but she was out of luck. She didn't want to pull out her knife, not just yet.

"Aren't you the picture of innocence?" he said, licking his lips with anticipation.

"Don't come near me. I'm no use to Madam Lafoe if you take away my innocence."

"I have no intention of taking that. There are other ways to satisfy, my dear. Something you'll learn pretty quick working 'round here."

Trepidation ran down her spine. The look in Bruno's eyes was unholy. "Stay away from me."

"I don't think so," he said as he reached for her leg.

She pushed at him. His grin was sinister. He snatched both her ankles and pulled her down the bed toward him, the blankets bunching around her. She fisted her hands, trying to fight him off. He grabbed both of her hands with one of his, his body holding hers in place while his free hand groped at her corset. She screeched, but he only became more excited.

"Boy, you are a feisty one, that's for sure," he said. "I'm going to enjoy this."

"No," she yelled again, trying to kick him off but she couldn't stop him.

Suddenly, he stepped back and released her hands. Louisa scrambled to get away, but she was flipped onto her stomach. One hand was braced against the back of her neck while the other fondled her backside. She blinked back tears. She was stronger than this. This would not end here, not while she had fight left inside of her.

Louisa reached one hand into her corset and ripped the knife from inside, holding it in her palm. She would find the right moment and slice him. He would regret ever touching her. She tried to scoot away, but he slapped her backside, a sharp sting left in its place. She had to make him stop. With a strength and resolve she didn't know she possessed, she pushed her arms up under her, pulled her knees up, and got into an almost crawling position.

He murmured appreciatively, as if she had just done something correct. "That's right, baby. You're one fine piece of beauty. I knew you'd like it."

Louisa didn't know what he was talking about, but this was going to stop now. With a powerful thrust, she took her foot and rammed it back with all her might, hitting him right between the legs and into his soft flesh.

He screeched, the sound roaring through the room like a tornado yanking all from the earth before he fell to the ground and moaned. She spun around, holding the knife at her waist. If he came at her, she'd cut him.

When he didn't immediately come toward her, she crawled off the bed. Bruno lay on the floor, writhing in pain. Her corset hung was cockeyed and out of place. Her shift was torn, and her stockings were ripped. She had to get out of there. There was no way she was staying, not if this was what she had to look forward to.

Grabbing a sheet off the bed, she wrapped it around herself as best as she could when his hand grabbed her around the ankle and threw her to the floor. The knife fell from her hand. Kicking at him, her heel caught him in the face, and he yelled once again.

Rushing to stand, she tried to reach the door, but it was too late. He grabbed her around the waist. She clawed and scratched at him, but she had angered him beyond measure. He slapped her across the face and threw her back onto the bed.

He stalked toward her. "That was a big mistake, you hussy.

You're going to pay for that." He inched forward on the bed, the mattress bowing under his immense weight, when someone called his name behind the door.

"What?" he hollered, his anger intensified.

"Bruno, are you in there?" a soft voice said.

He jumped off the bed, ripped open the door, and yelled at the person on the other side.

Louisa crawled to the side of the bed farthest from the door, holding onto the sheet in fear. She didn't know what had stopped him, but she was afraid she had only gotten a brief reprieve.

Bruno spoke to whoever stood in the hall and then looked over his shoulder. "This ain't over. I've got something to do, but I'll be back. I expect you to be waiting willingly when I return, otherwise you'll regret it."

With that ominous statement, he left her, the door clicking as the lock caught.

Louisa sank onto the floor, shaking. She had just avoided something painful and repulsive, but she knew it wasn't over unless she could find a way out of this room. She didn't know where Luke or the marshals were, but she couldn't wait. She had to save herself.

She went to the drapes and pulled them back, thinking maybe she could escape out the window but was dismayed. Thick, round bars covered the windows. They didn't budge no matter how hard she pulled.

"Arghh," she cried, banging her fists against them. She looked around the room for another exit and saw a door next to the fireplace. Pulling the sheet up over her shoulders, she scurried to it, grabbed the door handle, and twisted. It wasn't locked. She yanked it open and cried again in frustration. It was only a small room filled with clothing.

All of a sudden, women screamed and glass broke elsewhere in the house. Had the marshals finally come inside and taken

Connie? She banged on the door, yelling for help, but it was no use. No one came.

Frustrated, she headed back to the small room. Whatever was happening was out of her control, but she'd feel better if she were wearing more than a corset and shift. Maybe it'd keep Bruno away, although she was fooling herself. He was not a man who'd be deterred by a few pieces of modest clothing.

She chuckled ruefully. She knew it was ridiculous, but it made her feel a bit better. Going inside, she rifled through the clothing, but most of it was more risqué than what she was wearing. Finally, she came across a pair of men's trousers and laughed out loud. Men's trousers in a parlor house seemed a trifle ridiculous. She could imagine a man running out of the parlor house, naked as the day he was born, leaving his clothing for her to find. She'd thank the man if she ever met him.

Dropping the sheet, she yanked them over her slim hips. They were long and big around the waist, but she could work with them. She rolled up the cuffs and then looked for a belt. Seeing a silk robe, she grabbed the tie and put that through the belt loops, tightening it around her waist and knotting it into place. Now, if she could only find a decent shirt. Tossing clothes over her shoulder, she yelped with joy when she found a dirty, worn shirt underneath a pile of colorful petticoats. Throwing it over her head, she tucked it into the trousers and buttoned it.

Now shoes. She still wore one of her satin slippers. She kicked it off and got onto her knees, throwing the frivolous ones to the side until she found a pair of sturdy boots. They looked a little big, but at least they wouldn't be too small. Sitting back, she thrust one foot and then the other into the boots, quickly tying up the laces until they were snug around her ankles.

Striding out of the small room, she felt more confident and in control. She looked around for a weapon, her knife was still missing, and found nothing except a couple of chairs resting against the wall. Picking one up, she decided it was light enough to handle. It was also heavy enough that if wielded properly, could incapacitate Bruno long enough for her to escape.

She carried it to the door and stood next to it, ready to belt Bruno when he came back. She wouldn't let him touch her ever again, not without a fight.

Luke crept down the second-floor hallway, at the opposite end of the house from Connie's office. Walter, Harry, Ben, and Michael were causing a distraction on the main floor while he hunted for Louisa. The marshal listening behind the door of Connie's office had been waylaid by one of her guards and hadn't been able to get away until Louisa disappeared. It had taken them far too long to respond, but the marshal had confirmed that Connie confessed to his pa's murder. The man had then given the signal, and the remaining marshals had invaded the place. They were looking for Connie while he hunted for Louisa. The marshal had said that one of Connie's goons had taken her from her office but didn't know where.

As he listened at closed doors and peered into open ones, his instincts told him Louisa was locked up tight. Connie wouldn't have wanted to lose her again, but he needed to find her before Connie's man did something regrettable. He just had to find a room with a locked door. It couldn't be that hard to find.

He turned the last corner, the plush rug under his feet muffling his footsteps, and reached the last door at the end of the hall. It was locked. Running his fingers around the doorframe, he couldn't find a key. He only had a few more minutes before someone came up those stairs. With any luck, it would be someone on his side, but he couldn't take that chance.

With nothing to lose, he stepped back and, with as much force as he could muster, he slammed his foot against the wood. The wood splintered, and the door flew open. A woman screamed, and a chair crashed to the ground.

"What the hell?" he muttered.

"Oh, Luke, thank heavens it's you. I thought it was Bruno, and..."

"Did he hurt you?" Luke placed his hands on Louisa's forearms, looking her over for any signs of trauma.

"Yes... No," she said.

He pulled her into his arms and held her tight. He had almost lost something precious tonight and wasn't willing to put her in danger again.

"What was that?" A voice yelled.

Footsteps pounded down the hallway. They only had moments to disappear.

"We've got to go, now! Follow me," he said, pulling away.

She grabbed his hand and led him to a hidden door on the left. There was an old servant staircase behind it. This house appeared to have hidden doors all over the place. With careful steps, they crept down the stairs and emerged into the kitchen, where a bunch of women sat eating at a large round table. Surprised at their entrance, Pauline stood, her face as red as her hair. "Go back to your room, Louisa." Her eyes flitted back and forth between Louisa and the door.

Louisa looked at the woman with disgust. "Never. I'm done with this place."

Pauline stepped forward and raised her arm. A black derringer was gripped between her fingers. She pointed it at Luke. "If you don't want me to kill your lover, then I suggest you do as I say."

"No," Louisa said, defiantly stepping in front of Luke until the gun was pressed against her chest.

Luke was horrified. She was reckless and cared little for her safety. If she made the wrong move, Pauline was liable to shoot her dead on the spot.

"Louisa, no," Luke said, but she didn't listen to him. She never listened to him.

"Pauline, it's over. Madam Lafoe is done. You need to save yourself. Shooting me or Luke"--Louisa tilted her head toward him--"will surely put you behind bars. You don't want that."

Pauline's hand shook, and she dropped her arm, her body wilting in front of them. Luke stepped forward and carefully pried Pauline's fingers from the derringer.

"Let's go," Luke said

The other women sat in their seats, fear etched on their faces, but none of them made a move to stop them.

He gripped Louisa's hand and the two of them ran outside to the horses he had waiting for them. His heart pounded. He hated leaving his friends and brothers behind, but they knew what to do. Over the past two days, they had discussed all manner of ideas and the consequences of every scenario. The one thing they all agreed upon was Luke would get Louisa to safety once Connie confessed. What he hadn't told his friends and brothers was that Louisa questioned everything, but he did agree she would go with him more willingly than anyone else.

Thirty-One

November 5, 1900

Their horses pounded down the muddy road out of town, toward Mt. Helena. The night sky was lit up by bright stars. Dirt clumps flew behind them as they headed toward the dark forest at the base of the mountain. For a moment, Louisa thought they had gotten away, but the whiz of the bullets flying past her ear told her otherwise. Chills raced along her spine. Her hands trembled, and she had to concentrate to stay on the saddle.

Louisa took a moment to glance over her shoulder and immediately wished she hadn't. The men following were closing in on them. She moved forward in the saddle, squeezed her knees against the horse's side, and prayed to the heavens above that they'd get away.

"Follow me!" Luke shouted.

She nodded, although he wasn't looking at her. Fear and panic tightened her throat, making it hard to breathe, but she couldn't give in to the urge.

A few moments later, they rounded a sharp curve that took them out of sight of Connie's men. Luke slowed his horse and then veered him onto a hidden path. She followed suit. Thick trees and brush shielded the opening, making it barely visible. The narrow, rocky trail needed careful navigation. Her eyes had adjusted to the darkness, but the dense trees and the overgrown brush made the path nearly impossible to see.

Once shielded by the overgrown shrubbery, Luke gestured for her to bring her mount close. She nudged her horse forward until she rested next to him. He put a finger to his lips.

Her chest was tight, her fingers clenched the reins, and her fingernails dug into the soft skin of her palms. Discovery was only a breath away, and with the slightest movement of them or their horses they'd be found. Their pursuers' horses galloped toward them. They halted just outside the opening to the trail. Leather creaked, horses neighed, and the men murmured unintelligibly.

Louisa held her breath and prayed hard, for they only had the two revolvers in Luke's belt and the small derringer Luke had grabbed from Pauline. She didn't know how many bullets were in the guns, and she certainly had nothing in her pockets. She hadn't been able to locate her knife when Bruno had knocked it from her fingers back at Mon Petit Amour.

The men talked for a few moments and then continued past the opening, the click clack of hooves fading in the distance. She exhaled, her hot breath turning to steam as it hit the wintry air.

"We aren't safe. We need to keep moving," Luke whispered.

The snorts from their horses sounded loud as Luke led them along the hidden trail. After some time, the canopy of trees opened to a large clearing. A small, rustic cabin rested against the hillside illuminated by the sudden shifting of the half-moon from behind the clouds. No movement or lights came from inside the cabin. It appeared empty.

She dismounted and tied her horse to the railing, running her hands down her steed's side. She'd have to give it a good brushing once they made it back home, as well as a few carrots and sugar cubes.

Luke climbed the steps to the porch, opened the door, and waited for her. She rubbed the horse's muzzle one more time and went inside. Luke kept the door open while he looked for a candle and lit it. The flame flickered, throwing shadows against the walls, but the faint light did help to ease her trembling.

The clean cabin held a small table with two chairs nestled under the window, and a wide bed rested in the opposite corner. Large pillows and a thick blue and brown quilt covered it. The bed looked mighty comfortable. If she hadn't been aware of the danger following them, she might have climbed onto it and fallen asleep. The night had been long, full of surprises, and was nowhere near over.

"Where are we?" she asked, watching his every move.

Placing the candle on the table, Luke peered outside before closing the door and throwing the flimsy latch. It wouldn't stop anyone if they were found, but it gave her a measure of comfort, which is likely what he had intended.

He pulled a white handkerchief from his vest pocket and used it to wipe the mud from his cheeks and forehead. He held it out to her, but she shook her head.

"Harry offered me the use of this cabin years ago. He owns it but never comes here. He told me I could use it whenever I'd like. I come here to think."

"Are you sure it's a good idea that we came here?"

"Where else should we have gone? I don't have a plethora of places I can take you to keep those men from finding us." His tone was harsh and made her sorry she had asked.

Swallowing back her distress, she said, "Do you think they'll find the opening to the trail?"

He peered out the small window, his legs spread, his back straight. "It's hard to spot, even on a sunny day. I knew if we came around that corner far enough in front of 'em, they likely wouldn't see us leave the main road."

"How long will we stay here?"

"Through the night. In the morning, I'll look around, make sure no one is waiting for us on the main trail. If it looks safe, we can head back to town, straight to Walter's office. Everyone should be waiting for us there."

"Did the marshal hear her confession?"

Relief crossed his eyes. "Yes, we've finally got her. He'll be able to verify what you heard."

The past two days of planning had paid off. She smiled wide, and with a sudden burst of joy, she ran to him and threw her arms around his neck, squeezing him tight.

He stiffened, and she immediately backed away. "Oh, I'm so sorry. I didn't mean..."

"No apologies. It's been a harrowing night. You should rest," he said, placing his hand against the back of his neck. Luke seemed distant, and Louisa's heart broke at what had changed between them.

"I wouldn't be able to sleep. My heart is still racing a mile a minute. Until I know for sure she is behind bars, I think my anxiety will keep me from getting any rest."

He walked to the other window and looked outside, his eyes scanning the dark meadow in front of the cabin. He walked around her, checked the door next to the small kitchen, and then shoved a table in front of it, all the while avoiding her gaze.

"You said no one would find us here," she said, her tone defiant.

"And they shouldn't," he muttered, throwing his hands in the air. "But I can't make any promises. I'm not a magician, Louisa. This has been a nightmare from start to finish."

"But we finally got her. You can rest assured, knowing the woman who killed your pa has been arrested."

"Tonight could have gone so wrong. I could have lost you." His jaw was clenched, his eyes hooded.

Blood drained from her face. "What do you mean?"

"Don't act coy. We've been dancing around each other for weeks. I thought after that night where we... where we..." He stopped, anguish in his eyes. He breathed heavy and then started pacing in front of her.

"Where we went further than we should have? The night where I thought things had changed between us for the good. You've barely spoken to me since you found Harry in the parlor with me." She was being rash with her words. Her foray into the parlor house world had lowered her inhibitions.

"Did something happen between the two of you?" He avoided her gaze, looking over her shoulder as though he were afraid of her answer.

"No, nothing. The only man who means anything to me is you." She put her heart on her sleeve and prayed he wouldn't reject it.

"Then what did I stumble on?"

"He thinks I'm a whore," she cried. "He arrived before you came home and... and backed me into the wall, touching my face. If you hadn't knocked on the door when you did, I'm not sure he wouldn't have done more."

He scowled. "Why haven't you said anything?"

"What was I to say? He was your friend. You've depended on him to help you find Connie. I wasn't about to interfere. Harry is a despicable man who makes my skin shiver with revulsion. I don't want anything to do with him."

"I can't believe—"

"That is exactly why I haven't said anything. Why would you believe me over him? It was better for me to be quiet and avoid him as much as I could."

"You know what I think?" His face was flushed and his stance was wide as though he were preparing for a fight. "He's been a loyal friend for years, but I also know..."

"Know what?" she demanded. She didn't want him to think she asked for what he had done. "Would you rather I left, disappeared? Did I act as one of Connie's girls and you no longer want anything to do with me?"

His gaze was piercing. "No, of course not." He spat the words out and balled his fists.

"Then what is it?" she yelled. "Why can't you tell me what you're thinking?"

He closed the distance between them, driving her back against a wall. Her heart pounded. He stood so close she could reach out and touch him. The heat from his body seemed to jump from his skin to hers. She glared at him. She would not touch him, nor let him kiss her, not until he told her what he was thinking.

He lowered his head until his forehead lightly touched hers. His breath was warm on her cheeks, sending tingles to every inch of her body. Her body hummed in eager anticipation, goosebumps prickling her skin, but she would not capitulate.

"I... Why are we doing this?" he asked. His eyes were dark and half open. He licked his lips.

Thoughts tumbled through her mind as she searched his face for any idea of how he really felt. Her heart nearly burst from the look in his eyes. She had lost so much since her mother and father passed away. She loved this man with every part of her being, but until he told her what he was feeling, she couldn't reveal her heart. He was a savior, helping those who needed it, and she didn't want to just be someone he saved. She wanted to be his equal, his lover.

She raised her fingers to his face, lightly running them along the rough edge of his chin.

He chuckled, low and husky, sending shivers up her spine. He knew she had given up. His fingers touched her upper arm before running them to her hand, his fingers tangling with hers. She should push him away, but she wasn't able to. She couldn't forget the times they kissed—how her skin shivered, how her belly had tightened, how her toes had curled in her shoes.

"Things have been difficult, but I have this... this feeling deep in my gut that I just can't stop," he murmured.

A fire seemed to flame inside of her. "I'm your housekeeper. We agreed that until Connie was caught, we'd not go any further," she murmured.

"It made sense at the time, but now things have changed. What do you want?" he whispered.

His voice burned straight through to her core, her skin sensitive to his touch, and her head spinning with possibilities. "I... I want you," she blurted. "Do you want me?" If he wouldn't say it first, then she would.

"Oh, I definitely do," he said before placing a light kiss on her cheek.

Louisa trembled. The kiss sent shockwaves through her. She felt it all the way to her toes. It was as though sparks flew from her fingertips.

She looked into his eyes, her desire for him heavy. They were alone. She wanted to hold him, touch him, and explore what they could have together. She removed her hand from his and placed both arms around his neck, one hand cupping the nape, her fingers curling into his soft brown hair. She pulled his head close and placed her lips against his.

Her heart sang with joy when he returned the kiss. His arms wrapped around her waist and pulled her snugly against him. All rational thought disappeared at the speed of a falling star. Lights exploded in her mind as his full, plump lips devoured her almost as though he was drinking from a bottle of wine––smelling, swirling, gulping the sweetness.

Their bodies fit together like a tight glove. Her curves nestled into the rock-hard planes of his body. She wanted this, had craved this for so long. He was safe and comforting.

Breathing hard, he pulled away, his breath continuing to tangle with hers.

"I guess we're going to do this?" he murmured.

She nodded.

He stepped back and then, without warning, swept her up

into his arms. A squeal emerged from her lips, and her body soared with excitement. She relaxed against him and held tight. Tucking her head into his neck, she dropped one, two, three kisses against his warm skin. He strode to the bed where he gently laid her down. His hands were reverent as he brushed strands of hair away from her face.

"I've been waiting for so long. You're amazing, and I can't wait to make you mine."

Anticipation raced through her. This was what she wanted, what she yearned for – this and the joy that was to follow. He didn't even have to touch her. The look in his eyes was her undoing.

He slowly flicked open the buttons on his shirt, his eyes dark with need when the horses neighed. Luke stopped, his head turning toward the sound. She sat up in bed and panicked.

Someone was outside.

They had been found.

Luke grabbed his revolvers from the table where he had dropped them while Louisa scrambled off the bed. Her flushed cheeks and swollen lips made his heart ache. He'd had every intention of making Louisa his and was ashamed of himself. He shouldn't take her innocence in an old cabin while they were being chased by men who were determined to kill them. She deserved more than that. He had to be better than the men who frequented brothels.

He looked out the window. "They found us."

The yard in front of the cabin was full of men on horses, at least five that he could see. He didn't know how they'd found them. They should have been safe in Harry's cabin. He shoved the revolvers in his gun belt and ran a hand through his hair. They were outnumbered and outgunned.

Louisa stood by his side, her body warm, her face determined.

"Do you think we can fight them?" she asked, holding the small derringer he had pulled from Pauline. She sure didn't shy away from a fight, another reason he loved her.

"Luke?"

"What?" He hadn't realized the depth of his feelings and prayed they'd get out of this mess so he could tell her how much he cared for her, how he wanted her to be his wife.

She turned her head and caught his gaze, her eyes full of questions. "I said, do you think we can fight them?"

"I don't know. How many bullets do you have?"

"Not many." She flipped open the chamber of the derringer and scanned it. "There are only two."

"I've got eight." He had checked each one when they had arrived at the cabin knowing if anyone found them, they would be in trouble. "That leaves us only ten shots."

He peered out the window again, trying to see in the dark night. The five men had dismounted and were scattered throughout the yard, some behind barrels, others standing in full view of the door, their revolvers pointed straight at it. He bowed his head, not knowing how it had come to this.

"What are we going to do?" Louisa whispered.

"There's only one thing we can do."

She narrowed her eyes. "All right, I'll go to the other window and try to stop two of them. That should leave you just enough bullets to take down the other three."

Startled, Luke looked at Louisa and the firm set of her shoulders. If the situation weren't so dangerous, he would've laughed. He was touched she thought they could fight their way out of this, but he wasn't a gunslinger. They'd need far more than ten bullets to take out the men scattered outside in the clearing. There was no doubt those men had far more ammunition than them. "We can't. There's no way we'll come out of this alive."

She pushed him, and he stumbled back a few steps. "I'm not

letting them take me. She'll want her revenge, and they will kill me."

He tried to grab her wrist, but she stepped out of reach. "Please. We don't have a choice," he whispered.

"Yes, we do," her voice was raised in anger.

"No, we don't." And before she could fight him, he pulled the derringer from her hands.

"Give that back," she said, trying to grab it, but he held it out of reach.

"No. It's better if we live to see tomorrow." He shoved the derringer into the back of his pants to keep his hands free.

"Better for who?" She stomped her foot in anger, her eyes sparking dangerously.

"I'll try to work out a plan, but for now, we're going to give up without a fight." He placed his hands lightly on her shoulders, careful not to alarm her.

"No!" she said, her lips curled into a vicious frown.

"Louisa, listen to me. I can't take the chance that something will happen to you. I couldn't live with myself if you were hurt or worse." He wiped a lone tear from her cheek, but she shook her head.

"You don't understand. She was seething with rage, and she *will* make me pay."

"She should've been arrested by now."

"Then who are those men out there? They wouldn't have come after us if she was in the marshal's hands."

He sighed, his fingers tightening into her soft skin. "I don't know. Maybe something went wrong. Maybe she had a plan in place for something like this, I just don't know." He could see the pain in her eyes and he wanted to fix it, but he couldn't. "I promised I would protect you, but I can't do that with what we have." He clenched his jaw, his mind made up. "If they take you away, I'll find you. I found you once. I'll find you again. At least this way, we'll have a fighting chance."

Her shoulders slumped, and disbelief, anger, confusion, and heartbreak crossed her face before the fight fell from her. He pulled her into his arms, lightly kissed the top of her head, and held her close for a long moment before removing a white handkerchief from his pocket. He unlocked the latch, pushed open the window, and held it out the window. He waved in surrender.

A man yelled from outside, "Throw your weapons out the window and come out with your hands held high. Don't try anything, or we'll shoot."

Luke looked at Louisa. "Are you ready?"

Her gaze was unwavering, solid, and strong. "No, but I'll agree to your wishes."

"Stay behind me until I know they aren't going to shoot."

"You don't need to protect me, Luke."

"I have to, Louisa. I..." He looked into her eyes, trying to say more than just words. "I love you."

Her eyes widened. "Luke—"

"Shh"––he placed a finger over her lips––"Don't say anything now. Please don't fight me on this. If you ever repeat those same words back to me, I want them to be returned in a moment where we weren't facing..." He couldn't finish that statement and instead smoothed out a non-existent wrinkle on the collar of her shirt. "Please."

"If anything goes wrong, I'll do what I must to protect you." She placed her fingers around the lapels of his shirt, pulled him close, and placed a sweet, gentle kiss on his lips. Placing her lips against his ear, she whispered, "I love you, too."

She dropped her hands and stepped back, then straightened her shirt and threw back her shoulders. "Let's get this over with."

"We ain't got all night. Y'all better step outside in the next ten seconds, or we'll come inside and get you ourselves," a gruff voice yelled.

Resigned, Luke tossed his two revolvers and the derringer outside the window after removing the bullets.

He opened the door slowly and yelled, "We're unarmed. Don't shoot."

Stepping outside with his hands held high, he kept Louisa slightly behind him. Taking but three steps outside, he stopped in shock. Harry was standing off to the left.

"Harry?" he said as his arms were wrenched tight behind his back.

Harry's smug smile sent unease through his limbs. Another man snatched Louisa, and the leer on his face was enough to make Luke's blood run cold. It was the man Connie and Pauline had called Bruno. He thought he had killed the man. Harry had been the one to clean up that mess, or so he believed.

"Don't hurt her," Luke said, glaring at Bruno, his attention diverted from the man he had once called friend.

Bruno chuckled, the sound menacing and diabolical. "Don't ya worry about what I'm going to do to her. She's going to get everything she deserves." With that, he pulled her hair back and kissed her roughly.

Luke growled and tried to break free of the man holding him, but it was useless. His heart sank, his spirits plummeted, and he wondered if he had just made the biggest mistake of his life.

The next thing he knew, something exploded in the back of his head, and the world disappeared.

Louisa wrenched her lips from Bruno's, broke one arm free, and tried to slap him, but he stopped her. His piercing gaze caused terror to explode into a horror so frightening it was a wonder she was standing. He yanked both hands behind her back and held them both with one hand while the other grabbed her chin and twisted her neck hard. He was furious, and she was going to pay. As she fought to get away, he let go of her chin. She twisted and saw Luke slump to the ground.

"What did you do to him?" she yelled, dragging her heels in the dirt as Bruno hauled her away. She was helpless against Bruno's iron-tight grip. He reached for the reins of his horse, twirled her around, and pulled her face to him, his fingers grinding into her chin. "If you don't stop, he's as good as dead. You don't want that, do you?" His eyes were wide, the scar on his cheek reminding her that he wasn't a man to trifle with. Spittle flew from his lips and hit her cheeks as anger changed the contours of his face. He looked like a madman who had no bounds.

Louisa knew without a shadow of a doubt that Bruno would order Luke killed if she didn't cooperate.

She shuddered, quit fighting him, and nodded.

"Good, that's smart of you," he said.

"Wait, Bruno." Harry sauntered over to Bruno, his movements slow and methodical.

Louisa's fear grew exponentially. "Harry, what are you doing here?"

Harry's lips twisted into a cruel smile, a cold glint to his eyes. "I don't need to explain myself to a whore."

"I'm not—" He reached out and slapped her across the face, silencing her immediately. Her face smarted. Louisa blinked furiously to hold back the tears. She would not let him see her cower.

"Whores keep their mouths shut and their legs wide open. I suggest you get used to your new place in life."

She glared at him but didn't say a word. He was not a friend of Luke's and never had been. Her instincts were correct. Harry was a despicable man. Connie had likely bribed him, which would explain why Luke never seemed to get close to her.

"Wisely staying quiet," Harry drawled. "That'll likely save your life." He lifted her chin.

She wrenched her face out of his grasp.

He chuckled. "Still feisty. Someone will pay a good price for you, I'm sure. It's too bad I refuse to take second-hand girls."

Harry looked back to the man holding Luke and said, "Get

him and take him back to the brothel on fifth street. I'll meet you there later. Bruno, you know what to do with her."

Bruno pushed Louisa onto the saddle and mounted behind her, holding her tight. She had nowhere to go. He grabbed the reins and urged the horse forward. As they left the clearing, she turned and gasped in horror. Helpless to stop them, they dragged Luke to a horse, his head slapping against the ground. There was nothing she could do. This could be the last time she ever saw the man she loved beyond anything else. Her heart clenched. Pain like nothing else pierced her soul.

Luke had said he would find her, but if he didn't survive whatever those men had planned, her future was as good as over. Luke was going to be killed, and it was all because of her.

Thirty-Two

Murmurs, harsh whispers, and heavy footsteps fought to gain a foothold in Luke's scattered brain, but it was like a sledgehammer pounded over and over again in his head. He couldn't focus. Slowly, he separated the sounds, and the events of the night and early morning returned. He tried to open his eyes, but they refused to cooperate, and then he heard *her* voice and stopped moving. Somehow Connie had escaped the marshal's capture and their plan had gone awry.

"Nathan, he needs to disappear, but it has to look like an accident," Connie hissed. "I'm done dealing with him. I finally had that girl, and he and his brothers ruined it once again. They've pushed me too far. I've had enough. He's to be dealt with... now!"

"Why can't I just kill him and dump him in the river?"

"Because..." she paused, a sigh emitting from her lips. "There would be too many questions if he were found. I can ill afford that. His family will raise all kinds of hell if there's any evidence of murder. There's too much scrutiny as it is. If it looks like a misfortunate accident, the mayor and sheriff will not doubt my claims."

Luke squinted to see what they were doing when Nathan made a fist and hit the wall. The enormous crash made Luke jolt in his restraints, but they were so focused on one another, they didn't appear to notice.

"Yes, ma'am," Nathan mumbled.

"Bruno will help. He's done it before, he'll do it again. Besides, the fewer questions, the better. Let me know when it's done."

"Where are you going?"

"To the warehouse to deal with Louisa. Bruno should have her back there by now." She rubbed her forehead before placing her hands on her hips. "She's to be turned over to the fire chief in an hour. This'll shut him up and put her in her place. He'll break her spirit, of that I have no doubt." Her grin was evil and caused goosebumps to prickle Luke's skin. "Normally I'd warn him from hurting her, but considering what she's put me through, I don't care what he does to her. She'll rue the day she went against me."

She murmured something more to Nathan and then a door slammed. Luke wanted to jump up, chase after Connie, and tear her limb from limb, but he was groggy from the knot on the back of his head. Plus, he couldn't fight with ropes bound tightly around his wrists. He barely had the energy to lie there and wait for the right opportunity, if one ever arose.

Nathan gave an order to another man and then a foot slammed into his side. Luke grunted and pulled his legs to his chest, trying to block any additional kicks. His eyes closed against the pain surging through every part of his body.

"Knew you were awake."

Luke wrenched open his eyes and found Nathan crouched in front of him.

"You heard everything, didn't you?"

Luke just glared at him. Nathan wasn't stupid, and there was no point in denying it.

"Thought so. Well, at least I don't have to explain things to you now, do I? Although I have to tell you, I can't wait to get my hands on that woman. Bruno said she was a hellcat. If he'd had more time, he would've broken her spirit." He smacked his lips, an unholy glint in his black eyes. "She sure is delectable, don't you think?" He smacked his lips again and laughed maniacally. "Of course you do. I'm sure you've had a taste of her."

Nathan stood and rubbed his mustache. "She's got quite the body. I can just imagine having her on my bed. It'd be all I can do to not just explode right there from excitement."

Luke's loathing for the man increased tenfold. His head was clearing as anger built to a fever pitch. Once Luke had Louisa back, he'd eliminate Nathan and Bruno and enjoy doing so.

"Don't have nothing to say, do you? Has she shown you her wares already?" Nathan cackled. "I'm sure she has. She entered the house to become a whore, so I guess it stands to reason she would've shown you everything as well."

Luke stretched his hands against the restraints as Nathan droned on and on about Louisa and tried to see if there was any slack in the rope. He pushed to sit, scrambling with little success to make it unnoticeable. A vile grin lifted Nathan's ruddy cheeks. He stepped within inches of Luke. "Oh, I don't think so. You ain't gonna do anything. Not while I have breath left in my body."

Nathan punched Luke, knocking him against the floor. He then grabbed Luke by the upper arm. Luke's shoulder screamed at the pressure of Nathan's thick fingers digging into his skin, and he yanked Luke to stand. His hands were still bound behind his back.

"This has been fun, Seymour, but it's way past time for your untimely accident. You've caused too much trouble."

He forced Luke toward the door. Looking around, Luke realized he was in the run-down kitchen of the brothel he and Harry had searched just a few months past. Harry had been involved in Connie's plot, and Luke had never seen it. He trusted the man and Harry had deceived him.

No laughter, no music, no sounds filtered through the house. It appeared to be empty, which seemed to suit Connie's plans. There was no one and nothing to help him out of the mess he found himself in. As Nathan dragged him to a covered carriage, it was clear no help was coming, and dread settled deep inside of him. He was as good as dead.

Nathan opened the carriage door and threw him inside. Luke stumbled and hit the floor hard. Nathan said something to the driver, then climbed in behind him, pushing him forward so his face hit the seat. Using his knees to push himself up, Luke collapsed into a seat. He looked at Nathan in the dim light as Nathan lit a cigar, the flame from the match lighting up the sneer on his lips. His eyes were black, soulless.

The carriage rumbled down the street at a fast clip when the horses skidded to a stop. Nathan cursed and pulled out his revolver. "You make the wrong move, and I won't hesitate to shoot you no matter what Connie wants."

With those ominous words, Nathan opened the door and stepped outside. Then all hell broke loose. The carriage shook and gunshots roared through the night air. Gunshots were heard often near the seedy brothel, so there'd be no help from the law.

Luke threw himself to the floor as a bullet whizzed through the open window. The sounds of yelling, screaming, cursing, neighing horses, exploding rocks, and splintering wood filled the once-quiet night. The carriage shook like the earth had reached up and threw it across the open field. It was a wonder it didn't shatter into a million pieces around him.

Then all went silent. Luke's hands were bound, and he was weaponless. Luke was sure he'd taken his last breath and wished there had been time for one more moment with Louisa, but at least he'd been able to tell her how much he loved her.

The carriage door was yanked open. A black-gloved hand grabbed him by his collar and pulled him outside into the cool night air. Luke squirmed and kicked in a futile attempt to escape. He was bound and determined to not let this be the end of his life. He had to find Louisa and save her from Bruno. He wanted to live the rest of his life with the woman who had forced back his pain and anger, and replaced it with love. The man pulled him forward into the light from a single street lamp.

"What the hell?" he said, his words muffled as his brother, Ben, pulled him into a tight bear hug. His younger brother, Michael, stood next to him, a mischievous grin lighting his face.

Ben pulled out a knife, turned him around, and cut the ropes around his wrists. Relief and gratitude filled him. His brothers had pulled him out of numerous scrapes over the years.

"You trying to get yourself killed?" Ben barked.

Stretching his arms and rolling his wrists, he pushed his hair back from his forehead. Luke grimaced. "I hadn't planned on it. How did you find me? I thought for sure I was done for."

"When the marshals failed to grab Connie, they interrogated the girls in the house." Ben frowned. "One of them told us about this place as well as a number of other brothels and saloons she owned. We split up and have been searching all of them, and arrived just as you were shoved into the carriage."

"I'm glad you found me, but we don't have time. We need to leave and find a warehouse Connie owns."

Ben touched his arm. "Luke—"

Luke brushed him off. "I don't know where it is, but it can't be that hard to find." He paced, rubbing the back of his neck.

"Luke—"

"I overhead the goon who took Louisa. He was going to take her there."

"Stop, Luke," Michael said. "She should be fine by now."

"What do you mean?" He was confused. He didn't understand how she could have been found so quickly.

"Harry convinced one of the girls at Mon Petit Amour to tell him where Connie would take her. He should have rescued her by now, and we're to meet back at Walter's newspaper office," Ben said.

"No," Luke shouted. An evil foreboding circled around him.

"I'm sure she's safe and back at the newspaper office by now," Michael said.

He ran to the horses tied to the hitching post. "What's wrong?" Ben asked, running toward him and grabbing his arm to stop him, but Luke shook him off.

"Harry can't have her. He's involved."

"Involved in what?" Ben said, grabbing his horse and mounting just as quick. Michael followed suit.

"Harry was at the cabin when Louisa and I were found. Somehow he's been in Connie's pocket all along."

Kicking his horse in the sides, he leaned forward and prayed he wasn't too late.

Thirty-Three

Louisa sat on the plush brown sofa in Walter's newspaper office, a heavy blanket around her shaking shoulders. The sun was still hidden behind the mountains and would be rising soon. She hadn't slept since Walter had rescued her from Bruno, only to be thrown back into the lion's den when Harry had surprised them. She tried to suppress a yawn.

Louisa couldn't get warm. Chills ran up and down her spine, and her toes were numb inside the too-large boots. Harry sat in an armchair on the other side of the room, his arms crossed. His hat was pulled low across his brow, but the sinister smile on his lips frightened her. Blood dotted his sleeve, one tail of his shirt hung outside his trousers, a few buttons were missing from his shirt, and his trouser leg was ripped to the knee.

He was going to either kill her or rape her, of that she was certain. She didn't know what he had planned, but it wasn't going to be anything pleasant. Harry had forced them both down the hall to a second office where he'd made her tie Walter to a chair. He then dragged her back to Walter's office and had been watching her ever since.

She had never been so relieved when Walter pulled her from

underneath Bruno's dead body just hours before. When the gunfight had broken out, Bruno kicked his horse in the side, and they had taken off at a gallop. Then the horse had stumbled and thrown them both. She had slammed into the dirt, rolling to protect herself. A moment later, Bruno had yanked her to her feet, then shoved her forward when she had tripped, and she had fallen to the ground.

A gunshot blasted through the air, and a bullet ripped through him. He'd toppled toward her, his bulky body falling heavily over. She had lain stunned, his body smothering her until his weight was lifted away. Before she could take a deep breath, Walter had pulled her up. His smile had been a welcome sight. He had led her quickly to his horse and told her the men agreed that when they found her, they were to meet at Walter's newspaper office.

When they arrived there, Walter had ushered her inside and up the stairs to his office. She had just stepped through the doorway when Harry stepped out of the shadows, grabbed Walter around the neck, and placed a long knife to his throat. After Harry made her tie him up, he had forced her to sit, and he stared at her with menacing eyes.

Not able to take the silence any longer, she asked, "What are you going to do with me, Harry?"

He raised a brow. "Don't you worry your pretty little head. You'll find out soon enough." His rough voice sent chills along her spine. He stood and walked around Walter's desk, his fingers flipping papers away.

"I thought you were Luke's friend." She had always known something was wrong with him, but she had never contemplated that he'd been deceiving Luke.

His mocking grin unsettled her further. "Friends come and go, but money is all that really matters."

She was skeptical of his reason. There had to be more. "You betrayed him for money?"

"Can you stop?" he yelled as he slammed his fist against

Walter's wooden desk, the piles of papers jumping and scattering with the force of his blow. His face was blistering red, and his chest was rapidly rising and falling.

The loathing in his voice was scathing and horrific. It scared her almost more than Bruno had.

"Why are you such..." he stopped, ran a hand through his hair, and tried to straighten his clothing, but it was of no use.

She didn't understand why he hated her so much. She had done nothing to this man. Her fear receded and anger replaced it. If he was going to kill her, then he might as well do it now, for she wasn't going back into Connie's hands.

Her fingers relaxed, and she dropped her hold on the blanket. Her spine straightened, and she stood, her eyes focusing on the despicable man in front of her.

"Why am I what?" she said, her voice cold and emotionless.

"Don't test me, young lady."

"Don't speak to me like that," she said, her eyes flashing, her skin tightening with resolve. She'd rather die than be raped repeatedly by men as repulsive as Harry.

Harry's hands rested on the top of the desk, his hat having fallen from his head. His frame was bent, taut like a string pulled between a bow––tight and controlled, but with just enough force that it might spring back and explode.

"I'll speak to you any way I please," he bit out. "Sit your pretty little backside back on that sofa or I'll—"

"Or what? If you're going to kill me, then do it now."

He ever so slowly lifted his head, his fingers scratching across the wooden desktop until they curled into a fist. Straightening to his full height, he loomed like a bear, tall, ferocious, and fearless. He moved around the desk and strode right in front of her, standing within mere inches of her. Her hair practically stood on end from the dangerous energy emanating from him.

"All tough now, aren't you?" he said, this time his voice so low she had to strain to hear him.

Glaring at him, her hands gripped her waist. If she let go, she might wrap her fingers around his neck and squeeze until the breath left him. "I've always been tough."

He scoffed and lifted a finger to her cheek. She wanted to shrink from his touch, but she wouldn't give him the satisfaction.

He chuckled mirthlessly, watching her intently. "I don't know about that." His voice had dropped to a whisper. "You won't be so tough after I'm done with you."

Evil radiated from the man. If she didn't fight against him with everything she had, she'd never live to see another day, never hold Luke in her arms, and never have any children of her own.

"You're quiet and timid now that you know I speak the truth."

"You're an overgrown oaf, a bully," she muttered.

Harry laughed and grabbed her by the arm, his fingers pinching her skin, and pulled her up against him. He grabbed her chin, placed his cheek against hers, and whispered in her ear. "I may be, but I'm not a whore who'll sell her body to the first man who paid the least bit of attention to her."

Rage surged through her like a flash of lightning dropping from the thundering night sky. Before she could think through the potential consequences of her actions, she slapped him hard across the face.

His head swung from the force of the blow, and then time slowed to a crawl. He released his grip. She stumbled back. He slowly turned his face toward her, his jaw opening and closing as he reached to touch his cheek. His jaw snapped and cracked as he rubbed at the red sting that graced his skin.

"Well, well, well, you do surprise me."

His eyes narrowed and his breath quickened before he grabbed her shoulders and ground his mouth against hers, her screams strangled in her throat.

Louisa was sickened and shocked at Harry's angry kiss. His fingers dug into her shoulders, the painful pinching paling in comparison to the ardor evident between his legs. He backed her up against the wall, his hips pushing into her lower belly, his grip strong and vicious.

"I'm going to enjoy this," he said.

She had pushed him too far, and now she'd pay the price. She had no doubt he was going to rape her. Harry grabbed her shirt and tore at it, ripping down the front, the buttons flying across the room, clattering onto the floor. He pulled open her shirt when suddenly, a pounding up the stairs stopped him. He whirled around, grabbed the knife he had dropped in the armchair, and grasped the back of her neck before she had a chance to move.

"You scream and I'll cut you from neck to belly," he hissed in her ear.

Connie walked in. She was alone.

She took in Harry and Louisa with one glance. "You little brat," she said, her voice scathing. "You've caused me nothing but grief."

Harry kept his hold on the back of her neck and dragged her to the sofa where he forced her to sit. "Don't move."

Her hands shaking, she tried to close the front of her shirt, but the buttons were missing. She closed the loose flaps as best she could, shoving the ends in her trousers. She had pushed Harry too far and enraged him further, but she would be darned if she'd show him any more of her skin.

Harry strode across the room and kissed Connie's cheek before moving to stand behind Louisa again. There was something more between Harry and Connie than anyone had realized, and whatever it was would not be good for either her or Luke. Louisa had no doubt that when they were done with her, Luke would be next if he wasn't already dead. She had to blink back tears at the thought. She couldn't lose her composure now.

Taking a breath, Louisa said, "Why?"

Connie tilted her head to the side. "Do you really need to ask that question, you impertinent little whore? You left my employ after all the time and money I spent on you. You will not escape me this time."

"I'm not a whore, and I won't be one."

"You really don't understand how these things work, do you? You'll never leave, and you will pay for what you've done."

"I'll never agree to that," Louisa growled. She started to stand but Harry shoved a hand on her shoulder, keeping her in place.

"I didn't ask for your agreement," Connie drawled, raising an eyebrow. "You'll be taken whether you want it or not."

"No. I'll fight you every step of the way." She wrenched herself from Harry's grasp.

"Perhaps, but some men like women who are a bit spirited. They'll love to break it out of you."

Louisa's blood ran cold. If she let Connie take her from Walter's office, her life would be over. She'd never see Luke again.

"Now, Harry, grab the insolent wench and let's go. I'm leaving Helena, and she's coming with me."

Harry grabbed Louisa by her upper arm and ripped her off the sofa. She tried pulling away, digging her heels in, but it was no use. His grip was strong. He pulled out his knife again and held it against her cheek. "You don't have to be pretty for what Madam Lafoe has in store for you, so just give me one reason to cut you."

Suddenly, more footsteps pounded up the stairs. Connie cursed under her breath, pointed her finger at Louisa, and said, "This isn't over. You will pay for this." She ran to the door and turned one more time. "Harry, distract them. You know where to bring her." She then ran out a door at the back of the office and disappeared.

"You utter a word about Madam Lafoe being here and I'll kill you. Then I'll kill whoever is behind that door. I'll enjoy every second of it."

Harry pulled her in front of him, holding her like a human shield. The door flew open, and Luke and his brothers burst into the room, revolvers in their hands, their faces fierce with anger.

They stopped when they saw Harry had a knife against her chest, her body pulled up against his so they'd not be able to get a clean shot. If they tried, they'd hit her instead.

Luke took in the room with one glance. His once good and loyal friend, Harry, held Louisa with a knife in his hand. He didn't see Walter and feared something untoward had happened to him.

He wasn't about to lose the woman he loved, even if it would cost him the chance to end Connie once and for all. On the race to the newspaper office, he had known his life would mean nothing without Louisa in it. His vendetta against Connie had to go. With any luck, she'd be caught and face her crimes, but his priorities had shifted. The weight he'd been carrying for years lightened with the knowledge he had too much to live for. He couldn't continue to chase after Connie when his focus needed to be on Louisa and a future they could have together.

"Let her go," Luke said, his stance firm, confident. He pointed his revolver straight at Harry. He would not hesitate to shoot his old friend.

"She's a whore," Harry roared. He had become agitated, his eyes flitting back and forth, spittle dripping from the corner of his lip. Harry yanked Louisa closer, trying desperately to prevent anyone from getting a clear shot.

"I don't know what's going on, Harry, but perhaps we can talk this through." Luke had to calm or distract Harry to keep him from further harming Louisa.

"No!" Harry slammed his fist, still holding the knife, against the wall behind him. Plaster fell to the ground, the crash making everyone nervous, dust floating in the air.

Louisa swallowed, caught Luke's eye, and blinked back her tears. He hated seeing her this way, but she stood determined and resolute with a madman holding her hostage. She was far stronger than he gave her credit for. Time and time again, she showed she wasn't afraid even when she should be.

Luke took a small step forward.

She gasped and said something under her breath that only Harry could hear.

"What did you say?" Harry said, looking down at her. He returned the knife to the skin above the neckline of her shirt.

"Nothing," Louisa murmured, trying to appease the man.

He wrenched Louisa closer to him. "Don't lie to me!" he screamed.

"I'm... I'm sorry. I didn't mean anything by it," Louisa said.

"Harry!" Luke called, trying to distract him. "Let her go. Take me instead. She has nothing to do with this."

"She has everything to do with this. She ensnared you in her trap, making you forget your purpose, your revenge."

"Then why did you start working for Connie? She's the reason for all of this." He didn't understand what had happened for Harry to change his allegiance. Had everything been a lie?

"Because, I needed the money, and it was the only way to stop *her*"--Harry's knife pierced Louisa's skin--"from getting her sneaky hooks into you. You're going to let me take Louisa from here, and—"

"I don't understand." Luke shifted from one foot to the other. His mouth dropped into a deep frown.

"You were supposed to marry Eliza!" Harry screamed.

"Your sister?" Luke dropped his revolver a bit.

"Yes, my beloved baby sister." Harry's face fell with a pain Luke recognized.

"She's just a child, Harry."

"No she's not, not any longer. She's of age. I told her you'd marry her on her twentieth birthday." He raised his eyes, pleading with Luke to understand.

"I never agreed to this." Luke said, pinching the skin between his brows.

"You would have. She loves you, always has. I have to make her happy."

Luke had to tread lightly. Something had gone wrong with Harry, and if Luke didn't say the right thing, Harry could hurt Louisa or worse. Luke held his other hand out as though in acquiescence. "Of course you do," Luke said. "You care for her. You love her. But there has never been anything between us. I would never touch a child, Harry. You know that."

He had met Eliza about five years ago, after first moving to Helena. She'd been precocious, and had followed him and Harry around demanding attention as any child would. He had never given her any reason to think he was the man for her, but Luke didn't believe now would be the time to point that out. It would only antagonize Harry further.

"She's all I have left. I have to protect her, and she wants you"––his face changed from sadness to disgust––"so she's going to get you."

"But—"

"No," Harry said, his grip tightening again around Louisa's neck. "There's no discussion. This whore will die now, or you'll let us go so I can take her to Madam Lafoe. Then you can be free of her clutches, free to marry Eliza, and I'll have the money to live the way I should. Why do you get everything you want when I've had to scrounge for what little I have?"

"I'll marry Eliza, if you let Louisa go." Luke would say anything to get Harry to release his hold on Louisa.

"I don't think so," Harry roared. "I ain't stupid. You think you can fool me." The hand holding the knife moved away from Louisa's skin. He waved it in the air, his movements frantic.

Louisa caught Luke's eye. It was as though she was speaking to him without words. Before he could stop her, she slammed her elbow into Harry's belly and stomped on his foot. Harry screamed and relaxed his hold on her.

She ducked and dropped to the ground.

Luke took a shot, the noise burning his ears.

Then a second and a third shot blasted into Harry from Ben and Michael's revolvers. Harry jerked, grunted, fell back against the wall, and then slowly slid to the ground. Blood bloomed over his chest and arms. Scrambling, Louisa stumbled to get away.

Luke shoved his revolver into his gun belt and ran toward Louisa, scooping her into his arms, raining kisses along her cheeks. He ran his hands along her shoulders, down her arms, his eyes scanning her to make sure the blood on her shirt was not hers.

"Were you hit?" he asked, his voice torn with anguish. He had instinctively known she would do something. She had trusted him to make sure his shot counted.

"I'm fine." Louisa placed her palms over his cheeks and her green eyes gazed into his. "I love you."

"I love you," he said, his heart singing with joy that she was unharmed.

Ben and Michael ran toward Harry, removed his weapons, and pulled his body into the hall. They then left them alone.

"I prayed you would get here in time," she whispered.

Luke grinned and ran a thumb across her cheek, his touch gentle. "I've made so many mistakes, and I was so consumed with finding Connie that I almost lost something far more important. You." His eyes dropped to her neck and saw a drop of blood. He lifted a finger and brushed at it. "He nicked you."

She placed her hand over his, holding it near her heart. "It is just a scratch. You need to quit worrying."

He sighed. "You're right, but I've—"

Shaking her head, she said, "Shh, there's no point in second guessing the past. If you hadn't been chasing her, you would've never pulled me from Mon Petit Amour to begin with. I'll be forever grateful you were sitting in the audience watching me, although you did get quite a show." Her face turned bright red with embarrassment.

"So am I, although I would have preferred not everyone saw you that way," he said.

She chuckled. "Me too, but what's done is done." She wrapped her arms around his neck and held him tight.

"Is anyone going to come untie me?" Walter yelled.

Luke pulled away from Louisa. "Is Walter here?"

Louisa blushed. "Oh yes, I'm so sorry. I forgot he was." She pointed out the door. "Harry pulled him into the office at the end of the hall where he made me tie him up. He threatened to kill both of us if I didn't do as he said."

Luke gently pushed away a strand of hair on her cheek, kissed her forehead, and then promptly ran down the hall to find Walter glaring at him.

"It's about time," he grumbled. "Can you untie me?"

"Why didn't you call out earlier?" Luke asked as he pulled out his knife and cut the ropes around Walter's wrists and ankles.

Walter massaged his wrists once free and pointed to a rag on the floor. "That deranged fool shoved that in my mouth, and I just now managed to spit it out."

"It's good to see he didn't do any more damage to you."

"He did plenty, I'm afraid." Walter grimaced and touched the back of his head. "The last person I expected was him. I thought he was your friend." Walter looked at him side-eyed.

"So did I," Luke said.

"What happened?"

"I wish I knew. It's like he'd gone mad. He wanted me to marry his sister, claims he promised me to her. I think he was also jealous of what I had. I remember him being quite overtaken with my home, but I didn't think much of it. Perhaps I should've."

"Did you touch his sister?" Walter's eyes were pointed, examining him.

"Walter, I'd never. I barely knew the girl. I met her about five years ago when she came to town to visit with Harry. She was young, a child really." He thought Walter knew his morals, but considering everything that had happened recently, it was a fair question.

"Did you get her?"

"Louisa—"

"No, not Louisa, Madam Lafoe. She was in the office earlier."

"What? No, I never saw her."

Luke turned to look at Louisa who had followed him inside the room. "Was Connie here?"

"Oh, yes. I'm so sorry. With everything that happened, I just wanted to, well…" she blushed. "She ran out just as you and your brothers came inside."

"No reason to apologize." Luke smiled to let her know she had done no wrong. Everything had happened so fast. "Harry was erratic. You had no idea what he would do, but we need to go." He grabbed her hand and pulled her from the room.

"Walter," he called over his shoulder. "Harry's dead in the hall. I'll send the US Marshals to get the body once we find Connie."

"Don't worry about that," Walter replied, his voice fading as Luke ran down the hall and to the stairs with Louisa next to him. "I'll take care of him."

Thirty-Four

L ouisa followed Luke down the stairs and out the front of the newspaper office where Ben and Michael stood waiting for them. She had met them officially the day before when they'd discussed the plan to catch Connie. Luke had sent an urgent message to his older brother, Ben, who had dropped everything at the family ranch to come help. Michael lived in Helena and had been just as willing.

It had been a long night, and it was hard to believe it was already early morning. The sun was just beginning to rise off Mt. Helena. Red, yellow, and orange streaks scattered across the mountain tops and across the valley as far as she could see. They were all exhausted, but rest would come later after Connie had been dealt with.

While they had discussed all of the potential ways things could go awry, they hadn't been able to think of everything. Hopefully, it wasn't too late to catch Connie. Louisa knew that Luke needed closure more than anything else.

"Ben, Michael," Luke said. "Connie was here." He waved back at the newspaper office.

"When?" Ben said.

"She was here right before you arrived," Louisa said.

"Did she say where she was going?" Ben said. His brows knitted together.

"No," Louisa said. "She told Harry that he knew where to bring me, and then ran out the door and down the back stairs. She must've had a horse or carriage waiting to whisk her away."

"And Harry's dead so we can no longer ask him." Luke ran his fingers through his gloriously soft brown hair, his free hand still holding hers tight. He didn't appear to want to let go, and she felt the same way. Stepping close to him, she snuggled against his side. He looked down at her, his smile telling her of glorious things to come.

"Should we head back to Mon Petit Amour?" Michael said. "The US Marshals might have gotten more information from her girls about where she might've gone."

"It probably wouldn't hurt," Ben said. "We need something to go on. I'd hate for her to get away once again."

"Let me take Louisa back to my place," Luke said. "She'll be safer—"

"No," Louisa said. "I'm going with you. It'll save time if I do."

"Louisa, I don't know if that's a good idea."

"The place is full of US Marshals. I'm likely safer with you than back at your place, especially with Connie still missing." She gazed at Luke and implored him to listen to her. "Please. I won't get in the way, but I don't want to be left alone."

"I don't think this is the best idea. I want you safe," Luke said.

"I think we're way past the point of anything being safe for me, don't you agree?"

Luke's eyes shifted back and forth as though weighing the truth of her words against his protective instincts. "Are you sure you want to go back there?" Concern crept into his gaze.

"No, I absolutely don't want to go there, but if I can help bring Connie to justice, then I'd like to help."

"Luke, this no doubt isn't my place, but I've learned over the

years not to argue with the ladies. Elizabeth has taught me that."
Ben held up a finger. "But Louisa, you've got to do everything we
say. We still don't know how safe the place is."

"I'll do whatever you all say," Louisa said.

Luke nodded, and with that, all of them mounted their
waiting horses. Luke pulled Louisa onto his horse behind him, and
she wrapped her arms around his strong waist, resting her cheek
against his warm back. They galloped toward the parlor house and,
with any luck, to Connie.

A few minutes later, they slowed their horses to a stop in front
of Mon Petit Amour. There were a number of horses, buckboards,
and tumbleweed wagons sitting in front of the building as well as
US Marshals mingling around the property.

Louisa followed Luke inside Mon Petit Amour after he failed
to convince her to wait. Luke and his two brothers' faces had
boiled red with frustration at her stubborn nature. It was almost
comical how alike they were. Luke shared some of the same
features as his brothers, but he had green eyes in contrast to the
dark brown of his brothers. Their mannerisms were the same as
well as the width of their shoulders. She wondered if Ben's wife,
Elizabeth, fought him at every turn, and it made her grin to think
that she did.

As they stepped through the wide front doors of Mon Petit
Amour, they found a madhouse. Women were huddled in the
corners, against the walls, and on the sofas as US Marshals searched
the premises, their voices low, their eyes hard as they sent all the
women to one room. Men in various stages of undress waited
while they were each interrogated.

Ben moved ahead of them to speak with a tall man in a black
suit, a wide-brimmed black hat, and a string tie around his neck.
Another older man with white hair who wore a star on his coat's
breast pocket stood next to him. Ben shook both of the men's
hands and then gestured them forward.

"This is Marshal Banks"--he pointed to the tall man--"and Sheriff Fleming." He pointed to the older, white-haired gentleman.

Luke had mentioned Sheriff Fleming weeks before, but Luke had told her that he'd disappeared and another sheriff had been put in his place.

"Sheriff Fleming," Luke said. "You sure are a welcome sight. We've missed you around here."

The sheriff grinned. "It's good to be back."

"Did Connie return?" Luke asked.

"No, we haven't seen her since she slipped away," Marshal Banks said.

"She was at the newspaper office about an hour ago," Louisa said.

"She was?" Marshal Banks said, looking at her through kind eyes.

"Yes. Luke's friend, Harry, grabbed me and Walter Owens, the newspaperman. Harry restrained Walter and then held me hostage 'til she arrived," Louisa said, gripping Luke's hand.

The memory of Harry trying to hurt her was still too raw, but the men had to know what happened.

Marshal Banks's eyebrows rose. "Where did she go?"

"I don't know. As soon as she heard Luke and his brothers run up the stairs, she disappeared. By the time I was able to tell Luke what happened, she was gone." Louisa wondered if she'd made a mistake in not speaking up sooner, but if she had said anything while Harry was holding her, she might not be standing here now.

Marshal Banks shook his head. "That woman appears to be slippery as a snake. We're holding her sister, Pauline, upstairs. Maybe she can give us some answers or perhaps point us in the right direction."

They walked upstairs to Connie's office. There was a dark presence permeating every inch of the house as though evil lived there, and she supposed it had. When Luke had found her hours ago, she had prayed it'd be the last time she would step inside the place.

Now she was back again. At least this time, she was with Luke and well-armed lawmen.

Another marshal stood outside guarding the office. Marshal Banks stopped and spoke to the marshal on guard for a moment before gesturing them to follow. They found the elegant Pauline sitting on a chair next to the window with a tall, scowling marshal standing guard over her. He had a long, black handlebar mustache that gave him a severe expression. They weren't going to give Pauline a chance to escape.

"Marshal Banks, how much longer are you going to keep me here? I've done nothing wrong," Pauline murmured.

"You've done plenty, and you're not going anywhere until you give the Seymours and myself some answers," Marshal Banks said, his legs spread, his hands on his hips, pushing away his coat to show his doubly-loaded gun belt.

She raised her eyes and glared at them, her eyes flashing with irritation. When her gaze landed on Louisa, she stood. "What is she doing here?" Her fingers clinched the edges of her skirt.

Luke said, "She has every right to be here, considering what your sister did to her."

"Don't you think it's the other way around? She's the one who caused this mess." Spit flew out of Pauline's mouth before she shuddered and ran one hand along her red hair, patting down any strays. Then before anyone could stop her, Pauline rushed toward Louisa, her fingernails raised. A marshal grabbed her around the waist and held her back. Her screeches of rage were ear-piercing and irate, startling everyone in the room. It took a moment before she stopped fighting.

"Well, Pauline, you're an irate harpy, aren't you?" Marshal Banks said. "Are you done?"

Pauline glared at Marshal Banks, her eyes shooting daggers at him and everyone else.

"I suggest you sit in the chair, or I'll have one of my men restrain you. I don't cotton to that type of behavior."

The marshal let her go, walking away from her while Luke stepped in front of Louisa. She appreciated his protection, but Louisa wouldn't have minded getting a hand on her. Pauline may not be Connie, but she was just as culpable as far as Louisa was concerned.

Pauline ran her hands down the sides of her hips as if to smooth her skirt before she calmly went back to the chair and sat like she were a lady at a holiday ball.

Marshal Banks turned to the marshal with the handlebar mustache and asked, "Has she told you anything yet?"

"No, sir. Nothing. She insists she doesn't know where her sister has gone."

"Has anyone seen her?" Marshal Banks asked.

"None of the girls we've interviewed so far have seen her for hours. The only thing we know for certain is, when we raided the place, she rushed here in an all-fire hurry, talked to that one over there"––he pointed to Pauline––"then packed a bag and left. No one has seen her since."

"Thanks. Keep interviewing the remaining girls and see if anyone saw or heard anything else."

"Yes, sir." The marshal strode out of the room.

Marshal Banks turned to Ben. "She must've heard we were coming."

"How did she get wind of the raid?" Ben's hand rested on the gun belt around his waist. The men were all armed to the teeth. What she wouldn't give to have a pistol at her hip.

"It had to have been Harry," Luke said. "None of us knew he had been involved."

"The man with the curly black hair?" Marshal Banks asked. "I thought he was a friend of yours."

"So did I," Luke said. "Turns out he had been in Connie's pocket all along."

"Well, that sure explains a few things. I'm actually surprised that Louisa was able to get her to confess to killing your pa," Marshall Banks said, "especially if she knew we were coming."

"I must've angered her enough to cause her to lose her composure," Louisa said.

"Or she was so confident, she didn't care if the marshal overheard," Luke said.

"Well, while that answers some questions, it doesn't solve our problem. She's gotten away again," Marshal Banks said.

"What's it going to take to get that woman behind bars?" Luke ran a hand through his ash brown hair.

"I don't know, but we'll get her. This time, we have her for kidnapping. She won't be able to avoid that charge." Another marshal walked inside the room and whispered something in Marshal Banks's ear. Nodding, he turned back to Ben and Luke. "We've also disrupted her cash flow. She only has so many places she can hide."

"What about her?" Luke asked, pointing to Pauline.

"She isn't talking," Marshal Banks said.

"Mind if I give it a go?"

"Be my guest," Marshal Banks said, stepping out of the way and waving toward the woman who was their only link to Connie.

Pauline stared at them in defiance. Her back was straight, not a red hair out of place. Luke snatched a wooden chair, spun it around so the back was to his front, and straddled it in front of Pauline.

"So, you're Connie's sister?" His arms rested across the top back of the chair, his body relaxed and nonchalant. Louisa knew he was anything but. There was a fury brewing just below the surface of his calm demeanor.

"Yes, I am," Pauline said, her tone defiant.

"I guess you could say I'm your brother-in-law, then."

A small smile lifted the side of her lips. "I don't think so."

"Well, she was married to my brother, Stanley."

"Was she?" Pauline said, her eyes flashing with a look that vaguely resembled humor.

Louisa found a plush armchair in the back of the room and sat. She was afraid she was going to fall over with fatigue, but she wouldn't give Pauline the satisfaction.

Luke unwrapped his arms from the chair and leaned back, his bone-white fingers gripping the wooden sides. Louisa was surprised it didn't break under the force of his grip. "I'm not sure I understand what you mean." His nose wrinkled in confusion.

Pauline laughed before responding. "I hate to disillusion you, but she was already married before she met your brother. He isn't her husband and never was. Besides, he was only a means to an end." She fingered a red curl resting against her bodice. "Of which you should be aware."

It took a moment before Luke responded. He shifted his jaw and straightened his back, the anger simmering like a boiling pot of oil. Instead of losing his composure, Luke forced a smile and stared at the petite woman sitting in front of him. Louisa had to give him credit. From what little she knew, Connie had put his family through considerable heartache.

"Where did she go?" he asked through gritted teeth.

"I don't know." She giggled. Her hand grasped the gold necklace she wore, fingering it slowly and reverently. "And if I did, I certainly wouldn't tell you."

"Why wouldn't she tell you where she was going?"

"She doesn't tell me everything, Mr. Seymour." A scowl raised across her lips but then suddenly disappeared.

"So, she left you holding the saddlebag to this mess?" he said, gesturing to the marshals.

"She didn't leave me anything. This is an honest business. One in which I have a license to operate." She grinned widely.

"She's wanted for murder. Everything will be confiscated."

She chuckled again, her mouth opening wide as the laughter roared out of her like a freight train. For such a small woman, she had a ferocious laugh. "No, it won't," she said, her voice hard and clear.

Luke tilted his head to the side and glared at her but kept quiet, waiting for her to make the next move.

"Connie doesn't own Mon Petit Amour," Pauline said.

"Of course she does. She's the madam here. Everyone knows that."

"That is where *you* are wrong. Everything here belongs to me and has for quite some time. I haven't broken the law. You can't take this from me. In fact, my lawyers should be here soon."

Luke looked at Marshal Banks. "What is she blathering on about?"

"I don't know," Marshal Banks said. "This is the first I've heard of it. Do you know anything about this, Sheriff Fleming?"

Sheriff Fleming had been quiet, contemplative, standing against the wall. He appeared to be just as stumped as the rest of them. "No. Before I was ousted, Madam Lafoe tried to bribe me, but I didn't fall into her clutches. Not two months later, the mayor had me replaced with that... that." Sheriff Fleming's face grew red, his lips sputtering out the words. "With that corrupt sheriff."

"Don't worry none about him, Sheriff Fleming, he's being taken care of as we speak," Marshal Banks said. "You'll be replacing him as soon as he's arrested. The mayor understands the precarious position he's put himself in and is fully cooperating."

Pauline interrupted and stood. "Gentlemen, as much as I'm enjoying this delightful hugs-and-kisses reunion with you all, I have a business to run. If you will allow me, I'll show you the deed which demonstrates Mon Petit Amour is mine."

Marshal Banks nodded. She deliberately, but seductively, walked toward her desk. Sitting in the leather chair behind it, she opened a drawer and pulled out a folder. Riffling through the papers, she removed a few pieces and handed them to Marshal Banks. She sat back, an evil grin on her striking face.

The Marshal glanced through the paperwork, his face going white.

"She's right. This proves she owns this place and has for years."

"That isn't possible," Ben said. "Those could be fake documents. We know Connie had no problem forging my pa's will, so forging a deed is well within her skills."

"Gentleman, everything has been recorded at the courthouse. It'll be easy enough to prove once my lawyers have arrived." She leaned back in the chair, a self-satisfied smirk on her face.

"Did you check the documents in the courthouse before all of this?" Luke asked.

"We planned this raid within the last twenty-four hours. I trusted your family's word," Marshal Banks said. "I had no reason to believe otherwise, but clearly I was wrong in assuming."

"Even so, she's got to be responsible for some of this mess," Ben said, pointing his finger at Pauline.

Before Marshal Banks could respond, the door opened and two men in blue suits, one tall, one short, each holding brown leather satchels, strode into the room.

"Marshal Banks, Mr. Seymour, please meet my lawyers." Pauline waved toward the two men. "They will answer all of your questions."

Pauline said no more, and her lawyers made it clear that unless they had a reason to arrest Pauline, they were to leave the premises immediately.

Luke stood and turned to Louisa. "I think it's time we leave. It doesn't appear we're going to find any additional answers here."

Louisa rose from her seat and went to follow Luke but then stopped. She had something to say to Pauline and walked toward her and her two lawyers.

"May I speak to Pauline for a moment?"

Pauline looked at the lawyers and nodded. They scurried to the other side of the room, waiting to do her bidding.

"What can I do for you, Louisa?" She arched her brow.

"I just wanted to let you know that if you harm any of the girls in this house, you will pay for it. Mark my words."

Pauline chuckled. "There's nothing you can do to me. You're nothing but a harlot, just like the rest of them."

"I'm not even close," Louisa said.

"Oh, you are," Pauline said, stepping forward until her lips were near Louisa's ear. "You may not have lost your virginity, but you've been trained. You spent time in this house, and you had every intention of becoming one. Just because you never laid with a man doesn't mean you're a proper lady."

Pauline's words pierced straight into her soul. While she'd tried to deny it, Pauline was right. Would Luke really be able to look past her decision to enter a parlor house? Trying to control the tremor in her voice, Louisa said, "You're wrong and I'll prove it."

Pauline laughed softly against Louisa's ear. "When you realize you belong here, please do return. My door is always open to girls like you." She ran a long, thin finger against Louisa's cheek. "You'd fetch a high price and could command any amount you chose. Don't forget, your innocence is still worth a lot of money, and I'd be happy to make sure you got every penny you'd want for it."

With that, Pauline stepped away and turned back to her lawyers. She dismissed Louisa with a flick of the hand. Louisa swallowed back the nausea that threatened to overwhelm her. The horrible truth of Pauline's words made her loath herself. She worried that Luke would resent her one day for not being the lady she had been raised to be.

Thirty-Five

Luke followed his brothers and Walter out of what was clearly now Pauline's office, Louisa's hand held firmly in his. She had stopped to have a word with Pauline, and when she returned, her smile had dimmed. The light that had been shining in her eyes had disappeared. It was as though she had retreated inside of herself. He didn't know what Pauline had said to her, but he could imagine it wasn't anything pleasant.

The two of them hadn't been able to say more than a few words to one another, and while they had declared their feelings, he sensed there was more to be said. Unfortunately, it would have to wait as much as it pained him. He just prayed Louisa hadn't changed her mind about how she felt.

Walter stopped to talk to some of the women huddled in the corner of the hallway while the rest of them went down the stairs. Walter would likely scribble in his notebook any and all information he could glean from those inside the house. The story would make a big splash, especially if they could find Connie. Walter had gotten the story he wanted, just not by Luke's hand. It was the one chance Luke had to prove he could have a headline, and he'd blown it. But that was the least of his worries now. Connie still had to be caught.

The parlor off to the right was empty of anyone, so their group went in there to reconvene and decide their next steps. Their faces were solemn and resolute.

"What are we going to do now?" Luke said, looking at Marshal Banks and Sheriff Fleming.

"I need to go back to my old office," Sheriff Fleming said, his jaw tight. "I've got to unravel the mess my predecessor left behind."

"You're not going to look for Connie?" Luke asked.

"I can't. Not right now," Sheriff Fleming said. "I know how you feel about her, Luke, but there's more I've got to attend to. The marshal here"––he pointed to Marshal Banks––"won't stop 'til we find her. She has more charges against her at this point." He doffed his hat and then strode out of the room.

"What's your plan, Marshal?" Ben asked.

"My men are still interrogating some of the women. With any luck, one of 'em will have some information we can use." The marshal leaned up against a settee, his arms crossed.

"Did she own any other buildings, or other places of business?" Luke asked.

"I'll need to go to the courthouse and see if I can't get that information. They should be open for business in an hour," Marshal Banks said, his expression grim. "In the meantime, you'll have to wait 'til we figure out our next plan of attack."

"Pauline has to know more." Luke gritted his teeth in anger, his jaw tightening. "She's been involved for months. If she owns Mon Petit Amour, Connie was bound to have kept her in her confidence about some things."

"That may be true, but she ain't saying a word. She clammed up tighter than a toad's ass," Marshal Banks said. "Her lawyers were quick to stop the questioning."

"So she can try to have me killed, be involved in taking Louisa, and we can't do anything about it?" Luke asked.

Ben cursed under his breath. "She isn't who we really want, Luke."

"But she's involved." Luke knew Connie was the real criminal, but it just didn't feel right knowing that Pauline was culpable in her own right and the authorities weren't as concerned.

"Do you want to continue to interrogate someone who isn't going to tell us anything, or do you want to find someone here who is willing to spill what we need?" Ben said, exasperated.

"That's not enough, Ben. I've been doing that for the past few months, and it was all for naught," Luke said.

"Luke, calm yourself. The marshals don't have any evidence against Pauline and can't hold her. Besides, the marshals were after Connie, not Pauline, so they weren't tracking her movements. There's nothing more we can do," Ben said.

"No!" Luke went to push around his brother, but Ben held him back. "She killed our pa. Don't you care?"

"Of course I care, but I can't go running into situations without thinking it through. I've got a family I have to think about, and so do you. Our sister is still missing. Elizabeth's brother, James, has gone to Idaho to find his children, and you're acting like an uncontrollable teenager, just like you did when Pa tried to take you to task all those years ago. Never considering others or what your actions would do to them."

Ben's words were harsh but had a thread of truth to them. He was ashamed of his past behavior and what he had put his pa through, but this was different.

"Luke, this has gone on long enough. You've been angry for over seven years. You've put your life on hold while you chased after her. You're never going to get her without all of our help," Ben said.

"I just need a little more time." Luke blew out a breath and paced back and forth in front of him.

"Are you two done hollering? Everyone inside this place is hearing the two of you fight," Walter drawled as he ambled inside the room.

Luke turned around and winced at the censure on Walter's face.

"While the two of you've been carrying on, I've been doing the job I thought Luke and I agreed upon when this whole mess started back in June."

Shame rolled through Luke like a vicious storm. He had been so consumed with finding Connie, he hadn't done what he had promised Walter when he'd first gotten the invitation to the auction. If he didn't get control of his erratic emotions, he could lose his job and Louisa.

Scratching behind his ear, he took a breath, and said, "You're right, Walter. I haven't held up my end of the bargain. My short-sightedness hasn't been good for anyone. It appears I need to take stock of decisions I've made, or else I'm going to lose something far more important." He walked toward Louisa who stood off in the corner of the room. She had been quiet, almost pensive while he ranted to his brother. She was seeing a side of him he wasn't proud of. If he wanted to be the man she deserved, he had to do better.

He held out his hand, and she took it without hesitation. They didn't have time to talk, at least not right now, but with any luck they'd have time soon.

He turned to look back toward Walter and found him huddled with Ben, Michael, and Marshal Banks, discussing something without him. He bristled, but then Louisa tightened her fingers around his, immediately reminding him that he couldn't get angry, not anymore.

Luke looked down at her, and she raised her chin, touching his cheek softly, reverently. "Go, talk with them. See how you can help."

"I—"

"Shh." She dropped her fingers across his lips. "We're fine.

We'll have plenty of time to talk. You'll never have any peace until she's behind bars."

He lifted her hand, still clasped in his, and kissed her knuckles gently. Giving her one more smile she let go and shooed him away.

Hours later, Luke and his brothers crept up to the warehouse they believed Connie might have holed up in. Marshal Banks and a few of his men had gone around to the back to keep her from running if she was inside. They weren't going to let her escape, not this time.

Walter had interviewed some of the girls. One of them had overheard Connie mentioning the warehouse on King Street before she escaped Mon Petit Amour with her remaining guards. The young woman had been scared senseless. Walter had promised no one would know she'd given him the information. Giving her a few dollars, he had patted her on the shoulder, and she proceeded to tell them what she knew.

Ominous dark shadows surrounded them and thunderous clouds covered the sun. They were in for a storm. With any luck, the thunder would obscure any noises they might make. Each of them were loaded with revolvers, knives, and plenty of bullets.

The warehouse appeared empty, but Luke wasn't giving up hope. It was an old structure that had seen better days, but it had to be the one. His skin prickled with anticipation. She had to be in there. He couldn't keep chasing after her. If she wasn't here, he had to let the past go. It wasn't worth it, and he couldn't take the chance that he'd lose Louisa.

Although it was the middle of the day, they hadn't seen a soul in over an hour. It was unusual and they were on high alert. There was no telling what they might find.

They crept up to the windows that lined the side of the building and peered through the grimy glass. Not seeing anything, they were ready to admit defeat when Ben heard a sound. He gestured for the rest of them to be silent, and the three of them inched quietly to a door. They each pulled out their revolvers and checked that they were ready. With grim determination, they slowly pulled open the door, careful to keep it from creaking.

The faint light made it difficult to see, but as their eyes adjusted, they heard two men arguing. Luckily, they hadn't seen Luke and his brothers enter the space. The three of them slipped behind a stack of crates to the right. The warehouse was large with boxes, crates, old wagons, plows, and a various assortment of farm equipment was scattered against the walls and in front of them.

"Are those her men?" Ben whispered.

"I can't tell. They're too far away," Luke said.

"Let's see if we can't get closer." Ben pulled back the hammer of his revolver.

Both Luke and Michael followed Ben's lead.

They quietly but swiftly moved across the wood block floor, behind the crates and wagons that lined the side of the building. Luke peered over the crates, trying to get a good look at them. The short one was in the shadows and he couldn't see his face, but the taller one turned. He had a thick red beard and long thin mustache. Luke didn't know his name, but he'd been the one who had given him the black eye back in April, the first time he thought he saw Connie.

He squatted next to Ben. "That's one of 'em."

"It is?" Ben said.

Luke nodded.

A door slammed behind them, and they quieted. They squeezed back further into the shadows, trying to stay out of sight.

Two more men came in through the same door Luke and his brothers did with a woman in their midst. The clouds outside prevented any real light from shining through the high windows of the warehouse. If it was Connie, he'd be thrilled. He couldn't imagine Pauline coming here, not with the marshals watching her every move. Luke needed to get a better look.

One of the men struck a match and lit a lantern before placing it on a crate near them. The four men and the woman moved around, murmuring harsh words until she stepped into the lantern's light. It was Connie.

Luke shifted and hit the edge of a crate. A box sitting at the top tumbled to the ground and crashed, breaking the still silence.

"What was that?" one of the men hollered.

"This ain't good," Michael whispered.

Standing next to the crate, Luke leaned over and took a shot. The sound was deafening. The boom was enough to make his ear drums ring, but he was focused. The bullet hit its target, and the man crumpled to the floor.

The three other men scattered, pulling Connie with them. Bullets flew, piercing into the walls, wooden crates, and windows, the glass shattering on impact. Luke, Michael, and Ben were somewhat protected between the makeshift wall of crates, and the men shooting back couldn't get a good look at their positions. Michael moved next to him and started shooting to the left of him. Luke looked once again over the crate. One man was trying to shield Connie. The other two had disappeared from his view.

Anger, like nothing he had ever felt before, punched through him. He burst out from behind the crates.

"Luke, what are you doing?" Ben yelled from behind him, trying to give him cover, but Luke didn't care. He was going to kill Connie if it was the last thing he ever did.

His bearing solid, his footsteps sure, his eyes focused on Connie and the man trying to protect her. He didn't know where the other two men were, but he trusted his brothers and the marshals who were likely already inside. They would subdue the men while he finally, after seven long years, ended Connie. He knew he should wait to have her arrested, but he didn't waiver. He was done. There was only one way to end this forever, and it was to end her life in the same callous manner she had ended his pa's.

The man protecting Connie stumbled back, a bullet hitting his arm. His eyes widened in fear at Luke's sharp gaze. The man's gun jammed. Luke shot a second bullet into his shoulder and the gun dropped, clattering to the ground. Connie's face turned ugly, but she slipped behind a crate before he had a chance to send a bullet her way.

Ben rushed to his side and stopped him.

"It's over, Luke, stop," Ben said. "She has nowhere to hide. The marshals are inside now. They'll grab her, I'm sure."

Luke's arms trembled, and he dropped them to his sides. It was finally over. She could never hurt his family again. Ben put his gun away, smiled and squeezed Luke's shoulder.

"Where's—"

A blast of gunfire ripped through the room, once, twice. Luke stumbled back. His gun fell from his fingertips. He looked down in shock. He had been hit, both in the shin and in the side.

Connie stepped from behind the crates, a revolver in her hand, and pointed it at Ben. "Don't even think about it, Ben Seymour."

Ben cursed but stood still. They had assumed she hadn't been armed. Once again, she had gained the upper hand. Luke's leg throbbed. He tried to stay upright, but he couldn't. His hands reached to stop his fall, but he fell forward, his good knee hitting the ground.

"Luke!" Ben yelled. Before he could move, another gunshot blasted through the room. Ben paused and held his hands up in surrender.

"Now, that's what I want to see," Connie yelled, gleefully. "You thought you had me, but you never will. I'll take down your family, each and every one of you. Your pa's ranch will finally be mine."

Luke tried to stand, but it was no good. His mind became fuzzy and he shook his head, trying to clear his brain to understand what she was saying. He forced himself onto his good knee, grabbed a crate next to him, and pushed until he sat on it. Then, he grabbed a handkerchief from his pocket and tried to stop the blood trickling from the bullet wound on his leg.

"The ranch will never be yours," Ben responded. "You won't get away with this."

"I've already gotten away with it. Once the two of you are dead, I'll kill Michael, and then I'll come after your wife and sisters. When you're all eliminated, the only family left standing will be me."

"You aren't family," Ben said.

Luke turned his head. He didn't know what she was talking about. Where was Michael? Had he been killed in the chaos?

"That's where you're wrong. Your pa and my pa were brothers. Cole Seymour ruined my life when he made my pa marry that other woman and forced my ma into that brothel." Spittle flew out of her mouth, anger causing her body to shake, but she held firm to that gun and stalked forward until the gun was pressed into Ben's chest. "I'll get what's mine after all these years, if it's the last thing I ever do."

Luke tried to stop her and reached for her leg, but she kicked at him, her shoe striking his injured shin. He bent over in agony, but he couldn't let her kill his brother, not while he had breath left in his body. Gathering what strength he had left, he heaved himself up and startled her, his bad leg screaming in agony, but he tried to keep his weight on his good leg. Her arm waved, but she didn't let go of the gun.

"Luke, no!" Ben shouted, but it was too late. She got off another round and hit his other leg. His body fell to the ground, crashing onto the wooden floor, useless. He had failed again.

Thirty-Six

November 8, 1900

L uke groaned. He tried to move but his body didn't cooperate. Piercing aches shot through his side and down his legs. Wrenching his eyes open, he only saw a white ceiling made brighter by the sunlight spilling through the windows. He winced and closed his eyes. He turned his head to the left trying to avoid the glaring light.

"Luke, Luke! He's awake." Ben's voice echoed in his ears, and he slowly opened his eyes again. Ben's lips lifted up into a wide smile. "Holy cow, Luke. You scared us to death."

"What happened?" he mumbled. His lips were dry, and his tongue felt like it had doubled in size.

"What?" Ben asked, his eyes darkening in concern.

"Water," Luke said. "Louisa?"

"Hold tight, little brother."

Ben moved out of his sight, and Luke could hear rustling on the other side of the room. The door to the room slammed open, rattling the wardrobe. He couldn't focus and his eyes shuttered close.

Whispers and the sound of feet shuffling could be heard as others joined Ben. Luke's head pounded something fierce. He couldn't concentrate.

A gentle hand touched his chin.

"Here, Luke, drink this," Louisa said.

Her soft voice was a boon to his ravaged body. She was still here.

Luke opened his eyes to find a glass of water in front of him. His beautiful Louisa cupped the back of his head and helped him take a couple of sips, the water cool against his dry mouth. He drank greedily for a few seconds before she pulled it away. "Slow now, you don't want to get sick. Give it a moment to see if your stomach can take it before we give you more."

He reached a hand toward her cheek, brushing his fingers against her smooth skin. "Are you all right?"

She chuckled. "I'm fine. I should be asking you how you feel?"

"Better now that you're here with me."

"Don't ever scare me like that again," she said, her voice gruff as she blinked back tears.

Luke nodded and then pushed to sit up but sharp, piercing pain ripped through his side and he moaned.

"Don't move," Ben said. "You're pretty banged up. Let me help."

Louisa moved away to give Ben room. Ben reached around his chest while Louisa shuffled pillows behind him. A few minutes later, Ben had pulled him up against the headboard of the bed, pillows cushioning the hard wood. Sweat lined his forehead. Each movement caused aches all over his body.

Louisa sat on the edge of the bed, careful not to jostle it too much. She took his hand and held it gently against her chest. Her eyes narrowed as she scanned him head to toe, as though to assure herself he was really all right.

"What happened, Ben?" Luke said. He couldn't remember much. His mind was blank. "How long have I been like this?"

"You don't remember?" Ben asked, standing at the foot of the bed. "You've been out now for three days. We weren't sure"––his voice cracked––"we weren't sure if you were gonna make it. You lost quite a bit of blood."

Luke closed his eyes and tried to recall. A dark warehouse, gunfire, and Connie. "Connie," he bit out. "Where is she? Did you get her?" Snippets of the events pulled at his memory. "Tell me she didn't get away."

Ben crossed his arms across his chest. "She didn't. We finally got her, although she nearly ended you."

Luke shuddered with relief, an enormous weight lifting off his shoulders. Then he remembered he hadn't been the only one in that warehouse. "Where's Michael? Are either of you hurt?" He couldn't live with himself if any harm had come to his brothers.

"I'm fine, nary a scratch on me," Ben said. "Michael has a few bruises. He got into a scuffle with one of her men, but he suffered no lasting damage either. He's resting downstairs." Ben paused as though weighing if he should tell him more.

"Whatever it is, Ben, you've got to tell me. I can see it in your eyes."

Ben sighed, his fingers scratching at his neck. "Harry's alive. When Walter went to drag his body out, he discovered Harry was still breathing. Not sure how Michael and I missed that, but he's still kicking."

"I'd like to—"

"So would the rest of us," Ben said. "Although he ain't doing too well now that he's gonna rot in prison. Turns out he's been in cahoots with Connie for quite some time. He'd been reporting all of your activity to her as well as leading you on some wild goose chases in an effort to keep her real plan in motion."

Luke shook his head. "I can't believe I thought he was my friend."

"Yeah, I'm sorry to say he wasn't and hasn't been. He wanted the money he thought you had and well, you know he wanted you to marry his sister."

Luke nodded. "Yeah, it sure surprised me."

"Well, it's a little more complicated. Eliza somehow stumbled into Connie's clutches and found the place not to her liking."

"Can you blame her?" Louisa muttered. "I felt the same once I realized what I had gotten myself into."

Luke's eyes widened. He thought she didn't want anyone to know about her choice to enter Mon Petit Amour.

She caught his eye. "It's all right. Your brothers know everything and don't hold it against me."

Ben smiled. "Considering how much Louisa has fussed over you and, dare I say, doctored you better than any doc I know, we couldn't be more grateful to her. We don't care that she might've been a *guest* at Mon Petit Amour."

Louisa giggled, her face blushing bright red.

"Anyhow," Ben said, "Connie would only let Eliza go if Harry reported your actions back to her. He thought if he could get Eliza away from Connie, then you could marry Eliza and his sister's respectability would return. Not to mention Connie promised him a good sum of money to end you."

"I had no idea. He had me completely fooled." Luke shifted on the mattress and cursed when he bumped his leg. The pain was something fierce, but he forced back the moan that bubbled in his throat. "What about Connie? Tell me she's behind bars."

"No, I'm afraid not," Ben said.

"But you said we got her." Luke's anxiety increased.

Louisa patted his hand, trying to comfort him.

"We got her, but not like you think. She's dead," Ben said. "She got off another shot when you tried to save me, but then Michael shot her in the neck. She died minutes later."

Relief surged through him. It was finally over. "She's truly gone?"

Ben grimaced. "Yes, she is. Although truth be told, I really wanted to talk to her. Find out what she meant about being family."

Luke tried to remember what she'd been saying while they were staring each other down in that warehouse, but a lot of that was now a blur.

"I'm not sure I remember," Luke said.

"Sounds like she was Uncle Howard's daughter, or at least that was what she claimed."

"What does Pauline say about it? Have you interrogated her?" Luke asked, intrigued at what might have been behind Connie's vendetta against the family.

"Yes," Ben said. "She's claiming she doesn't know anything about it and pursed her lips tighter than a fresh oyster. She ain't talking and insists she's had nothing to do with the whole mess. She's not telling us if she was really Connie's sister by blood or not."

"She's lying," Luke said.

"Oh, we're sure she is, but the marshals got nothing to hold her. No proof she was involved, but we'll keep an eye on her."

Luke's eyes were heavy, and he struggled to keep them open. "Sorry, Ben. I'm not sure what's wrong with me."

"You've got three bullet holes in you, that's what's wrong," Ben said. "But luckily enough, Louisa was able to stop the bleeding before it got too bad. She says you'll survive, but you're going to be laid up for quite some time."

He looked at her. Her auburn hair hung around her shoulders in thick curls, just the way he liked it. "Thank you, Louisa. This ain't the first time you've patched me up."

"I'm sure it won't be the last, although I'd really rather we stop with the bullet wounds," she said, her eyes twinkling with mirth, a devilish grin on her lips.

He chuckled but his energy waned. Louisa and Ben swam like

fast moving clouds. He tried to speak but couldn't. His eyes fluttered close.

Louisa stood in the hallway, leaning against the door to Luke's
room. He had fallen asleep after talking with her and Ben far
longer than he should have. When he had first opened his eyes,
relief had surged through her. Ben had gone downstairs to give her
a few minutes alone, giving her a grave smile before leaving her be.
Her legs shaking, she slid down the door until she hit the hard
wooden floor. Pulling her knees to her chest, she wrapped her arms
around them, silent sobs wracking her frame.

She had held back the tears for days, trying to see him only as a
patient that needed tending to. She hadn't allowed herself to think
anything beyond tending to his wounds and praying he would
survive. Now that he had, she had reached her breaking point.

Ben had told her how Luke had stepped out in the open, away
from the crates protecting him, to take Connie on himself. He had
put himself in grave danger, and it could have ended much differently. A part of her understood why he did it, but the other part of
her was angry. He had almost been killed, and by the sheer grace of
God, he had survived.

She had told him she loved him, and he had said the same to
her. Considering everything that had happened, she wasn't sure if
he'd said it in the heat of the moment or if he had truly meant it.
They hadn't had any real time to discuss their feelings or what it
meant. To know she could have lost him made things even more
difficult.

Sniffling, she rubbed her nose and eyes into the folds of her
skirt. She was a blubbering mess and leaving her skirt just as
disheveled, but she had to compose herself. It wouldn't do to let
anyone see her cry. They were depending on her to care for Luke,
and she couldn't do it if she fell apart. Michael was resting in

Luke's parlor downstairs, and he needed her attention as much as Luke did. He had been pretty banged up, too, but luckily stood stronger than Luke had and would recover much quicker.

Walter had gotten his headline and Harry was locked up, never to hurt her again. She ached for what it meant to Luke. He had thought Harry was his friend, his confidant but had been betrayed. However, she was glad Harry was in jail. He had always given her a bad feeling, and while she would never tell Luke who he could be friends with, she was glad she didn't have to say anything now.

"Louisa?" Marie's soft voice interrupted her self-pity party.

Louisa tried to wipe her eyes surreptitiously, but when she raised her head and caught Marie's gaze, she knew she'd failed.

Marie knelt next to her, her hand touching Louisa's shoulder in a gesture of friendship. "Are you all right?"

Louisa shrugged and tried to smile but failed again.

"Ben said Luke woke up, and he believes Luke will be all right once he's healed. Did I misunderstand?"

Louisa shook her head. "No. Luke will be fine, or at least he'll recover from his injuries."

"Then what's caused all of this distress?"

Louisa's eyes filled with tears once again. "Marie, I just... what if he..." She thrust her palms across her face, viciously wiping them. "I'm sorry. I..."

"Oh, Louisa." Marie wrapped her arms around Louisa's shoulders and let her cry. After a few more minutes of silent tears, Marie said, "It's been too much for you, hasn't it? We should have called the doctor, not made you tend to his wounds."

Louisa pulled back. "No one made me do anything. I had to help him. I love him."

Marie smiled and pushed back stray hairs behind Louisa's ear. Her touch gentle, considerate, kind. "Of course you do, and he loves you, too."

"Does he?" Louisa asked, grabbing Marie's hand frantically. "What if he said that because he thought we would be killed?"

"If you only saw the way he looks at you when he thinks no one is looking. His gaze is intense, and he can't keep his eyes off you. That man loves you more than anything else."

"Then why did he endanger himself to go after... after that woman?" Louisa cried.

"I don't know. You'll have to talk to him about that when he's stronger. But make no mistake, that man loves you."

Thirty-Seven

November 16, 1900

Luke was chomping at the bit to get out of his bed. Both Louisa and Ben insisted he was to stay, but he was done lying there like a fat cow enjoying the hot sun. As far as he was concerned, he was healed enough. He couldn't stand to stare at the four walls of his bedroom any longer. He hadn't had a moment to talk with Louisa alone for days. Whenever she came near him, she was either with Ben, Michael, or Marie.

It would be darn near comical that she wouldn't stay in the room alone with him if he didn't ache to talk to her, to truly tell her how he felt. He could feel her pulling away, and it was all his fault. She had questions about the day Connie was killed, but he wasn't sure he could tell her why he had acted so recklessly. He'd thought when he had pulled her from Harry's arms that he was done making mistakes. His rage over Connie's actions had pulled the red over his eyes. He hadn't been able to stop until it had been too late.

Only through the grace of God and Louisa's fine doctoring was he alive. He just needed the chance to tell her that, and if he didn't get it soon, he was going to rip someone's head off in sheer frustration.

Yanking at the bedclothes, he looked at the bandages on his thigh and shin. They hadn't bled in days, and according to Louisa, there was no sign of infection. The only time he'd gotten out of bed was to use the chamber pot. Louisa insisted he use it, and he hadn't wanted to argue with her. It stopped him from walking far. Ben was the lucky one to help him, embarrassing as it was. The last time he had used it, his legs had shook. It had been uncomfortable but not as bad as Louisa feared. He was determined to get up, find her, and sort out the mess he had created.

Dropping his legs over the side of the bed, he held onto the bedpost to test his weight. Taking a small step forward, he grimaced but found he could withstand the pain. The bullets hadn't done any lasting damage.

Shuffling to the wardrobe, he pulled it open being careful of the stitches on his side. He found a pair of trousers, and with a bit of maneuvering, he was able to pull them on. He worked up quite the sweat while doing it, but it was a small price to pay if he could finally have a real conversation with Louisa.

He pulled out a blue chambray shirt and had just shoved his arm into one of the openings when his bedroom door opened.

"Luke," Louisa cried. "What are you doing out of bed? You get right back in there this instant."

Michael had followed in her wake and grinned when he saw the look of consternation on Luke's face.

"I'm fine, Louisa," he growled and immediately regretted his tone.

Her eyes lost their twinkle and a scowl lined her lips.

"I'm sorry," he said. "I didn't mean to be gruff with you."

She swept past him, yanked at the pillows on his bed and proceeded to fluff them, ignoring his pleading tone.

Michael held out his hands and said, "Let me help you back to bed, Luke."

Luke glared at his brother. "I'm not an invalid. I can walk on my own. I'm not getting back in that bed. Why don't you go back to... to wherever you came from."

Michael grinned. "Well, that might be a problem, seeing as how I was at the ranch about twenty-eight years ago."

Michael's sense of humor and easy-going attitude made Luke laugh most times, but in that moment it infuriated him. He glared at his brother again. Michael's smile dropped and he held up his hands. "Um, how about I go?" He backed out of the room and closed the door behind him.

"What did you say to him?" Louisa asked, turning her pointed gaze on him. She had straightened the sheets and blankets on the bed. Her movements were angry.

"I just encouraged him to go somewhere else," he muttered, not liking the look in her eyes. He took a step forward and couldn't hide his grimace. He might have overdone it.

"You're hurting," she said.

He hadn't been hiding the pain very well. "I'm fine."

"You may be, Luke, but you won't recover if you don't get back in this bed... right... now."

He couldn't hide a grin at her annoyance with him.

She placed her hands on her hips and glared at him. "Do you find this funny?"

Wiping the smile off his face, he said, "No, I don't." He hobbled to the bed, his footsteps slow, wincing with each step when he stumbled. He fell onto one knee, his hands grabbing for the bed, the blankets falling with him to the floor.

"Luke!" Louisa ran to him, dropping to the ground to help him.

He was embarrassed and tried to push her away, but she swatted his hands away.

"Stop," she ordered. "You will let me help you."

He ducked his head and muttered obscenities. "Am I just a patient to you?"

"What?" she asked, pushing away the hair from his forehead. "You are more than that." She placed her hands on her knees and stood. Putting her hands under his elbows, she helped him to stand, bearing his weight well. He hated that he was not as strong as before and that he had to depend on her to help him when he couldn't stand on his own.

"Whatever you're thinking, you can stop it right now," she snapped.

He startled at the vehemence in her voice. She was far too intuitive.

Louisa wrapped her arm around his waist. "Let me get you into bed."

Not wanting to upset her any further, he let her lead him back to the soft mattress. He sat on the edge, and her hands went to his waist to undo the button. He stopped her with his hand and raised an eyebrow. She stilled and then blushed.

"What do you think you're doing?" he whispered, tucking a hair behind her ear, his fingers lingering on her neck.

"I'm sorry," she mumbled.

She stepped back, but he grabbed her wrist and pulled her close. He had opened his legs and pulled her between them. He rested his hands on her hips.

"Don't apologize to me, Louisa."

She avoided his gaze, instead looking down at her hands which rested precariously close to the seam between his thighs.

Taking a breath, he said, "Why are you avoiding me?"

Her eyes jumped to his. "I haven't been."

"Don't lie to me. I thought we had moved past that."

"I've never lied to you, Luke." Her eyes flitted away.

"Then don't start now."

He could see her throat working as she swallowed hard. Something was bothering her, and he didn't know what it was.

"Can you tell me why you don't come up here unless one of my brothers is with you, then?"

"Because it isn't proper for us to be alone," she said, her breath quickening.

"That didn't bother you when we first met."

Her face went bright red. She wrenched herself away as though she were trying to avoid his touch. Her hands gripped each other, the knuckles growing white from the pressure. She paced back and forth in front of him. He wanted to go to her, but he could barely stand and had to wait for her to come to him.

"You could have been killed," she cried, raising a fist to hide her tears.

"But I wasn't—"

"No," she said. "You ran straight into the gunfire, not caring for your own wellbeing. If you'd been killed, what do you think that would've done to me? I thought you loved me, but did you love me when you put your life in danger?" Tears bloomed but she blinked them back, keeping them at bay. "Or maybe you never loved me and just said those words in the heat of the moment."

He hung his head in shame. "I'm sorry—"

"Don't apologize to me," she yelled. "I don't want that. I want you to not get yourself killed." She stomped her foot. "How can you say you love me and then don't have any regard for your safety? Look at yourself. You have three bullet holes in you, and this isn't the first time. You've also been beaten too many times to count." She whirled around, her back straight, her arms crossed as she hugged herself.

He let her words settle inside of him. She was right. Holding back his groan, he forced himself to stand and shuffled to be near her.

"Go back to bed," she said, sensing he was right behind her.

He ignored her words. He raised his hands and placed them gently on her shoulders. She tried to pull away, but this time he held fast. He pulled her back against him, wrapping his arms lightly across her chest, and put his lips toward her ears. "I made a mistake. I can't say that I won't do it again, but I could have taken more care."

"I can't live with knowing that you'll put yourself in danger." Her voice broke, but she seemed determined to not let him see her cry. Sniffling, she wiped her nose, and he grinned behind her ear.

"I have no reason to do that, not anymore," he said.

"How can you know that?" she said.

He carefully turned her around, trying not to jostle his wounds. All the movements were sending sharp pains down his legs and along his side, but he wasn't going to stop. He had to fix this.

He gazed down at her, his hands on her upper arms. "You're right, I can't make that promise. We live in a world where there is danger. I'm reckless and impetuous, but I love you with my whole heart. I promise you that I will be careful and considerate. I won't run into burning buildings or up to random skunks. I'll try and stay away from hornets' nests as well."

She quirked a smile and then tried to hide it.

He ran his thumb against her bottom lip. "Is that a smile I see?"

She tried to bend her neck to avoid looking at him, but he stopped her. He placed the same thumb against the bottom of her chin, forcing her to look at him.

"I can't tell you how sorry I am that I scared you. I can promise you I'll always love you, always care for you, and I'll do my best to make sure no harm ever comes to you again."

She shuddered. "I love you so much. It was so hard to see you bleeding from multiple wounds. I had no idea if I could save you."

"You saved me the day I met you. While I couldn't seem to stop hunting her, you burrowed into my life, and have brought me more joy and happiness than I've had in over seven years. I've been so consumed with anger and hurt at what Connie did to my family, and I let it override my good sense." He kissed her forehead, his lips lingering on her soft skin. She shivered before wrapping her arms around his waist and buried her face in his neck.

"I'm still mad at you," she mumbled. "I should make you grovel, beg me for forgiveness."

He chuckled.

"Don't laugh," she said.

"I'm not laughing at you, I promise."

She looked up at him with a side-eyed glance and then smirked. "I can't stay mad at you. You're hurting though, I can see it in your eyes."

"I'd rather be hurting than hurt you ever again."

Her eyes solemn, she placed her fingers across the hollow in his throat. "I can't lose you."

"I'll do my best."

"Oh, you," she said.

He grinned. "Does this mean I'm forgiven?"

She buried her head in his neck, but he could feel her smile. She mumbled something that he couldn't quite hear.

"Hmm," he said, "what was that?"

She giggled. "Fine, you're forgiven... if..."

"If what?"

"If you kiss me."

"I'm sure I can do that."

"Can you?" An impertinent smile lifted her plump lips, a small sigh emitting from them as she clearly saw the heat in his eyes.

He wanted to savor her, to love her, and to spend the rest of his life with her. "Yes... I... can," he said, his voice low and gruff before he slowly bent his neck until his lips touched hers.

Epilogue

⤙∾⤚

December 17, 1900

Louisa stood in front of the tall, gold-lined mirror dressed in a simple white satin gown, her cheeks pink, and her green eyes twinkling. She beamed with joy, and her hands trembled in anticipation. In just under an hour, she would be Mrs. Luke Seymour. There were moments where she wondered if it were all a dream. But then Luke would smile at her, hold her hand, or whisper sweet words in her ear, and she'd know that it wasn't a dream but a dream come true. She lifted a shaking hand to adjust her veil when a loud knock sounded at the door.

Louisa looked over her shoulder and saw Marie smiling at her. "Stay there. I'll see who it is," she said.

"If it's Luke, tell him it's bad luck to see the bride before I walk down the aisle."

She smiled at the thought of her beloved coming to see her before the service. He'd been right anxious the past few days, afraid she'd change her mind. No matter how much she had tried to reassure him, he still had worry in his eyes. She had forgiven him, but there was still a part of him that worried she would find him unworthy of her love.

He had also spent the last several weeks recovering and trying to make it up to her. She had thought it was too soon, but he insisted he could stand at the altar and wait for her. He said, he didn't have to move and had the cane to help him stand if needed.

"Don't you worry. If it's Luke, I'll send him on his way," Marie said, laughter in her tone.

Turning back to the mirror, Louisa adjusted the simple gold chain around her neck. She wanted to look perfect.

"Luke, what are you doing here?" Marie's voice was filled with joy. "I was just telling Louisa I'd send you away. It's bad luck."

"I'll cover my eyes and won't take a peek."

"Why should I trust you?"

Luke murmured something that Louisa couldn't hear.

Marie chuckled. "Hmm, I suppose if Louisa says it's all right, but you'll cover your eyes."

Marie pulled the door fully open, took hold of his elbow, and led him to a chair he could lean against if necessary. He held one hand over his eyes while the other held the cane Louisa had insisted he use until he was fully recovered. He hadn't wanted to argue with her so had done as she asked.

"Don't peek or I'll have your head." Marie then scooted around him and closed the door behind her, leaving them alone.

"What are you doing here?" A giggle at his antics burst from her lips. "You aren't supposed to see the bride before the ceremony."

"I know, which is why my eyes are closed." He dropped his hand and his eyes were squeezed shut. "See? They're closed tighter than a lid on a cask of beer."

She walked to his side and grabbed his hands, holding them close to her chest. "Oh, all right. Just don't open them. Promise me."

He smiled. "I promise I won't, but I had to come and see you before the ceremony. Or rather, I had to come and talk to you."

"You haven't changed your mind, have you?" she asked teasingly, although she knew he never would. She knew he loved her with all his heart, and she loved him with the same intensity.

"Of course not. I just had to tell you something."

"Oh, and what's that?"

"Just..." his voice grew tight and his face grew red. "Just that I love you and can't wait for you to be my wife." He pulled her close around the side of the chair and kissed her sweetly, never opening his eyes. Then, he pulled back. "I wish I could see your face right now."

"Luke, I—"

"Oh, and one more thing?" he said, letting go of her hands.

She placed a finger against her throat. "What's that?"

He pulled a folded piece of paper from his coat pocket, his fingers fumbling to grab it while keeping his eyes closed. He held it out for her to take.

Taking it from his fingers, she looked at the paper and then back at him. "What's this?"

"Open it." A wide grin lifted his cheeks, making him look like a child who had a great secret to tell. He was bouncing on his feet, or rather on his cane, his body taut as he tried to stand upright. She knew it was difficult for him to stand for long periods of time, but he seemed determined to give her the paper.

She opened the note and started reading. Her mouth fell open with shock. "What... I can't believe this. Is this true?" Her eyes watered.

"Yes, my love. It arrived at Marie's place just yesterday. She thought it best if I were the one to give it to you."

She held the paper tight against her chest. It was an acceptance letter to attend medical school back East. She was speechless.

"I wish I could see your face right now."

She squealed and jumped around in a circle, her dress flowing around her. It was a wonder she didn't trip and fall. She stopped and gently cupped his cheek. "If you could, you would see how much I love you, Luke Seymour, but how? It's so far away."

His fingers rested against her shoulders, squeezing lightly. "Seems only fitting that we go together. I'll find work there. Walter said he has a few contacts and could help get me a job at a local newspaper."

"But your family?"

"They'll still be here when you're done. I'm hopeful you'll want to come back here when you're done with school, but I'll be happy living anywhere as long as you're there with me."

"Oh, Luke," she cried. "How can I thank you?"

"By meeting me at the altar. I'll be the one in the black suit waiting for you, my soon-to-be doctor of a wife."

My Dear Reader,

I hope you enjoyed Luke and Louisa's happily ever after. If you'd like to learn more about me and my novels, sign up for my newsletter at www.nicoleneiswanger.substack.com.

All my love, Nicole

About the Author

Nicole is a Senior Business Analyst by day, a reader during meal time, and a writer while watching historical dramas. She rediscovered her passion for writing during a summer vacation when her husband's truck died. While being stranded for five days with nothing to occupy her time she began writing. She writes American Western Historical Romances set in the heart of Montana and Idaho with swoon-worthy cowboys and feisty, independent women.

Please get in touch
www.nicoleneiswanger.substack.com
nicoleneiswanger@gmail.com

Help other readers find this book by writing a review with your favorite retailer or by sharing on your favorite social media platform.

Also by Nicole Neiswanger

Thundering Mountain Ranch Series

Beneath the Thundering Sky

Thundering Mountain

Thundering Meadows

Thundering Ridge

Thundering Snow

Thundering Sunset - **Available January 15, 2026**

www.ingramcontent.com/pod-product-compliance
Lightning Source LLC
Chambersburg PA
CBHW020537020726
47494CB00006B/1799